THE AFTER PARTY

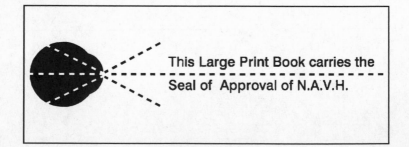

This Large Print Book carries the
Seal of Approval of N.A.V.H.

THE AFTER PARTY

ANTON DISCLAFANI

THORNDIKE PRESS
A part of Gale, Cengage Learning

GALE
CENGAGE Learning·

Farmington Hills, Mich • San Francisco • New York • Waterville, Maine
Meriden, Conn • Mason, Ohio • Chicago

GALE
CENGAGE Learning®

LIBRARY OF CONGRESS CATALOGING-IN-PUBLICATION DATA

Names: DiSclafani, Anton, author.
Title: The after party / Anton DiSclafani.
Description: Large print edition. | Waterville, Maine : Thorndike Press, 2016. |
    Series: Thorndike Press large print basic
Identifiers: LCCN 2016015529 | ISBN 9781410489883 (hardback) | ISBN 1410489884
    (hardcover)
Subjects: LCSH: Upper class families—Texas—Fiction. | Debutantes—Texas—Fiction.
    | Socialites—Texas—Fiction. | Social status—Fiction. | Large type books. |
    Domestic fiction. | BISAC: FICTION / Contemporary Women.
Classification: LCC PS3604.I84 A69 2016b | DDC 813/.6—dc23
LC record available at https://lccn.loc.gov/2016015529

Published in 2016 by arrangement with Riverhead Books, an imprint of Penguin Publishing Group, a division of Penguin Random House LLC

Printed in the United States of America
1 2 3 4 5 6 7 20 19 18 17 16

*For Peter Smith, who was with
me the whole time I wrote this book,
and in memory of Peter DiSclafani,
1928–1990*

PROLOGUE

It's the women who still ask me about Joan.
Young women, who have stumbled upon
her story and my part in it. Old women,
who used to admire her photographs in the
gossip columns: Joan the jewel, a glimmer
on some man's arm. Frank Sinatra's, Dick
Krueger's, Diamond Glenn's. They want to
know who she was. First, I tell them, she
was Furlow Fortier's little blond darling.
From the very beginning, she was adored.

Then she was Houston's most famous
socialite. They won't ever know what it was
like to stand in her presence, but I try to
paint a picture. There wasn't anything
subtle about Joan, a woman born to be
looked at. She was slender, but she wasn't a
twig. Her dresses clung to her, drew attention to her shapely hips, her strong arms,
her famous bosom. Wherever she went,
champagne flowed like a fountain. She
made people happy. She was beautiful,

certainly, but she was more. She was lit from the inside.

I stop here. They want to know how she disappeared. But I can't tell them that.

I don't say that loving her was my earliest instinct, my first memory. I was her best friend since infancy, her modern-day lady-in-waiting, her sister in all but blood.

She disappeared for the first time in 1950 when we were seniors in high school. It didn't take us long to figure out that she had run away to Hollywood to become a star. And if you had stood in a room with her at that time you would have been sure she'd make it. Because she was everyone's dream, in those days; why not some studio executive's? She was gone for a year, trying, and then she returned, and life as we all knew it resumed its orbit, with Joan at the bright, hot center. She disappeared in a thousand small ways after Hollywood. For a day, for an evening, for a week. Even when she was with me it felt as if she were vanishing.

It was the one constant in our friendship: she would leave and I would look for her. Until I would not.

In the beginning, we were both Joan. Joan One and Joan Two when our nannies dropped us off at River Oaks Elementary School for our first day of kindergarten. Our teacher, a young blond thing who was teaching rich babes their ABCs and colors until her beau finally proposed, paused as she was going through names. Paused at us, the two Joans. One fair, one dark. One, it seemed evident, even at this young age, destined to be beautiful; the other one dark, with clear, even features. Pretty enough.

"What is your middle name?" she asked me, the dark girl.

"Cecilia," I replied. I was five years old. I knew my middle name, my address, my telephone number.

"And you?" she asked, kneeling before Joan, taking her tiny hand and holding it as if a fragile bird.

I removed Joan's tanned hand from the teacher's grasp. I didn't like people taking liberties with my friend, even then. I was used to people wanting to touch her. I understood, but I didn't like it.

"She doesn't have one," I said, and Joan nodded cheerfully in agreement. She wasn't scared of strangers, or big men with deep voices, or anything really. She'd started swimming lessons the year before and was already diving off the high board at the pool.

"I don't."

9

"Well," the teacher said, her hands on her hips. In my memory, she wears a pale blue dress dotted with delicate flowers, her hair in a modest bob. I could see the lacy edge of her slip when she knelt down to speak to us. It was 1937, and she must have been desperate to be married, desperate to teach her own children the ABCs, to identify for them the many hues of the bright and colorful world.

"Let's say you're Cecilia from now on. No, Cece. Has a nicer ring to it. And you" — she smiled at Joan, reassuringly — "don't worry, you're still Joan."

Our mothers weren't friends, but they were friendly. We'd met because our nannies, Idie and Dorie, were sisters. They'd wanted jobs close together, in River Oaks, and they'd gotten them only a street apart with Mary Fortier and Raynalda Beirne, two very different kinds of women. Their differences stemmed from money, as so many differences do. Mary, Joan's mother, had grown up poor and plain in Littlefield, Texas. She was in high school when she met Joan's father, fifteen years older than she and already wealthy. Mary understood the magnitude of her good fortune, the unlikelihood of her escape from dusty, dead-end Littlefield. Joan was born when Mary had thought her childbearing years were through. She made Furlow a daddy, Mary a mother, and both parents seemed forever grateful to her for the gesture. Furlow, an oilman from Louisiana who kept making money right through the Great Depression, believed in divine providence, the way that lucky men often do, and Joan's late arrival into the world was proof of his blessed life.

My family was rich, too, but not like the Fortiers. My mother had her inheritance, and my father was an executive at Humble, but he wasn't a diviner of oil like Furlow Fortier. My mother's married life was a steep decline from her childhood. She'd grown up with maids and butlers and nannies in Savannah; in River Oaks she employed one maid and one nanny, and lived in a house that wasn't even close to being the biggest.

But still, both women had named their firstborn daughters Joan. The gesture seems hopeful to me now. Joan: such an elegant name. And strong, too: they must have felt like they were bestowing their tiny babies with men's names. Perhaps they hoped their daughters would inherit a man's world, with a man's privileges. Probably they thought nothing of the sort. Joan was the fifth-most popular name for little girls in 1932. Mary and my mother named us Joan just like everyone else did, because that's what people do, generally: what everyone else does.

But back to that first day in kindergarten. That night, after my nanny, Idie, had fed and bathed me and my mother had come to tuck me in, I told her that my name had been changed. She was furious, naturally. My mother was always furious. But the name stuck, and from then on Joan got to be Joan, and I was Cece, less a name than a sound, a whoosh of air, twice; a near-whistle.

I got used to it.

CHAPTER ONE

1957

Joan sat in my living room, on my squat orange sofa, sipping a dirty gin martini, her usual drink. It was her second, but Joan had always held her liquor like a man. On this hot, humid day in May — summer comes early in Houston, always — our lives were still normal. By August Joan would be gone.

Joan and I lived five minutes from each other, still in River Oaks, the most beautiful neighborhood in all of Houston, house after spectacular house. You felt like you were a person who meant something, if you lived in River Oaks. The lawns so big they could have been pastures, the houses so grand they could have been mistaken for castles, the gardens and esplanades so manicured they could have belonged to Versailles. There were other nice neighborhoods in Houston, sure, but West University wasn't quite rich enough and Shadyside wasn't quite big enough, more like a collection of houses than a neighborhood. River Oaks was another world. You entered its borders and found yourself in a land both spectacular and unending.

I was twenty-five, the mother of a young child, and I spent my days tending to my house and making social calls and generally fulfilling the role of a wealthy young housewife. Not that any of us women in River Oaks were anything besides housewives. What else would we have done? I belonged to the River Oaks Garden Club, to the Junior League of Houston, to the Ladies' Reading Club. Joan did, too, though she was careless with her memberships, rarely came to meetings. But no one would have thought of revoking her memberships. She was Mary Fortier's daughter, and Mary had ruled River Oaks in her day. And besides, I would have raised holy hell.

Lounging on my couch, Joan wore a brown shirtdress from last season, cinched at her waist with a red belt. The dress was all wrong: meant for fall, too big in the shoulders, a stiff material that did her no favors. She had no style when it came to clothes; I had always dressed her for evenings out. Or the ladies at Sakowitz sent over full outfits, from shoes to dress to un-

14

derthings to earrings, a black-and-white Polaroid of the ensemble clipped to its sleeve.

I was always the better dressed of the two of us. Today, even though I'd only left the house once, for a Junior League meeting, I wore a knee-length, pale blue taffeta skirt that moved with me as I walked, sprouting from my waist like a flower. It made me bolder, to wear fine clothes.

All I had to do was lean forward and touch the hem of her skirt and Joan rolled her eyes.

"I think what you want to say is let's put that up forever and forever. Send it to the clothes graveyard." She set her martini on the little chrome-and-glass drinking table I pulled out for cocktails, clasped her hands behind her head, and stretched. There was something mannish about the way Joan moved. She wasn't careful with her gestures, her limbs. She looked around the living room, at everything but me. She was bored.

"Where's Tommy?" she asked, in a bright, false way that made me think I had misread her completely. Maybe Joan wasn't bored. Now that I was noticing, her famous brown eyes were a little swollen.

She saw me staring and raised her eyebrows.

"What? Is there a piece of chicken in my

15

teeth? I had chicken enchiladas again for lunch today at Felix's. With a side of lard. Pretty soon I'm going to turn into an enchilada . . ." She trailed off, plucked an invisible piece of something off her lap.

"Are you all right?"

"Are you sure there's not a piece of tortilla?" she asked, batting away the question with a joke. She drew her lips apart, revealed two neat rows of beautifully white teeth. For a second I forgot what I had been asking Joan, and then why I had asked her in the first place.

"Tommy?" she asked again.

I called for Maria. A moment later she appeared, dark and petite, Tommy on her hip. Maria was our housekeeper, technically, and she helped with Tommy. People — the women in our circle — thought it strange I didn't have more help, a nanny for Tommy, and though it bothered me that people might think we couldn't afford a nanny, I didn't want one. The idea of holding Tommy up to more scrutiny from a stranger, even a stranger in my employ, unnerved me.

"He can walk," I chided. "Tommy, come see Miss Joan."

If Tommy ever did start speaking, *when* he started speaking, he might as likely speak Spanish as English because of Maria. She

16

and I communicated in a tangle of words and gestures.

The servants Joan and I had grown up with were all colored, with a few white country people mixed in. Most of the servants in River Oaks were still colored, descendants of that first generation, but I'd scoured Houston for someone who didn't remind me of Idie.

Tommy stared at me, then held out a hand for Joan. He was three years old, just, and still hadn't uttered a single intelligible word. He loved Joan. He loved a lot of things: Water, dogs, slides. A book about a flying monkey. The way I patted his cheeks and kissed both of them, left, then right, the very last thing before I tucked him in at night. And yet sometimes, to me, only to me I hoped, there seemed to be a vacancy in his gaze, an absence.

Joan crossed the room in three big strides and took Tommy from Maria's arms into her own.

"Why walk when you can be carried?" she sang while she fussed with his collar, smoothed his pretty brown hair against his head.

I watched them and felt happy. Joan herself seemed happier.

It was an easy thing, to feel happy with

Joan. My husband, Ray, was where he belonged right now, at his office downtown. But he would come home soon, and later, after Joan and I had changed and Ray had put on something more comfortable, we would go out on the town. Pretend we were young again. Tonight there would be dinner and drinks at the Cork Club. There would be dancing, joking, general feelings of goodwill amplified by champagne. Wherever Joan went, the drinks were on the house and people were desperate to be near her, to know her, to catch her eye.

But of all the places in the world she could be, she was here, with me. In my living room, holding my little boy's hands in her own, trying to teach him how to dance. In a second she would ask me to put a record on.

There was always a future, with Joan. Another moment to look forward to. Tommy glanced at me and I smiled; he seemed to be, if not dancing, exactly, trying. Like he understood what Joan was asking of him.

Joan sat on a shaky fence that summer. All the girls we'd used to float around with had married, produced children, fallen neatly into the ranks. Like me. Since high school Joan had enjoyed a reputation as a wild

18

child but that didn't matter so much in Houston, not when you were young. Not if you had money; beauty helped, too. And Joan had both. Another town wouldn't have forgiven her Hollywood jaunt — who knew the men she'd been with, or what she'd tried out there. But Houston was magnanimous in all things.

Yet she wasn't eighteen anymore. And last month in the powder room at the Confederate House I'd heard Darlene Cooper tell Kenna Fields that Joan Fortier was getting a little long in the tooth to wear her hair in a high, blond ponytail like a little girl.

I'd stayed in my stall, stared at the black-and-white striped wallpaper, mortified. A better friend would have marched out and told Darlene Cooper, whose husband, everyone knew, was light in the loafers, exactly what she thought of her and her cheap gossip and cheaper dress. Darlene had been in our circle since high school. She should have known better.

But I'd been hearing a lot of murmurs about Joan lately. A man was a game she tired of playing after a month or two. Nobody used to care that she hadn't had a serious boyfriend since high school — but now that she was getting older people were noticing. It was time for the great Joan Fortier to settle down, was the general feeling.

But I had to pick my battles. This one didn't seem worth fighting, that's what I told myself, but really I thought perhaps Darlene was right.

After Joan danced with Tommy, she went home to change. She reappeared several hours later, running across my lawn in a blue velvet dress and pearl earrings the size of walnuts.

I'd slipped outside when I heard her Cadillac pull up and watched her leap out of the pale green car before Fred, her chauffeur since forever, could assist her.

"Ta-da," she sang as she approached, barefoot, ignoring the neat brick path to march instead straight through the grass. Her heels were in her hand, her face unmade, her hair undone: she looked like she'd just gotten up from tanning by the pool. Which she probably had.

I tamped down a flare of irritation; she was forty-five minutes late.

"We've got to get moving," I called.

She smiled, gave an elaborate shrug, kissed me on the cheek. I could smell her coconut tanning oil.

"Did you even take a shower?" I asked. "A bath?"

She shrugged again. Her eyes were unfocused, like she'd been in the sun too long.

"What's the point?" she asked, and walked past me into the house, dropping her shoes — Ferragamos — onto the hardwood floor of the foyer.

I made her sit at my vanity and, mindful of Darlene's ponytail comment, fixed her hair into a French twist. I applied a little powder to her forehead but skipped the rouge because her cheeks were already red.

"If you stay out in the sun too long," I said, "you'll turn into a lobster."

Joan ignored me, fiddled with a diamond bracelet Furlow had given her when she'd turned twenty-three.

Joan's parents still lived in Joan's childhood home, Evergreen, her father in his eighties and losing his mind, Mary his faithful companion turned caretaker.

"Sit still," I murmured as I filled in Joan's brows with pencil. These days, Joan only tolerated makeup when I applied it. I knew her face better than my own: the mole at her right temple that was somehow pretty instead of distracting; the sharp cheekbones; the faint scattering of freckles on her forehead that emerged only in the summertime.

"Did you hear about Daisy Mintz?" she asked.

Of course I had. Daisy Mintz, née Dillingworth, had caused quite a stir in River Oaks three summers ago when she'd left to marry a Jew from New York. Her parents had disowned her, briefly; apparently the Mintz fortune had soothed their outrage. Just last week I'd heard from our friend Ciela that Daisy was asking for a divorce. Mr. Mintz had been unfaithful, which was a story as old as time itself. Older. I couldn't help but be bored by it.

"What did she expect? She chose glitz and glamour and money. A stranger, practically. And it all fell apart." Joan said nothing. "Anyway, it sounds nasty," I continued. "He wants the child to stay with him. Ridiculous," I murmured, as I smoothed a dot of foundation onto her chin. "Children belong with their mothers."

"She's going to get a lot of money," Joan said abruptly. "Tons."

"And?" We all had a lot of money. "That child's going to grow up with parents who hate each other. What did she want with him?"

"Maybe she loved him."

"Maybe she was being shortsighted," I countered.

"Oh, Cee," Joan said, "don't be such a yawn." Her voice was easy; I wasn't offended. I *was* a yawn, between the two of us. I didn't mind.

"I might be boring, but at least my life's not a wreck."

"Daisy Dillingworth Mintz," she said. "Stranded on the great island of Manhattan."

"You're flushed," I said, feeling her forehead with the back of my hand.

"Am I? Must be the weather. It feels like the sun came out just for me."

"Maybe it did," I said, and Joan smiled, and there was such an understanding between us, such a feeling of grace.

It went without saying that summer was Joan's favorite season. She loved to swim, to dive, to do anything that involved water. The rest of us wilted a little bit in the heat, even though we were used to Houston's climes, but Joan seemed made for it.

"She got to see the world," Joan said, and at first I didn't know what she was talking about. "Daisy," she said, impatiently. "She got to do whatever she wanted for three years."

"I hope she fit a lifetime into them."

The Shamrock Hotel was wildcatter Glenn McCarthy's green baby. Sixty-three shades to be exact: green carpet, green chairs, green tablecloths, green curtains. Green uniforms. The hotel sat next to the Texas Medical Center, which Monroe Dunaway Anderson had founded and bequeathed nineteen million dollars to in his will. It was like that, in Houston: there was money everywhere, and some people did very good things with it, like Mr. Anderson, and some people built glamorous, foolish structures, like Mr. McCarthy. Mr. Anderson *helped* more people than Mr. McCarthy, certainly, but where did we have more fun?

The rest of the country was worried about the Russians, worried about the Commies in our midst, worried about the Koreans. But Houston's oil had washed its worries away. This was the place where a wealthy bachelor had bought himself a cheetah and let it live on his patio, swim in his pool; where a crazy widower flew in caviar and flavored vodka once a month for wild soirees where everyone had to speak in a Russian accent; where Silver Dollar Jim West had thrown silver coins from his chauffeur-driven limo, then pulled over to watch the crowds' mad scramble. The bathroom fixtures at the Petroleum Club were all plated in twenty-four-karat gold. There was a limited supply of gold in the world; it would not regenerate. And Houston had most of

24

it, I was convinced.

We valeted our car and headed straight to the Shamrock's Cork Club; Louis, our Irish, gray-haired bartender, was there, and he handed me a flute of champagne, Joan a gin martini, up, and Ray a gin and tonic.

"Thank you, doll," Joan said, and Ray slid a coiled roll of money across the bar.

That night we were all in attendance: the aforementioned Darlene, dressed in a lavender dress with, I had to admit, a beautiful sweetheart neckline; Kenna, Darlene's best friend, who was very nice and very boring; and Graciela, who went by Ciela. Ciela had been a scandal when she was born, the product of her father's affair with a beautiful Mexican girl he'd met while working in the oil refineries down in Tampico. His ex-wife had been rewarded for his sin — she'd received the biggest divorce settlement in Texas history. All of this was old news, though. There had been bigger divorce settlements since then, much bigger. It was Texas: everything bigger, all the time.

Ciela's father had married the señorita, was still married to the señorita, which perhaps would have been the greater scandal, if he weren't already so powerful. We all had that in common, save me: powerful fathers. And husbands who would become powerful. And we were going to go there with them.

Darlene kissed Joan on both cheeks and then turned to me, "Long time no see, Cece," and then laughed uproariously at the repetition. She was already loaded. "You look like Leslie Lynnton herself," she said, and even though I looked nothing like Liz Taylor, aside from the dark hair, I was pleased. We'd all seen *Giant* at least three times, were titillated by the fact that the James Dean character was based on Glenn McCarthy himself, even though we publicly hated Edna Ferber and her portrayal of Texas.

Ciela, whose hair was now so blond and coiffed she looked as Mexican as Marilyn Monroe, was on the arm of her husband, and Darlene's and Kenna's husbands were across the room, smoking. My own husband was at my side; Ray was quiet, a little bit reserved, most comfortable near me. He wasn't shy, exactly, but he didn't feel the need to be the center of anything, a rarity in our crowd.

The night wasn't full of possibility for us wives, like it used to be, like it still must have been for Joan. Yet the champagne was crisp and cheerful, the men were handsome and strong, and the music buoyed our spirits. I was wearing a beautiful silver dress, strapless, cinched at the waist. (Ray made a good living at Shell but my mother had left her small fortune to me, and because of it I wore astonishing clothes. My one extravagance. My mother had always refused to touch the money, thought my father should earn more. And so it was mine, granted to me in a legacy of bitterness, in lieu of parental attention. I was determined to spend it all.) My wrist was encircled by my fourteenth-birthday present, a delicate diamond watch I only took out when I was feeling hopeful. Later tonight we might venture outside, to the Shamrock's pool, which happened to be the biggest outdoor pool in the world, built to accommodate waterskiing exhibitions. Joan loved to dive from their high board, said it felt like flying. Or maybe we'd make our way to the Emerald Room, the Shamrock's nightclub.

I chatted with Ciela, who had a daughter, Tina, the same age as Tommy, about whether or not we'd send our children to preschool in the fall (I wouldn't — I couldn't imagine throwing Tommy to the wolves like that) as we watched Joan hold court ten feet away, laughing and smiling and acting like it all came so easily to her. Which it did. Ray stood next to me and he watched her, too, and I wondered what he thought of Joan Fortier underneath his unvarying calmness.

"What do you think she's saying?" Ciela asked, following my gaze. Her scent was a combination of Chanel No. 5, which all our husbands gave us once a year, on Valentine's Day, and hair spray. I'm sure I smelled much the same, with a little bit of Tommy's bubble bath mixed in. Ciela's husband, JJ, a tall, gregarious man from Lubbock whom I found a little forward, was at the bar, getting a drink.

Joan was a little *too* bright, tonight, for my taste. A little wired, a little too close to out of control.

"Who knows with Joan," I said, and took another sip of champagne.

JJ came up behind Ciela and kissed her cheek. She acted surprised, as if he'd come from nowhere. I smiled, allowed JJ to kiss my hand; then Ray's arm was around my waist, and he was pulling me toward the floor. Ray would never kiss a woman's hand. That was one of the things I liked about him: he wasn't interested in pageantry.

"Would you care to dance?" he asked, and I smiled, let him lead me to the shiny wooden floor. He put me instantly in a better mood. A four-piece band played something slow; I didn't recognize the music but that was beside the point. I finished my champagne and deposited the empty flute onto a silver tray balanced on the white-gloved hand of a colored waiter.

Ray loved to dance. It was the reason he tolerated these nights out. If not for dancing he'd have liked to be at home, sipping a neat scotch, reading one of his presidential biographies. But on the dance floor he was a different man. I felt small in his arms, though I was nearly as tall as Joan, who was five foot eight; but Ray was six foot three and broadly built. I fit neatly into his embrace. I was attractive but not beautiful, and I was honest enough with myself to acknowledge the distinction. I was still slender, but pregnancy had softened my edges, made my face fuller, given me more weight and heft, anchored me to the world. My hair was a fight, eternally swollen by the Texas humidity, but after hot rollers and my weekly salon appointment it tended to frame my face becomingly. My dark brown eyes were my best feature, almond shaped and bright; Ciela had once said they were the envy of us all, and though she had been drunk when she said it, and probably didn't remember saying it in the first place, I did.

"This is *fun,*" I said, and Ray gathered me

to him. The Cork Club was filling up, with people we knew and people we didn't. That was the fun of this place: only the richest and the brightest were granted admission, and you never knew who you'd see.

The band started playing something fast and Ray twirled me out the length of his arm, and in the second before he brought me back in I saw Joan out of the corner of my eye. Joan, with a man I didn't recognize. I rested my chin on Ray's firm shoulder and watched them. Joan had turned her back to the room, which was unlike her. It seemed as if she were hiding her companion.

The rest of us wanted true love and a husband, and if not true love then a husband would do, but Joan had always been content to spring from one man to the next. The papers adored Joan: she was featured regularly in their gossip columns — the *Houston Press*'s "The Town Crier," the *Chronicle*'s "Gadabout" — usually with a man and a photo. But those men weren't serious, and they weren't strangers.

"Stop watching Joan," Ray whispered in my ear, and I turned my attention back to him. Joan, if I'm being honest, was a minor tension in our marriage, mainly unspoken.

"I'll only look at you for the rest of the night," I said.

"Now you're talking," Ray said, and twirled me out again onto the floor in response.

Ray had promised the night we were engaged that he would never leave me. And he had asked I promise the same thing, which I thought was absurd. Men left women; women never left men, not unless they were stupid, and I wasn't stupid.

Now he spun me out and grinned a little crookedly, as he did when he'd had a drink, his big hand warm and firm as he caught me again. He continued to watch my face. Ray often surprised me with the things he noticed. He was attentive in a way I'd had to get used to. He could walk into a room and read me in a second. Half a second.

"Cee," he said now, "have I lost you?"

"I'm here," I said, and leaned in closer to Ray so I could watch my friend without Ray's noticing. She wasn't right tonight; I'd known it since this afternoon. I could see the man better now. He was tall and meaty. And he was certainly a stranger. He wasn't handsome. But handsome didn't matter to Joan. "I'm like Jesus," she said one time, when I asked her how she could date men so clearly unsuitable for her. "I love them all."

A pair of dancers swung into our path,

31

blocking Joan and her stranger. Ray kissed my cheek and I closed my eyes and I was lost in the music, in the press of bodies, in Ray, for a moment or two.

When I opened my eyes I was dizzy, but I had a perfect view of the tall man leaving through the door next to the stage, which led through the bowels of the club and hotel, straight to a stairwell; the stairs rose to the Shamrock's rooms.

I scanned the club for Joan, and spotted her near the bar, smoking a cigarette, laughing. I was relieved to be wrong.

Then Joan extinguished her cigarette in an ashtray, dropped her lighter into her satin clutch, and followed the stranger through the door. I wasn't wrong.

Life should have shown me by now that I was powerless against Joan. She was a grown woman, a grown woman who was used to getting her way. Nobody had ever told her no: Not her parents, certainly. Not a teacher. Certainly not a man. Joan Fortier did as she liked. I was only her friend.

CHAPTER TWO

I was fifteen when my mother died. It was December, nearly Christmas. A week after the funeral, Joan and I were still in my mother's house, skipping school, sleeping until noon each morning, falling asleep as the sun rose. Joan had already told me I would come to live with the Fortiers at Evergreen. I wanted to, fervently, but I didn't quite believe her. Joan loved me, and I loved Joan, but Mary and Furlow were not my parents.

Furlow had come to Texas from Louisiana to make his fortune when he was a young man, and decided to stay. Texas could do that to a person: you came for a visit, then looked up one day and found you'd never left. He'd built Evergreen for Mary's wedding gift. It was a graceful plantation-style mansion with enormous columns flanking the porch, replete with rocking chairs and black-shuttered windows. He'd named it after his beloved magnolias, which lined the driveway.

Furlow and Mary wanted me to live with them because I took care of Joan. I had access to places they did not. But I didn't know that then. Then, it was second nature to follow Joan around at parties, to make sure she met curfew, to cut styles I thought would suit her from *Harper's Bazaar* and give them to Mary to order.

I was asleep in the home I'd known since birth, Joan next to me, lightly snoring (you wouldn't think a girl like Joan would snore, but she did), when the doorbell rang. At first I thought it was my mother. I sat up in bed, disoriented, my mouth dry from the sweet white wine we'd drunk late into the evening. The line from the song we'd been listening to all fall circled my brain: *That's when I'll be there always, not for just an hour, not for just a day.*

Of course it wasn't my mother. My mother was dead.

"Cece?" Joan sat up beside me. Her voice was slurred from sleep. She rested her warm cheek on my shoulder, and for a moment we were still. The doorbell rang again, but I made no move to stand. There was no one in the world I wanted to see. I just wanted to sit there, with Joan next to me, and forget all the things that awaited me. My mother's lawyer had been calling to make an appointment. There were her things — things upon things upon things, Limoges boxes and antique perfume bottles and an endless wardrobe — to sort through. My father, at his permanent room at the Warwick, might as well have been in Switzerland. He was with his mistress, I knew. A woman named Melane, whom he would marry and take to Oklahoma as soon as the ink had dried on my mother's death certificate. I didn't blame him, but I didn't want to see him, either.

Joan rose at the third chime. "Let me," she said, and picked up her robe from the floor.

She returned a moment later with Mary, who surveyed the room, lifted the empty bottle of wine from my bureau, and made a face. Joan, out of Mary's line of vision, imitated her, and I stifled a laugh.

Mary was now the secretary of the Junior League; next year, my mother had said, she would be president. My mother didn't understand Mary Fortier: Mary wasn't beautiful, didn't come from money, and yet she was powerful. A woman like Mary didn't fit into my mother's worldview. Mary should have been uncertain, full of doubt.

"It's time to go," Mary said. Of course I didn't call her Mary. After I'd lived in her home for a few weeks she would tell me to call her by her first name, tell me that we no longer needed to stand on ceremony. But the offer didn't strike me as genuine, so I avoided saying her name at all.

I sat on the bed like a child and watched them sort through my things, nodded or shook my head when Joan held up a purse, a blouse, a pair of flats.

"Of course we'll come back later," Mary said, "and pack up the rest, but this will do, for now."

I knew that I would never come back. Strangers would box up my remaining possessions and bring them to me; everything else, except for the family Bible and my mother's jewelry, would be sold at an estate sale.

"Fred's day off," Mary said, when she opened the driver's-side door, which was what she always said when she drove. It might or might not have been true.

Mary liked to drive, even though it was far more acceptable for a woman of her station to be driven.

I got into the backseat, and Joan, instead of riding up front with her mother, sat next to me. I closed my eyes and didn't open them again until Joan touched my knee.

We were turning onto Evergreen's red gravel drive; I felt the crunch of the pebbles beneath the tires.

"Your new life," Joan said.

"Yes," I said. "Thank you."

Joan laughed, but when she spoke, her voice was serious.

"You don't ever have to thank me, Cee."

A week later Joan convinced me to go out. I hadn't been around anyone my own age besides her for months. Darlene, Kenna, and Ciela had come to my mother's funeral, but I'd barely spoken to them.

"It'll be good for you," Joan said, dabbing on the lightest coating of lipstick — any heavier and Mary might notice.

Joan, as a sophomore at Lamar High School, had already been asked to be on the homecoming court. She was a cheerleader, too, one of two underclassmen on the squad. She ate at the center table of the cafeteria, surrounded by the football team. She was invited to every party, every dance. Without Joan I would have been no one, a girl on the fringes of the popular group by virtue of the fact that her family had money, that she lived in River Oaks: a girl with a forgettable face, a forgettable name. But I was saved from this fate because I was Joan's best friend. I ate lunch with her, went to parties with her, generally benefited from standing at her side. I might have been jealous but I didn't want the spotlight, didn't need it. I needed Joan, and I had her.

Puberty struck some girls like a match. At fourteen years old, a freshman, Joan had breasts the size of melons. That's what I'd overheard a boy saying, one day after school. She was already the most beautiful, the richest, the most charming, the most everything. Now she had a figure like Carole Landis, too. A figure most of us knew, even then, we would never come close to having.

Joan had grown right into her body. Other girls who developed early stooped their shoulders, carried their books in front of their chests, but Joan? Our first day of high school Joan wore a brassiere with pointed cups, like the movie stars did. She hid it in her purse and changed in the bathroom.

This particular night she wore a familiar dress, baby blue with a flared skirt. I'd never seen her necklace before, though. It was a tiny gold star with a diamond chip in its center. It hung in the dip between her collarbones like a glimmer.

I touched it on the doorstep of the house where Fred had deposited us.

"What's this?" I asked.

"Oh," she said, "Daddy gave it to me."

"For what?"

She shrugged, and I understood she was embarrassed, to have a father who gave her gifts for no reason — for being Joan — when my own father, for all intents and purposes, might as well have not existed.

Joan rang the bell. When nobody came to the door, she finally opened it, revealing a throng of high schoolers. A boy Joan had been seeing, Fitz, snagged her and they headed upstairs almost as soon as we were inside, while I stood by the punch bowl until I mercifully spotted Ciela. We chatted about nothing and tried to pretend we weren't watching to see who was watching us.

"Joan's been up there for a long time," Ciela said. She was wearing a short-sleeved plaid dress with a collar. It almost looked like a school uniform, except it was skin-tight. Ciela dressed like a siren but wouldn't even let her boyfriend, a senior, touch beneath her bra. I felt a little flare of jealousy — she looked like Lana Turner tonight.

I was drunk on grenadine and whiskey; the house, in Tanglewood, was gauche and brand-new. You could practically feel the light blue rug turning brown beneath all our feet.

"She and Fitzy are talking," I said.

Ciela eyed me. "You really don't know what they're doing up there?"

"They're doing whatever they want," I said. "Joan's doing whatever she wants." Defending Joan was a sharp reflex.

Ciela nodded, took a measured sip of her punch. "She sure is," she said finally. She smiled at me. "She sure is."

Just then Fitz appeared at the head of the stairs and motioned to me; I left Ciela there like we hadn't been in the middle of a conversation.

"Joanie's a little upset," he said when I reached him. I grabbed the stair rail for balance — I was drunker than I thought — and watched Fitz run a hand through his thick black hair, lick his chapped lips. This close I could see little bits of dead skin clinging to them.

"Where is she?" I asked.

He nodded in the direction of a closed door at the top of the stairs, which turned out to be a bathroom.

Joan was sitting on the edge of the tub. A candle was burning on a shelf over the sink, an awful cloying smell. The room was dark except for the flare of the wick but I knew it was Joan, sitting in silence. The dark had unnerved me since my mother died.

I flipped on the light and Joan turned her face from me, an unusual, somehow terrible gesture. I noticed right away her necklace was gone.

"What happened?"

She shrugged. Her shrug seemed exaggerated, sloppy, but still somehow elegant. She was drunk, too.

"Nothing," she said.

I sat on the toilet lid, so close to Joan our bare calves touched.

"You've lost your necklace." I tapped between her collarbones, the hollow where it had sat, and she jumped. When she looked at me her eyes were unfocused.

"Where were you last?" At first she wouldn't answer, acted as if she hadn't heard me.

"The room at the end of the hall," she finally said. "It looks like somebody's little brother's room."

It *was* somebody's little brother's room, done up to look like the Wild West, with horse-shaped pillows on a bunk bed. The bottom bunk was unmade, though the rest of the room was neat as a pin. I spotted Joan's necklace on the pillow, its clasp broken.

I went back to the bathroom, knelt down,

and held her chin between my pointer finger and thumb and made her look me in the eye.

"Did he hurt you?" I asked.

For a moment it seemed as though she was on the verge of telling me something. But then she shook her head. Smiled.

"Fitzy? God, no. I'm just tired and sozzled. Help me up." She held out her hands and I took them; when we were standing I folded the necklace into her palm. I never saw her wear it again.

That was the first time I remember being aware that Joan had secrets. At first, Joan told me about her private life: The boys she kissed; the first time, in eighth grade, she let a boy touch her bra. The way Fitz had turned hard beneath her hand. But she told me less and less, as we grew up. Sex became Joan's private world.

That night I fell asleep next to Joan, to the familiar sound of her breathing. I woke in the middle of the night and sat straight up in bed. I couldn't shake the feeling that something bad had happened to Joan in that little boy's bedroom, something she was keeping from me.

"It's okay," Joan said, sleepily, from the bed next to mine. "It'll be okay, Cee. It'll be okay."

■ ■ ■ ■

I grew accustomed to life at Evergreen. At first it seemed strange; within a month it was home. How quickly the young forget. And though I never quite felt like Mary and Furlow's daughter, I grew to love them. I like to think they grew to love me.

CHAPTER THREE

Joan did what she wanted to do; she always had. When she was young, this had aligned with what Mary desired: Joan wasn't rebellious. And Mary wasn't a prude. Our curfew was generous. We could accept as many dates as we liked, attend as many dances as we wanted, go to as many parties as we cared to. Mary wasn't *on* Joan, the way my mother had been on me. We came and went from Evergreen as we pleased, driven by Fred, funded by Furlow. She had accounts at the stores and restaurants we frequented and everything we bought was charged to them. The transactions remained invisible to us.

But Joan began to change our senior year of high school. She told me less. She snuck out of our room more frequently after I had fallen asleep. I'll never forget waking up in the room we shared, the yawning feeling of panic and isolation when I realized her bed was empty.

And then debutante season arrived. We had all been anticipating the ball for years. Since we were children. Joan had been as excited as the rest of us the summer before, when we began our preparations.

"This dress," she said, during one of her fittings, rubbing the white satin between her fingertips.

"This dress what?" Ciela had asked.

"It's like we're getting married. Like we're getting paraded in front of all Houston's eligible bachelors so they can pick and choose among us."

"That's the idea," Ciela said, and laughed, but her voice was taut in a way only I noticed.

It both was and wasn't the point. We would be paraded, of course, and though a certain young, handsome bachelor might take a shine to us, we wouldn't be married for another three or four years at least. Two at the earliest.

We all fussed over our white dresses, spent hours with the seamstress, who worked miracles; we all rehearsed our curtsy, our "Texas dip," over and over, the motions so practiced by the end we might have curtsied to the president himself in our sleep.

Joan was dating — of course — the captain

of the football team, a dark-haired boy named John. She spent more and more time with him that fall, less and less time with me, with the rest of the girls. Ciela had said the week before, in the cafeteria as we picked at our lunches, that Joan seemed bored by us. She had begun to disappear from our center table during lunch hour — I assumed to be with John, though I didn't really know. I'd glared at Ciela until she'd held her hands up in mock surrender and halfheartedly apologized, but I couldn't help but think she might be right.

"The effect will be stunning," I heard Mary say to Joan one morning, as I was coming down to breakfast. It was a month before the ball, which would be held at River Oaks Country Club in December. Evenings we ate in the formal dining room, mornings at a small pine table in the breakfast room, which was separated from the kitchen by a narrow swinging door.

"You'll look ethereal," Mary continued. "Like a blond angel." She had been up for hours, sipping coffee. She always waited to have breakfast with us.

Joan muttered something as I entered the kitchen. She was hunched over a piece of toast. When she saw me she rolled her eyes.

"Good morning," Mary said, and took in

my outfit. She'd make us change if she thought our skirts were too short, our blouses too flimsy. Satisfied, she turned her attention back to her daughter, while Dorie, who now worked as a maid, wordlessly offered me a bowl of oatmeal, a ramekin of raisins, and a glass of milk, without meeting my eye.

Idie was the younger of the two sisters by seven years, and she was delicate and pretty where Dorie was thick and sturdy, with a man's jaw. I always felt I'd gotten the better of the sisters.

Dorie had never really liked me, and she liked me less after my mother died and Idie left my family's employ. But still, I felt a certain affection for her. I knew she missed having Idie down the street, as I did.

"Sit up, Joan," Mary said. "You'll develop a permanent hunchback if you sit like that. Spines are very suggestible." She smiled at me as I sat down. "Joan and I are having a little tiff."

"Oh?" I looked at Joan. It was Friday, football season, so she wore her navy cheerleader's outfit, the blue sweater emblazoned with a red *L,* her hair pulled back in a pert ponytail and tied with a red bow. She didn't look ethereal — she was too solid for that — but she did look like a blond angel. A very tan blond angel.

"Yes, I'm afraid we are. Joan has decided she doesn't want to debut. Doesn't want anything to do with the ball, apparently."

I choked a little on my oatmeal, and Joan gave me a tiny, almost imperceptible scowl. But this was news to me: how was I supposed to defend Joan when I was blindsided by her choices?

"It's silly," Joan said, drawing her spine straight, calmly tightening her ponytail. The only sign she was furious was her knife, clutched in her hand.

My feelings were hurt. Of course they were. We'd been talking about the ball since we were children. The past few months we'd talked of little else: Dresses, invitations, escorts. How we would wear our hair. And now, apparently, Joan wanted nothing to do with it.

"Silly?" Mary asked. Her voice was high, her cheeks flushed. It was unusual, to see Mary unmoored.

Joan made an odd, strangled noise, but in an instant, she seemed to compose herself. She waved her hand. "It's fine," she said. "I'll go."

"You should —" Mary began, and Joan interrupted.

"I said I would go." Her manner was

48

falsely cheerful, and I understood this was worse, not to let Mary fight the fight.

"In Littlefield," Mary said quietly, "I didn't even know what a debutante ball was." She laughed, and looked toward Joan hopefully. Mary had made herself vulnerable, which she did not often do. Joan turned her head to me, and rolled her eyes again.

Mary saw, of course. She was meant to see. She turned hard again, in an instant.

"Of course you'll go," she said with finality. "You'll go and you'll like it. Or you won't. Either way, you'll behave."

I was embarrassed for Joan. Mary spoke to her as if she were ten years old. Joan stared at her plate. I couldn't tell if she was going to cry or erupt in rage. Just then Furlow's frame filled the door, and I was half grateful for the interruption, half annoyed that I wouldn't see how this would play out between Mary and Joan. I quelled the outrageous impulse to giggle as Furlow settled down to the steak and eggs Dorie had just placed in front of him.

"Joanie," he said, after he'd cut a piece of steak and dipped it in the runny yolk. Furlow's breakfast had always disgusted me. "Lonny wants you to hand out a prize at Houston Fat. Prize heifer, something along those lines. You'll need to pick out some-thing fancy to wear." He laughed, winked at me when he realized I was the only one looking at him. Both Joan and Mary were staring at their place mats.

Furlow was nice to me, treated me like he treated everyone: as someone he need not concern himself with too much. He moved through the world like a man who owned a great big piece of it. He had been named one of Texas's fifty wealthiest men for a decade running.

The Houston Fat Stock Show and Rodeo was Houston's biggest event, held every February, and everyone went. My ears burned a little bit at the news that Joan had been tapped to present an award. She would be dressed to the nines, would float out into the dusty arena, where everyone would watch her, admire her.

"Oh," Mary said, "Joan isn't interested in any of that. She finds all that business" — she waved her hands in the air, as if shooing away flies — "silly."

Furlow put his fork down, looked from his wife to his daughter. He began to say something but Joan interrupted.

"I'll do it, Daddy," she said sweetly. "It'd be my pleasure."

Furlow's handsome brow relaxed, and he

smiled at Mary. I couldn't quite read the tension that existed between the three of them, but I understood that it was Joan and Furlow against his wife.

Mary stood. "Of course you will."

Joan watched her go, her face blank. Furlow, for his part, finished his breakfast in silence. But his eyes never left his daughter.

I understood that Furlow should have followed Mary. That he was choosing Joan by staying put.

On the way to school we sat in the backseat of the silver Packard, piloted by Fred. For a while Joan wouldn't speak. She didn't get mad often — why should she? Her life was so easy. She herself moved so easily within it. But when she did get angry she turned quiet.

"I didn't know you didn't want to go."

She shrugged. "I don't care about the goddamn ball."

I waited a moment. "What do you care about?"

She looked at me. "Sometimes I hate her." She looked away. "I'm sorry. You don't even . . ." She trailed off.

"Have a mother?" I was stunned: Joan never apologized. "No," I said. "But that doesn't matter. Tell me." It was all I ever really wanted, for Joan to tell me: something, everything.

I could see Joan deciding, whether or not to explain further. I thought she wouldn't, and I leaned back into my seat, disappointed. But then she spoke.

"I hate her world. President of the Junior League, treasurer of the Garden Club." She paused, looked out the window. "Biggest bitch in River Oaks."

"Joan!" I'd never heard Joan speak of her mother like this.

"What? I hate her world, and I think she hates me." She played with one of the charms — a solid-gold swimmer, in a swan dive — on her charm bracelet.

"She doesn't hate you," I interrupted. "She just doesn't understand you."

"What's there to understand? I don't want to be her."

"Why?" Mary's life seemed nearly perfect, except she wasn't beautiful. It had occurred to me when I was a child that if she and my mother could have become one person, *she* would have been perfect: my mother's beauty, Mary's power and social prowess.

Joan was that person, I realized now. Beautiful and powerful. She would be like her mother, inherit her mother's position, and her beauty would only amplify her power. There was nothing more she could want, nothing more that girls like us desired.

"It's what you want, isn't it? The same friends, all your life. The Christmas party every December, the Fourth of July picnic every summer. Galveston for a change of scenery. A luncheon every week. Children," she added, almost as an afterthought.

She wasn't trying to be mean, but her words stung. I did want children. We all wanted children. We needed families or else we would float away; we needed homes to put them in. But I didn't say any of that. I felt silly, suddenly.

"You'll be my friend all my life," I said. *I hope,* I thought to myself.

"Of course I will," Joan said, impatiently. I had lost her. "If you don't know what I mean, then I can't explain it. Anyway," she said, and opened her purse, removed a tube of lipstick that was too dark to wear around Mary. Flashy, she would have called it. I reached into my own purse and pulled out my compact, held it steady while Joan drew her lips into a grimace and painted them deep red.

"What *do* you want?" I asked, and Joan's eyes darted from her own reflection to my face, surprised.

"I want what you don't want," she said softly. "I want to leave."

"Why would you say that?" I asked, my voice shrill. I thought of our debutante gowns, both made in Paris — a place Joan had talked about us visiting together next year after graduation. Mine was off the shoulder, Joan's was delicately gathered and tucked at the waist. They were both silk. They were both the kind of dress you wore once in a lifetime if you were lucky.

"Oh, I don't really mean it." But she was only mollifying me. "Here," she said, "let me do yours," and without thinking I stretched my lips over my teeth and let her paint them a garish red I would wipe off as soon as we arrived at school.

"You say you want to leave. But where would you go?"

"Somewhere I've never been. Somewhere no one could follow me," she added.

She meant Mary, I supposed. But I couldn't help inserting myself into the sentiment: somewhere you can't follow me.

"What would you do there?" I asked quietly. Joan simply gazed at me. She was in another world this morning.

"Things I've never done before," she said. We were pulling up to Lamar. A classmate, Daisy, waved at us; Joan returned the wave and smiled brightly, as if she hadn't just fought with Mary, as if she hadn't just told me she wanted to leave all this — including me — behind.

We were walking up the stairs of the school when Joan suddenly grabbed my sleeve.

"Where did you get this outfit?" she asked. I was wearing a garnet-red dress belted at the waist, with pearl buttons down the front.

"Sakowitz."

"But where did *they* get it?" she asked, with a shake of her head.

"I don't know where they got it. Maybe Houston."

"But where did they get the *idea* from? Not from Houston. Where do you get your ideas from, for clothes?"

We had reached the top of the steps; out of the corner of my eye I could see Ciela waiting for me. We had homeroom together.

"From magazines, I guess? *Vogue, Harper's* . . ." Tears came to my eyes, even though I knew it was ridiculous to cry. But I didn't understand what Joan was asking.

"Yes," she said. "Yes!" Her face was very close to mine. "Exactly. I want to go where the ideas are."

"You want to go to New York? But you don't care about clothes."

She stamped her foot, and I could see her so clearly as a child, mad because she hadn't gotten her way about something. "New York, Chicago, somewhere big. Somewhere else. And not for the clothes. For the world."

She kissed me on the cheek, her breath hot in my ear, and then she was gone. John was waiting for her just inside the glass doors, and she deposited her books into his arms and patted his shoulder. I noted that she did not kiss his cheek. She was careful about what she did with boys when she was watched.

"Nice lips," Ciela said when I reached her, and I brought my hand to my mouth, embarrassed. "What was that about?"

I shrugged. "Joan thinks she wants to go to New York." I felt mean; there was a certain pleasure in revealing Joan's plans to Ciela, making them seem frivolous.

Ciela laughed. "New York? What would she do there?" I tried to picture it: Joan on a busy street corner, waiting for a taxicab. My idea of New York came from movies. How could she want crowds and filth when she had Evergreen? There would be so many people; she'd have to blend in among them. And would she really want to? Here, she was a star. I could see her just ahead of us, in the hallway, her arm threaded through John's. The throngs of us — girls and boys, in various stages of becoming men and women — parting for John and Joan, our king and queen. John could have been any good-looking man. He was replaceable. But Joan was not.

"I expect," Ciela said, as she turned into Mrs. Green's room and I turned into the restroom across the hall, "she'd meet a lot of men."

CHAPTER FOUR

1957

Have I established our group well enough? Everyone was the same. There were hierarchies, of course, of wealth and family and beauty. But none of us were too far from the center. We were the sons and daughters of oil, some of us more directly than others. Joan, for instance, had oil in her name; so did Ciela. The rest of us had fathers and husbands who worked for people who had oil in their names.

Except for River Oaks and a few other neighborhoods, the Bayou City was nothing more than a charmless swamp out of which a lot of tall buildings had suddenly sprung, watered by oil.

Esso, Shell, Gulf, Humble — our men worked downtown in tall buildings, wore full suits and ties even in August. If you were a lawyer you lawyered and if you were a doctor you doctored for the oil company

58

men. You met at the Houston Club to drink amber liquor and broker deals. I'd seen oil, once. When we were young, eight or nine, Furlow had taken Joan and me up to one of his oil fields in East Texas. We were supposed to go to a Fun Club movie at the theater, which we did some Saturdays; usually it was a cartoon and a clip about the war, but there had been a polio scare — a child who lived near the ship channel had recently been diagnosed — and our mothers didn't want us going anywhere near a crowd.

Furlow let us dip our fingers into a barrel. Me timidly, because I didn't want to get my sundress dirty — there would be a price to pay, later — Joan without a second thought. It felt like nothing much — "Oily," Joan had said, and Furlow had laughed, but I had held my hand to the sun and considered it: Joan had oil, and I did not.

There wasn't an old guard in Houston. Our parents were it. We would have been laughed out of the society registers in most places in the country but in Houston our names meant something, even if they only went back a generation. In Houston *we* meant something, and we knew it, and we were careful with our positions. We might have gotten silly when we drank but we tried never to get sloppy. We didn't do drugs. We kept our prescription painkillers at home, in the medicine cabinet, where they belonged. We didn't follow strange men into bathrooms and swallow what they placed in our palms. We knew that some people did, in other places: New York, Los Angeles. The big cities. But us? Alcohol was enough of a drug for us. It took the edge off. It made us come alive.

We didn't do strangers, either. That's why Joan's man was particularly unnerving to me. There were new people, sure, of course, all the time. Business associates of our husbands who'd just moved to town from San Diego, from Oklahoma City, once even from London. We admitted them because they had been properly vetted. We knew them from somewhere.

So many stories start when a stranger comes to town. Including this one, though not in the way I thought at first. I wouldn't understand our story — how it truly began — until years later, when I was far enough away to see it clearly. Perhaps a stranger only reveals what has been there, hiding in plain sight, all along.

Ray, for his part, was bored with the idea that Joan should be more careful. "Isn't Joan always talking to some man?" he said when I brought it up the morning after our night out. "Never seemed to hurt her before." He was looking at something slightly beyond me, as was his habit when irritated.

I didn't call Joan because I was careful with her; there were certain things she didn't tell me, at least not right away, and this man seemed to be one of those things.

Monday morning I woke and pulled the covers around my shoulders — Ray liked to turn the air-conditioning unit on high at night — and tried to push her face from my mind.

What would she be doing at this very moment? Sleeping, in her own bed. I hoped she'd left the Shamrock carefully, through a back door. I hoped they'd left separately. I felt Ray stir beside me, and then I thought of all the things I needed to do today. Call Darlene and ask if she wanted to go to the Garden Club meeting together. She could always be counted on for things like that. Take Tommy to the park. Write a grocery list for Maria — she went to Jamail's every Monday. Plan our menu for the week.

I tried to keep myself busy, always. When I wasn't busy I could feel myself getting dangerously close to a despair that always seemed to be there, just beneath the surface:

I thought of it as the ground beneath a car. When I was a teenager I'd gone on a date with a boy who wasn't from River Oaks; the car he'd picked me up in was so beaten up I could see the road through the floorboard. The sight had made me unbearably sad, and I'd feigned illness.

"My stomach," I'd said. "It's a little tender."

"Tender," he repeated quietly.

He turned the car around silently, returning me to my surrogate family, my borrowed home. The moment had stayed with me. His pitiful face, angry and hurt; the quickly disappearing ground beneath my feet.

Now I had a house to run, a maid to manage, a husband and child to tend to. It was infinitely better never to see the dirty ground beneath the floorboard. It was there, of course, but why linger on it?

Life before Tommy seemed scarcely worth remembering. What had I done with all that time?

Most mornings I rose before six, so I could get breakfast together for Ray before he left for work. Ray could have gotten breakfast together himself, of course, but I tried to live my life exactly the opposite of how my mother had lived hers. I rose, brushed my teeth, and smoothed my hair into a loose bun. Most women I knew wouldn't let their husbands see them without makeup, but I liked to think Ray and I were closer than that. I tapped Ray on the shoulder as I was leaving — "Rise and shine," I whispered — then stopped at Tommy's room. He was waiting for me, standing up in his crib in his blue, footed pajamas, waiting to be lifted. His silhouette in the dim morning light always moved me. He was most affectionate now, would allow me to nuzzle his cheek, dot his forehead with kisses; he loved threading the tie on my silk robe through his fingers.

It was time for him to move into a real bed, but I didn't want to do that until he spoke. It seemed safer this way, to keep him contained, until he could call out if he needed me. Today he rested his warm cheek on my shoulder, and we stood there for a moment, completely still. It would be my only still time that day.

When Ray joined us we were in the kitchen, Tommy in his high chair with toast. Ray gave us each a kiss and took a seat before the plate I had set for him, and Tommy, at his side, held out his hand, waved it, and looked at Ray expectantly. *Ask for it,* I thought, but did not say. It was something I'd heard other mothers say to their children, though of course they said this to children who spoke. But Ray knew, and spooned some of his eggs and a piece of his bacon onto the high chair tray.

"Ciela invited us to Clear Lake in August," I said instead.

"A whole weekend with JJ."

I smiled. "I'll be there, too. And Tommy. And I think a few other couples."

We ate in companionable silence, Ray skimming the paper, occasionally reading things out loud to us.

"Are we done?" I asked Tommy, while I wet a rag. "Yes," I said, "we are," as I scrubbed his face clean. He held out his hands, so I could do those next. Those were the kinds of gestures that made me hopeful.

We were all so used to each other in the mornings. I never remembered my parents talking like this, chatting for an hour over coffee. It meant something to me, that Ray and I could pass time so easily. And everything was more hopeful in this early light, even this morning, when Joan had tied up my brain in knots. That Tommy didn't try to speak to us, even babble; that he seemed more interested in his high chair, in his hands, in the bird outside the window than us — well, he was our son. Whatever he gave us seemed like enough.

Even now, though, I wondered when Joan would call. Had I called her one too many times this week? All friendships have boundaries. I believe that: then, now, forever. One woman is more powerful than the other. Only subtly more powerful. Too big a difference, like with me and Darlene, and a close friendship never has a chance. But even in the deepest friendships, like mine and Joan's, one woman always needs the other woman less. Joan didn't spend her days wondering when I would call. If she wanted to hear my voice, she picked up the phone.

The next afternoon Darlene returned my call about the Garden Club meeting — we were beginning to plan next year's Azalea Trail, where outsiders came to River Oaks and toured our homes — and managed to invite herself over that evening for cocktails.

"It's just that it's a weekday," I said, trying to find a way out of the cocktails, standing in Ray's office on the second phone extension, an extravagance.

It was a poor excuse — we entertained on weekdays. But I didn't particularly care if I offended Darlene. I absentmindedly pulled one of Ray's books from the shelf. A biography of Abraham Lincoln.

"Maria's home sick. And it's a busy week."

In our group I was known as the one who pulled no punches, who told it straight, who didn't particularly care about hurting feelings. Joan laughed at this depiction, said I was the most sensitive soul she knew, and maybe I was but occasionally all the various songs and dances that came with being a woman exhausted me. At that very moment I was tired; Tommy was going to be up from his nap soon and I had promised him a trip to the park. I wanted nothing less than to entertain Darlene over gimlets.

"Is it? For me, too. And is it a busy week for Joan as well?" She sounded gleeful. I could picture her at this exact moment: three miles away, in her black and white living room, twisting the phone cord through her fingers. She would be wearing white; though she wouldn't admit it, she liked to match her furniture when she was home. Absurd, but true. Smiling — she would be smiling. Grinning, like a cat. Because she had me.

An hour and a half later, after a rushed trip to the park, where Tommy had stared at other children playing but allowed me to push him in the swings, Darlene sat in my living room, in Joan's spot on my beloved orange couch, which I'd custom-ordered from New York.

Ray, home early from work, was outside, grilling steaks. When I'd told him Darlene was coming over, and that I was irritated, he'd shrugged and mixed me a shaker of gin gimlets.

I could see him from here. He was whistling — I could imagine the tune. Tommy was playing quietly with a wooden train set he carried around with him. He'd been devoted to this particular train set, a Christmas gift from Ray's parents, since December. Ray's parents were kind but completely loyal to Ray's sister, Debbie, who lived in Tulsa with her four stair-step children, each blonder than the last. We saw them once a year, at Christmas. I'd never seen Debbie's home, but I imagined that it was as boring and perfect as Debbie herself. It had been clear, from the very beginning, that the Buchanans would dedicate themselves to Debbie, not Ray, and not, by extension, me. They were only following the time-honored rule: upon marriage daughters remained loyal to their mothers, while sons switched their allegiances to their wives.

I had the gimlets waiting in a chrome shaker, a small plate of crackers, pickles, and cheese beside it. I owned a new Russel Wright cocktail set, squat glasses emblazoned with ruby and gold bubbles, but I wasn't using these on Darlene. Darlene got the clear glasses — though I was cutting off my nose to spite my face. Darlene would have noticed the sharp barware, unlike Joan.

I'd greeted Darlene at the front door and now she sat across from me. She wore slim white capris and a sleeveless white blouse; her eyes, which had always been small, almost beady, were thickly lined with kohl, and her cheeks were luminescent with rouge. I'd never seen Darlene without makeup. She was one of those women who made up her face first thing, took it off after her husband was asleep.

I hated her, suddenly. I nodded at her small talk about so-and-so in the Garden Club, the giant divorce that was coming her way, and took a sip of my gimlet. I kept the gin in my mouth a second too long, until it burned, before I swallowed.

"So tell me, Darlene," I said. "What's the news?"

She traced the rim of her glass with a painted finger, pale pink.

"Well," she said. She paused, took her own sip of gimlet, drew the moment out to capacity. "A man was seen leaving Joan's house Sunday afternoon." She raised an eyebrow and couldn't stop herself from smiling.

"Was he?" I tried to hide my shock. Joan *never* took men to her home. She went out, with men. And if it was the man I had seen with her at the Shamrock, it meant that not only had she taken him home — I did a quick calculation — she had been with him there for over three days.

I tried to calm myself. I looked around my living room: orange and white with pops of blue. Everything was spare, modern. Gone were all traces of my mother's world: Old, ornate Victorian settees and cabinets. Dark, drab colors. The feeling that you were living with borrowed furniture, which led to the constant reminder that you were living on borrowed time.

This was how a room should be — new and fresh and utterly carefree. I'd worked on it with a designer shortly before we moved in. It was the room that got the most light, the most sun, the most energy. I loved it. Ray had carried me over our threshold and delivered me into it as a young bride. I remembered feeling at home here, for the first time in my life. It was the only place I'd lived that wasn't Joan's or my mother's.

I could feel Darlene watching me; her drink was running low. I could have poured her another; that would have been gracious.

I leaned in close, and kept my voice low.

"Oh, Darlene," I said, as if I were speaking to a small child. "That was a business associate of Furlow's. But I think it's time for you to go home. Tommy's bedtime, soon." I stood, adjusted my belt. I'd had to get completely dressed and waste an outfit for Darlene's visit. Not my best outfit, but still. I watched Darlene try to assemble the various pieces — what had just happened, exactly? How had she gone from being the bearer of valuable information to getting kicked out of Cece Buchanan's home before her drink was even done?

I waved good-bye from our front door as Darlene backed out of the driveway, wincing as she edged onto the vulnerable grass by the mailbox. She wasn't a good driver. None of us were, really. We weren't supposed to care about cars or driving so we didn't.

I worried for a second that Darlene would call Kenna, or Ciela, or someone further out in our group — Crystal Carruthers, or Jean Hill — and tell some sordid secret about me. But I wasn't a ninny. I'd never revealed anything essential about myself to anyone but Joan.

Besides, I understood Darlene. She was neither mean nor nice, smart nor dumb. She wasn't spectacular in any way, but she aspired to be. Joan was spectacular. Joan was a target. Always had been, always would be for women like Darlene. I wasn't spectacular, but neither was I worthy of envy, except when I stood near Joan.

Darlene would go home, kick off her shoes, pour herself a glass of wine, fold herself onto that white leather couch, and call Kenna, recount my insult, casting herself in a virtuous light — "I was only trying to help poor Joan!" — and she and Kenna would talk for half an hour, an hour, while their maids prepared dinner and the nannies bathed the children, and by tomorrow Darlene would have forgotten all about the time Cece Buchanan practically threw her out of her house.

I could have been meaner, I could have told her what I really thought instead of simply forcing her to leave. Most of us wanted what we couldn't have. Darlene wanted to be more popular than Joan. I wanted Tommy to speak.

I also wanted Joan to behave herself. She was already the talk of the town. If Darlene knew a man had left her house, everyone did. I would tell whoever asked that he was a business associate of Furlow's, but no one would believe me.

I stood outside for a moment longer.

Inside would be a series of chores — dinner, bath time for Tommy, bed, a book he would show little interest in. Assembling all of it, cleaning it up. Making small talk with Ray. But I felt powerful after I defended Joan. I surveyed my lawn, the neat circle of ivy enclosed by our driveway, the white day-lilies and pink four o'clocks. Soon everything would wilt and die in the Texas heat. But not quite yet.

Ray and I sat by the pool after we'd put Tommy to bed. The temperature was more pleasant out here at night.

"I put Tommy in front of Roy Rogers," Ray said. "He seemed to like him."

"Who wouldn't like Trigger?" I asked, and Ray gave a chuckle. I didn't want to discuss Tommy tonight. I wondered how much interest he'd shown in the television. Ray and I were divided over our son: he couldn't bear to think anything was wrong with him. "I was slow to talk, too," he'd say, or: "He'll be a football star, not a rocket scientist."

"What's in store for you tomorrow?" Ray asked, which is what he always asked in the evenings. I listed my plans: lunch with the ladies, the Garden Club meeting. The minutiae of a marriage; the minutiae of a life. It was these minutiae that comforted me. I'd never had someone so interested in me, before Ray. Joan wasn't meant for the small things.

I touched his hand, lightly, and he turned to me with unexpected intensity.

"Do you think Tommy is lonely?" he asked.

I could tell he'd been waiting to ask this question. Or, not this question, exactly: the real question he wanted to ask was when we could start trying for another child. It was, if not quite yet a problem, a small issue, something to be tiptoed around. Most of our friends started trying again when their first child was two. Any earlier suggested an accident. Any later suggested trouble. Tommy was already three.

My secret was that I needed Tommy to start speaking first. I wanted assurance that our next child would speak, too; I wanted to be certain. I could never say this to Ray, but I wondered if Tommy's silence wasn't a reflection of how I cared for him. If I wasn't warm enough, maternal enough; if Tommy could sense something I could not. I had learned the value of silence from my mother, after all; the less I said, the less likely she was to take offense.

Ray would tell me this was nonsense, that I was devoted to Tommy, that anyone could see how much Tommy loved me. I wanted to believe that it was nonsense, but sometimes, in dark moments, I could not.

"He has his Mother's Day Outs," I said, and I could sense Ray's disappointment, that I would not answer his question, that I would not engage. But how could I? I was ashamed: that I was not more hopeful, that the thought of another child stirred fear in my heart instead of love.

"That's true," Ray said quietly, and I leaned back in the lawn chair and closed my eyes. The air smelled of chlorine and freshly cut grass and four o'clocks. A summer smell.

Another night, I told myself, I might have worked up the courage to answer Ray differently. Honestly. To give him a little glimpse of my heart. But tonight I was occupied with Joan, and I could not muster the effort required for such a serious conversation.

Ray stood, leaned down, and kissed me on the forehead. "Night," he said. "Don't stay up too late."

"I won't," I promised.

I would go in, soon. I was exhausted, and the day would begin again in a few short hours whether I was well rested or not.

CHAPTER FIVE

1957

As soon as Maria was in the door the next morning, I was out. "Be back soon," I called over my shoulder, and slipped outside before Tommy knew what I was doing. He wouldn't throw a tantrum, but sometimes he clung to my leg and cried, and when he did this I found it nearly impossible to leave.

A gardener edged the lawn across the street, slow and methodical. Otherwise the neighborhood was still, too early for children to be about, splashing in pools or running through sprinklers. River Oaks was a neighborhood for families, with yards meant for sprawling games of hide-and-seek, for swing sets. The backyards, anyway. The front yards were meant to be seen.

Joan's house was five times too big for her — she was the only single woman in all of River Oaks who did not live with her parents. I'd always thought her husband would move into this home when Joan married, but no decent man was going to want Joan if she truly was keeping company with strange men.

I drove by my childhood home on my way to Joan's, owned now by a family I'd never met. An old colonial, it sat proud and tall like a soldier, with white columns and long windows and plantation shutters. I remembered my mother sitting at one of those windows, smoking a cigarette, telling me that smoking was trashy, that if she ever found me with a cigarette she'd wring my neck. Yet she had caught me, once, and she hadn't wrung my neck; in fact, she hadn't seemed to care at all. Right now the Confederate jasmine my mother had trained to a trellis was in bloom. I used to be able to smell it through my bedroom window.

I rang Joan's doorbell and listened to the electric chime reverberate through the tall-ceilinged house. Her home was Spanish style, sprawling, with a red tile roof and a rose garden that overlooked the pool. She never stepped foot in the garden.

I waited. I might wake Joan, who wasn't an early riser, but I didn't care.

Sari opened the door. She was German, and had been with Joan since our days together after high school. Every other maid in River Oaks was colored, but somehow Mary Fortier had found her daughter a German maid.

"Here for Joan," I said, and Sari frowned while she said hello. She was old enough to be my grandmother, and I don't think I'd ever seen her smile. Sari made Germany seem like a place you'd never want to visit. Usually Joan opened the door herself.

I saw Joan's white cat, deaf as a doorknob, pad languidly across the tiled entryway and I knew, suddenly, that Joan was upstairs with him. The stranger with the unhandsome profile. Darlene had said he'd been seen leaving on Sunday; this meant he was coming and going as he pleased. There was no unfamiliar car in the driveway, at least.

"She's with someone, isn't she?" I reached out and rested a hand against the doorframe.

Sari looked at my hand, then at me.

"She is indisposed," she said. I could smell the scent of freshly baked bread wafting in from the kitchen. I could see beyond Sari into Joan's spacious foyer, a vase of fresh yellow roses from the garden on the entryway table, next to a silver tray stacked with yesterday's mail. The pile was tall with magazines and I recognized the red corner of *Time,* which Ray subscribed to. Joan was the only woman I knew who made a point of reading it, regaling us at our ladies' lunches with the news of the day.

"I know she's here," I said, hating the way my voice sounded, plaintive, jealous even. I knew Sari well enough to know she would tell me nothing, but I was getting frantic at the thought of Joan in there, with him. Who knew what he wanted with her? And what did she want with him?

Joan wasn't a child. She knew better than this.

I backed away from the door. "Tell her I was here," I called out. I lifted my hand in a wave.

Once, when we were little girls, playing at Joan's — we were nearly always at Evergreen, with Dorie and Idie — I looked up from the moat I was building in the sandbox and Joan was gone. We must have been about four, young enough that the memory is hazy but old enough that I know it happened. Idie and Dorie were sitting in the shade of a giant oak with glasses of lemonade, chatting; I remember feeling relieved because they appeared so unconcerned.

I stood, the sand I had not minded sitting in a moment ago suddenly irritating, nearly unbearable, and went to Idie.

"Where's Joanie?" I asked, and I must have sounded worried because Idie paused, held my hand in hers for a moment. She and Dorie smelled of the same lotion, which was confusing to me because I loved only Idie. I understood from a young age that Idie knew how to manage my mother, how to navigate her moods, how to shield me from her. I preferred Idie's company to my mother's, to almost anyone but Joan's. She was an adult in whose presence I felt safe, though of course I would not have put it in those terms when I was a child. Then, I simply knew I loved her.

"She's inside," Idie said. "She'll be back."

"I want her." I could feel tears bite my eyes.

"You can't have her." Dorie's voice. I backed into Idie's knees and wrapped her arm around me. Dorie was stern, older than Idie and more dangerous. Joan and I rarely crossed her. "She's in the house. She'll be back soon. But until then, you can't have her." She leaned back in her chair, done with me.

The threat of crying had disappeared. Fury had replaced it.

"I *can* have her," I said, "whenever I want her."

Idie began to laugh first, then Dorie, shaking her head. "Is that so, child," she kept saying, "is that so."

But of course, I couldn't have Joan whenever I wanted her, then or now or any time in between. It was a lesson I should have learned early: that Joan was never entirely mine.

CHAPTER SIX

1957

A few nights later I lay in bed, wide awake, and knew I would call Joan. She had been so good for so long. But this behavior — stealing up to a hotel room at the Shamrock, taking a man to her house, spending *days* with him — it alarmed me. I'd almost lost Joan once, the year she'd come back from Hollywood. I hadn't known how to help her.

This time I'd left her alone for as long as I could, hoped she would come to me. It didn't serve me well to ask too many questions of her. But she had not come to me, and so I left my sleeping husband and padded down the hall to his office.

I checked on Tommy first — was it possible to pass your child's room at night and not peek in to make sure he was still breathing? He was, deep, even breaths you could set a clock by.

After all the old, creaky hardwood in my

childhood home I'd made the designer put fluffy beige carpet everywhere but the kitchen. On top of that lay shag rugs in vibrant colors, scattered about the house. It was impossible not to walk softly in my house.

I closed the door to Ray's office behind me, poured myself a finger of his nice scotch, and drank it in a single swallow. I hated the taste but liked the effect.

I had nearly given up and set the phone back in the receiver when she answered.

"Hello," she said. "It can only be Cece, calling this late." She didn't sound drunk. She didn't sound anything. She sounded like herself, perhaps a little annoyed.

I sank into the soft leather chair behind Ray's desk; my bones felt liquid.

"It is Cece. I —"

"Of course it is." She exhaled, and I knew she was smoking. I associated smoke — the smell of it, the sight of a woman bringing a cigarette to her lips — with Joan.

"Remember when you taught me to smoke?" I asked.

"Is that something you can teach?" she asked.

"We were at Evergreen. I think we were thirteen."

"Twelve," Joan said, "we were twelve," and

82

I was so pleased she remembered. "You threw up in the grass and I was so worried I'd killed you." She laughed. "But you're tougher than that."

"You took care of me," I said. "You made me change so Dorie wouldn't smell anything on our clothes, and then you convinced our mothers to let me sleep over, even though it was a school night."

"You didn't want to go home," Joan said. "You never wanted to go home."

It was true: I never did. The smoke had made me sick, and I had vomited behind a garden shed, and Joan had rubbed my back and given me a cold washcloth for my forehead, and I had gotten to sleep next to her that night.

"I used to steal Daddy's cigarettes," she said. "He never counted. Mama did." She sighed. "And now my daddy doesn't know who I am."

"He still loves you," I said. I believed it was true. Loving Joan was Furlow's instinct.

She was quiet for a moment. "I suppose he does. I don't know. It's late, though. Very late. I would never call you this late. I might wake Tommy."

I waited. My face felt hot.

"So what did you want to know tonight? Am I okay? I'm fine. I just need some time to be alone."

"But you're not alone," I said. I traced the rim of the heavy crystal glass.

Joan was silent. When she spoke she sounded resigned.

"Have you ever wondered how many lifetimes you've spent worrying over me?"

"I'm your friend."

"I have a mother," she said, as if she hadn't heard me. "I have a mother to worry over me. I don't need two."

I felt her words physically: a blow to the chest. Or no, it wasn't that: it was whatever the opposite of that felt like. A sudden, sharp elimination of air from my lungs. Like a puncture. Did she know her power? Surely she did. Surely she must have.

"But you're a doll to worry," she said, just when the despair was about to overwhelm me. The trick of our friendship, perhaps: Joan could be mean, she could be irritable and she could be short and she could treat me in ways I would never treat her. But she never went too far. She always came back.

"Just be . . ." I trailed off. "Just be careful. Please."

"And now I have to go." And then she was gone.

There was no chance I'd sleep now. I stood, drew my finger over the spines of

Ray's books. Pulled one out. Reshelved it without registering a single thing about it.

All these years later, I understand that worrying about Joan was a little bit like being in love. Her absence was painful. Hearing her voice, seeing her face — I felt new. I felt completely revived.

Ray wouldn't like this: Me, calling Joan in the middle of the night. Drinking scotch straight, like a man. I was angry at myself, too: it was three o'clock in the morning! I would have to be up in three hours, and I had wasted time on Joan, on Joan's problems, on Joan's life. I stood. "Enough," I said.

I checked on Tommy once more before sliding under the covers next to Ray. She would come to me in time. She always did. The man would go away. They always did.

I should have gone to her at that point. If I'd known all that was to happen in the coming weeks, I would have. Perhaps it would have stopped nothing — Joan had started on her particular course long ago.

Some would say she was only fulfilling a destiny. But destinies can be changed. Joan had, after all, changed mine.

CHAPTER SEVEN

Joan ran away the spring of our senior year of high school. A week before she truly disappeared, I followed her at lunchtime. She'd stopped showing up at the cafeteria and I was tired of her leaving, tired of not knowing where she went. I slipped out of typing class and waited behind a bank of lockers for the bell to ring and Joan to emerge from Home Arts.

She was the first person out the door and she was alone, which surprised me. Joan was usually surrounded by a throng. Now she seemed pensive, her arms wrapped around her books. It was easy to follow her blond head through the hallways, darting into a crowd of people when it seemed like she might turn around. But she never turned around. It never occurred to Joan to be careful.

She rounded the corner and went through an open door into the gymnasium, where we had our pep rallies and watched basketball games. Where Joan had cheered, a million times. I remember the rectangles of light cast by the high windows and Joan walking through them, her books still pressed against her chest.

I flattened myself against the cold wall, next to the door. The gymnasium was huge, meant to seat hundreds, but today it held only two people: Joan, and me.

I stepped out of the shadows.

"Joan," I said softly, and she cocked her head but then another figure rose from the bleachers. We were three, not two. John, I thought at first, the senior Joan had been dating for a few months; but John was taller than this boy, held himself differently. This was a boy I had never seen before.

Joan went to him. I had a strange feeling in my stomach; I knew without knowing. Joan ascended the steps silently; when she reached him he kissed her hard, his hand behind her head. I'd never seen anyone kiss like that, openmouthed, the desire on both sides equal, clear. Joan wasn't shying away — she was pushing back. She was hungry, too.

"Let's get rid of these," he said, and though I could not see him, I could hear him clearly. His voice was low, tense. He took Joan's books and dropped them on the metal seating. I felt sure someone would come — I held my breath for one second, two — but no one did.

Joan wore a pink cashmere sweater, short-sleeved; he ran his hands over her breasts, lightly at first, then harder and harder until Joan moaned.

I'd never heard a sound like that from her. And then she was kneeling, he was pushing her down, and she was still moaning. I thought of her bare knees on the bleachers, the pressure of his hands on her shoulders. He unzipped his pants, hurriedly, clumsily — I was shocked by what I saw — and put himself in her mouth and then he stroked her cheek, the gesture weirdly tender.

I felt faint. His eyes were closed. I couldn't see Joan's face.

When Joan stood up, I turned to leave but the boy spoke. "You, now," and his words echoed around the empty gymnasium. He put his hand beneath Joan's skirt — I'd chosen that skirt for Joan, at Battelstein's, for the way it had complemented her waist — and Joan made another sound I had never heard her make before, and she made it again and again and she leaned her head back and he put his other hand behind her neck, and at first I thought he might hurt

88

her but then I saw he was only helping her stand.

I could see her taut throat, the curve of her breasts beneath the sweater. They were locked in a strange dance, and I didn't understand it, who was leading whom, or maybe nobody was leading, maybe this was a dance that had no rules.

There was a noise outside the door, an errant shout. Joan turned toward me. I closed my eyes as if closing them would make me invisible.

But she turned away again and I slipped out the door, made my way down the empty hallway and back into the noise and bustle.

A week later, in the aftermath of her absence, I would wonder if she had gone somewhere with this boy. I saw her over and over, sinking down to her knees. But I didn't even know his name. I felt sure I'd never seen him before. I looked for him, in the lunchroom, between classes, but I didn't know who I was looking for. A boy who was shorter than John. A boy who had been touched by Joan.

Joan ran away while I was in Oklahoma City for Easter, enduring a tense, awkward visit with my quiet father and his idiotic new wife, Melane. Melane, who had been his long-term mistress before she became his wife, laughed at everything she said, and everything he said, everything anyone said, and served silly little canapés instead of dinner. Their house was big and boxy, decorated with Melane's knickknacks, with none of Evergreen's solid walls or old family portraits or sense of history. But she was easy to be around, as my mother had not been.

When I returned to Houston, Mary, not Joan, met me at the airport. I remained calm as she escorted me through the busy lobby, full of people arriving, people departing; I took deep, even breaths like Idie had taught me to do when I was a little girl and something had upset me.

Fred stood next to the car, waiting for us in his black uniform; he tilted his head, gave me a small, sad smile, and my fear was confirmed: Joan had left.

"Tell me right now," Mary said, once we were in the backseat of the car, "tell me everything."

"Joan's gone," I said, almost to myself. I looked out the window, at all the travelers returning from their own unpleasant Easters. Weary women in pastel hats, men in suits, clutching the hands of their thrilled, happy children. Travel was still exciting for them; they didn't know the people they loved would abandon them, eventually. They didn't know that love was not a fact. I pressed my forehead to the window and swallowed a sob. Who did I have left?

What did I know? I told Mary I knew nothing, wiping tears from my face that Mary pretended not to see. I tried to concentrate on her questions; I tried to understand what she was asking of me. But it wasn't true that I knew nothing. I knew that Joan had drifted away from me. That her plans for the future had stopped involving me. The penthouse apartment we were to live in after graduation; the correspondence course we were to take, unseriously, that summer; the parties we were to throw: her heart hadn't been in any of it lately. She had said she wanted to leave Houston, to go to where the ideas came from, and now she had succeeded.

That night, I fell asleep surprisingly easily, exhausted from the day. I woke up and it was still dark through the curtains; I looked at Joan's bed and for an exasperated moment thought she had sneaked out to meet a boy, and then I remembered.

The panic was overwhelming. My throat tightened and I gasped for breath. My scalp and hands tingled. My lips went numb. I dug my fingernails into my cheeks, and the pain brought some relief.

I went in the dim light to Joan's closet and found the dress I had last seen her wear, a pretty purple-and-yellow plaid with capped sleeves. I put it on.

The dress hung loose on me and smelled like Joan. I climbed into her bed, pulled the sheets over my head. Had she looked at my empty bed before she'd left this room? Had she imagined me in Oklahoma City, enduring my father and his wife, and felt sorry for me? Or was she glad that I wasn't there to interfere with her plans? Had she thought of me at all?

I fell asleep thinking of Joan. I woke thinking of Joan. I wore my own clothes downstairs, of course, but at the breakfast table Mary stared at me, startled, and I thought for a second I'd forgotten to change. I looked down, at my own hunter-green skirt.

"Your face," Mary said, and I felt my cheek.

"Oh," I said. "I must have scratched myself in my sleep."

"There's blood on your face, Cecilia. You should wash it off."

The scratch was small; once the blood was gone you almost couldn't see it. But it felt strangely satisfying, to see that I'd hurt myself. I wanted to show the world that

92

Joan's departure had scarred me.

But I was too practical for that. The world would only think I'd lost my mind.

After that, I slept in Joan's clothes when I was particularly lonely. No one ever knew.

Every day, Stewart, the Fortiers' butler, stacked the mail into a neat pile and left it on a silver tray in the foyer, and every day I looked for a letter from Joan. A month after she disappeared a postcard arrived, a picture of a field of bluebonnets on the front.

I'm fine, it read. *Don't look for me. I love you all.*

I turned the postcard over. The postmark read Fort Worth, but I knew Joan was not in Texas any longer. She was in New York. She was in Hollywood. The rumors were varied. But I only knew she was nowhere near me.

I wanted to rip the postcard in two but instead tucked it back into the sheaf of envelopes and slipped into the downstairs powder room before Stewart or Mary saw me snooping. The mirror in there was a Fortier antique, its surface dotted with black marks of age. I could hardly see my reflection in the dim light.

Who would see me, now that Joan was gone?

93

■ ■ ■ ■

I waited for my own postcard, my own signal. An acknowledgment at least. She couldn't send it to Evergreen, so perhaps she would send it to Ciela. "Gotten any unusual mail?" I asked Ciela one day, as we were leaving school. Fred waited for me at the bottom of the steps. "No," she said slowly. She could see straight through me, but I couldn't help myself.

There were hushed meetings between Mary and Furlow in Furlow's office. A private detective was hired, then another when the first found nothing.

I would never tell anyone else about what Joan had said to me about wanting to leave Houston. I would never tell anyone about what I had seen in the gymnasium. It became clear, in those months, that Mary's plans for Joan had been more concrete, more realized and nuanced, than I had ever known. I once heard her say to Furlow that Joan was "meant to be something the likes of which the world has never seen." But she didn't mean the world. I knew that even then. She meant Houston, and her plans did not involve Joan living elsewhere, far from her parents, in an orbit they couldn't influence and control.

I sleepwalked through the next month and graduated from Lamar High School without Joan next to me. My father flew in from Oklahoma and we had a sad lunch at Sonny Look's afterward, just the two of us. I missed Joan with a blinding intensity. I could not see my way forward without her. My father offered to take me back to Oklahoma City and I all but laughed in his face. What would I have done there? Served canapés with his wife? I needed to stay here for when Joan returned.

"But what will you do, Cecilia?" my father asked, his forehead creased.

"Is now the time to start worrying about me?" His face fell. I'd forgotten how sensitive he was. He wasn't a good man but he wasn't a bad man, either. Mainly, he had been no match for my mother.

"I'll manage," I said, and patted his forearm, awkwardly. We took great pains to avoid touching each other. "I always have."

I wonder now how my life would have unfolded if I had moved back to Oklahoma with my father. Established a life for myself in a different world. A world without Joan.

"Well, Cecilia," Mary had said, one morning a month after graduation, as I ate my oatmeal alone at the breakfast table. I'd been spending my time as Joan and I would have spent it, had she been here: going every morning to the pool, shopping, seeing movies with the girls. Occasionally Mary, Furlow, and I had joyless cocktails before dinner. "I think it's time."

I rested my spoon on the wide rim of the bowl, dabbed the corners of my mouth with my napkin before meeting Mary's eye.

"Time?" I asked, though I knew exactly what she meant.

"Time," Mary said. "Time to move on from Evergreen. I'm sure you're tired of living with us old fuddy-duddies." She laughed. And then, as if just noticing me, cut herself short. "You do know what I mean, don't you, Cecilia? I mean move into the penthouse. Move into the penthouse and wait for Joan." She pressed her finger to her lips. "She can't stay gone forever."

I wanted to weep. I dumbly looked around the breakfast room, at the pine table where Joan and I had sat a hundred — no, a thousand — times. At the armoire that housed extra china. And then at Dorie, who stood at the door to the kitchen, watching me. I wanted Idie. I could smell her. I remembered how perfectly I had fit underneath her chin when I sat on her lap as a child. Dorie shook her head before she stepped back into the kitchen, the gesture nearly imperceptible, but I understood: the Fortiers were not my family.

With Joan gone, it was easy to forget that Mary and Furlow weren't my parents. I slept in their daughter's room. I ate meals with them. They'd given me a gold charm bracelet for graduation, a gold "J" dangling from a link. "It's your real name, is it not?" Mary asked, when I touched the letter with my finger. She'd kissed my cheek, and I'd felt loved. It was a rare moment of affection from Mary. Mary was kind to me, but I would not have called her affectionate. Yet I felt like I deserved her affection: I was behaving more like a daughter than Joan. I was good, as Joan was not.

Mary stood over me — towered, a woman like that always towered — and I wanted her to touch me so desperately I could almost feel her hand on my shoulder. She did not.

She remained standing longer than necessary. She gazed at me, not fondly, exactly, but not meanly, either. I couldn't discern it. Things were not as they seemed, I felt, suddenly. Things were being kept from me. And then as quickly as the feeling had come over me, it disappeared, because Mary leaned down and kissed my cheek.

Mary and Furlow were generous; where I would go was never in question. But now I understand that generosity had little to do with it. They wanted everything in Joan's life to be the same, so that when she returned she could slip back into it as if she had never left in the first place.

By the next day I was in downtown Houston. It was July, blazing; before I mustered the energy to get dressed I sat in front of the window unit in my bra and panties to cool off. Ciela had come over to help me unpack — though there was nothing to unpack. All my clothes had been hung neatly in my closet, all my toiletries placed in the stainless-steel bathroom cabinet. I had been relieved to see that all Joan's clothes were there, too.

It never even occurred to me that I should spend my own money, waiting for me in a bank account downtown, and get my own place. My inheritance, already substantial, had grown since my mother's death, due to the wise investments of faceless men. I wasn't as wealthy as Joan, of course, but I could take care of myself for the rest of my life if I needed to, and live well. I hated the sight of the monthly statements that arrived in the mail from the Second National Bank of Houston, tucked them away, unopened, in the drawer of my nightstand. Instead of a mother binding me to the world, I had a stack of papers stamped with numbers I never read.

Ciela walked in, took one look at the large glass windows, and dubbed the place the Specimen Jar.

There had been whispers, lately, that the feds were going to try Ciela's father for money laundering, but Ciela seemed impervious to them. She had grown into herself, as the saying went; she moved across a room like she had an audience, like Joan had. Like Joan still did, wherever she was, unless her magic was less potent outside of Houston.

Ciela would blossom while Joan was gone. She would be featured in the *Press* every week; she would be Houston's go-to girl. Then Joan would return and replace her.

"You'll never feel alone, at least," Ciela said, with a smile, leaning her forehead against a window.

That was true. I felt watched, though no one could possibly see me up there, on the fourteenth floor of one of Houston's tallest buildings. And there was a live-in maid, too, Sari, though we mostly avoided each other.

Ciela left and the doorbell buzzed again

so quickly I was sure she'd forgotten something.

"Come in," I called.

Instead of Ciela there was Furlow, standing hesitantly in the doorframe, even though he owned the place. I jumped up to welcome him and he kissed me on the cheek, tentatively.

"How do you like it here?" he asked. His hat was still on his head; perhaps a sign that he wouldn't stay long. I hoped so. I didn't think I had ever been alone with Furlow.

His skin had begun to show age, but the years had not clouded his blue eyes; it was easy to see the handsome man he had once been in the contours of his face, in his thick, silver hair. He had celebrated his seventy-fifth birthday before Joan left.

"Cecilia?" he said, and I realized I hadn't answered his question.

"I like it," I said, and nodded, though what else could I have said? Joan's absence felt like a death. It felt worse than a death, because when my mother died I'd had Joan, and now I had no one. Furlow could have asked me anything, and I would have told him what I thought he wanted to hear.

"May I?" he asked, and gestured to the sofa I'd just straightened, a sofa he had never laid eyes on before but had, nonetheless, bought. I nodded. I watched as he sat down on the low-slung sectional. A designer had done the space in the newest style, and it was sleek and modern and utterly unlike any place I had ever lived. I felt like I was living in a hotel lobby, though it had only been a day. I would get used to it, just as I'd gotten used to Evergreen.

Furlow looked out of place. He wasn't a man made for the low proportions of modern furniture. He needed heft and weight to his furniture: a distressed leather chair with a tall back, a mahogany wardrobe in which to hang his cowboy hat.

"Joan's been gone for three months," he said, and I nodded. This was a fact, though it seemed impossible. "I came here alone, without Mary, because I wanted to know if Joan had been in touch."

"The postcard," I said. I cleared my throat. "With the flowers." I understood him, but I wanted to buy myself time.

"I meant privately."

I smiled, and tried not to cry.

"She has not," I said. And she should have! I should have been lying; Joan should have written me a letter, made a phone call. Sent a note for me to Ciela's house. Something, anything. I should have received some signal, some sign that I still mattered to her.

It had become harder and harder to take for granted that Joan loved me, that Joan was simply careless with her affections.

Furlow studied Houston's skyline. What a different view, I thought, than Evergreen's copse of trees, which were visible from every window. Did he imagine Joan looking from a window? Did he wonder, as I did, what his daughter saw, wherever she was?

"I had hoped she had. I had hoped you might be able to tell me something of her happiness."

Such an odd way to phrase it. "Her happiness?"

"Her happiness has been the only thing I have ever concerned myself with. Unlike her mother." He smiled faintly. This was a side of Furlow I had never seen before — quiet, contemplative — and it made me nervous. He continued to speak.

"Mary thinks we gave Joanie too much. Let her have too much freedom. But a girl like Joan," he said, spreading his hands, "what else were we supposed to do? Do you know a movie agent took Mary aside after the debutante ball? He happened to be there, one of the girls was a cousin of his. He thought he could make Joan famous."

He looked straight at me.

"Do you think that's where she went? To

Hollywood?"

My face flamed red. This was the first I'd heard of a movie agent. Joan had told me nothing.

"Maybe." I tried to make my voice sound hopeful. I thought of the boy in the bleachers. I thought of John, who'd been smitten with Joan. I imagined Joan at a casting call, like I'd read about in magazines, surrounded by other beautiful young women. Hollywood seemed as good a guess as any.

Furlow sighed, took off his hat and put it back on. "Mary thinks that's where she's gone. I just don't know why she didn't tell us. I would have let her go."

He would not have let her go.

"I gave my girl *everything,*" he said, and the emotion in his voice caught me off guard. "Everything," he repeated.

And still she had left. Furlow stared at me. Joan, leaving his world, without permission: he could not make sense of it.

After Furlow said good-bye, with no more information than he had come with, I went into my new, modern bathroom, with a showerhead so wide that standing underneath it felt like being caught in rain.

I studied my reflection. I wasn't surprised Joan had been singled out among all us debs.

In that moment I felt like nothing so much as a paid companion, the spinster, the homely friend from one of the Victorian novels we'd had to read in English class. Except my companion, my purpose, my reason for existence, had jumped ship.

"Hollywood," Ciela said one night, near the end of the summer. We sat on the white leather couch in the Specimen Jar's living room, playing mahjong with an old Bakelite set I'd discovered in a closet. We were still in our bikinis, robes untied. We'd spent the day by the pool, as we'd spent most of our days that summer. How I would have spent them had Joan been here.

Mary had called me to Evergreen the day before, to let me know that they'd found Joan. She was, as Mary had suspected, in Hollywood. And she was not planning to come back any time soon.

"Yes," I said, "Mrs. Fortier said she's trying to become a star." I tried to keep my voice casual.

"The great mystery is solved," Ciela said, and I didn't like her tone, but I liked that she was making light of Joan and her ambition, turning them ridiculous. She didn't belong in Hollywood. She belonged here, with me. All our plans, all our schemes: We

104

were going to go out every night, become regulars at the Cork Club. We were going to spend two weeks in the Hill Country. We were going to escape to Galveston when the heat became unbearable. We were going to Paris next spring, where Joan was going to lead us around the city and practice her French. We were going to come back to Houston and find handsome, older men — not the boys we had dated in high school — and go on double dates. We were going to live the lives we had been imagining since middle school.

But Joan had changed her mind. She hadn't picked up the telephone. She hadn't picked up a pen. She hadn't even relayed a message for me through Mary. Had I done something wrong, offended Joan in some profound way? I racked my brain. Had she seen me that afternoon, in the gymnasium? Had I spent too much time with Ciela, become too close to her? Had I defended Mary too staunchly? But none of my offenses, real or imagined, were big enough to merit Joan's departure. I knew that. Her sudden exit, her new life, her reluctance to return to Houston — none of it was because of me.

"It must hurt your feelings that she didn't tell you," Ciela said. She was looking at me sympathetically. "I'm sorry, Cece."

I almost told her. We were very drunk and it was very late. Despair. The word was on the tip of my tongue. It wasn't a word I remembered ever using before. It was a word for women in novels, for heroines in film; it wasn't a word for Cece Beirne from River Oaks, Texas.

But that's what I felt, wasn't it? Not hurt; hurt was how I had felt when a photographer had come to Evergreen to take the Fortier family Christmas picture and it was a given that I would not be in it. Hurt was how I had felt when my father and his new wife had not remembered my birthday, even though I hadn't truly expected them to. Hurt was another thing entirely. You could forget a hurt feeling; you could forgive it.

When Joan left I felt emptied out, a particular kind of hollowing I had felt when my mother died.

"Cece?" Ciela said, waiting for my response. Did she care about me, or did she just want the dirt? I wondered. Did she want me to tell her that Joan was not the girl I thought she had been? That our great friendship was a farce?

She had benefited from Joan's absence, after all, invited now to every party, every opening, every concert. She'd even appeared in the "The Town Crier" last weekend, leaving the Cork Club. It would have been Joan's picture, if Joan had been here.

I took a deep breath. "You can't tell a living soul," I said. "Mary Fortier would have me beheaded." I drew a finger across my neck. Ciela watched me with a knitted brow, her head tilted. "I knew. She told me everything."

"Everything," Ciela echoed, and I wasn't sure if she believed me, but it didn't matter. I had closed the subject of Joan.

CHAPTER EIGHT

1957

I was soaking my delicates — I liked to wash them myself — in the laundry room, listening to the soft thud of Maria's footsteps as she played with Tommy upstairs. The phone rang, and I rushed to the kitchen to get it.

"Hello?"

"Cece, can you hear me? This is Mary Fortier," she said, even though I'd known who she was the instant I'd heard her voice, deep and firm, a man's voice, with a Littlefield drawl she'd never tried to undo. I'd always liked that about Mary: she'd tell you in a second she'd grown up without two nickels to rub together.

"I can hear you." Like most people over a certain age, she didn't quite trust the telephone. I drew my fingers across the rows of canned vegetables: corn, green beans, beets. We hadn't built a backyard bomb shelter, like our neighbors the Dempseys, but I had more canned foods than we'd eat in a lifetime.

"Good. Joan's indisposed this week" — at this I froze; did she know what Joan was up to? — "but Furlow's been asking about her. He wants to see her, and I thought you might be able to come instead. Would you consider it?"

"I'll be over this afternoon," I promised, "with Tommy."

I dressed Tommy in his navy-blue sailor suit and combed his hair with a little bit of Ray's pomade. "So handsome," I said, when I was done, and Tommy gave me a tiny smile, which made my day. My week, even.

I slowed down as we approached Evergreen, set back from the road, screened by those enormous magnolia trees. It was one of the biggest houses in River Oaks, second only to the Hoggs' mansion, Bayou Bend, on Westcott. It had been designed by Staub and Briscoe and built on two lots; its magnificent gardens were the work of Ruth London herself. Furlow had originally intended Evergreen as a country estate, a retreat from the crush of downtown Houston, but after Evergreen was completed he and Mary decided they never wanted to leave.

Furlow had been heir to a Louisiana family fortune, made on cotton and sugarcane, divested before, as he called it, the War Between the States; the fortune had multiplied, then been largely lost by a reckless father before Furlow came into his own. I couldn't think of a more classic Southern coming-of-age story. Furlow liked to think of himself as a Southern gentleman from another world turned Texan. He wore Lucchese cowboy boots and a custom-made cowboy hat, even now.

Furlow and Mary lived at Evergreen alone these days, with a dozen servants to help Mary keep an eye on her declining husband. Once Furlow had roamed all the way to one of the entrances of River Oaks; Fred had circled the neighborhood for hours before he found him.

I felt a peculiar mixture of dread and longing as I turned into their red gravel driveway. All these years later, I still felt privileged to be invited here, though I knew I should have outgrown such feelings. I knew people thought my attachment to Joan strange. It would have been normal for me to grow up and scale back my devotion to her. But our friendship was different from other friendships. My own husband didn't understand it. He was a man, after all. He wasn't capable of female devotion.

Now I felt disoriented, anger at Joan bubbling up though I tried to tamp it down.

My hair looked frizzy in my compact and I tried to smooth it down. It was curly and I wanted it to be straight, and I wasted a lot of time in my youth trying to make it that way. I tilted the compact and checked my lipstick, my light swipes of rouge. I had good coloring — even, olive skin and red lips, courtesy of my mother — so I didn't need much makeup.

"Mommy's biding her time, isn't she?" I asked Tommy, who was looking out the window. "Let's go see Uncle Furlow and Aunt Mary. Let's show them what a big boy you are."

I stepped across the gravel, noted the satisfying crunch beneath my shoes. The work that went into this place astonished me. The gravel was raked, by hand, every evening. There were servants' quarters out back — Little Green, Mary used to call it — where six full-time employees lived. My mother used to seethe over the servants' quarters; *I* had that, she used to say. That's how we used to live. What use does Mary Fortier from Littlefield have for a ladies' maid?

I used the front door, instead of the side

111

door I would have used with Joan. I hesitated at the doorbell, Tommy on my hip — was I standing on ceremony? But it was a thousand degrees outside and I could feel my hair getting bigger and bigger the longer we stood there so I rang the doorbell, and almost immediately Stewart answered. Mary appeared behind him and ushered me in, took my pocketbook and kissed my cheek. I murmured hello to Stewart, who, in the way of all Evergreen servants, barely acknowledged me. He had always been thin, a meatless kind of man; now, in his old age, he looked positively concave.

"Hello, dear," Mary said. She looked me up and down in her appraising, affectionate way.

She wore an ordinary skirt and blouse, her uniform. If she had been born in the era of pants, she would have worn nothing else. The only hint of her wealth: a diamond the size of a cherry on her ring finger. And of course in the way she carried herself, as if the world would bend to her, which it always had, since she'd married Furlow.

She used her lack of beauty to her advantage. No one expected a plain woman to want so much. Mary commanded a room in such a way as to suggest that good looks were frivolous, a symptom of superficiality.

Still, she took pleasure in Joan's beauty. I remembered getting ready for our junior prom, glancing in the bathroom mirror and being startled by the reflection of Mary, standing at the edge of the door and watching us — watching Joan. It would be easy to say that Mary was jealous of Joan's beauty. But what I saw that day, in Mary's expression, wasn't jealousy. It was pride, a specific brand of wonder.

"Aren't you something, today," she said, nodding at my sundress. It was a simple style that covered my upper arms and fell to my knees. "This way," she murmured now, "Furlow's in his office."

Furlow sat behind his massive mahogany desk, looking at a magazine, and from this vantage point you would not have known his mind was turning to cotton. He looked like the handsome Furlow Fortier of my youth: aged, of course, his hair white, his cheeks striated with the deep lines earned by spending most of his young life on oil fields. On the desk there was a single picture, in a silver frame: Joan, as a little girl. She sat on a pony, grinning at the camera.

I was nervous, suddenly, hesitated at the door, but then Mary's hand was on my back, pushing me forward.

"Joan?" Furlow asked, looking up. The

magazine he was gazing at was a gossip rag, mainly pictures, something he wouldn't have looked twice at in his old life.

"No, Furlow," Mary said firmly. "It's Cece, Joan's best friend. She's married to Ray Buchanan. She's like another daughter." She walked across the room to Furlow as she spoke, and I stood there, dumbly. She smoothed Furlow's collar, helped him stand and walk to a chair, and gestured for me to take the one across from it.

"She lived with us for a few years in high school — how many was it, Cece?"

Like all capable women, Mary had a memory like an elephant's. But she wanted me to speak.

I cleared my throat. "Yes, for two and a half years. After my mother died and my father moved away. Every Sunday we used to eat outside. Dorie would serve us fried chicken and biscuits on paper plates. We loved it."

Mary looked at me for a moment. It was a misstep to mention Dorie, who had left the Fortiers' employ under mysterious circumstances years earlier.

I wanted to take back the reference to Dorie, but then Mary spoke.

"Dorie and Idie took such good care of you and Joan for such a long time."

The last time I'd seen Idie was at my mother's funeral; at the end of it, in the receiving line, she'd hugged me and it had felt so familiar I'd had to bite my cheek to stop myself from crying. I wanted her to never stop touching me.

Furlow had perked up at the mention of Joan. I saw with a pang that he was dressed beautifully, in well-ironed linen slacks and a soft blue knit shirt, his boots shined to within an inch of their life. Tommy squirmed on my lap and I put him down, looked to Mary to make sure it was okay; she nodded. There wasn't a third chair so she perched on the edge of Furlow's desk, like, I couldn't help but think, a chaperone.

Tommy backed up until he found my knees. His hand was in his mouth, as was his habit in any new situation.

"He's shy," I said. "Let's take your hand out of your mouth." I regretted not bringing his train to distract him.

Furlow clapped his hands, suddenly. "He's a delightful boy!" he said, laughing. "Delightful!" I flushed with pleasure.

Furlow leaned forward. "Who are you?" he said softly, to Tommy, and when I looked at Mary she shrugged, a smile playing across her lips. "It's better to laugh at it than cry over it," she always said, whenever Joan or I was upset. I hadn't thought of her saying that in years. But once upon a time, during our theatrical high school years, she had said it often.

"It's the highlight of his week," she said, and I thought she meant this visit, with me and Tommy, but then she went on, "when Joan visits."

"I can imagine," I said.

"How is she these days?" Mary asked.

"She?"

"Joan," she said, with a careful casualness, and I understood all at once that Mary had invited me to Evergreen to find out what I knew about Joan.

"Oh," I said with a nervous laugh. "I'm sure she's fine. When I spoke to her the other night she was," I said. "Fine," I added.

Mary nodded, and I couldn't tell what she knew: Had she already heard that Joan had a man at her house and called me over to find out how far the gossip had spread? Or did she know only that her daughter was absent? At least Furlow would never learn anything of Joan's behavior. He would not have been able to comprehend it.

"Has she been in touch?" I asked, after a moment, but Mary only gazed at me benignly.

"We're gearing up for a hot summer," she

116

said. We passed the time watching Tommy with Furlow, chatting about nothing. Tommy was wary of Furlow at first, but by the end of the visit he sat in Furlow's lap.

As I stood by the front door, preparing to leave, Mary gave me a firm hug. She didn't touch lightly, in the way of most women.

"Thank you for coming, and for bringing the boy. It did Furlow some good," she said. But she gripped my hand and did not let go.

There was nothing I could do to help Mary. I didn't know what Joan was up to, was the truth. I didn't know how long she was planning on staying away from Evergreen, or why she stayed away in the first place. Surely she knew how much she meant to her parents, Furlow especially. I had been anxious for Joan, but now I was angry. Joan was an adult. She wasn't nineteen anymore; I shouldn't have been worried about failing her. She should have been worried about failing her mother, her father. And me.

I helped Tommy into the car and slid into the driver's seat. Joan had been so kind to me when I'd first come here. Had been so kind to me as my mother lay dying. But she had been more than that. She had shown me, and my mother, compassion beyond her fifteen years. And now she couldn't tear herself away from her romance, her sex — whatever you wanted to call it — to reassure her father, her father who was losing his mind but still yearned for his child.

CHAPTER NINE

I can recall every inch of my mother's body, even now, all these years later. What happened to her was not a thing you forget. The first time I saw her wounds, when a nurse was changing the bandages, I ran into the bathroom and vomited. It looked like a child had gone to work with a pair of scissors, not like the careful handiwork of a surgeon. I was grateful my mother was asleep. The nurse had looked at me sympathetically.

"You'll get used to it," she'd said, but I never got used to it. My mother had gone into surgery with a hard knot in her left breast, which her doctor had discovered after she had complained of a burning sensation. She woke up in the hospital and both her breasts were gone. She was thirty-six years old. She couldn't lift her arms because the muscle had been taken along with her breasts. Carrying her to the bathroom back at home was nearly impossible, because she couldn't cling to my neck, so she used a bedpan. And it was only me there to help her — she wouldn't tolerate the nurse the hospital sent, and Idie's presence was only permissible if my mother was so knocked out by drugs she no longer cared who saw her.

And the thing was, I understood. Which is not to say I didn't resent this sudden intimacy with my mother — I did — but I understood why she didn't want strangers in her presence. I understood why she only tolerated me. She loved me, because loving me was a biological fact: I was her daughter. She was my mother. She had no choice. When my mother fell ill I would have told you that she didn't love anyone. But dying laid bare her animal instincts.

Strangely, she tolerated Joan. Or at least, she ignored Joan when Joan came to sit with her, turned her head on the pillow and fell asleep. When I remember my mother dying I remember her in her bedroom, on her back because she didn't have the strength to turn to her side, her head tilted away from the person sitting next to her, which was usually me. Her head on her beautiful pillow, her bedroom as pretty and neat as it always had been. I was rarely allowed to go in there when I was a child, and as a young teenager I had no interest. But now I spent most of my time with my mother, waiting. Lifting her head so she could swallow a pill; grinding the pill into dust and spooning it into her mouth with applesauce when she was too weak to do that. Bringing her a bedpan, helping her relieve herself. Sponging the debris of death — her skin was covered in a granular substance, almost like sand, during her last few weeks — from her body.

The intimacy embarrassed me, but I had no choice.

"You're good to her," Idie told me once, over grilled cheeses and tomato soup. And it seemed such a strange thing to say, because what else could I be? There was no future with my mother, no past: we were simply two bodies in a room, one dying, one well.

Before my mother's illness my concerns had been typical: School, which I had all but dropped out of for now. A boy named Charles who was very devoted to me, though we had never touched. Joan. We could spend hours talking about Charles, or whatever new boy Joan was seeing. We could spend hours talking about whether or not Ciela meant to be so sharp-tongued, or if it was just her personality. I understood I would return to these concerns, to that life, after my mother died, but for now I put aside my former life as easily as a book that didn't quite hold my interest.

The doctors spoke to my father, not me. He came to the house three times, and each time he sat with my mother, alone, for half an hour or so. I could hear them quietly talking from outside their door. I had briefly harbored a hope that my father might return to us for good for at least as long as my mother was alive, but when he came his presence in the house felt odd. I was always glad when he was gone, when it was just me and my mother in her room, Idie beyond the door.

The last time, my father sat with my mother and then found me in my bedroom. She'd had a difficult day, been unable to keep even water down. Sometimes I thought she didn't want to keep anything down, didn't want any part of this to be easy or comfortable. That she wanted to punish herself, and me, as she was dying.

But when I told her my father was there she was strangely calm.

"Do you want to see him today?" I asked. "He can come back another time."

She gave a short laugh. "I better see him

while I have the chance," she said, and I understood she was referring to both my father's history of running away and her own situation.

My mother had been beautiful all her life. When we went anywhere together — to the gas station, to my school to meet the principal, to my riding lesson — men stared, made any excuse to be near her. Sometimes my mother entertained their attentions, and sometimes she ignored them. Beauty, after all, had not kept her husband near, had not made her richer than the homely Mary Fortier. It should have. But it had not. And yet I understood, from a very young age, that my mother had not wanted my father near. She, like most unhappy people, wanted contradictory things.

Illness turned my mother into a grotesque. The incisions where her breasts had been wept, constantly, and her chest looked like a bombed, pitted country. Her skin was gray. Wrinkles appeared overnight. She aged thirty years in a day. Once I caught her looking at her reflection in the silver coaster I kept next to her bed.

"Do you want a mirror?" I asked.

I thought she might cry, but then she laughed.

"I think I've seen enough." I rose, but she

shook her head. "Stay a moment."

I did what she asked. I did anything she asked, in those days. Always.

"Days are gods to years," she said. "Time will fly. You'll forget this."

I shook my head. I would never forget.

Back in my room, my father knocked, gently — his knock was unfamiliar, as his footsteps had been outside my door.

"Come in," I said, and he opened my door gingerly, stepped inside. It was the first time he'd been in my room in I couldn't remember how long. Ever? No, surely he had been in there at some point. I watched him take in my room, which was still done in different shades of pink, or, as my mother called it, rose, accented with little flourishes: a collection of sterling silver card cases that my mother had been collecting since she was a little girl; five Limoges boxes; a picture of Cary Grant I'd cut from the pages of *Photoplay* and taped to the wall. My father looked relieved when he saw the picture, proof that his daughter was normal. She liked Cary Grant. She had crushes on movie stars.

Because the truth was that my father didn't know me at all. How could he have? He was a little softer around the middle than when I'd seen him last, and balding now. He stood at the foot of my bed, awkwardly, waiting for something. I felt an unexpected tenderness for him, which is what I'd always felt for this man who was my father, for as long as I could remember. I was never angry at him for leaving. I understood why he wanted to be somewhere else, why he could not take me with him. Children belonged to their mothers.

"Cecilia," he said, "are you fine?"

What a strange question. *I* was fine. It was my mother who was not fine.

"Fine," I said, and felt a rush of anger. I looked down at my pretty manicure, which Joan had done last night. I looked up again. "I have help," I said. "Joan. Idie."

"From what Idie says, your mother won't let anyone else help."

I said nothing.

"Your mother is going to die, Cecilia. Soon, I think."

I wanted him gone, out, disappeared from our lives. Of course I knew my mother would die soon. Nobody had ever told me — doctors weren't frank, in those days, especially not with teenage girls — but I wasn't an idiot. There had been no hope in her hospital room. No reason to think she might leave that place a well woman.

"I know," I said.

"Well," he said, after a long moment. "Do

125

you need anything from me?"

I shook my head. "Nothing," I said.

He stood against my doorframe, half in, half out. He did not know what to do with his hands. My father was neither short nor tall, neither handsome nor homely. He looked like any man, every man. My mother had been a catch. They had met through her older brother, who had been my father's fraternity brother at the University of Texas.

"What was she like when you met her?" I almost clapped my hand over my mouth. The question had come, unbidden, into my throat; it felt like it had asked itself.

But my father didn't seem surprised. "What was she like when I met her?" he mused, staring onto the yard, where our gardener was weeding a bed of camellias. I cut some every afternoon, brought them into my mother's room, and floated them in silver bowls.

"She was a sight to behold," he said. And I sighed impatiently. I knew that she had been beautiful. I wanted more.

My father glanced at me, but I couldn't read his expression.

"She was smart, too. Smart as a whip. Could cut any man down to size in a second." He laughed. "I suppose a lot like she is now."

126

I nodded. I'd never heard him speak so affectionately of my mother. Perhaps it was easy to speak well of the near-dead.

"All right," my father said, and took his hands out of his pockets, then put them back in. "I should get going. I should ske-daddle."

He walked over and kissed me on the forehead.

I used to think that my father had married my mother because of me — because she was already pregnant with me. But when I was thirteen I found their marriage certificate in my mother's files, which proved that was not the case.

Suddenly he turned halfway around so I could see his profile.

"I asked your mother to marry me after we'd known each other for three weeks. It was 1931. Everything felt like it was falling down all around us. And then there was your mother. She seemed . . . untouched." He shrugged. "I don't know, Cecilia."

Through the window I watched him leave, tip his hat at the gardener, open his door, and slide into the car. All while my mother lay two doors down, dying her slow and painful death. My father would die pain-lessly, in his sleep. His wife who loved him by his side. Clean, smooth sheets beneath him. My father was someone who moved easily through the world; my mother was not, never had been.

And who was I? I wondered that, then, sitting on my pink matelassé cover, leaning forward to catch the last glimpse of my father's blue car as he drove away. How would I move through the world?

CHAPTER TEN

1957

I was standing near the sink, listening to the rain and holding a plate with half a tuna fish sandwich and a cup of fruit cocktail on it, when Maria spoke.

"There's a man here," she said. I joined her by the window, from which you could see the front door; there was a person standing there, in a shapeless coat, soaking wet, trying to shake the water from his hands, his hair.

We weren't expecting anyone. Not in weather like this. And nobody dropped by without calling these days, not with children who napped.

"It's Joan," I said. Maria shook her head, but I recognized the way she stood.

"A man," Maria insisted.

The doorbell rang.

I ran my tongue over my teeth to check for

bits of bread and tuna as I opened the door.

I would act a little peeved, I decided. Joan would act sheepish. Just a little bit. She would apologize, tell me where she had been — or maybe she wouldn't, maybe she would make an easily dismantled excuse — but I wouldn't care. I would take her into the kitchen, her distinct odor of cigarette smoke and sun trailing us, and she would be kind to Tommy, she would be happy to see him, and I would forgive her.

When I opened the door she was smoking a cigarette, or trying to; she was too wet to light it properly. She looked awful: thin, mascara running down her cheeks — why was she wearing mascara in the first place? — her hair falling around her face. I leaned forward to hug her and she stiffened but let me touch her anyway, and I confirmed my suspicion: her hair hadn't been washed in days.

"Joan," I said, "come in. Right this instant," I continued, when she stood there, hesitating, as if she were going to stand on my front steps and I were going to stand inside my warm, dry house. She stood there another moment.

"Now," I said, and something in my voice made her obey.

I took her wet coat, which was indeed her

old Burberry trench — I'd seen it a million times — and led her into the kitchen, where I meant to make her tea, or coffee, something warm.

"It's been a few days," she said, as she sat down at our table, in Ray's spot, the best spot, with a view of both the kitchen and the big bay window. Her voice sounded completely normal. She plucked a napkin from the holder, her compact from her purse, and went to work on the mascara smudges. She was fine.

I was suddenly infuriated.

"It's been two weeks," I snapped. Joan looked at me, her face tilted as if she were nothing more than a curious child. "Two weeks," I said. I stood there with my hand on my hip, and I was aware of the ridiculousness of my pose, as if I were a schoolteacher and Joan was my bad pupil. I sat down across from her.

"Should I make us tea?" I asked, and sighed.

Joan shook her head. It occurred to me that Joan didn't really want to be here at all. It was starting to seem like that, more and more as we sat there.

"I was with an old friend," she said finally. "From my Hollywood days."

I felt my cheeks turn hot, my palms

131

dampen. I took a deep breath before I spoke.

"I didn't know you had friends from your Hollywood days."

Joan lit a cigarette in a single, practiced motion. She looked like Kim Novak when she smoked.

"I don't have many. But I have some."

She turned her head away as she said this last part; she didn't want to make eye contact. It wasn't like Joan, to provide explanations, to account for herself. My instinct had been correct: this man meant something to her.

"So this is something serious."

"Did I say it was serious? He's an old friend. Just an old, old friend."

"So that's where you've been. With your old friend," I said, surprised by my own sarcasm. I'd been worrying about the wrong thing: a stranger, not someone with whom she had some mysterious history. Though a stranger might have been preferable; it would have been temporary.

She gave a hard, short laugh. A peculiar laugh. Everything about this moment was bizarre. There was no warmth between us, no understanding.

"Yes, with an old friend, but not like that." She tapped her cigarette against the rim of

Ray's ashtray. I felt shaky, panicked. Joan was lying, keeping a secret from me again.

"But not like what?" I persisted. "What are you doing with him?"

"Do I have to spell it out? We aren't fucking, Cee." She turned and looked outside. The rain had stopped, and you could see by the soft glow of the clouds that the Houston sun would be out again before you knew it. A moody morning, a bright afternoon. In Houston, anything could be erased.

"He's an old friend, that's all. I ran into him at the Cork Club. He was here for business and we got to talking about times gone by." She stood, stubbing her cigarette in the ashtray, drawing out her slim cigarette case to retrieve and light another. "He's gone now. He won't be back."

I almost laughed. Did she really think I would believe they weren't, as she put it, fucking? I knew all of Joan's habits. Men she wasn't fucking held no interest for her.

Hollywood was a wound. We never spoke of her year away. She'd left me. She'd never apologized, never offered any good explanation for why she'd not let me in on her plans. And now *old friends* were appearing? I went to light Joan's new cigarette; my hand shook. Joan looked at it, then up at me. But he was gone, I reminded myself. He was no longer someone I needed to worry about.

"Why'd you tell me, then?"

That got her attention. "What do you mean?" She fiddled with the diamond bracelet on her slender wrist.

"I mean, why bother coming over and telling me if you're not going to tell me the real reason he was here?"

Joan studied me, as if she'd forgotten, and then remembered, who I was. *I'm your friend,* I wanted to say, though "friend" was a flimsy word for it.

For an instant I thought she might confess. For an instant I thought she might tell me everything. But then she smiled, and the old Joan returned. She leaned over the table and kissed my cheek.

Just then Tommy peeked around the corner of the kitchen door. "Go see Maria," I said, and then I checked my voice — this encounter with Joan had rattled me — "or you can come see Miss Joan. Would you like to come see Miss Joan?"

Tommy disappeared from view except for his small hand, which lingered on the doorframe.

"I don't know where Maria is," I muttered under my breath. Joan wasn't in the mood for children today. My questions were already frustrating her, and I didn't want to irritate her further.

"It's fine, Cee," Joan said softly. She stood. "Come see Miss Joan," she said, and walked to the kitchen's entryway, knelt on the floor, and placed her hand over Tommy's.

The soles of her shoes were badly scuffed. Her hair, held in place by a metal nest of bobby pins, hadn't been brushed in days. "Come see Miss Joan," she said again. Tommy's hand disappeared.

"He won't come," I said. "He's being shy today."

Joan ignored me. "Tommy," she called. "Please." Her voice sounded plaintive. It made me want to cry, though I did not understand why, exactly.

Tommy's head emerged, a small smile on his lips. He'd been playing a game with Joan. Joan had won.

"Oh," Joan said, and gathered Tommy to her, "you love Miss Joan, don't you?"

Tommy's cheek rested on Joan's shoulder. His hand toyed with her earring.

I was glad Joan had found some person to take comfort in, today.

CHAPTER ELEVEN

My mother began to lose her mind after my father's visit. There were moments of clarity — when she asked clearly for water, or another blanket, or called me by my name — and other times I felt certain she didn't recognize me. Idie had warned me about this: "The mind leaves the body first, Cecilia."

A few days after my father's visit, Joan came over after school, as she did most days. Being in close proximity to death — my mother upstairs, us in the kitchen drinking Dr Peppers and eating cocktail sausages out of the tin, our favorite snack — didn't rattle her.

"Mama told me your father was here last week. You didn't tell me." But her voice wasn't accusatory. She picked up the last sausage. Chewed, swallowed. She seemed so strong, so vibrant and present. My mother could barely take a sip of water without coughing.

I shook my head. "Only for a little while. I think it's the last time he'll come."

I wondered, briefly, how Mary had known, but Mary knew everything.

"My father doesn't want me to live with him," I said, abruptly. Joan had stood, opened the refrigerator. She was always starving after school. "He said something about me staying on here, with Idie."

She turned, a jar of pickles in one hand, a loaf of bread in the other. Joan was never confused. She took the world in stride. Nothing surprised her. But *I* had surprised her, just now. She couldn't fathom a world where a father would not want his own daughter.

Her expression infuriated me. I took a deep breath, tried to remind myself that Joan was silly, a little girl in certain matters.

"Why did you think otherwise?" I asked. I could not keep the anger from my voice. "You know how it is. You know how he is."

"I'm sorry, Cece." Her voice was low. "You'll come live with us, at Evergreen."

I closed my eyes and heard the clink of the jar as she set it on the counter. She came to me and hugged me, from behind. And I wept.

■ ■ ■ ■

That night I woke to the sound of my mother moaning. I was sleeping on her chaise longue, with a thick cashmere blanket that had been in her bedroom since I was a little girl. It was from Scotland, she used to tell me, and I wasn't to touch it.

Now the blanket, sturdy for all its softness, was my one real comfort at night. I associated it with sleep, when I could wrap myself in it and let myself go dead to the world for however long my mother did not need me.

Usually I slept in spurts: an hour here, half an hour there. But tonight I had closed my eyes at midnight, and my watch read 4:13 a.m. when I opened them and held my hand to the window to see the time by moonlight. The watch had been a gift from my mother and father last year, presented to me in a slim red box from Lechenger's for my fourteenth birthday. The piece was much too nice for a fourteen-year-old, a gold bracelet with diamonds framing the delicate watch face, and I had kept it in my sock drawer until recently. I'd never felt before the need for a watch; at home Idie kept me apprised of the time. At school,

teachers. But now my mother needed medicine on a specific schedule; now I needed to
always know the time.

"I want a bath," my mother said, after I
held up the glass of water I had just poured
to her lips. She shook her head, pressed her
lips together in a line.

"A bath," she repeated.

And her voice was filled with such longing, such desire, that I did not know how to
say no. I should have said no. Or I should
have, at the very least, fetched Idie, to help
me. But my mother would have screamed
at the sight of her, so what would have been
the point?

"All right," I said, "a bath. Let me draw
the water." And I stood, Idie's words — let
me draw the water — strange in my mouth.
It was Idie who had drawn my bath for years
and years, until I was old enough not to
need her. I couldn't remember my mother
ever doing it for me. I slipped my watch off
and left it on her bedside table among the
collection of pill bottles that stood sentry.

My mother's tub was porcelain, iron-
footed. Pretty, as everything she owned was
pretty. She had often retired to her room in
the evenings, and I could hear the water
running for a long time, and then silence,
and then the drain, and so I had come to

understand without ever being told that my mother liked long baths. I did not. I didn't have the patience.

I retrieved the glass bottles of pastel liquids from underneath the sink, along with the green dish of bath salts, a silver spoon nestled within. I had put them there when the nurse had asked me to clear the bathroom of anything unnecessary.

Now I had the feeling someone was watching me as I worked, putting a little bit of this and that into the water as it ran, trying to create the most perfect scent. I felt like a sorcerer. And then it was time to get my mother.

She is like my child, I caught myself thinking as I wrapped my arms around her back and lifted her to a sitting position, supporting her head with my hand. One day, I will carry my child like this. And then my mother's smell rose up, and the thought, which had been tender, turned grotesque.

I half carried, half dragged her to the bathroom, and then I stood in front of the mirror and used her reflection to help me undress her. We had long ago exchanged her silk nightgowns for thick, flannel pajamas, which were so unlike my mother. I had called Battelstein's and had them send over the smallest size they carried in men's. My mother was always cold, always freezing, and now, as I drew the top over her head, slid the bottoms off her hips, she gasped.

My naked mother was pressed against me. Her spine was so pronounced her vertebrae looked like joints from a child's building set. The place where her chest would have been pressed into mine, her bone against my flesh. I felt nothing. No tenderness, no pity. Just a strong desire to deliver her safely into the tub.

And I did, somehow. She lay there for a long time, moaning, almost imperceptibly, with pleasure. I propped up her head with a folded towel, and every so often I opened the drain to let out a little water and refill the tub with more hot water. It was satisfying work, because my mother was satisfied.

I don't know how long she stayed in the bath. I wouldn't remember my watch until the next morning, when it was light out. In my memory, it is hours, but that is impossible. The hot water would have run out long before then. My mother wouldn't have been able to tolerate the same position for so long. Or maybe she would have, since she was buoyant in the bath as she wasn't in her bed, her hips floating to the surface like two small, perfect apples. Maybe my memory is correct, and we sat there for hours, my mother's eyes closed against the light, me testing the water, over and over, until my own hands were prunes.

"I'm ready," she said, at the end of it. She sounded sleepy. She sounded nearly happy.

I crouched over the tub and began to lift her, but it was harder to handle her wet than dry. I hadn't wanted to drain the bath first, knowing she would be cold.

I dropped her. It happened quickly, as those things do. One second she was half out of the tub, her torso wrapped in a towel; the next second she was splayed on the tile floor, an inhuman keening emerging from deep inside her throat.

I screamed for Idie. I screamed as loud as I could, so loud I could not hear my mother.

Idie was good in a crisis. As soon as I saw her I stopped screaming; then my mother started, furious at Idie's presence, and in pain. Idie examined her quickly, ran her hands down my mother's arms and legs while my mother lay there on the bath mat, the towel barely covering her.

"I'm sorry," I murmured, over and over again, intercut by Idie's "Hush."

"Her shoulder," Idie said, when she was finished. My mother had gone mercifully silent, closed her eyes against the sight of us.

"I don't think it's broken," she continued. "Wrenched." I touched her shoulder as lightly as I could, but my mother still flinched. Already there was a bruise blossoming. It seemed impossible: my mother's body was so weak, so spent, how could it possibly have worked up the energy for a bruise?

She submitted to Idie's help: we carried her to the bed, dried her, dressed her, deposited her beneath the covers. We were lit only by the narrow glow of my mother's bedside lamp, for which I was grateful, because this way Idie couldn't see as clearly how ravaged my mother's body had become. But still she must have seen what had become of my beautiful mother. I felt both protective and ashamed of her.

Yet it was easier, much easier, to handle her with another person. Every time we moved her, even slightly, she whimpered, and I cursed myself for not being more careful. I had never caused my mother's pain before. Before, I had only relieved it in some way — with medicine, a heating pad, a massage. Mostly medicine.

I was near tears, but I did not want Idie to see me cry.

"Do you want me to crush it?" I asked,

holding up her pain pill, "or can you swallow it?"

I asked the question a dozen times a day. There were various pills, for various ailments. I kept a chart to keep track of it all, which I had drawn on graph paper from geometry class. I'd taped it by her bedside table, on the side closest to the window, where she would not see it. She would have hated it, something like that taped to the beautiful wall of her beautiful room. She would have thought of the residue the tape would have left when it was removed. Or perhaps she didn't have the energy to hate anymore, to consider things like tape residue. Perhaps it was a salve, to believe that she did.

When my mother answered she would say, "Swallow." When she did not, I would crush the pill. My mother would not look at me. So I turned from the bed, placed the pill in the bowl of the mortar, and lifted the pestle. When she spoke her voice was clear, as it had not been in a long time.

"Crush me a thousand more. Deliver me from this."

I glanced at Idie, who stood near my mother's feet, close enough to help me, far enough away that my mother might not notice her. Her face revealed nothing.

"Stop," I said. "Stop it."

"Her." My mother lifted her chin in Idie's direction. "Tell her to leave."

I looked down at the applesauce I held in my hand, then up at Idie. I didn't want her to leave, but I needed her to. She nodded, and slipped out the door, closing it softly behind her. I felt a surge of love.

"There," I said, "it's as if she was never here in the first place." I spooned the applesauce into my mother's mouth. It felt like I was depositing food into the mouth of a corpse. There was no resistance when the spoon met her lips, no sign that she knew she was being fed except the faint contraction of her throat when she swallowed. I began to cry. I hadn't cried in front of her since I was an infant — maybe the errant tear here or there, but not like this. I felt my shoulders heave. I felt desperate. How long could we do this? I could hurt her again, easily, and it could be worse next time. I wasn't meant for this. I wasn't good at it.

My mother opened her eyes. "It's time," she said, as if she'd read my mind. She moved her hurt arm, and winced. I knew she was searching for my hand, so I gave it to her. She held it with more strength than she had mustered for weeks. I don't think I'd ever felt as close to her. And perhaps

145

that's why I did what I did: this closeness.

"A dozen," she said, and nodded to the applesauce, which I held, half-eaten, in my hand. "And I'll go to sleep."

I couldn't do it. I took the pills and the mortar and pestle into the bathroom early that morning, while my mother drifted in and out of her endless half sleep. That was as far as I got.

Idie found me at the breakfast room table, a bowl of grits in front of me. I had no appetite. I'd lost ten pounds since my mother had become ill. My clothes slid around my frame, meant for a bigger version of myself. I wondered, as I sat there, the grits congealing into a solid mass, whether I'd gain the weight back after she died, or if I would continue to become smaller and smaller. It seemed possible, that I might disappear. I hardly cared. I didn't know any girls without parents. There were girls with stepparents, though that was rare in those days, even in Houston. But every girl I knew had a mother attached to her, a mother we all knew, and saw; a mother who made sure she did not disappear.

Idie took my grits from me, replaced them with a cup of hot coffee and a cinnamon bun.

"Eat," Idie said, and I tried. She sat down next to me, with her own cup of coffee. She wanted to say something about last night, I knew. But I was too exhausted to help her say what she needed to say.

"The Lord will take her when it's time," she said finally, and touched the small gold cross that rested in the hollow of her collarbones, the only jewelry I had ever known Idie to wear. Her voice changed when she spoke of God. Her entire bearing shifted, into something more serious. I didn't like it. I especially didn't like it now, my mother upstairs, so close to death I had to wet her tongue every hour or it dried up like a sponge.

I nodded. It seemed like the path of least resistance.

But still I could feel Idie watching me. After a moment she spoke.

"Has she asked before?"

I was too exhausted to lie. "Yes," I said. "She started asking a week ago. Maybe longer. I can't remember."

I looked up at Idie then, and was surprised to see that she seemed pleased. Then I understood why. I hadn't done anything to help her so far. I was a good girl, in Idie's eyes. I knew right from wrong. She rested her hand on top of mine. It felt good to be touched by a person who wasn't sick.

"It's not for man to interfere with God's work," she said, and I nodded again, feeling my throat constrict.

"I'm not," I said. "Interfering," I continued, in case she didn't know what I meant. "I can't."

I dropped my mother on a Friday, and Idie was picked up at dawn on Sunday by Dorie and Dorie's husband for church in their big blue Lincoln, a hand-me-down from the Fortiers. She would not return until the following morning. My mother stopped speaking after that night. She moaned, and screamed, and made other sounds, but the last words I heard from her were her request to go to sleep.

Joan came over that evening so I wouldn't be alone with my mother, and I made peanut butter sandwiches for dinner, and then Joan poured us each a glass of my mother's sweet white wine, and we sipped that in my room while listening to Frank Sinatra's "Always" over and over on the record player — Joan, half propped up on pillows, repositioning the needle just as the song ended. I fell asleep on top of my bedspread. I woke up once, briefly, to find Joan covering me with a blanket. I should have risen, then, and gone to my mother. I should not have left her alone. But I did.

The next time I woke up, it was to my mother's screams.

"What in the world?" Joan gasped, though it was not really a question.

I knew what I needed to do. I needed to jog down the hallway into my mother's room and tend to her. She was in pain; that much was clear from her screams, which were subsiding now. But I did none of those things. I didn't even sit up.

"Listen," I said, and put my finger to my lips. "She doesn't have the strength to scream for very long." And then I closed my eyes and shook my head. "I can't do it, Joan."

Joan said nothing. She was sitting up, so I only saw her back, not her face.

"She wants me to give her more pills." There — I had said it. "She wants the pills to kill her," I said, searching for the correct words.

"I knew what you meant," Joan said, and turned so I could see her handsome profile, lit by moonlight. "And?"

"And," I murmured. My mother's screams had stopped. I began to sob. Hysteria rose in my throat. "I dropped her. She wanted a bath and I dropped her. She was so slippery in my arms. Like a baby. I wanted to hold her but I dropped her. I —"

"Hush," Joan said. She turned so I could see her completely. "Mama says she'll be gone within a week."

"A week," I repeated, and swallowed a sob. It seemed like an interminable amount of time. "I tried to grind up the pills, but I couldn't do it. I took them to the bathroom and emptied them into the mortar but I couldn't make myself." I shook my head. "I could not."

Joan studied me for a long time. "I don't think," she said finally, "that a week makes any difference."

And is this what I had wanted all along? I don't know. I can't say, even now.

"It will be a terrible week," I said, just to make sure I was understanding her.

"Then let's make it tonight."

It was easy after that. I did not think of Idie, of how fervently she would disapprove of what I — of what we were doing. I thought only of the task at hand. I went to my mother's room and retrieved the mortar and pestle, the pills. I handed them to Joan, who stood just outside the door, then went to my mother, who was watching me. Her gaze seemed alert. I like to think that she understood. Her covers were around her waist, and she was shivering. I went to pull them up, to cover her arms, which she liked, and she gave a low, wild warning sound. I understood it meant I would hurt her if I touched her.

"I won't touch you," I said. "I promise."

My mother was terrified. She sounded like an animal and watched me like an animal.

"I promise," I said again.

Joan knocked on the door. It had happened faster than I thought it would.

"Joan is going to come in. She's going to feed you. And you'll let her, won't you? You'll let her do what I can't." I laid my hand over my mother's as lightly as I could. She tolerated my touch. It was cold, and covered with tiny grains. Her skin, sloughing itself. "Come in," I called to Joan.

There was an instant — when Joan held the first spoonful to my mother's mouth — when I did not know if my mother would eat from Joan, but then she opened her mouth, proof that she understood. That was how it seemed to me, anyway.

After it was finished Joan left. I retrieved the cashmere throw from the chaise longue and climbed onto the bed, very, very carefully. My mother had told me all my life to move more quietly, to walk more softly, to speak in a more subdued voice. To move through her house in a way that did not call attention to myself.

That night I was so quiet I don't think she knew I was there.

CHAPTER TWELVE

By December of 1950, Joan had been gone for over eight months. Some days I woke and it was as if she had died. The world was less interesting now that she was not in it. Occasionally I mustered the energy to put in an appearance at a party, meet the girls for lunch, but mostly I rose at noon and wandered around the apartment until the television programming started at five. Once a week, or so, when I felt Sari watching me too closely, I left and went to the movies: the Majestic or the Tower, caught the matinee. I closed my eyes in the cool theater and imagined Joan into the films: Rubbing shoulders with Patricia Neal. Being held by Humphrey Bogart.

I was starting to accept that she might never come back. I hadn't slept in her clothes in months. I was starting to see my life, my future, without Joan, and I did not know what that future held. I didn't know how long the Fortiers would allow me to stay in the Specimen Jar. I didn't know where I would go once I left. I could have bought my own house. I could have bought three of them. But I didn't want to live anywhere without Joan.

Ciela begged me to come out on New Year's Eve. "You can't stay cooped up in here," she said. "It's not healthy. And it's the best night of the year!"

I shrugged.

"Cece," Ciela said, pulling me off the sofa. I'd been sitting there nearly all day, staring into space and paging through old copies of *Vogue.* I couldn't concentrate enough to read anything. "I insist."

The party was at a junior's house in Galveston. I pretended to sleep on the drive down, so I wouldn't have to talk. I opened my eyes as we crossed the bridge onto the island, in hopes we might pass by the Fortiers' beach house, but we did not.

I regretted agreeing to go as soon as I stepped out of the car. The old gang was all there, and I didn't like how they looked at me.

"Long time no see," Kenna said, and from Darlene: "Has Joan been cast yet?"

"She has a better chance than any of us," I snapped, and wrapped my fur stole around my shoulders. The air had a chill to it.

"Easy," Darlene said, in a tone that was meant to mollify but only served to further infuriate me.

"Come on," Ciela said, shooting a glare I was not meant to see in Darlene's direction. "Let's go outside."

I followed her to the beach. I was drinking a very potent gin and tonic, though I'd been drinking so much lately, alone, late into the night, that I barely felt it. A crowd of boys smoked cigarettes around a bonfire; I recognized some of them but couldn't bring myself to care.

"Got a light?" Ciela asked, and Danny, a football player with sculpted sideburns, swooped in and lit her cigarette.

I stood there, content to listen, while Ciela flirted and held court.

I shook my head when another boy approached and offered me a beer. I held up my gin and tonic, annoyed. I didn't want to talk to anyone tonight. I wanted the world to leave me alone.

But he didn't leave, instead stood next to me and looked out over the water.

"It's nice here, tonight, huh?"

I turned to him.

"Say something else," I said.

He laughed. He thought I was flirting.

"Something else," he said, and then I was sure: this was the boy from the gymnasium, the boy who had touched — done more than touch — Joan.

"You're him," I said.

He stopped smiling. "Who? Do we know each other? I go to Lamar, I moved here last year . . ." He was rambling. He had no idea who I was. Just a strange girl who was making him nervous.

I shook my head. "Never mind." I touched his forearm, and he looked at my hand, curiously. He took a step backward, but I moved with him.

His skin felt smooth beneath my hand. His arm was nearly hairless, scattered faintly with freckles. He wasn't particularly attractive. He was average. Average height, average looks. Like a million other boys.

"Why you?" I asked.

"Hey," he said, and held up his hands. "I've gotta split." He hurried away, back up to the house, and I watched him go, watched the boy who had made Joan feel such pleasure.

He was no one. He had meant nothing to Joan. She had not gone anywhere with him. Somewhere in the back of my mind I'd thought maybe she had. I laughed out loud. I knew nothing, about Joan or anything else.

Only that she'd run away by herself. She was so brave, Joan, so daring. The only place I went by myself was an empty movie theater in the middle of the day, and even then I felt embarrassed.

I took off down the beach. "Cece?" Ciela called, but I waved her off.

"I'm going to take a walk. I'll be back," I called. "I promise."

The shoreline was littered with bonfires; I was probably trespassing. But I didn't care. "Miss," a man called, as I passed by a cluster of men and women smoking cigarettes by the water's edge. "Miss!"

I ignored him. I imagined myself at this time tomorrow, still walking, on the side of some highway, my heels digging blisters into my feet. I didn't know Joan Fortier at all, and so much of my life hinged upon her. What did anyone care if I walked forever? I was a girl with a father in Oklahoma whom I hadn't seen in months. A girl without a mother. A girl with no real purchase in the world.

A tap on my shoulder; then the ragged breath of the man who had tried to get my attention a moment earlier.

"You're one fast walker," he said, and I was about to turn away — I wanted nothing but to keep moving forward — when he held up my stole.

"You dropped this."

I stared at the fur. I could live without it. But I was suddenly grateful to have it, grateful to this man for noticing.

"Thank you."

"You're welcome." He leaned forward, seemed to take an accounting of my face. I felt tender toward this handsome man who watched me like he had all the time in the world. Like I was the most important girl in the world.

"I'm Cecilia. Cece." I held out my hand.

He took it. "And I'm Ray. Ray Buchanan. Why don't you come over here for a moment and catch your breath?" He gestured up the shore, to a pair of Adirondack chairs that looked, in that instant, very inviting. He had dark brown eyes and thick, almost feminine eyelashes. He stood aside, swept his arm out in a signal that I should go first. That he would follow me.

I went.

Ray was enough to make me believe in God. He appeared and I stopped being lonely. He occupied my mind, my body.

Three days after we met we were fooling around on the couch in his small brick house in Bellaire. The Specimen Jar was nicer, but it wasn't more comfortable, and anyway, Sari was always there. Ray was kissing my neck, his arms around me, his hands in my hair, when I suddenly spoke.

"I have no one," I blurted. I'd never said those words before, not to anyone.

Ray pulled back to look at me. "What do you mean?" he asked. He was still fully clothed, but my top was off, crumpled beneath the coffee table, my bra straps around my elbows. Ray touched my breast, gently. "You're —" he said, and then paused, as if he didn't have words for what I was.

"I'm beautiful?" I asked, a smile on my lips. It was what men said, when they were moved: that the woman they were with was beautiful.

"I mean, yes — but no." He shook his head. He needed a haircut. He wore his hair short, in the fashion of the day, slicked back with a little pomade. It was an unforgiving style, but Ray had a jawline like an ax. I'd already thought of how our children would benefit from that jawline. My curls, his bone structure.

"You're not alone," he finished.

Joan left, and Ray swooped in to fill the void. "He's a good match," Ciela said. My father came through on business and took us to lunch. "A good man," he said. Darlene drunkenly gave me her approval: "You've found the last good man in Houston!"

Good. That was the word everyone used to describe Ray. And it was true.

He'd never done anything truly bad. He told me the saddest moment in his life was when his childhood dog died, when Ray was sixteen. He loved his mother, went fishing with his father, kept in touch with both his high school and college friends. He never talked about work, even though he worked like an animal, said he preferred to leave that world at the office. I knew all the big things about Ray, but it was the little things that moved me: The way he asked gas station attendants how their day was going, and meant it. He was the first man in a room to stand when a lady walked in, but not in a lascivious way. He pulled her chair out before she even knew she wanted to sit. He smiled benignly at conversations I knew didn't interest him.

He mixed a mean Manhattan, looked great in a pair of swim trunks, kept quiet about politics in mixed company. And he wasn't scared off by my odd circumstances, the way a lot of men would have been. Men wanted their wives to be saints, not orphans with fathers who had open affairs.

Almost as soon as I'd met him I wanted to marry him. I wanted to start a life with Ray Buchanan. He would propose soon — I was sure. I'd already met his parents. We'd stopped by a display window of rings at Lechenger's, and he'd asked which one was my favorite. I'd pointed to a pear-shaped diamond.

The facts of our lives matched up, too: We both couldn't imagine living anywhere but Houston. Ray, because he worked in oil; me, because nowhere else felt like home. We both ran in roughly the same crowd. Ray's crowd was older, but Ciela had, of course, heard of him. He made a good living. He had to work, but his job combined with my money meant we would always live well.

The four months we spent together while Joan was gone are a happy blur, mostly. Sex, four times a day. Once, I'd put my hand on his lap, underneath his jacket, during a matinee of *Sunset Boulevard.* Our love had felt immediate, powerful. I missed Joan — I composed letters to her in my head, telling her all about my new life — but I learned to turn all the attention I had spent on Joan toward Ray. He didn't understand my relationship with Joan, with the Fortiers — "You mean this place is owned by the Fortiers?" he asked once, when I'd made dinner for him at the Specimen Jar, on Sari's day off. "And you live here alone?" But I suppose it was easy for him not to press the issue while Joan was gone. Easy to ignore a person you'd never met. It must have seemed to Ray — as it did to me — as if she would never come back.

And as for my part: I kept quiet about Joan. I told Ray she was my best friend since infancy, that she'd run away to Hollywood. If he asked whether I was in on the plan, I was going to lie, I was going to tell him yes, just as I'd told Ciela.

"She wanted to see the world beyond Houston."

"But you don't need to see that world, too, do you, Cece?" he asked, taking my hand, and I realized he cared nothing about Joan Fortier. He cared only for me.

I smiled and shook my head. "No," I said. "I have all I need right here." And it was true.

CHAPTER THIRTEEN

And then, spring of 1951, one year after Joan disappeared, she was back. She returned with little fanfare. I opened the door one evening to go out — to meet Ray for dinner at the Confederate House — and there she stood, a slim red purse hanging from her forearm, a delicate hat perched on her head.

I had known she was coming. Two weeks before Easter, Mary and Furlow had called me to Evergreen and informed me that Joan's adventure was over. They had tried, Furlow especially, to make light of the situation. "She wanted to be a star," Mary said, her voice arch, and though I wouldn't have said she was mocking Joan, she was coming close. "But then she learned the world has enough stars," Furlow said, forcing a laugh. "And I think she also learned that a life without money is no fun."

So Joan had been cut off. I only wondered

why it had taken so long.

"I know you've been waiting a long time," Mary said, as she showed me to the door. "But now she's coming! Are you excited?" Her voice was falsely bright, as if I were a child to whom she'd given a long-anticipated treat.

"Yes," I said, "of course." The answer left my lips immediately, but the truth was more complicated. It was like being excited to see a ghost. Waiting suggested hope, and I had stopped hoping a long time ago that Joan would return. I moved around the Specimen Jar with her things — her maid, even — greeting me at every turn. It reminded me of living at my mother's house that week after she died, before I went to Evergreen. Now that Joan was returning, it felt impossible, like she was rising from the dead: how could a person, a person I had loved more than anyone else on earth, disappear so completely from my life, only to reappear a year later? It felt like magic, like sorcery. The idea of her scared me. How would I act in her presence? I no longer understood what she expected of me, nor I of her. I didn't know which way she would tip the delicate new balance of my life: I was in love. I had learned to love someone besides Joan.

But of course I wanted her desperately. I wanted to see her: to sit next to her, to touch her shoulder. Her shoulder that had surely been brushed by a dozen strangers since I had last seen her.

I wanted these things like you want to be held when you are a child: I wanted them instinctively. I wanted them from some deep place I could not name.

Sari and I had been waiting for days. I just didn't know exactly when Joan would arrive.

"You're here," I said, staring at her, standing there uselessly, my arms at my sides. I was struck by how unchanged Joan appeared. The moment could have gone on forever — but then she stepped through the door and wrapped her arms around me. That was all it took. Joan wanted me.

She pulled away and surveyed the room. "Quite a place," she murmured, and there was some awe in her voice, at least.

"I'll be right back," I said. I had to slip away, call Ray, tell him I couldn't meet him. "I had plans. But I don't need to go anywhere, tonight." I took Joan's hand between mine. I needed to feel her skin; I needed to convince myself that my ghost was actually here. Joan didn't seem to notice my nervousness. Or my happiness. She had removed her hand from mine and was introducing herself to Sari, whom she had never met; now she was sitting on the couch, smoothing the leather beneath her palm, smiling grandly, then standing up again, opening the sliding glass door and stepping out onto the balcony, gasping theatrically.

"Oh my," she said, "this view!" She stood, and spoke, as if she were in front of an audience.

I'm not an audience, I wanted to say. *It's just me, Cece, your friend from birth.*

I called Ray and then joined Joan back out on the balcony. "We're not staying here," she pronounced. "Let's go out, just the two of us. To Maxim's."

I called Ray again after we returned home, standing at the counter while Joan undressed in her room, the phone pressed to my ear. I was still drunk on what had seemed like gallons of wine from Maxim's famous, never-ending wine list. I wanted to hear Ray's voice. I'd wanted all night to be with him. It hadn't just been the two of us, like Joan had said; by the end of the night, a dozen other people were clustered around our table.

"She's in fine spirits," I said. "She's happy to be back, I think."

"And you?" he asked. "You sound a little

down in the mouth." *This* was what it meant to have someone in my life who loved me. Joan had been the star all night. Furlow and Mary had been finishing up their meal when we'd entered, and they'd lingered a little bit, watched Joan say hi and chat with all the people who came up to our table, watched her tell them that Hollywood had been fun, but not as fun as Houston. But Ray only wanted to hear about me.

Joan meant nothing to him. Now I was the star.

"It was nice," I said, "but I wished the whole time I was with you."

I don't know what I had expected. An apology, perhaps? I tried to tell myself that Joan had her reasons, that surely they were good ones.

I had imagined the conversation we would have — I would be hurt, a little angry, and Joan would say she was sorry, she was so, so sorry, and explain herself. Reveal the reason that could possibly make her departure and absence and silence understandable. But that had not happened. Joan spent most of her mornings in her room, with books — reading was a habit she seemed to have picked up in LA — then, as evening approached, she would emerge, and move around the Specimen Jar with greater and greater animation. This Joan would give no explanation. Nor would I ask. I felt lucky to have her back, and that would have to be enough.

A few days after she had gotten back, though, she opened her bedroom door and called me in. The books rested in a neat stack on her bureau.

"Help me get dressed?" she asked. "Let's go out tonight." She wore a pale pink robe and sipped a gin martini, which was now, apparently, her drink of choice. Before she'd left she hadn't had a drink of choice.

"In Hollywood," she said as she stood, her voice faraway, "we went out every single night. Even Sundays. We had so much fun, Cece. I felt alive."

Tell me what you did, I wanted to say, *tell me what took you away from me for so long.*

"Ray's excited to meet you," I said instead. It seemed important to say his name. I missed him, even when it had only been a short time since I'd seen him.

I dressed her in my clothes, a black gown that was a little too big for me. She filled it out in a way I never could. It wasn't something I would have worn anyway — I had probably bought it for Joan in the first place.

In the car, Joan watched Houston pass by

our window.

"It's the same," I said. "It waited for you."

I wondered as I said it. Had Houston waited for Joan? Was it capable of waiting for Joan? Tonight, at the Cork Club — how would she be received? All our old gang would be there, along with Ray. I wanted Houston to be the same for Joan. I wanted Joan to be the same for Houston.

The closer we got, the brighter Joan seemed to burn. She was sipping whiskey from a flask like the ones boys used to bring to high school dances.

She offered it to me and I took a sip, because I wanted to please her. I was relieved to see, if not quite the old Joan — this Joan held herself at a remove — some version of her returning to me, as if the ghost of Joan were now clothing herself in flesh.

"Mmm," I said, though I hated it. I wondered what Fred thought of what we were doing back here. If he disapproved, if he cared at all.

Ray was waiting for us at the door. When I saw him I broke into a smile, and the night turned more promising. Going out with Joan had always, since we were teenagers, stirred me into a state of nervous excitement. I never knew what she would do. I never knew where the night would take us. Ray's presence, I realized, was reassuring. I knew what he would do.

"That's him," I said to Joan, pointing as we pulled up to the entrance. "That's Ray."

Joan watched him for a moment, silently, and I began to panic. If Joan did not like Ray, if she didn't approve of him, he would be ruined for me. I tried to stop myself from thinking it — surely Ray mattered more than what Joan thought of him — but I knew it was true.

"He's a doll," she said, and grinned at me. "A doll."

She jumped out of the car and ran up to him, me trailing a step behind, her heels clipping the pavement.

"Well hello," she said when she reached him. "I hear you've been taking good care of Cece while I've been gone."

"Yes," Ray said, a little uncertainly, and I slid beneath his arm, put my hand on his chest. Ray seemed buoyed by my touch. "It's nice to meet you," he said, and tipped his head.

"The pleasure's all mine," Joan nearly sang, and patted her hair before she nodded to the doorman, who swung open the door with ceremony, as if he understood her

170

importance. And who knows, perhaps he did.

It was a Saturday night; the place was packed. I scanned the room and saw a roped-off section in the corner. I could make out Glenn McCarthy, in his sunglasses and leopard-print ascot. He was sitting around his regular table with glamorous blondes and a few unsmiling men. I wondered if they were his bodyguards.

I stood a few feet behind Joan. She stopped as soon as we were inside, backed up a little bit, and I wondered if she was frightened, if she wanted to leave. If returning to all this — all these people, all this noise, all the smoke and shimmer — was not, in fact, what she'd wanted. Too much, too soon, perhaps.

I stepped away from Ray. "It's okay," I whispered, and touched Joan on the back. "Stay with me."

She looked at me with an odd little half smile I couldn't read. Should I have left her alone? I looked at my friend, dressed in my gown, her hair in a high ponytail I'd done myself, and felt despair. I knew no one, and no one knew me.

"Thank you," she said. It was all I needed; I felt euphoric. But then she gathered herself, threw back her shoulders, and marched straight through the center of the room, her hand extended, waving at the people who watched as she passed. And who watched her? Everyone.

"So that's Joan," Ray said, coming up behind me, encircling me with his arms.

"Yes," I said lightly, slipping out of his grasp. "That's Joan."

Half an hour later and she was sitting at Mr. McCarthy's table, the glamorous blondes shooting her dirty looks. An hour later and his leopard-print ascot was around her neck. Somehow she didn't look foolish. She looked fun.

"Looks like she picked up a few tricks in Hollywood," Ciela said, furiously smoking a cigarette. We were standing at the bar, with Ray, watching Joan. "She hasn't even said hi yet. Too busy with Diamond Glenn."

Just then Joan caught sight of us and waved, and before I knew it she was running across the room, throwing her arms around Ciela's neck.

"Long time no see!" she said, and laughed.

"That's for sure," Ciela said. "I didn't quite make it out to Hollywood last year."

But Joan didn't take the bait; she was too enlivened — too drunk — to take offense.

"This place is so goddamned ugly!" Joan said loudly, and I checked to make sure

172

Glenn McCarthy wasn't in hearing distance.

"Joan!" I hissed. The snobs from Dallas might have called it the Damn-rock, but we were proud of the Shamrock, which was emblematic of everything about Texas we held dear. It was bigger and better and brasher, and of one thing we could be absolutely certain: there was no other place like it in the world.

"What? I'm going to fall asleep to visions of green tonight. I want to come to a nightclub that reminds me of Paris," she said, "or Monte Carlo! Not a leprechaun's fantasy." A waiter placed a glass of champagne into her outstretched hand. "They're keeping me well-oiled," she said, and winked.

Ciela chortled. "Paris? Monte Carlo? You've never actually *been* to either of those places, have you, dear?"

Joan shrugged. "I've read about them. Seen plenty of pictures. Taste is taste. And if you'll excuse me . . ." And with that, she reentered the melee.

"She reads!" Ciela said. "She looks at pictures. 'Taste is taste,' " she mimicked, and glanced at me, waiting, but I couldn't do it. I couldn't mock Joan.

"She's just excited," I said. "She'll calm down."

Ciela sighed. "You'll have to excuse me, too," she said. "I need to visit our most vulgar of powder rooms."

"Is Joan always like this?" Ray asked, after Ciela had left.

"Like what?" I asked, though I knew exactly what he meant. I took a sip of my champagne. "Let's dance," I said, because Ray loved to dance.

"Okay," Ray said, "but slow down a little bit?"

I smiled. "I don't want to slow down!" And we were out on the dance floor, where I could go as fast as I wanted.

A few hours and a few glasses of champagne later and Ray and I were sitting at the bar, me practically on his lap, when Ciela ran up, breathless.

"You've got to come see this," she said giddily, and motioned outside, toward the pool, and I knew immediately she meant Joan.

She was already halfway up the steps to the high diving board by the time I arrived. There was no way for me to get close — there must have been two hundred people on the patio next to the pool, ladies in their glimmering evening dresses, men in their slim-fitting suits, watching Joan as she ascended the steep spiral stairs. She was still in her heels. One hand gripped the railing; the other held a glass of champagne. I should have been terrified, but I wasn't. You could feel the energy of the crowd, watching Joan. Elated. We were all waiting for what came next.

The Shamrock's diving board wasn't your ordinary diving board — there was a low board, a medium board, and a high board a good thirty feet above the water. Joan had executed beautiful dives from the high board, it was true, but she'd been in a bathing suit, and she hadn't been drunk.

I squeezed Ray's hand.

"What in the hell is she doing?" he asked, and I shrugged impatiently.

"She's going to the top," I whispered as she climbed. But no, she stopped at the middle board. I let out a breath I hadn't realized I was holding.

She slipped off her heels and threw them into the pool, where they bobbed to the surface, and someone let out a hoot and a holler. She kept climbing.

"She'll kill herself," Ray said, and I brought my hand to my mouth.

"No she won't!" I said. *She's just having fun,* I started to say, *she's just being fun,* but the crowd's cheers drowned me out.

When she reached the top of the stairs

she tilted her glass of champagne, drained it, and gave the crowd a wide, beatific smile. Then she walked slowly to the end of the diving board. She stopped at the very edge, bobbing up and down; stretched her hand out; and let her champagne glass follow her shoes into the pool.

And then she bent her knees, once, twice, raised her arms above her head, and dove. Ray gasped behind me; I could feel his breath on my neck. It was a beautiful sight: she leapt from the board in a perfect swan dive, toes pointed, my black dress shearing the air, and entered the water so quietly she barely made a splash.

The crowd broke into a wild cheer. "A perfect ten," someone shouted. "Champagne all around!" another person yelled.

"Let's get this lady a towel," Glenn said, and the crowd roared again as Joan surfaced and backstroked cleanly to the shallow end. The next day there would be a picture of Joan on the front of the gossip section, standing at the edge of the diving board, poised.

"I'm a little tired," Ray said, "do you think we could go?" I was torn: I didn't want to miss anything — I'd missed an entire year! — but Joan was surrounded by people now. I couldn't even see her, just the place where

I thought she was, at the center of the throng.

"Yes," I said, "let's go to your place."

He ushered me out to the valet stand, and then a voice behind me. Joan's voice.

"You're leaving?"

I spun around. She was shivering, one of the Shamrock's thick green robes wrapped around her shoulders.

"Yes," I said. "Ray's tired."

She stared at me for a second. "Don't go," she said softly. "Don't leave me."

Ray's car was pulling up and he looked at me quizzically. What could I do? I kissed him good night and told him I'd see him tomorrow.

Joan's hair was plastered against her cheeks. She'd lost an earring — luckily only a piece of costume jewelry. Fred appeared and once we were in the car Joan leaned her damp head on my shoulder.

"Sleep with me," she said, when we were inside the Specimen Jar, "please," and I did so, gladly, helped her out of her wet dress, tucked her into her bed, then slid in next to her. The sheets were cool and smooth against my bare legs. The pillow was soft beneath my cheek. Joan was warm and heavy next to me. I found her hand underneath the covers.

"Did you have fun?" I asked, struggling to keep my eyes open. It was four o'clock in the morning. A new day had already begun.

"Oh," she said, "I was just showing them a good time. But yes. Yes, I had fun."

Ray proposed the next week, at his friend's beach house, where we'd met.

We stood on the damp sand of Galveston's shore and Ray got to his knees. I thought about how he was ruining his pants; then he slid a pear-shaped diamond, flanked by two round sapphires, onto my left ring finger, and I stopped thinking about his pants.

I held my hand away from me, like I'd seen so many women do in the movies. I'd never really liked the ocean — it was Joan who loved the water — but now the dull roar of the waves slapping the sand, over and over again, sounded lovely and comforting.

I thought of my mother and father. I didn't know how he had proposed, but surely she must have loved him, in that moment; surely she must have believed their love was certain, would cushion them against life's slings and arrows.

Something occurred to me. "Did you ask my father?"

Ray stood, held me to him. "No," he murmured. "I'm sorry — I thought —"

"Good," I said. He didn't deserve to be asked.

Joan was back. She would help me plan my wedding. And Ray was mine forever. My life, it seemed in that moment, was perfect.

"I'll never leave," Ray said, his voice thick with emotion.

And then he made me promise I'd never leave him, either.

"Never," I said, "never, ever," and in that moment, I believed nothing more.

A month after Joan returned, I slipped into her room to see if she had one of my blouses. I saw the same stack of books on her bureau, untouched.

CHAPTER FOURTEEN

Joan had been back for nearly a year — nine months — when the Fortiers threw their annual Christmas Eve party. The mayor was there, several city councilmen; Hugh Roy Cullen was in attendance, the cherry on the sundae, one of the richest men in Texas. Joan's name had been on the invitation, along with her parents'. For the briefest instant I'd wondered, as I'd slid the thick card stock from its envelope, if my name would be engraved next to Joan's. But of course not.

I comforted myself with the thought of the parties Ray and I would throw, once we were married.

Evergreen glittered. Pine boughs woven into the grand staircase railing; little white orbs twinkling on every bush, every window-sill and eave. Joan glittered, too, a bottomless glass of champagne in her hand. She wore a red silk dress, its bodice so tight it was a second skin.

I stood near the Christmas tree, with Ray. We would be married that summer, at Evergreen. The next party I attended here would be my wedding reception.

The tree was two stories high, decorated with little candles in silver holders. I was sipping spiked eggnog, fiddling with one of the candles, passing my finger through its flame.

"Are you impressed?" I asked Ray. It was the first time he'd been inside Evergreen. He saw Joan of course, when we were all out together, but he preferred to spend time with me alone. And he was working feverishly at that point, trying to prove himself at the company, so our nights together were sparse anyway. To me, it was ideal: I had Ray and I had Joan.

"By?"

I thought he was trying too hard to act nonchalant. "All of it! The cooks have been slaving in the kitchen for a week. The gardeners worked until three in the morning to make sure the yard was perfect. The —"

Ray placed his hand over mine, quieting it. "Joan's drunk as a skunk. Look at her. She can barely hold her head on straight."

We watched Joan for a moment. She was,

indeed, gesturing widely, dipping and bobbing her head, but she wasn't drunk. She
was tipsy, animated.

"She's always like that," I said. "She can
handle her liquor."

"Hmm. Think you can find a way to
introduce me to Cullen? I wouldn't mind
showing my face to him."

At the end of the night, after Ray had left,
pleading exhaustion, I wandered out back,
tired and drunk, passing a cluster of old
men whispering and smoking Cubans. They
nodded furtively in my direction as I passed,
and I suppressed a giggle at their self-
importance. It seemed impossible that Ray
would ever be that old.

I would wait and leave with Joan, whenever she was ready. Soon, Ray and I would
leave parties like this together, as a couple.
Soon, he would go nowhere without me,
nor I without him.

A swing hung from an oak tree, and I sat
on it tentatively, not quite sure it would hold
me. But it did, just as it had when we were
children. There was our sandbox, covered
now, unused for years.

I thought of Idie, how kind she had been
playing with me near that sandbox day after
day. And it occurred to me, sitting there on
our old swing, that I hadn't seen Dorie in

ages, not since Joan had left. Now Joan was back and Dorie was not.

In the car going back to the Specimen Jar, I was alone with Joan again: the smooth leather seats, the dry heat radiating from the dashboard, the back of Fred's bristly, gray head. I loved this car in winter.

"Jesus Christ," she said, "what a spectacle. What a spectacular spectacle," and giggled. She squeezed my hand. "Was Ray grumpy, darling?"

I shook my head. "No. He's just a little quiet tonight."

"A quiet man is a boring man," Joan said, lighting a cigarette; in the flame I saw her eyes, unfocused. "But you've got to love a boring man. No trouble with a boring man."

I let her go on. Every time she called Ray boring I pressed my lips together, but I knew she meant nothing by it.

"I'll be married this time next year," I said.

"You sound sad," Joan said quietly.

"Do I? I'm not. I'm happy. But we won't ever live together again. Remember how we used to say we'd marry brothers, and live in houses next door to each other?"

"I do," Joan said. "I do." She laughed. I laughed, too. The idea, which had seemed so plausible to our ten-year-old selves, now seemed utterly absurd.

"Things will change," I said.

"Of course they will," Joan said. "But, honey, you know you can't marry me, right?"

I was prepared to be hurt, was already, but then Joan grabbed my hand.

"Ray loves you. You can't really ask for more than that, can you?"

I shook my head. It was true: Ray loved me, and I couldn't, shouldn't ask for more than his love, his loyalty.

"Let's go to Shailene's," she said abruptly. "Fred, take us to Shailene's!"

Did I want to go? Did it matter? We were going to Shailene's, where I hoped there would be a booth and Joan would want to sit down in it.

I watched River Oaks, perfect as a little town in a snow globe, houses lit, ornamented trees with presents underneath visible from the street. Then the globe started to spin and I leaned my head against the soft seat.

"Joan," I said suddenly, as the question had just occurred to me again.

"Yes?" she murmured.

"Where's Dorie?"

She said nothing. I opened my eyes, expecting to find her looking out the window, her attention caught by something other than me. Instead I found her watching me intently.

"She's gone," Joan said.

"Gone where?"

"Just gone," Joan said softly, and slipped out the little ashtray that lived in the door and stubbed her cigarette into it.

Servants came and went all the time, of course. But still, Dorie had been like a mother to Joan.

Joan had closed her eyes, and I did not push the matter because I did not want to disturb her.

And yet, I knew she was lying to me.

CHAPTER FIFTEEN

1957

A week or so after she showed up rain-soaked on my front porch, I saw Joan again at the Petroleum Club. All the girls went there for dinner once a month; it was something of a tradition, started by Darlene. She was there, of course, along with Joan and Ciela and a few others at the end of the table. Tommy was home with Ray. We all placed our orders — steak was what you got there, what each of us ordered that night, red in the middle — but when Philip, our waiter, stopped by Joan she asked for champagne.

"I'm not in the eating mood, tonight, not especially. I'm in the champagne mood. A magnum," she pronounced, and smiled brilliantly at the table. "I want to do something special for my girls." Philip was gray-haired and quietly capable, had been our particular waiter for as long as we'd been coming here.

He didn't have to ask Joan what kind of champagne she wanted. The most expensive kind.

"What a treat!" Darlene exclaimed, even though we were already drinking cocktails, had martinis and Manhattans and, for those of us who drank more moderately, daiquiris lined up in front of us in a neat row. I wanted so badly to roll my eyes. Darlene wore a white strapless dress with a gold lamé belt, a choker of pearls around her tan throat. I thought she looked like a snake, one of those nonpoisonous ones with rings around their necks.

I turned as Philip passed behind me — "Miss Fortier will have a steak, too. Rare," I said, and he nodded and I was grateful that the transaction had passed so quietly between us.

I myself was drinking a daiquiri, because Joan had clearly been loaded when she'd arrived at the restaurant and I'd wanted to set a good example. A lot of good that had done: Joan had already had two martinis, and was generally drinking like there was no end in sight. She could hold her liquor but sometimes it seemed like she didn't want to. Tonight was one of those nights.

The room was watching us. This was a place you came because you wanted to be

187

seen. And we did, I suppose. Want to be seen, I mean. It wasn't even a question, where we would go each month, where we would sit once we were there. We would elicit murmurs and glances as we paraded through the room. Each of us, but Joan especially, and she would say her own hellos and darlings and can you believe it's been so longs. Joan basked in the attention, of course, we all did, but it was Joan that everyone wanted to see. Her recent dalliance seemed not to have affected her reputation; neither Darlene nor the other girls made any mention of it. Joan had gotten lucky.

"She's on tonight," Ciela murmured.

I turned to her, glad that she had not heard me order a meal for Joan. I knew that I worried over her too much, fussed over her like she was a child. But someone had to.

I smiled, took a sip of my daiquiri. "She's just happy," I said. "She likes it when we're all together."

Ciela shook her head, gazed at me for a moment. "Everyone should have a friend like you, Cece."

Joan heard that last part. "Everyone should have a friend like Cece! I'll toast to that!" And she raised her martini and clinked glasses with Darlene and Kenna, who sat to her right and left, spilling a bit of her drink as she did it, not bothering to wipe it up; then they were off, bantering, talking and laughing about nothing.

I wasn't feeling particularly festive. Tommy hadn't wanted me to leave, and for that matter, neither had Ray. "Joan beckons, I assume," he had said when I told him I couldn't back out. Joan had returned to her old self since that rainy afternoon in my kitchen, a brighter version, even, but I hadn't quite caught up with her. Her absence over the last two weeks had changed something in me; her absences always did.

Ciela and I were idly chatting about our children, our fallback conversation, when Darlene brought up the Daisy Dillingworth divorce. It had gotten nastier, last week — pictures of Edwin Mintz and his mistress leaving a Broadway play had been published in the *Chronicle*.

"Nothing about it's natural," Darlene said. "She didn't stick with her kind. And now she's reaping what she sowed, isn't she?"

"Well, she sure is," Joan said, in a falsetto voice, and Darlene beamed before she realized Joan was mocking her.

"Daisy will bring the boy back here, I bet," I said, hoping to ease the tension that had

189

settled over the table. "River Oaks is the perfect place to come back to, the perfect place to raise a child." I was rambling, but I believed it: Daisy needed to be near her family. A place where she and her child would never be alone.

"I think River Oaks would be hell to come back to after New York," Joan said. "And that child? He should stay with his daddy in the city. At least there nobody would care he was a half Jew." She looked at us evenly, as if daring us to disagree. And she seemed as if she wanted to say more. Tell us what fools we were, how vapid and provincial we had all become.

Darlene laughed — a high-strung poodle, barking.

"River Oaks isn't hell." I paused. I could feel the table watching me as I tried to regain my composure. "And I think people would be kind. He's a child — he doesn't belong in New York. He needs his mother." It was true I didn't know many, or any, Jewish people, but I knew Daisy. And I knew without a doubt that River Oaks was a better place for a child than an anonymous, dirty city.

Joan lit a cigarette, took a drag before responding.

"Does he? In some cultures children are

raised communally, by the whole tribe. A thousand people to tuck you in at night."

"Did you read that in *National Geographic*?" I asked.

Joan tilted her head, gauging me. I didn't usually bite back.

"Yes, yes I did." Joan wasn't sitting where she could see Ciela roll her eyes, but I wished she were. I wished she could see how mentioning the *articles* she read, the places she wanted to go — all the ways in which we were not enough — won her no favors among us. "We had Dorie and Idie," she continued. "They were like mothers to us. Better than our mothers."

I gasped, stunned that she would mention Idie so casually, in front of all these people. Part of me wanted to fight Joan, say something nasty, not let her get away with it. But the bigger part of me wanted to pacify her.

"It sounds hard to manage, doesn't it?" I asked lightly. "A thousand parents."

Joan twisted her cigarette into her ashtray.

"Oh, Cee, don't be such a bore. I was just teasing."

Just then an army of white-coated waiters filed over, sliding plates with their balloon-like silver lids in front of us. I heard Joan murmur as the lids came off and revealed our bloody steaks, the trails of fat glistening

191

in the candlelight.

"Oh, Phil," she said, playacting at disappointment. "Honey, I didn't order a steak. Take it back, will you? Give it to a more deserving soul."

"Of course," he said. And he was moving to take the plate when I spoke.

"No," I said. "It's not a mistake. You need to eat something."

"You ordered me a steak?" Joan asked brightly, her face stretched into a smile that looked hideous to me.

"I did. You need something to soak up the poisons, don't you?" This was an old joke, something Sari had always said before we left for a night out, when we were living in the Specimen Jar.

Joan gazed at me and I stared back. Darlene fingered the pearls of her choker excitedly; Kenna pressed her hand to her mouth as if to suppress a smile. I was furious, suddenly, that Joan was antagonizing me when she should have been going to great lengths to make sure I was happy. She'd ignored us all, including the Fortiers, for two weeks! None of us behaved that way, not me nor Ciela nor Kenna nor Darlene. None of us but Joan. I thought of Ray, at home. Tommy sleeping soundly in his crib. You didn't marry and have children for pleasure, for fun; you married and had children so you could be an adult, so you could have something to worry about besides yourself. But not Joan.

"Take it away, Phil," she demanded. And so he did. I watched him as he held out his hand; another waiter soundlessly placed a silver cover onto it; he re-covered the steak, whisked it from Joan's presence, as if it were a nuclear threat.

But then the rest of us were still faced with our nuclear threats, quickly losing heat; hot, tasty fat turning cold and chewy.

We needed a word to break the tension. From Joan, Joan who would not provide such a word in a million years. I don't think, truly, that it would have occurred to her. She was used to making messes, not cleaning them up.

"I, for one," said Ciela, "am absolutely ravenous. Tina was busy throwing a temper tantrum during lunch and I barely had a thing to eat." She held up a gold fork, a piece of steak stabbed through its tines. "It looks delicious." She tasted it. "And it is."

I was so grateful. Joan wouldn't look at me but the pall of tension that had settled over the table disintegrated, almost instantly. The alcohol helped. So did the anticipation of our evening. No one wanted it ruined.

The steak in my own mouth tasted like tears. After I had sat for an acceptable amount of time, and everyone else was chatting, I quietly excused myself and made my way to the bathroom. The attendant, mercifully, was on a break, so I sat on the little brocaded settee and tried not to cry. I tried to focus on the gold fixtures, to distract myself from Joan.

I should have left her alone. I shouldn't have fussed, shouldn't have worried, shouldn't have made a scene.

I went to the mirror and opened my mint-green clutch, fished around for my powder and lipstick. I was wearing an off-the-shoulder dress, made of netting. I'd ordered it from New York; no one would have it here for at least a season. I had matching shoes on, too, high heels covered in the same mint-green silk as my clutch. I had felt like a million bucks when I'd left the house, and now? Now I felt like nothing, no one.

I was pretty enough, as my mother had said, and I knew how to put myself together. I wondered, not for the first time, what my life would have been like had I been outrageously beautiful. Ciela was nearly as beautiful as Joan but she was missing something, that special, final spark. Darlene, Kenna, the rest of us — we were all pretty enough.

Well, Darlene was, as my mother liked to say, half homely, but she knew her way around makeup.

Perhaps, I thought, as I patted powder on the circles beneath my eyes, the hollows of my temples, my life would be exactly the same. I didn't have it in me, to act like Joan. But who knew. Perhaps beauty would have changed me.

The door groaned and I put a little smile on my face. I was expecting the bathroom attendant, hoping for Joan. Instead I got Ciela.

"Hello," I said to her reflection as she came and stood next to me.

"Such a waste," she said, and tapped the faucet. "Think of the pretty gold earrings you could have instead."

I laughed, though I wasn't in the mood.

"I'm sorry I made such a fuss," I said.

"Did you?" Ciela asked. "Make a fuss, I mean?"

"I should have known better." I studied Ciela in the mirror, bold and blond with a hint of something exotic in her lips and eyes. She licked her finger and gave each of her eyebrows a swipe. I could tell she wanted to say something. That was why she had come in here, wasn't it? But I didn't want to talk about Joan. Ciela would not understand.

"Sometimes," Ciela said, "I try to imagine your life. Joan Fortier's handmaiden. It gets exhausting, I imagine."

I watched my face crumple; I tried to relax it, tried to smooth my expression, but Ciela saw.

"Is that what people say about me?" I asked. "I'm not. I'm not Joan's handmaiden. I'm her friend."

Ciela looked at my hand. I hadn't realized I'd been fiddling with my compact. "I didn't mean to upset you. I just meant —" She hesitated. "I just meant that sometimes Joan can be cruel. Or maybe 'cruel' is too strong a word. Insensitive. Sometimes Joan can be insensitive."

I almost laughed.

"Cruel? Insensitive? You have no idea what Joan is like, not really. Do you know how kind she is to Tommy? She hides that part of herself. She's different with me." I gathered up the contents of my purse. "I know her the best of anyone in the world."

"I don't doubt you do."

"Then don't presume other things," I said. "Don't presume you know me. That you know Joan."

Ciela's expression was mild. She played her cards close to her chest, always had. My hand was on the door when she spoke again.

"Do you know what she's acting like, tonight?" She gestured, as if at something beyond the walls of the ladies' room. As if at Joan.

I needed — I *had* — to hear what she thought.

"She's acting like she did when she came back from Hollywood."

"When she became Houston's star, you mean?" Ciela was jealous.

"When she was wild, Cece. When she was high as a kite and slept with anything within walking distance."

"When she was young and beautiful," I countered. "When she had Houston by the tail."

"If that's what you want to call it," I heard Ciela say, but I was already out the door.

Later that evening we all went back to the Shamrock and sat outside, by the pool. Ciela had begged off when we left the Petroleum Club, and I thought about doing the same thing but hadn't. I watched Ciela go and envied her a little bit: she wasn't worried she might miss something. It was like this: What was at home was known. My sleeping husband and child. And what was out here, in the great big world of the night,

197

was yet to be revealed.

Fred drove us all over and Joan had taken the front seat, and whether she did this so she wouldn't chance sitting next to me, whether Joan thought that far in advance, or if that was something only women like me did — well, I couldn't quite read her mind.

There were a hundred people scattered by the pool, upon which floated little green candles. I halfheartedly chatted with friends of Darlene, who'd just moved to the area.

"The heat is unbearable," a woman — Bettie, I think her name was — said. She was slightly chubby and a little snobby, her patrician manner undercut by how she had squashed herself into a dress two sizes too small. There were women who could carry their weight — Kenna was a little on the heavy side, a little Marilyn Monroe–ish — and women who couldn't.

"You'll get used to it," I said, and yawned. I checked my little watch. Three o'clock in the morning. "If you'll excuse me, I need to refresh."

But I didn't need to refresh. I needed not to be having insipid conversations with insipid women from Connecticut. I searched the deck for Joan but didn't see her. She must have been inside, either by design —

avoiding me — or because that's where the night had carried her.

My feet had been aching all night, which was the price you paid for beautiful shoes. It was late, and I was drunk, so I took them off and sat on the edge of the pool, careful to lift my dress from the back of my thighs so it wouldn't catch on the concrete, and dangled my feet in the ice-cold water. The relief was so sudden, so pleasurable, I nearly moaned.

And then Joan was behind me. I could feel her before I saw her. I could smell her, her particular absence of perfume. Sometimes she wore perfume and sometimes she didn't. I always noticed. It's impossible to describe someone's scent but I'll try: she smelled like day-old citrus, the brace of vodka, and her mother's powder.

"I thought I'd lost you," she said when she sat down. She slipped off her own shoes and placed her feet in the water. "Praise be to Jesus," she said. "This feels heavenly."

"I was out here the whole time," I said. "You didn't lose me."

"For God's sake, Cee. It's just something I was saying." She sounded tired. "You shouldn't have ordered the steak."

"It was just a steak." I could feel the heat rising in my cheeks.

"I didn't want it."

"But you needed it."

"Did I? How strange, that you know what I need better than I do."

"I've ordered food for you before," I said finally. And I had. It didn't seem like something she would have minded a month ago.

"Maybe I'm different now." She splashed her foot in the water, dimming a nearby candle. "Maybe things have changed."

I laughed. "Things never change. I'm always here, you're always there. We're always at places like this, late at night when we should be asleep."

And what I wanted to say, but did not: *I'm always waiting for you.*

I felt a large presence behind us. A man — I knew without looking. "Oh," Joan said. Her voice changed, became higher, unserious. "You again!"

"I'm back," he said, and something about the way he said it chilled me. But perhaps that's only now. I realized Joan had lied to me. *This* was the man I had seen her with at the Cork Club, the old friend she'd said was going back to Hollywood. The man I'd thought was gone for good.

He helped Joan stand. He dwarfed her. Joan was not a small woman, but he was even taller than Ray, with hands that made Joan's disappear.

He wasn't young — forty, maybe — but he still had his light brown hair; big, almost womanly lips; and the kind of ruddy complexion that suggests a constant state of too much sun or too much alcohol. His eyes were pale.

"This is Sid," she said, and then she leaned into him, brushed something off his shoulder. It was true: they were, as she had put it, old friends. More than that, obviously. They knew each other well.

He gazed down at me. I reached my hand up to shake his and he took it, held it firmly for one second, two. "A pleasure," he said distractedly, and I knew he didn't have the faintest idea who I was. Just one of Joan's girlfriends.

As he held my hand I understood exactly the kind of man Sid was. He reeked of sex; he wasn't even interested in me and I could feel his appetite through the faint pressure of his skin.

"We're off?" Joan asked, and another piece of the puzzle slipped into place. She'd planned to meet him here, planned all along to go home with him.

"One second," he said, and held up a cigar. "This needs smoking."

Joan laughed. I hated how she sounded: like a silly, stupid girl.

"You said he'd left," I said, once Sid was out of earshot. She shrugged; I wanted to slap her. "You said you hadn't fucked. Not that I believed you. But why lie, Joan? Why?" I'd provoked her again and this time I didn't care. I wanted a fight.

But when Joan spoke she didn't sound angry. She sounded sad.

"He did leave. But then he came back." She held up her hands.

"And your plans? With him?"

"The fucking? You show entirely too much interest in that, Cece. You always have." I thought of that day in high school, when I had seen her in the gymnasium with the strange boy. I looked down, embarrassed.

"I'm your friend," I said.

"Woe be to you."

"Joan?" It was Sid, calling her from the bar. Her sad, tired look vanished. She was the Joan everyone knew again: always ready for a good time, another drink, another party, another man.

I loved the other Joan, the Joan beneath the Joan.

Once they were gone I was tempted to submerge myself in the pool, dress be damned.

202

Instead I took my feet out of the pool and shook them off, one by one. Stood, slowly. Scanned the crowd for Darlene and Kenna. It occurred to me that Fred would have left with Joan, so we would have to find another way home.

I sighed. I wanted the other Joan back.

CHAPTER SIXTEEN

It was New Year's Eve. More precisely, the dawn of New Year's Day, a week after the Fortier Christmas party, 1951 tipping into 1952. Ray had just deposited us at our building, and after a sweet good-bye to my fiancé, Joan and I sat on the rooftop deck in our dresses and stoles with glasses of champagne, watching the sun light Houston's skyline. We'd had a good night together, a fun night. Ray had been there at my side, of course, along with our friends and Joan's ubiquitous suitors, yet she and I had finally slipped back into the easy relationship we'd shared before she had left. That's what it felt like to me. That sense, with a friend you love, that you could tell her anything, everything. That confidence that she would understand.

"Are you happy now?" I asked her.

"Happy?"

"Now," I said, "this instant." I gestured to

the world beyond the rooftop. "There's all this to see." I *wanted* to see it, in that moment. My father, my poor dead mother — they all seemed very far away right now, minor in their distance.

I turned to my friend, put both hands on her bare forearm. Her skin was dry beneath my palms.

She looked down at my hands, curiously, then up at me.

"Joan," I said, "what happened when you were gone?"

Slowly, she gestured to the skyline. I looked, too. I tried to see what she saw. But all I saw were buildings bracketed by sky.

"What happened, Cee? A lot happened."

I waited. *This* was the moment I had been waiting for since she had come back.

"I went away, and then Mama and Daddy brought me back, because I had been a very bad girl."

I nearly stamped my foot in impatience.

"No, Joan. Tell me what happened."

"I can't," she said, and there were tears in her voice. "I don't know how to put what happened into words."

My hand tightened on her forearm. "Try. Please, try."

She nodded, and wiped her eyes with the back of her hand. She did not look beautiful in this moment, or unbeautiful; she looked like herself.

"I thought the world would be different outside of Houston," she said. "But it wasn't."

"What was it like?"

"I saw Ingrid Bergman there."

"Really?" I asked. "Isn't she in Italy?"

She shrugged. "She must have come back for a quick trip. She was walking into a café. I was sitting at a little table, drinking a cappuccino."

A cappuccino. A café. Ingrid Bergman, back from Italy. I didn't know if Joan was fooling herself or just trying to fool me. She had seen a woman, likely, who resembled Ingrid Bergman, but the real Ingrid Bergman had been exiled from the entire country, had earned the wrath and ire of everyone, from senators to housewives, for her affair with Rossellini.

"You don't believe me?" Joan asked. She knew me so well.

"No, no," I protested. "You just hadn't told me before. What did she look like?"

"She was gorgeous," Joan said, sharply. "Of course." Her voice dropped to a whisper. "I want to *be* her, Cece."

"You want to be Ingrid Bergman? Everyone hates her."

"Not in Italy. I bet they love her there."

"Maybe."

"You don't see it." She sat back in her chair.

"No, I —"

"It's fine. I bet she meets a dozen interesting people a night, two dozen. I bet her house — her villa! — is covered in artwork. I bet she can hardly sleep her life is so exciting. Hop on a train to London at a moment's notice. Eat gelato at midnight next to the Trevi Fountain. Kiss a stranger in front of a movie camera."

Her eyes were bright, and I understood.

"There are so many people who want to be famous," I said.

She looked at me, uncomprehending.

"In Hollywood," I went on. "But it's just luck, Joan. Lightning."

"Lightning," Joan repeated. "It doesn't matter, anyway." She rose, sweeping my hands off her arm in a neat gesture. "It's all in the past."

Joan was not Joan outside of Houston. The rest of us knew to stay here: we knew who we were, where we belonged. The problem was Joan's ambition, which was unfocused, silly. But she would settle down again. Mary had said so, and I knew she was right.

207

"It's not so far in the past. You left me." It felt like I'd been waiting months to say this to her.

She nodded, considering. "I did. But we're not girls anymore. Do you want me to say sorry? I'm sorry." But she didn't sound sorry. She sounded angry, though how could she have been angry at me? I had done nothing but wait. I had waited so faithfully.

"Did you think about me while you were gone?" I hated myself for asking, like some scorned lover. But I couldn't help it.

"I did," Joan said. "Of course I did."

"But not as much as I thought about you." It slipped off my tongue like a greeting.

Joan's hand was on the sliding glass door; it was only a matter of time — minutes, seconds — before she left again.

"It's not long until you marry Ray, Cee. He loves you. You'll leave this place. You should leave this place."

CHAPTER SEVENTEEN

1957

I woke the Saturday morning after our night at the Petroleum Club, certain I had dreamt of Joan. I was groggy, disoriented. It was half past ten when I emerged from our bedroom. Tommy grinned at me from the kitchen floor, where he was playing with mixing bowls. I had a headache the size of Texas, and my mouth felt like terry cloth.

"Hi, sweetheart," I said, leaning down to kiss his forehead. And to Ray: "Maria?"

"Washing clothes."

"Did everyone eat?"

Ray glanced at the red enamel clock that hung over the stove.

"Tommy and I have been up for three hours. Yes, we've eaten. Toast." There was an edge to his voice but I chose to ignore it. I was allowed to sleep in once in a blue moon. I was irritated, too, besides. We always had pancakes on weekends, but ask-

209

ing Ray to make pancakes was like asking the president to knit a sweater after he hung up with Nixon. Men didn't do those things, in those days. Yet I knew I was lucky that Ray enjoyed Tommy. It was a constant complaint, among other women, that their husbands treated their own children as if they were strangers.

I hated when Ray was moody. He wasn't, generally. He was quiet with other people — not the life of the party, by any stretch — but with me and Tommy he was open and friendly and kind. I don't think there was a mean bone in Ray Buchanan's body. I had plenty of mean bones, and he had none. Perhaps that's why I married him.

I poured cold coffee into a pot and put it on the stove. I harbored a small hope that Joan had called, that if she hadn't called yet she *would* call, and smooth over last night. What Ciela had said — that I was Joan's handmaiden — was a thread being stitched through my tired brain.

I went to the little yellow notepad we kept by the phone, decorated with bluebirds, and checked to see if there were any messages for me.

"She didn't call." Ray licked a finger and turned a page of his newspaper.

"Who didn't call?"

"Your friend," he said. I hated his tone, which was mocking, deliberate. "The great Joan Fortier." Still he did not look at me. "The woman who keeps you out until three thirty in the morning, and then occupies your thoughts the day after. The woman who kept you in a knot of worry for the past few weeks, when she was off doing who knows what —"

"Stop." Tommy looked up at the sound of my voice. Watched me, solemnly.

"Stop?" He set his paper on the table, carefully. Ray was the most careful man I knew. I was taken aback by his anger, his handsome face distorted into a series of separate, ugly tensions. "I'll stop. But then maybe *you* should stop. Stop pretending you're twenty years old. You have a child at home, Cee."

"I'm a good mother. A good wife." I tried to keep my voice low. I didn't want Maria to hear. Tommy was still staring at me in his solemn way; I offered him a tight smile. "And you're upsetting Tommy, besides."

"Don't use Tommy."

"Don't you dare," I said. My voice was shaking. "You like Joan," I said. "Joan's our friend."

He laughed. "God, Cee, this has nothing to do with Joan! It's you. She can manage

211

herself. She's an adult."

"She needs me."

"Then you should have married her." His voice was hard.

I gave a bark of laughter. "Don't be absurd. But she needs me," I repeated. "She's always needed me."

"*We* need you. Tommy needs you." Tommy swung his head around to Ray. "And speaking of Tommy, when are we going to have another child? 'The time isn't right, the time isn't right.' " He was mimicking me — I hated being mimicked. "When will the time be right, Cee? When Joan says it is?"

"We'll have another child," I said, "when this one starts to speak."

Ray stared at me. I'd gone too far. Even I could see that, furious as I was. He stood, picked up Tommy, who clutched a block in his little, perfect hand.

"In front of him?" Ray hissed, before he left the room.

The pan rattled; the scent of scalded coffee filled the room.

"Perfect timing," I muttered, as I emptied the contents of the pan into a mug, then stirred in milk. I liked my coffee black but I needed it to cool down, quickly, so I could drink it and clear my head and start to put together where I had gone wrong, exactly.

He kept Tommy from me all day. Fed him lunch, dinner, bathed him, read him a story. All the things I normally did, as if to say, *Look, you're not the only one who can care for him.* Ray never spent time alone with Tommy other than our monthly girls' night. That Ray could do all the things I did made me feel useless. I was Tommy's mother, Ray's wife: my twin purposes in the world. I didn't like feeling as if I could be so easily replaced.

I spent the day in the bedroom. I wanted it to begin again. I wanted last night to never have happened. I considered calling Joan but she wouldn't have been helpful in her current state. And anyway, there was no one to whom I could confess the things I needed to confess. That I was afraid my son was damaged. That my husband was jealous of my best friend. That I could feel my best friend slipping away from me and I did not understand why.

Sometimes Tommy woke in the depths of the night. I went to him, padded down the hall and took him from his crib and rocked him back to sleep. I knew he was awake by some animal instinct; Tommy did not cry, or call out for me, or even shake the sides of his crib. His not speaking was something deeper than simple silence: it seemed he did not want to be heard. I wondered how many times my animal instinct had failed me, and I'd slept while Tommy waited for me to come to him. I thought of my own mother, and the fear returned that some essential lack of warmth on my part was to blame for Tommy's silence.

Now I had said something that could not be unsaid. I couldn't help but think that I had shifted something between Ray and me irrevocably. It made me feel desperate. Late that afternoon I stood at my window and watched Ray outside with Tommy, in his sandbox.

Ray offered Tommy a shovel, and Tommy took it without looking up. I didn't think I'd ever felt so completely excluded from my child and husband's world. I pressed my forehead to the glass and felt like weeping.

I found Ray in his study late that night. He was drinking a glass of scotch, a thick book he wasn't reading set in front of him.

"I'm sorry," I said. "About Tommy."

He cocked his head. "I don't think Tommy understood you," he said at last. "He's too young. He'll speak. It's just taking him longer than it takes other children."

"I know." In that moment, I believed him. I felt so sorry, so miserable, I would have believed anything he said.

"I'm not mad anymore. I just don't understand." He took a sip of his drink. His face was relaxed, and I wondered how long he'd been sipping scotch. Ray always seemed so knowable, so clear, but now I wondered about all the things he thought, all the secrets he kept from me.

I didn't want to wonder. I didn't want to be upset. I wanted to do something instead of thinking about doing something. I wanted to be clear about the difference between the two. I wanted to go back to last night and behave differently: behave more like Joan herself. What did I care if Joan ate poorly? What did I care if Joan wasn't always the nicest, the most understanding, the most polite? *She* didn't care.

"Understand what?" I asked.

"Understand you."

I went to him. I kneeled beside him, put my hand on his chest. I wasn't usually so dramatic.

"You understand me," I said. "You understand me the best of anyone in the world."

He smiled faintly. "Do you think so?"

I put my hand on his thigh. Sex with Ray was the most familiar thing in the world, an old sweater. I wanted it to be different tonight. I wanted him to come back to me. I wanted to be a different woman for him. I wanted not to care. Most of all, I wanted not to care.

I unzipped Ray's pants before I could think about it. I felt shy, suddenly, and the idea excited me, that I could feel shy with a man I'd been with since I was eighteen years old. Ray put his hand on my forehead, and I thought he wanted me to stop but then I understood he was only brushing my bangs from my face. He wanted to see.

When I put him in my mouth he gasped. "Jesus, Cee." I didn't want to hear my name. I didn't want to open my eyes and see Ray's study in all its ordinariness. I tried harder to pretend I was elsewhere. He was larger and larger in my mouth and I was less and less myself. I was giddy with the possibility of what we were doing. Hopeful.

The next day Ray loved me again. He was shy with me, and I with him; we didn't discuss what had happened in his study, the utter surprise of it, but it was there with us all day long, the way good sex makes you feel like a slightly different version of yourself. And perhaps you really were a different version of yourself; maybe sex had to

216

change you.

Mercifully — mercifully! — he was out, running by his office to pick up a file, when the phone rang. It was Mary, speaking too loudly again.

She got right to it, which was her way. "Have you seen Joan recently?"

"Two nights ago," I said.

"Oh." She sounded relieved. "And?"

I was never exactly sure what Mary wanted from me. The truth, or a version of it that was compatible with her idea of Joan — or, rather, her hopes for Joan. When we lived in the Specimen Jar, had Mary truly wanted to know that Joan was taking shots of tequila from salt-rimmed glasses and popping Darlene's mother's old painkillers?

"She was fine," I said, my voice neutral.

"Fine?"

"Fine."

A pause. I could hear ice rattling in a glass and I knew Mary was drinking her afternoon tea: iced in the summer, hot in the winter, or what passed for a winter here.

She sighed. "I'm concerned, Cecilia. She's been off, gallivanting, and hasn't been in touch as much as I'd like. Do you think I need to worry?"

Mary never laid her cards on the table so quickly, so easily. Never made herself so completely available. She knew something.

"Worry about what, exactly?"

"Oh, Cecilia. I'm an old woman with a husband who doesn't recognize me half the time. I just want to know if my daughter is safe. I just want to know that she's being prudent."

What must it be like, to have a mother who worried over you like this? I felt a brief surge of jealousy. And then sympathy, for Mary. Perhaps my sympathy had been carefully elicited, perhaps not. I no longer cared.

"She's dating a new man," I said. "His name is Sid."

I heard a small intake of air.

"Mrs. Fortier?"

The other end was silent. I leaned against the counter, a cold sweat on my forehead.

"Do you know him?" I ventured.

This time she answered. "Yes. Sid Stark," she said. "Only by reputation." She'd gathered herself.

"And his reputation?"

"Fine," she said vaguely, taking my word. "Fine. And now I really must let you go, Cecilia. Thank you for your help. As always."

After I hung up the phone I felt a tug on my skirt. Tommy, careful enough to wait until I was done speaking to solicit my attention. I felt a surge of love so great tears came to my eyes. I picked him up and held him, his warm breath against my neck, the sweet scent of him in my nostrils. I was terrified for Joan. But there was nothing I could do until she came to me.

I lasted a day. On Tuesday I was up extra early to bake a chocolate buttermilk cake, Ray's favorite. Actually, I made two. By the time Tommy was awake the cakes were already in the oven.

I fried crispy hash browns and eggs over easy; my timing was perfect. Ray came downstairs, his tie in his hand, and kissed me softly — tenderly, even — on the cheek.

"Sit down," I murmured, a thrill moving up my legs, the smell of him — his aftershave, his toothpaste, his essential oiliness — in my throat.

He sat and I slid his plate in front of him.

"Like Simpson's!" he said, delighted. Simpson's was the little café we had gone to for breakfast when we were first married.

"Right down to the slightly burned edges."

And a smaller plate for Tommy, who studied the food, then picked up a chunk of hash browns between his thumb and pointer finger and delicately took a bite.

Usually this delicateness bothered me. I didn't like that Tommy seemed, unlike other children, so unwilling to disturb the world. But in this instant his carefulness was charming; Ray and I watched our son together, taking equal pleasure in him.

Ray laughed. "And what's that smell?" he asked. "An after-breakfast treat?"

"Hardly," I said. "Something for after dinner."

"Just for me? No special occasion?" He caught me around the hips, pulled me into his lap.

"Just for you," I said, letting myself settle into him. "Just for you."

I put together the layers of both cakes as Tommy played with his train on the floor, iced each one with buttercream frosting on my special cake stand that had been a wedding present. The plate spun on its stand, making icing a breeze. When I brought my homemade desserts to Junior League meetings the other girls asked where I'd bought them.

"There," I said, and stood back to admire the cakes, each on a pale green platter. Out of loyalty to Ray I poked toothpicks into the top of the slightly lopsided one, then covered it in tinfoil.

I felt a small, smooth hand on my calf. Tommy, who looked up at me mournfully.

■ ■ ■ ■

It was also out of loyalty to Ray that I left Tommy at home, with Maria. And, though it was impossible, Tommy seemed to *know* I was doing something I shouldn't. What did Ray care if I dropped off a cake at Evergreen? I asked myself as I drove. But of course Ray would care. It would break the lovely feeling that had existed between us since Saturday night. But he wouldn't know, I told myself. Couldn't know, unless he'd suddenly developed a sixth sense. And he hadn't, because he was a man.

I knocked on the side door, like I'd done most of my life. I planned to slip in and see if Mary was available, and if she was, I'd — well, I didn't quite know what I'd do. I wanted to see her. I wanted to hear her say that Sid Stark was no one to worry about. I tapped lightly on the ancient screen door.

Stewart opened the door and stood there, jacketless, his sleeves rolled up, a cloth napkin tucked into his shirt.

He followed my eyes and plucked the napkin from his shirt in an unhurried gesture.

"Hello, Mrs. Buchanan. How may I help you?"

"I'm sorry," I said, flustered. "I see I've disturbed your lunch. I was hoping to catch Mrs. Fortier."

I noticed Stewart's hands, held out, waiting.

I looked at them, then at Stewart's face, which was, as always, inscrutable.

"The cake? A treat for the Fortiers? Please, allow me." And before I could stop him he'd taken it from me. "I'm afraid Mrs. Fortier is out, with Mr. Fortier. I'll tell her you called."

"Thank you," I said, because there was nothing else to say. Stewart nodded, and beyond his shoulder I glimpsed the little table where he had been sitting, lunch things laid out.

He shifted his weight, almost imperceptibly, but it was too late. I had seen, despite his best efforts.

"Thank you," I said again, backing away, Stewart letting the screen door close inch by inexorable inch. "Sorry to interrupt."

I sat in my car and tried to keep the panic at bay. I'd just seen a face I hadn't seen in years. Dorie. She was back. And she had appeared at the same time as Sid. It meant something. It must.

CHAPTER EIGHTEEN

1957

Sid Stark — the name circled my brain like a shark. Along with Dorie's face. And Joan's. Always Joan's. I told myself, just as I'd done when I'd first noticed Dorie gone all those years ago, that servants came and went all the time. Dorie's absence, and now her reappearance, might mean nothing. Yet I knew things were being kept from me. I was sure Stewart had not wanted me to see that Dorie had returned, and I was certain not only that Mary did know Sid Stark, but that I'd heard fear in her voice at the mention of his name.

There was no proof that these events were connected, but everything was beginning to feel like a deception.

I called Ciela on Wednesday.

"I'm sorry about the other night," I said, right away, about our moment in the Petroleum Club bathroom. "I was a little tipsy."

"Is that what we're calling it these days?" she asked, but then she quickly relented. "It's fine. We all get a little 'tipsy' sometimes, I suppose."

She seemed surprised I wanted to bring Tommy over.

"To play with Tina?"

"Umm, yes," I said, "unless you have another child I don't know about?"

She laughed. I was making her uneasy. Tina and Tommy had never played together before because I had never allowed it. He needed to be around other children, I knew that, and he was, in a Mother's Day Out on Tuesdays, across town, with children whose mothers I had no chance of running into otherwise. Tuesdays were my dress-down days, where I wore pants from last season and little jewelry.

"Tina will love that. She loves little boys, have I told you that? Prefers them a million times to little girls. Just like her mama!" She laughed, casually this time. Ciela could be biting but she could also be gracious, graceful: she made you feel comfortable in her presence. She had none of Darlene's dumb aggressiveness, none of Joan's carelessness. I felt a surge of affection for her, on the phone.

"I didn't know that, but I hope Tommy

fits the bill." It wasn't just a thing I was saying, either. It didn't matter where I put
Tommy, across town or not: he didn't like
other children. He didn't dislike them,
either — that would have meant he had
preferences. He simply ignored them, played
by himself, gave wary, sidelong glances to
any child who approached him.

Tina was tiny and cherubic, with enough
words to ask her mother why Tommy was
so silent.

"Not everyone talks as much as you, doll,"
she said, and though she was trying to be
kind, the words felt like a slap.

"He's shy," I said, giving Tommy, who
stood glued to my knee, his hand in his
mouth, a little push. "He's chattier at
home." An absolute lie, the kind that hurt
no one.

Ciela and I sat in Tina's playroom, with
the fan going full blast. It was decorated as
a room in a castle. A pink castle, inhabited
by pastel princesses, which were painted on
the walls in various poses: granting a wish
to a child who looked very similar to Tina;
floating over a field of flowers that contained
a child who looked very similar to Tina;
hovering beside a child who looked very
similar to Tina.

"Christ," I said, when we'd ascended the stairs and Ciela had flipped the light on and I had absorbed the room. "It's a little creepy, don't you think?"

I instantly regretted saying it, but Ciela took my comment in stride, laughing lightly enough that I would not feel uncomfortable, but not so heartily that I might think she agreed with me.

"We went a little overboard, but that's what children are for, don't you think? To go overboard on?"

I looked at Tommy, who stood not a foot from me. It was equal parts thrilling and upsetting, the extent to which Tommy needed to be near me. I tried not to take too much pleasure in this need, but it was hard sometimes, to deny my son such a simple thing.

Instead of drawing him into my lap, I took his hand and led him to a plastic kitchen where Tina played. I had no illusions he would play with Tina, but I had brought his blocks with me, and if all went well Tommy would stack these blocks obsessively while Tina played with her miniature kitchen, and it would appear, to the unpracticed eye, that little boy and little girl were playing together happily.

We talked about Darlene's younger sister,

Edie, who was flying to Miami for a nose job. "Poor thing," Ciela said, "she needs it." We talked about one of Ciela's neighbors, Beauton, a woman I knew socially who had recently caught her husband with the housekeeper. "Old story," Ciela said, winking. We talked about the new house going up on the west side of River Oaks, which was going to be over six thousand square feet. "A monstrosity," I said, "though I wouldn't mind living in it."

We did not speak of Joan. She was off-limits, more so now because Ciela had criticized her last week. We all had our lines in the sand — Ciela would not entertain rumors about her father, for instance — and Joan was mine.

"How's Ray?" Ciela asked. "Jay Potter says he's on his way to running the place." She smiled, so I would know she wasn't jealous. Our husbands both worked for Shell, but in different departments.

"Yes," I said vaguely, "I think he enjoys it." I was surprised that Ciela seemed to know so much. I liked that Ray worked hard but I appreciated none of the details. I knew he worked on leases for Shell; I knew Thursdays were very hectic because his company closed deals on Thursdays and Ray came home very late, if at all. Joan came over those nights, or I took Tommy to her house.

Ciela nodded, and I wished I had a glass of wine in my hand, or a cocktail, though it was too early for either. A Bloody Mary or a mimosa, if we had been at a restaurant, but we weren't. It was nearly time for us to go. Tommy hadn't offended Tina by his lack of interest; the two were playing quietly, Tina speaking soothingly to a doll she was frying in a plastic pan, Tommy stacking his blocks.

I wanted to leave before Ciela said something about Tommy, or, worse, Tina did. "Little boy is strange, Mommy!" another little boy had said during Mother's Day Out pickup last week, pointing at Tommy; the mother had hushed her son, and looked at me sorrowfully, which was worse than anything she could have said.

I tried to bring his name up casually. I tried very hard to act like it was nothing big.

"Do you know," I said, "a Sid Stark?"

Ciela could make her face a mask and reveal nothing when she was so inclined.

"Ah," she said finally, and pressed a finger to her lips. "Ah. Joan."

I was transparent, one of those see-through fish at the restaurant downtown

228

that Tommy loved. "They have no bones," I liked to say to Tommy, "and very small brains."

I was grateful to Ciela for not saying what we were both thinking: that my purpose in coming here, for showing interest in a friend in whom I had not previously shown much interest, was suddenly very obvious. I couldn't remember the last time I'd been to Ciela's house alone other than for a party or a cocktail hour with the girls.

"I hate to disappoint you," she said, "but I don't know a thing about Sid Stark. Other than he and Joan are dating. Though I like his name. Has a nice ring to it."

"Oh." I smoothed my wet palms — I was nervous — on my skirt.

"We don't all," she went on, "live and die by Joan's dating life."

Her tone was cheerful, but the insult stung.

"I'm sorry," she said. "I didn't mean to be a bitch. You sound worried. Are you worried about Joan? I mean, of course you are — you're always worried about Joan. Last Friday at the Petroleum Club, for instance." She gave me a pointed look.

It was true. I was always worried about Joan. But that Ciela didn't have any information about Sid did not relieve me, as

229

maybe it should have. It made me more nervous.

"I don't know," I said. "He seems nice to Joan."

Ciela laughed. "I don't know this man from Adam, but of course he's nice to Joan. Why wouldn't he be? She has something he wants."

"What does Joan have that he wants?" I asked. Tommy approached me cautiously, a block in his hand. I pulled him close, glad to have him near.

"What do you think, Cece?" There was a rare note of contempt in her voice.

"You don't know what you're talking about," I said. I could feel my cheeks flush. Nobody *used* Joan — Ciela needed to drop the idea.

Ciela turned to check on Tina; a flash of tanned skin, an unmovable helmet of blond hair. I could glimpse her peanut-sized diamond earrings through her hair. You could identify how well we had done, how well our husbands had done, by the size of our diamonds and how many there were. Were they peanuts or walnuts strung together on a bracelet? A necklace? How far down did it dip between our breasts?

I felt my own ears. I had worn sunburst garnets, practically costume jewelry. Sometimes it was exhausting, remembering all the ways we measured each other. The ruler was long and precise.

Ciela turned back to me.

"Joan has something all of us want, doesn't she? Isn't that the trick of Joan Fortier? She makes you think you want to be her. And being with her is the next best thing," she added.

"There is no trick to Joan," I said. "She's just Joan."

"Do you really think Joan is as innocent as all that?"

"I do!" I said. "I —"

Ciela held up her hand, her small gold watch sliding down her arm. "I didn't mean to upset you. I only meant to say that it's not hard to see why any man would want to date a woman like Joan. For a little while. She would be fun, wouldn't she? And she wouldn't ask anything of you." She raised her eyebrows. "To be so free, like Joan! Free as a bird. I can barely remember a time before Tina. I can't imagine dating. I can't imagine a life that's not this." And she gestured to the room, to the horrible princess mural, to little Tina, who was putting Tommy's blocks into the oven; to Tommy, who was sitting in my lap, the edge of his hand in his mouth.

"Can you?" she asked.

I could, was the thing. I could imagine a life that was not my own. I didn't want to *be* Joan, but to say, then or now, that Joan's life didn't seem charmed — didn't seem nearly perfect, in certain ways — would be a lie.

I drove home from Ciela's and stopped at the Avalon drugstore for sundaes, where we sat at the counter. "Because you were so good," I told Tommy. No ice cream for me, of course; summer was here, season of wasp-waisted sundresses and barely-there bikinis. I watched Tommy bring his spoon to his mouth, his coordination sloppy. I would never stop worrying about him. And if we had another child, as Ray wanted, as I supposed I wanted, too, I would never stop worrying about *that* child, either, and it was such a strange thing, to understand you would worry about a child who did not yet exist. A phantom child.

Ray could always leave. Men did it all the time. I had no reason to think he would, and in fact his constancy was one of my keenest sources of pride. I had, unlike my mother, chosen a man who seemed intent on sticking around. There were pleasures in marriage, certainly, and I enjoyed them, but on certain days marriage felt like a long, unending slog. And sometimes the slog was pleasurable, when Ray and I were on the same page, when our life was unfurling in the way we thought it should; but sometimes it was sad and depressing and you never knew which it would be. We were so young. Would our marriage be a happy one? It was a question I asked myself all the time then. Only time would tell. Marriage, then, seemed like a waiting game: How happy would we be? At what point in our lives would other people be able to say of us, "The Buchanans are very happily married"? Or: "It's a troubled marriage." There was nothing in between; people didn't say, "Well, they love each other in an average sort of way; their marriage hasn't been disappointing but neither has it been the source of comfort and joy they had hoped."

Tommy's glass dish rattled against the table. My child was a disaster. I hadn't watched him closely enough and his cheeks, his hands, the front of his shirt were covered in chocolate syrup. He would mess up the car now.

"Tommy," I said. He looked up, attentively, his spoon balanced in his small hand.

Right now Joan was asleep, or by her pool, or in bed with Sid Stark. I would have traded places with her in an instant.

■ ■ ■ ■

I went to Joan's the very next day. Did you think I was capable of waiting, of letting Joan come to me? I was not. I at least knew that about myself, what I was and was not capable of in life. I was capable of secrecy. I was capable of great loyalty. I was capable of a kind of faithfulness that did not occur to most people. But I wasn't patient. I wasn't able to put things out of my mind for any period of time. The people I loved were always threaded through my thoughts, went with me everywhere: home after Avalon to put Tommy down for a nap; to Jamail's to pick up a few things on the grocery list Maria had forgotten; to the dry cleaner's for Ray's suits; home again to relieve Maria.

I waited until after lunch. The drive from my house to hers was short — three minutes, four minutes tops — and the world as I passed it in my car was still, not a person — a child playing in a sprinkler, a gardener trimming hedges — in sight. It was too hot. I drove with my window down, but the breeze wasn't much of a breeze. More of a dry, brittle blast of wind. I could have turned on the air conditioner — it was our first car that had it — but the icy temperature it produced felt unnatural, like I was on a tundra somewhere.

When I got out of the car I was already soaked with sweat.

I walked around the side of the house, admiring the beds of hydrangeas and crepe myrtles that Joan cared nothing about; I hoped to find Joan and avoid Sari entirely.

The wrought-iron fence that surrounded Joan's pool and backyard was solid, meant to keep out the reporters who used to lurk around the house. There had been an incident, an unflattering photograph, and the next day this fence was installed.

I knew where the key to the gate was, but as I circled behind the garden shed to retrieve it I noticed the gate was open a sliver.

Joan's leg was all I could see at first: her painted toenails, her surprisingly flat foot. (Wouldn't one expect Joan Fortier's feet to be perfect and small and arched? They were average-sized, flat, a little wide.) Then her leg, gleaming with oil. And then: well, the rest of her. She was naked as the day she was born, her entire body slick with oil. The smell came to me — coconut, tropical — and made me sad for reasons I couldn't name.

She hated tan lines. So did the rest of us,

but the rest of us were more discreet with how we tanned, where. The rest of us didn't remove our bikini bottoms. We tanned on our stomachs, our tops judiciously removed but still hanging loosely around our necks, so that we could, in an instant, refasten them should a stranger come knocking.

I wasn't a stranger. But still I wished Joan were more modest. I'd seen her naked so many times I couldn't count if I tried; I knew all the stages of her body, from little girl to adolescent to this: lean, golden thighs; the surprise of her pubic hair, darker and coarser than you would have imagined; her long, muscular torso; her heavy, unbeautiful breasts. Joan needed a brassiere for her breasts to be beautiful. Those and her feet were God's way of reminding Joan Fortier that she was mortal.

Joan didn't care. She never had taken any particular pleasure in her beauty. All the times I had eagerly unfolded the *Houston Press* and flipped past all the boring sections to "The Town Crier" and thrilled at the sight of Joan, looking beautiful and radiant at some event, on some man's arm, though she always managed to make it look as if the man were on *her* arm — Joan barely gave these photographs a second glance. "Will make Mama happy," she'd murmur. "She chose that dress."

The sight of her, naked, thinner than I'd seen her in a long time, a tall drink of something clear at her hand, undid something in my soul; I wanted to slap her, to shout at her, to tell her to put some clothes on and stop acting like a teenager. But I also wanted to watch her, to stand there for as long as I could and observe Joan as I never saw her: asleep and unguarded.

I slipped through the gate and Joan shifted. She wore cat-eye sunglasses.

"Cee," she murmured. "Come sit." She patted the space right next to her but I took a chair a few feet away, smoothed my skirt underneath my thighs as I sat.

She sat up a little, gazed, I thought, at me, though it was impossible to tell with the sunglasses. She laughed, and pulled a neatly folded towel from the table at her side — a towel Sari had left, I was sure — and draped it over her waist.

"I'm naked as a jaybird, aren't I? Of course, I wasn't expecting company." But the way she said it wasn't mean, and I felt a burst of relief so pure and instantaneous I wanted to cry. She wasn't mad.

"It's hot as hell," I said. "Hotter. You'll burn."

Her languid smile was beginning to unnerve me.

"Oh no," she said. "I don't burn. You know that by now. I tan, to a crisp. But I never get close enough to the sun to burn."

Beyond Joan was a table littered with half-full drinks and ashtrays. A magnum of champagne sat in a chair, like a person. I closed my eyes. Joan had been entertaining, with Sid. Last night, the night before — did it matter when? "Doll," I imagined Sid saying, "I have a few friends who are dying to meet you."

"Where's Sari?" I asked.

"Sari?"

"Sari, your live-in maid? The woman who hasn't left your side since the Specimen Jar?"

"The Specimen Jar," Joan said. "I'd forgotten how you used to call it that. I never really liked that name."

"Ciela's the one who named it," I said. "It just stuck . . ." I trailed off.

"It never really made sense to me," Joan continued, as if I hadn't spoken. "Because nobody could see us up there." She paused. "Butterflies in a jar," she contemplated further, something liquid in her voice.

That was our purpose. Joan's especially.

"Beautiful bugs, trapped in glass. I suppose we were Mama's specimens, now,

238

weren't we."

It was like that between us sometimes, as if Joan could read my mind, as if I could read hers.

"Yes," I said, slowly, considering, "I suppose we were. Or you were, anyway."

She laughed, her breasts rising and falling with her shoulders. One nipple was tense, puckered; the other was smooth as glass. I turned my head.

"I just came by to see if you were all right. I wanted to hear more about Sid." There. I'd said it. I couldn't unsay it now; his name floated between us.

"I sent Sari away," Joan said, finally.

"A day off?"

"Sure. A day off."

"She wouldn't have approved." I gestured behind Joan, to the mess, to the champagne bottle that sat in a chair like a small child. I took care not to include Joan's altered state, her careless nudity.

"No," Joan said, smiling. "That's something you two have in common." She raised her sunglasses, and squinted desperately, like some sort of underground creature. "Goddamn it's bright."

I stood. I was tired of this, tired of sitting there and pretending.

"Tommy misses you," I said. "And so do I."

I watched as Joan's eyes gradually adjusted to the sun.

"I'm right here," she said. "I haven't gone anywhere."

"But you have," I said.

"Cee." She stood, her towel falling to the ground. "Leave it."

My attention was caught by a figure in the background: Sid, moving through the house. He was naked; his nakedness thrilled and terrified me. His silhouette was muscular and broad. How is it possible to feel repelled by and attracted to someone simultaneously? It was as if I could feel his magnetism through the door. I could feel it the same way Joan must have felt it.

CHAPTER NINETEEN

One night in February 1952, when Joan had been back for just short of a year, the curtain had dropped. It was time.

I was tired, the kind of exhaustion that turns you half dead. Joan rarely slept that year, and neither did I. I had never in my life dabbled in drugs but I knew Joan must have picked up the habit in California. Mostly prescription drugs, I thought — I'd found a bottle of them in her lingerie drawer.

I tried to always watch her. I would stay with her as long as I could, until she disappeared from my sight at a party or a club, and then I would fetch Fred and we would drive from haunt to haunt in the dimly lit Houston night until we found her.

But I could not always watch her. That would have been impossible: Joan wanted to vanish.

It was a Sunday night. A nothing night; I

had hoped Joan would turn in early, that we could have Sari fix us ham sandwiches and stay home and watch *The Ed Sullivan Show.* Instead we had gone to Sam's, downtown. As Fred held our door open and we slipped out of the car I said a little prayer that Joan would want to go home early, or if not early, before the sun came up.

But I knew as soon as we walked into Sam's that we wouldn't be leaving any time soon. The night was busy, the air smoky, illuminated by candles and the tips of cigarettes.

Sam himself came up to greet us, dressed in a shiny gray suit too tight for his corpulent frame, his hair slicked back neatly to his skull. He was chubby and persnickety, tidy about his person, and his club was neat, too: there were never crumpled napkins beneath tables, stray cigarette butts outside of ashtrays.

"Joan," he said, and kissed her hand. She wore a ruby-and-pearl cocktail ring shaped like a teardrop on her left hand, a gift from her father. "Cece," he said, and waited, as if he had all the time in the world, until I offered him my hand. That I wouldn't offer it was unthinkable. Men touched women whenever they wanted, in those days. I was lucky it was my hand and not my cheek, my forehead, my lips. I didn't particularly like being touched by men. I liked when Ray touched me, and that was all.

Joan never seemed to mind. I brought it up once and she'd shrugged. "Lips are just skin," she'd said.

"And a penis? That's just skin, too, I suppose?"

She laughed merrily. "It's all skin. Though some skin is more pleasant than other skin."

Tonight Sam led us through the club, me a few steps behind Joan. Women stared, then turned their heads; there was generally something cold in their gazes. Men sat back, lit a cigarette, took in Joan as if she were a drink they'd just ordered. I was irritated; Sam was taking the most circuitous route possible. Finally we stopped at an elevated booth near the stage, where we were introduced to a man from Austin, whom I'd never met; he was talking to Darlene when we approached.

"Your hair," I said, "it's different." She'd cut three inches off, at least.

"I'll take that as a compliment. I need another drink." She sighed, and tilted her head toward Joan, who now had the man from Austin's attention. I hadn't bothered to remember his name.

I was surprised to see Darlene. We had

been a band since high school — Joan, me, Ciela, Kenna, Darlene — and most of the time we went out on the town together. But I also understood why a woman like Joan was especially hard on a woman like Darlene, who possessed neither looks nor charm. I can't remember why Ray wasn't with us that night. Maybe he'd had to work. I do remember thinking, even without him there, that I'd hit a good place in my life. After all the turmoil of my youth, it was a pleasant surprise. Joan had returned, I was engaged, and I would be the first one of us married.

"I didn't know you would be here tonight," I said to Darlene. Though I didn't particularly like Darlene, I was glad to see her. She was someone familiar, and I could spend the night chatting with her about nothing instead of trailing after Joan from person to person. Joan was in constant motion, darting from one person to the next in a way that suggested she was never satisfied. (At the end of the night, when we were alone in the backseat of the car, she often complained about how tiresome she found everyone. "Water, water, everywhere, and not a single drop to drink.")

"And yet," Darlene said, "here I am." She raised her hand at a passing waiter, nodded

244

to her empty champagne glass. In thirty seconds there was another one in front of her, and me as well.

"Compliments of Sam," the waiter said, as he set down the last glass, in front of Joan.

Darlene made a face; Sam had not sent her any compliments via champagne. And why should he? There was a good chance there would be a photographer outside at the end of the night, waiting to snap a picture of Joan; Darlene's would only appear in the columns if she happened to be next to Joan, in the right place at the right time.

Joan, who was listening to the man from Austin, briefly nodded her head at the waiter, apparently absorbed in her conversation.

Darlene stared at Joan, and I felt a surge of sympathy.

"She's just pretending," I said. "She's not really interested." It was true: in five minutes Joan would be off to another booth, the man from Austin left behind, wondering if he'd ever had a chance with Joan Fortier. No, I could have told him had he asked, he had not ever had a chance.

Darlene snorted. "Do you think I don't know that?" She took a long sip of her champagne; the red lipstick she left behind

245

on the glass was thick, striated. She must have been very drunk, I thought, to leave lipstick behind on a glass like that.

In six months Darlene would meet her husband, a man fifteen years her senior who *did* have to work, but only to manage his fortune. Darlene would find herself happy, for the first time in her life — that's what she would tell all of us, anyway. "I'm truly happy for the first, the very first time in my life!"

But for now she was a girl at a nightclub on an off night, waiting for love.

"How's Mickey?" I asked, hoping to change the subject. Mickey was the man she had been dating for a few weeks. Darlene was drunk enough that distracting her would be either very easy or very hard.

"Mickey." She snorted again. "He's not here, is he?"

I felt a warm hand on my shoulder, and picked up the scent of Chanel No. 5.

"Cece," Ciela said, moving into my line of vision. "Didn't think you'd be here tonight."

My cheeks turned hot. Ciela gracefully slid into Joan's side of the banquette. "You're all here?" I asked. It was worse that Ciela was in on the plans, had probably designed them. She mattered more than Darlene. I tried to catch Joan's eye but she

246

wouldn't look at me. She couldn't have cared less that all the rest of the girls had planned a night out without us. Without her, more to the point. "Kenna, too?"

Ciela removed a small silver compact from her alligator clutch, made a show of patting her perfectly coiffed hair.

"I just put her in a cab home, as a matter of fact. She had a little too much fun too soon." She rolled her eyes, and laughed. "We would have invited you two but I thought Joan mentioned something about plans." She lit a cigarette, exhaled over her shoulder, coughed a bit in a glamorous way that was completely contrived. She was lying, we both knew that. Joan never made plans. And Ciela had been smoking since she was twelve. Smoke only soothed our throats.

In December *Reader's Digest* would publish its "Cancer by the Carton" article and though we would feel guilty about smoking from that point on, we wouldn't stop. But for now smoking carried with it just pure, simple pleasure.

I lit my own cigarette. Ciela didn't seem disappointed to see us. But she wouldn't. Ciela had perfect manners. You never really knew what she was thinking.

"What I want to know," she said, smiling,

leaning toward me, but no, she was reaching for an ashtray, "is when on earth the great Joan Fortier sleeps!"

I glanced at Joan; if she'd heard her name, she didn't let on.

"Yeah," Darlene said, lighting her cigarette from Ciela's. "I want to know that, too."

The truth was that Joan never slept. The truth was that Joan seemed incapable of sleep lately; I often lay with her in bed until four or five in the morning, talking about nothing, chatting about the night we'd just had, the nights that lay ahead of us, undisturbed, a row of tantalizing presents. That was how Joan spoke of them: as if each upcoming night was a promise. She slipped into the future tense so often I no longer found the habit jarring. "We'll go to the Cork Club," she'd say, in her nightgown, her head resting on her pillow, her eyes staring straight up at the ceiling, looking at nothing, "and we'll bump into Larry and maybe he'll take us driving in his new car." And on and on. The truth was that I often drifted off to sleep and woke to find Joan gone, not even a note; the truth was I emerged from the bedroom to the disapproving glances of Sari, who had also failed to stop Joan from leaving. We were the same, Sari and I. Neither of us knew how to make Joan stay.

I realized Ciela and Darlene were waiting on an answer.

"Oh," I said vaguely, "she'll sleep when she's dead."

Darlene looked a little startled, her small, thickly lined eyes darting back and forth between me and Ciela, who just laughed.

"Won't we all," she said, and examined her cigarette. Joan rose, her hand on the man from Austin's elbow, and I chatted with Darlene and Ciela about nothing, keeping track of Joan out of the corner of my eye.

It had been nearly two years since we'd graduated, but we might as well have been in Lamar's vast cafeteria, picking at our sandwiches, watching Joan flirt with a boy at the football team's table.

And then Darlene was gone and Ciela and I sat alone at the banquette. The evening ended where it always seemed to: all eyes on Joan. The man from Austin had pulled her onto the small cabaret stage at the back of the club, and she was obviously very drunk, and maybe something else, but still she moved gracefully to the music, swaying and turning unself-consciously, as if she were alone. She wore a black strapless dress, elaborately crisscrossed at the bust with thick white ribbon. The effect was almost masculine, as if she wore a suit of armor around her breasts.

I turned to say something to Ciela but she was gazing at Joan. I tried to see what Ciela saw.

She was too thin — Ciela would have noticed how thin Joan had become. She seemed almost fragile, her wrists tiny, child-like; her waist dramatically drawn in as if she wore a girdle. But I had zipped Joan into that dress; she wore nothing under-neath. Joan at her best was more Rita Hay-worth than Vivien Leigh: being thin didn't suit her.

I glanced at the other patrons, the room filled with glittering bodies, all young except for the richest men, who were ten, twenty years older than us. Thirty. The man from Austin looked like he was in his late forties. There was not a single woman in this room over the age of twenty-five, I realized. If you were older than that you were at home, with a husband and a child. I thought of Ray, and felt a rush of unexpected relief. My days here were numbered.

All the glittering bodies were watching Joan. All the glittering bodies were capti-vated. I touched Ciela on the shoulder, lightly, and gestured to the room.

"They love her," I said, and it was hard

not to feel satisfied, not to take pride in Joan's beauty and charm. Hard not to take a smug pleasure in how the night had turned out: Ciela had tried to engineer the night for herself, tried to take Joan out of it completely, and look where that had gotten her.

Ciela turned to me. "Joan's troubled," she said. "She's in trouble, Cece."

I know, I should have said. Did Ciela think I didn't know? I knew how much she drank; I was the one who tucked empty bottles into my largest purse and secreted them out of the Specimen Jar, though of course Sari knew what I was doing.

"She's just having fun," I said, and I half believed it myself.

Ciela smiled, almost smirked, though Ciela was not a woman who smirked.

"Fun," Ciela said. "Do you really think that?"

Ciela considered me for a moment. I could feel her deciding.

"Yes," I said firmly, to put an end to the conversation.

Ciela left shortly thereafter, kissed me on each cheek like we were French. She glanced at Joan, who was behind the bar with Sam, laughing.

"Good luck with her," she said, "though I

suppose you don't need it."

I *did* need it. It was nearly impossible to make Joan leave a club, a bar, a party. I knew Ciela and all the others wondered why I stayed, why I did what I did.

"Just move out," Ciela had said, when Joan was in Hollywood, after I had met Ray. "Get married. Get your own place. It's not healthy, waiting for someone who might or might not be coming back."

She was full of advice, Ciela.

I made my way to the bar.

"Baby," a man called after me, "baby, come sit down." It was nearly two o'clock in the morning. The alcohol had turned to sludge in my blood. I wanted to go home.

I took a seat at the nearly empty bar, next to the man from Austin, who, predictably, was waiting for Joan to leave to make his exit. He seemed harmless enough. I don't know why I thought that, exactly — just that I had somehow learned, like every other woman on earth, to separate the men who might do me harm from the men who seemed likely not to.

"Joan," I said. She was whispering something to Sam, who was cupping her elbow conspiratorially. I was disgusted, though I knew exactly what she would tell me. *That's what men do, Cece. They're animals. Take it as a compliment.*

Now Joan was pretending not to hear me. I would be lucky to have her in the car by three.

"Joan," I barked.

She spun around and glared at me. Sam and the man from Austin sat up straighter.

"Leave," she said, and paused. "Leave me alone. Get out of here. I'll find my own way home."

I felt my face flame. She could be petulant at the end of a night, but she'd never spoken to me like this, certainly not in front of strangers.

Her eyes were bright, her pupils strangely large. Joan did not look like a woman who had been slamming drinks all night. She looked like a woman who could go on for hours.

I recognized the strangeness of her eyes and left anyway. "You left her there?" Mary would ask later. "All alone?"

Yes. I left her there. All alone.

"Fine," I said, and gathered my clutch, my stole. I took Fred away, told him to go home after he'd opened my door, that Joan could find her own way back.

I woke at eleven the next morning. I brushed my teeth; dabbed a cream Kenna had given me underneath my eyes, something she said was from Paris; took a pill that was supposed to make my hair thicker; and when I finally emerged from the bathroom, dressed in capris that hit my waist at just the right point and a soft blouse that exposed exactly the right amount of my collarbone, I felt better than I had in a long time. I'd made up my mind before I fell asleep to confront Joan: things needed to change. She needed to come home at a decent hour, she needed to drink less and be careful with whatever else she was doing or taking. And she needed never to raise her voice at me again among strangers. I was used to Joan's moods, but I could not tolerate a stranger seeing the private bits of our relationship. That moment last night now belonged to Sam and the man from Austin and the few people scattered at the bar. Joan had given it to them.

The light in the Specimen Jar was blinding; sometimes, during the brightest parts of the day, Joan and I wore sunglasses. I shielded my eyes and made my way to the kitchen, where Sari had set out my bowl of oatmeal.

I heard her thick-soled shoes against the tile before I saw her.

"Do you want anything else with your oatmeal? An egg?"

"No," I said. "Thank you."

She asked me every morning; every morning I said no, thank you. There were so many rituals, with live-in servants. Joan, when she emerged from her room — I glanced at the door, shut firmly against the light of the living room — would want something greasy, with meat, "to soak up the poisons."

Sari measured out coffee, poured a neat glass of orange juice, which she squeezed fresh every morning.

"Thank you," I said when Sari placed the small, pretty glass to the right of my cereal bowl; Sari made a low, aggressive noise.

Now I expected her to leave. This was our routine, when Joan wasn't here. When Joan was here, she stayed, and tended to Joan, who needed tending.

She stood beyond my frame of vision, waiting, it seemed, for something.

"Yes?"

"Remember Mrs. Fortier is coming to dinner tonight," she said. "With Mr. Fortier."

I'd completely forgotten. Mary never came to the Specimen Jar. It was Furlow who stopped by bearing gifts, to have a glass of champagne and sit on the rooftop deck, admiring Houston's hazy skyline. Instead,

255

Joan went to Mary. Something had changed in their dynamic; Joan was more in thrall to Mary than she ever had been, a change I mistook for closeness: I thought Joan needed her mother now, depended on her in a way that signaled their relationship was better. I knew nothing. Joan *did* need Mary, but not in the way I thought.

At five o'clock, two hours before Mary and Furlow were set to arrive, I knocked on Joan's door. There was no answer, and instead of knocking again I turned the knob and blinked; gradually the dark room revealed itself and I saw that Joan's bed was undisturbed. The books that had lived on her bureau since she'd returned were gone.

I thought she might be dead in the bathroom. I don't know what sense of dread compelled my brain to the worst possible outcome — but I was in the bathroom, the light flipped on, nothing but bright white porcelain and my own reflection before I realized how absurd the idea was. Of course Joan wasn't dead.

But she was gone, which presented two problems. The first: Mary and Furlow. The second: Joan's whereabouts.

Oh, I knew where she was. With a man, in his bed; or if not his bed, then a bed through the stage door, down the warren of halls, and up the stairs in the Shamrock. The man from Austin. I sat down on the edge of her white bed and put my head in my hands. He wasn't even her type. He was old, too old to deserve a body like hers, too old to even be in the same room with her. But it didn't matter. Any man would do these days.

I went to call Mary, for I knew that wherever Joan was, I would not locate her, then retrieve her, then bring her back here and make her presentable, within two hours.

I had been planning to go to Ray's after dinner, spend the night at his apartment. Now that was out of the question. He seemed irritated when I told him, but I didn't have time to placate him. I would deal with him later.

I would find her, but I didn't know that. If only all the people who searched in the world could know whether or not their looking would end in a reunion. I stayed up that entire night, after speaking to a reticent Mary — "She's gone, dear? I'm not alarmed, exactly, but I'm a little put out." I didn't know if I believed her. I could never read Mary. All that night and into the next day I heard Ciela echoing in my brain like an ache that occasionally dulled but never quite disappeared. *She's in trouble, Cece.*

It was six o'clock in the morning and I sat at the dining room table, staring at the beef tenderloin and roasted carrots resting in their own congealed fat.

The phone rang. I was waiting for Joan to call, hoping she would do so before I had to begin to search for her in earnest. I couldn't run from club to club, asking if anyone had seen her; I couldn't stop by Sam's and ask whom Joan had left with, and where they had gone; to do this would be to risk Joan's reputation, and though it was understood that Joan was wild and fast, a party girl, she was still a respectable woman who returned home after her nights out. It was my job to protect her from herself; it was for this that the Fortiers needed me, and loved me.

I snatched up the receiver. "Miss Cecilia," an unfamiliar voice said, "I need to take you somewhere."

I looked out the window into the black night, terrified. I wanted to hang up yet I could not, because this person might know something about Joan.

"Where?" I asked, in a trembling voice.

"This is Fred," the voice said.

"Oh," I gasped. "Thank God."

"Can you come downstairs in half an

hour?" he asked.

"Do you know where Joan is?"

Silence. "I might," he said.

I hurried downstairs and waited in the lobby before I saw the silver of the Fortiers' car.

We left downtown. The address was in Sugar Land, so we would be there soon. The sun had not yet risen, and the buildings' outlines were ghostly in the predawn light. The familiar sight of Fred's coarse gray hair, the stiff black collar that covered his neck — it calmed me. He wore his uniform even now.

"Not too long," he said. He had a Southern accent, but not a Texas drawl. He'd probably grown up on a farm somewhere, in the South, then moved to the big city in his youth.

Houston fell away quickly: high-rises gave way to large houses; then smaller houses with wide porches and dusty, dry yards; then empty land, purple spiderwort and violets just starting to bloom. I wrapped myself in my cashmere shawl and leaned my forehead against the cool window.

I wondered what Joan had seen as she'd driven this same route last night, or if she'd seen anything at all. I would ask her, I decided. A surge of hopefulness sparked its way through my limbs and I felt electric. I would make her understand why she had to be different, be better.

After another twenty minutes I saw a sign for Sugar Land, Texas, on the side of the road. One of Darlene's cousins lived here. We weren't that far outside of Houston, but it felt like another world.

It was not what I thought it would be. Is anything ever? We turned off the main road onto a dirt road and drove deeper and deeper into a vast expanse of what appeared to be a farm with no crops. The sun was almost out, now.

The car shimmied and swayed over the rocky path so violently I thought I might be sick.

"Rough territory," Fred said, and I knew he was trying to be kind, and I wondered what he must think of me, of this. He had his sources, clearly. I assumed another chauffeur had told Fred where Joan had gone. But I didn't really know, and I never would, because I couldn't ask him. Fred had ferried Joan from place to place for years, from the time she was a little girl. He knew, I realized, suddenly. He knew more than I. But I couldn't ask him, either, if he knew who Joan really was. Last month the *Press* had called her Houston's most eligible bachelorette, and printed a photo of her leaving the Cork Club, a man on either side of her. You could see me, too — not my face, of course. Just the side of my figure, clothed in a skirt made of netting and lace, dotted with crystals. It was one of my favorite pieces. When I wore it I felt like a person who could go anywhere, be anyone.

The road leveled out and we were on asphalt; it took a second for the dust to clear and the house to emerge: ranch-style, long and beige. Its plainness made me nervous. I had not expected to find Joan somewhere so ordinary.

There were no signs of life: I noted a carport, where the car would have been parked. The flower beds that edged the house were gutted, filled with dirt and gravel to keep the dust down. Curtains were drawn tightly against the windows. The house was nondescript and neatly kept. There was neither grass nor weeds, no shingles missing from the roof, and the brown trim around the windows looked fresh. It was clear someone tended to the place.

Fred turned the car off and looked back at me; for the first time that morning I saw his entire face. He looked tired. He must not have slept, either. I wondered if Mary had called him. "Do you want me to come with you?" he asked. "It's no trouble." And I knew we both saw the same thing in the house: it was menacing in its blankness, dead against the horizon.

"Just please wait for me," I said, even though of course he would.

The door was unlocked. I stepped into a carpeted foyer; to my left was a sitting room, with a brown sofa covered in plastic. A vase of artificial flowers sat on the coffee table, next to an open newspaper with a small glass of water resting beside it, on a coaster.

The house smelled like potpourri, and something burned, and — I almost cried with relief when the scent hit me — Joan. Her perfume first, and then her hair spray, which I had applied the night before, when I'd done up her hair in a French twist, then again right before we'd left the house, as a touch-up, to make sure she would remain exquisite throughout the night.

Joan had been here for hours now. Over a day.

"Joan?" I called. I walked down a dim hallway, beige, lined with beige doors. I imagined empty rooms lay behind them.

When I came to the door at the end of the hall I hesitated. I knew Joan was behind it, I knew it was a bedroom, but I didn't

262

know who else was with her. The man from Austin, maybe. But maybe not. I knocked, lightly at first, then harder. Last night I'd thought she might be dead in the bathroom, but now she really could have been dead. She could have taken too many of her pills. A girl we'd known of in high school — she hadn't run in our circle — had locked herself in her bedroom with her mother's prescription and a bottle of vodka; she'd died a week later. Joan might not have been trying to kill herself, but she'd been so wild lately she might have hurt herself accidentally. I pictured Mary's face, Furlow's. "Please be fine," I whispered. "Please."

The door was locked. I would have laughed if I weren't terrified. The lock was cheap — I found a nickel in my purse and opened it in one twist.

The room was bright, and it took a few seconds for my eyes to adjust. The source of light was an open window that looked out onto the backyard.

I saw only Joan, at first: her cheek pressed into the pillow, her neck turned at an odd angle, her blond hair still in its twist. My head spun. *She is dead,* I thought, *dead and gone.* But then the flutter of an eyelid: she was only sleeping. Her hair looked nearly perfect. I took quick, misplaced pleasure in my handiwork before I remembered that I had a job to do, that Joan's hair mattered not at all.

The room smelled of sex, and I noticed the fact of her nakedness and the two other bodies in the bed almost simultaneously. I tiptoed closer. On one side of Joan lay a man draped with a bedsheet; on her other side lay a man as exposed as Joan was, but facedown. I couldn't see either of their faces. The man who was covered had an arm flung over his face, and a long, purplish scar ran from his elbow to his wrist. I raised my hand to my mouth and stared at all of it. Tried to fit the pieces in front of me into a picture I could understand. The three bodies were inert, their sleep so deep it seemed unnatural.

I couldn't tell how tall these men were, or how much money they had, or if they were from Houston or somewhere else. I couldn't tell if they mattered — and which was worse, that they did or did not? I reached out to steady myself with the wall.

They had both touched Joan, at the same time. Used her. And she had been willing, she had presented herself up to them like an offering, a gift. *Have me any way you like me, boys,* I imagined her saying. *I'm Joan Fortier, and I don't care.*

Fred had known the address, but had he known what happened here? No. He would have stopped it had he known.

The room was bare except for a large painting of a herd of cattle surrounding a cowboy with his lasso raised, which hung above the bed. I wondered if Joan had looked at this painting, considered it. But Joan had not looked anywhere beyond herself, not for a long time.

"Joan," I said softly. No response.

"Ma'am?"

I turned at the sound of Fred's voice. His eyes were more gold than brown, which I had never noticed before. I didn't think I had ever been so glad to see anyone.

"Help me," I said, and the emotion in my voice surprised me. "I need to get her." I pointed at Joan, though it was of course obvious who I meant, a naked woman lying between two men. "I need to take her home."

He nodded. "Cover her," he said, pointing at the shawl I had forgotten I was wearing. I took it off and draped Joan as best I could from the foot of the bed; I took hold of her calf and squeezed, hard, until she moaned faintly.

Then Fred was at my side, directing me to grab one of her hands while he took the other; I tried to ignore the men on either side of me as we pulled Joan into a sitting position. I wrapped the shawl around her, but it was too small and there was too much of her. I thought ahead to how I would take the elevator upstairs and return downstairs with the long Burberry trench Joan wore when it was chilly. We would park in the garage beneath the building, where we had the least chance of seeing anyone.

Fred gathered Joan in his arms easily. "Joan," I said, and patted her cheek. She opened her eyes, briefly, and closed them again. There was a smear of lipstick on her pale cheek.

"She's in no state to answer," Fred said.

We were in the hallway when I noticed she was missing a diamond earring.

"One second," I said, and darted back into the bedroom, remembering the diamond-chip necklace, the little boy's bed with the cowboy sheets. I put my hand on the sheets to feel for the earring — it would be sharp beneath my palm — and when I looked up toward Joan's pillow I saw the man with the scar watching me. The hair on the back of my neck stood up. Fred was in the hallway behind me, Joan in his arms, waiting, and I was suddenly terrified for us — for me and him and Joan.

"She's a good girl," the man said, and though he spoke in a low voice I could hear every word he said.

"Evergreen," I told Fred, when we were in the car, Joan lying across the backseat like a child who had fallen asleep at a party, the shawl covering her, her head in my lap. "Take us to Evergreen."

He hesitated. "I think she needs to go to the hospital."

I found Joan's pulse. I could never take her to the hospital like this.

"I can't," I said, and bit my lip so I wouldn't cry.

"Yes, ma'am," Fred said. "To Evergreen."

Joan went away then, for a few months. A second disappearance, two years after she'd first run away, but this one organized by all those who loved her. Mary had come to the Specimen Jar and gathered her things, and once again Joan missed spring in Houston. She missed the magnolias blooming at Evergreen, great white flowers that were easily bruised. Mary used to float them in crystal bowls throughout the house. She said the scent reminded Furlow of his childhood, though I never heard Furlow say so himself.

"I found her like this," I told her, forcing

myself to look Mary in the eye and not beyond her at the striped wallpaper hung with giant watercolors of Texas landscapes: a field of bluebonnets, a desert. *This is not my failure,* is what I meant to say. Joan was already upstairs, in her childhood bedroom, sleeping. A doctor had come to the house, then left, but his nurse had stayed. She was with Joan now. Mary wore a pale pink robe, a matching nightgown. Peach, I would have called it. The color seemed uncharacteristically feminine.

"I see. And how did she get like that?"

Her voice wasn't accusatory, not exactly, but it wasn't kind, either. I remembered the man in the bed, how he had looked at me.

"You'll have to ask her," I said, and I would have given anything to be elsewhere, to be with Ray.

"I will," Mary said. "I certainly will." She turned to leave the room, but when her hand was on the doorknob she paused. "I trust this matter will go no further."

"It has *never* gone any further."

Mary nodded. "You're like a daughter to us, Cecilia. A daughter who behaves herself."

"But — what will happen to Joan?" I felt ashamed for asking, but I couldn't help myself.

Mary cocked her head, as if she'd heard something beyond the door. I listened, too, but all I heard was the light footfall of a servant, the chirping of birds outside. It was still late morning. She closed her robe over her nightgown with one hand.

"Do you hope to have children, Cecilia?"

I nodded.

"Children surprise you, in all sorts of ways." She turned to go. "Joan will be fine. She will always be fine." She said this firmly, as if there were no room for discussion. I wanted to believe her.

"But why? Why is she like this?" I was becoming hysterical. I wiped my eyes with the back of my hand. "What happened in Hollywood?"

Mary came to me and comforted me while I wept, smoothed my hair with her cool palm. But she told me nothing.

Joan missed the magnolias. She missed my wedding. Ray and I eloped, which nearly killed his mother but I wouldn't have it any other way. There was no reason to wait until the summer. Once Joan left, I wanted nothing more than to be married to Ray, to leave the Specimen Jar, to be so near to my new husband I could reach out and touch him whenever I wanted. I could not recite vows in front of an audience that did not include

269

Joan. And so we recited our vows in front of the justice of the peace and his secretary.

"Are you happy?" Ray asked, after we had been in our home for nearly a week. Already it had started to feel like mine. It was brand-new, designed by MacKie and Kamrath in the modern style, full of magnificent windows that ran the length of the walls. I was, I realized, hungry for ownership. I spent far too much money on pots and pans, on table linens, on furniture to sit in and artwork to hang. I bought a Noguchi coffee table from New York, a marvel of glass and wood; an Aladdin lamp that looked like a spaceship and cost about as much as one, too. But why not? The money had been sitting there waiting for me to spend it ever since my mother's death. Why had I waited so long?

I smiled at Ray. *Mostly,* I could have said, if I were being honest. I had a husband. I had friends. I had a beautiful home filled with beautiful things, in a beautiful neighborhood. I was twenty years old. I had my whole life ahead of me.

But I did not have Joan.

"Yes," I said. "I am very happy."

CHAPTER TWENTY

1957

I woke to Ray standing over me, holding Tommy on his hip.

"Cee," he said urgently. "Cee."

I tried to gain my bearings. I'd come into Ray's office because I'd been tempted to call Joan. Instead I'd allowed myself to revisit a past better left alone.

"I thought you'd gone out," he said, his voice a little softer. "I had no idea where you were."

Ah. He thought I'd been with Joan. But I hadn't laid eyes on Joan for a week. Not since I'd stopped by her house and seen her by the pool, naked. I'd called, but Sari had made excuses.

"No. Couldn't sleep. Got into your stash." I nodded at the crystal decanter, a wedding present from Darlene. "Not my best idea ever."

Ray smiled. All was forgiven. I hadn't been

271

with Joan. I was making an effort not to be with Joan, to live my life apart from Joan. I needed to let her do whatever she was doing with Sid Stark. I needed to pay attention to my own life, my own husband and child, in the meantime. I took Tommy from Ray — he came gladly — and noted that his diaper was leaking. Tommy wasn't potty-trained yet — I hadn't even tried. A mother from Mother's Day Out had raised her eyebrows at this fact last week, but I had too many other things to worry about, with Tommy.

"His diaper," I said, and looked at Ray, who was checking his watch. Then he kissed me on the cheek and was gone, just like that, and I thought how easy it was for men to disappear. For men and for Joan.

And of course it wasn't Ray's responsibility, to change Tommy's diaper. I was lucky he'd even attempted it. I took Tommy upstairs, my hip getting soaked as I walked.

"Are you tee-teeing right now?" I asked Tommy. He sighed, and patted my cheek. I sighed, too. My robe, silk, would be ruined. I laid Tommy on the changing table and removed his rubber pants. I saw immediately the problem — the diaper looked as if Tommy himself had fastened it with pins. Tommy watched me, solemnly. He reached

272

for my nose, and I leaned down, eager to feel the touch of his small, moist hand.

But I also saw how easy it was, to blame Ray for my own bad mood. He didn't know how to change a diaper properly because nobody had ever taught him. The nurses at the hospital had taught me. And Maria. Just as her name entered my mind — shouldn't she be here by now? — the doorbell rang, and Tommy grinned. My head ached.

"You like Maria," I said. "We all like Maria. Especially on mornings like this."

I spent the rest of the day tending to the house, fielding phone calls: from the president of the Garden Club, who wanted me to provide refreshments for next week's meeting; from Ray's mother while I was folding laundry, who called every few weeks because she "just wanted to check on things." She was kind, Ray's mother. And not overbearing — Darlene's mother-in-law had practically moved in after her baby had been born, and Ciela's mother-in-law had twice claimed that Ciela's cooking made her ill. Which was funny, because Ciela didn't cook — her maid did. Anyway, I liked Edith: she was levelheaded and serious, like her son. After we'd eloped, she and Ray's father hosted a small cocktail party for us, in honor of our wedding. They lived near Rice, in an expensive but unremarkable house — brick and black-shuttered. They had enough money to make them comfortable, but not nearly enough to make them seen. I liked this about them: that they were solid, the opposite of flashy. Edith stopped by once every few weeks and took Tommy for half the day. At the wedding party, Edith had waited until all the guests had left and taken both my hands and told me that she and Ray's father, Ed, thought of me as their daughter now. But it was just something Edith, tipsy from the champagne toast, was saying. She already had Debbie.

The Buchanans had done more for us than my own father, anyway. A few days after the wedding a fat check had arrived in the mail. He hadn't been to Houston in years. He'd never met Tommy.

I thought about Edith for the rest of the day as I folded Tommy's tiny shirts, sliced peaches for a cobbler, pushed Tommy in the park swings after the sun had dimmed. How would my life have looked if I'd had a mother like Edith? Would it have made me a better mother? Would Tommy be speaking by now?

The playground was deserted. "So nice, isn't it, Tommy?" I asked, savoring not having to talk to anyone. And then Tommy, who

274

had been playing in the sandbox, filling his little bucket with sand in one spot and taking it to another spot a few feet away and dumping it, all very seriously, according to his own system of logic — he spoke.

"Ma," I think it was. I *know* it was, because what mother doesn't recognize her own son's first word? What mother doesn't have it recorded on the deepest layer of her brain?

In a flash I was in the sandbox, holding his chubby cheeks between my palms.

"Again, Tommy! Please. Pretty, pretty please. For Ma."

Of course I wondered if I had imagined it. Of course. And I felt guilty for wondering, but it's impossible, isn't it, to spend so much time wanting one thing, and then not be suspicious of that thing when it arrives?

I was waiting for Ray by the door, Tommy on my hip. Since we'd come home from the park I'd spun around the house in a flurry of excitement, pointing things out to Tommy — "That's your rocking horse, Tommy. Say 'neigh'! That's Mommy's lipstick. It's what she wears to disguise her natural lip color, which isn't a shocking red. Can we say 'lip'? Or 'red'?"

Tommy watched me, and did not utter

another word. I almost told Maria but stopped midsentence, embarrassed. She might not believe me, and I wanted to savor this moment for as long as I could.

I couldn't help it, though; I wasn't entirely sure that Tommy had actually spoken, that I hadn't simply heard what I'd been wanting to hear for so long, what my friends heard from their children again and again — I saw the rest of his babyhood, then his childhood and adolescence and even his adulthood, or *especially* his adulthood, completely differently: he was going to be normal. I could taste his normalcy, so close it felt like a thing within reach. Tommy was going to be normal. He was going to speak to other little children. He was going to demand things from the little boys in the sandbox. He was going to say hi and bye to Tina. School, dates, dances, work: his life unfurled before me, thrilling and terrifying.

"He spoke," I said, before Ray had even had a chance to close the door behind him. I'll never forget the look on his face, a look that told me he'd worried, too, though he'd pretended he hadn't.

"I can't get him to do it again," I said. "Right, Tommy? Just the once. But he spoke. I know it. I heard it."

"What did he say?"

276

I told him. Such a normal, tiny word. Insignificant. More of a sound than a word, really. Ma. And we weren't country people — Tommy couldn't call me Ma. I would be Mother. But oh, what did I care what he called me? He could call me anything in the world and I would answer.

We stood there, grinning at each other. Tommy seemed to sense the significance of the moment, because he didn't move, didn't squirm or reach for Ray.

We felt like a family. That's what I remember thinking. And then I realized I hadn't thought of Joan since Tommy had called me Ma. And I was glad.

For a few days, life was bliss. We waited for Tommy to utter another word, another sound we could tease into a word. We were happy. We were hopeful.

We didn't really have a signal for sex. Sometimes Ray turned to me, and sometimes I turned to him. Our marriage wasn't passionless but it was a marriage, with a young child. When we'd started sleeping together I'd been shy, and Ray had loved my shyness. It was never something we'd spoken of but I could tell that he liked it when I would barely look him in the eye, when I was tentative about touching him.

But that night, after Tommy had spoken, I felt shy again. I went to bed with Ray and waited while he completed his ablutions in the bathroom. I was eighteen again, ready to give myself to this new man. Joan's face flitted briefly through my mind. But then it disappeared again.

"Cee," Ray said, and touched my breasts through my silk nightgown. I wore a silk nightgown every night, then; we all did. We needed our husbands to want us.

Moonlight illuminated the room, made it a series of soft edges. It was dark but I could still see the top of Ray's head as he rested his forehead on my breasts, as he lifted my nightgown and kissed my hip bone. I could see his narrow back, his long arms, the body that remained a surprise to me, even after all these years. I didn't see him naked all that often. He wore pajamas, showered and dressed before I rose. We were modest with each other. I never entered the bathroom when Ray was dressing. He paid me the same courtesy.

But now he was undressing me. He drew my panties off with his thumb. I tried to pull the sheet up but he stopped my hand.

"I want to see you," he said.

I let him. I let him draw my nightgown over my head, carefully, then lay me back down against the pillow. He was naked, too, and the sight of him, hard, next to my thigh, made me feel like a teenager again. Nervous but hopeful, as if anything could happen tonight, in this bed, with this man.

He put his finger under my chin, turned my face toward his.

But it was different now, of course, I wasn't a teenager. I felt closer to Ray than I ever had before. Closer to him than I'd ever felt to Joan. We had a child together, a life. Tommy had spoken, and Ray had believed me. I would have been skeptical if Ray had come home from an outing with Tommy and told me he'd uttered his first word. Uttered it unprompted, even. I would not have believed him.

But Ray always believed me. Such a rare thing, really. To have a person who both loved and believed you.

I raised my hand to Ray's cheek and let it hover an inch or two away from his skin. I didn't want to touch him; I wanted to almost touch him.

Ray murmured something I didn't understand, and maybe I wasn't meant to understand, and then he kissed my neck, my breasts, my stomach. He slid a hand between my knees and unclenched them with one neat motion; I hadn't realized I'd been holding them together.

And then his tongue was inside me, and I held my hands over his head, and the whole world disappeared, and it was only me and Ray and what existed between us because we had made it.

I was a better person after good sex. I felt understood, I felt loved, I felt wanted. It was easy for me, to put Joan out of my mind. To mostly not think about Sid Stark and his outrageous nakedness. To convince myself that Joan was not mine alone to worry about. She had her mother, and a formidable one at that. She had more money than God. She had a father who believed she was the best gift he'd ever been given. She had more than I did, certainly. Or at least: she had started out with more.

The next several days I continued to push Joan and her family from my mind. I felt like it was good practice, to live my life without her. Practice for when Joan went away for good. I remember the exact instant I caught myself thinking that: the thought that slipped, unbidden, into my head as I was cleaning the grout in the guest bathroom.

I was applying a bleach paste to the crevice between the bathtub and the tile floor — it was such satisfying work, a task like this. No messy conversations, no hurt feelings, no misunderstandings. I mixed baking soda and bleach until it achieved the right consistency — not too runny, was the trick — and then I called Maria away from polishing my mother's old silver, which she did every month, and we got on our hands and knees and applied the paste with a toothbrush to every square inch of grout. Which was a lot, because the entire bathroom, including all the walls, was done in an avocado tile.

I had felt inspired. "I've never thought to do this," I said to Maria as we got started. Over the years the grout had turned yellow; it was hard to imagine the white it must have been once upon a time. Tommy was upstairs, taking his nap. We had a good hour before he woke.

So there I was, on my hands and knees, in my jeans and one of Ray's old shirts, vigorously scrubbing the grimy line of grout between the bathtub and the tile floor, the smell of the bleach so strong it felt cleansing, like swimming in Evergreen's pool.

And then the thought slithered into my head, small and sneaky: This is good practice for when Joan is gone.

I sat up too quickly and had to brace

myself against the edge of the bathtub.

"Mrs. Buchanan?" I felt Maria behind me, deciding whether or not to touch me.

"I'm fine," I said, "I'm fine." I stood slowly. "Just a little dizzy."

In the kitchen, I poured myself a glass of water. I stood at the window and looked at the neat grass, freshly mowed. It would be a miracle if it made it through the end of the summer, if the heat did not kill it before then. It didn't matter how much water you gave it, how early you went out and set up the sprinkler. The sun killed everything in Houston, eventually. It had always been just a matter of time.

CHAPTER TWENTY-ONE

1957

You wanted to wear something at least a little bit patriotic for the Fourth, but you didn't want to be tacky. I decided on a pale blue Swiss-dot dress that tied around my neck. It hit just below my knees: any shorter and you were tasteless; any longer and you looked like a Pentecostal from the panhandle.

Today was Thursday, the beginning of a very long weekend. Everything would be closed tomorrow, the day after the Fourth. Houston was good at holidays. There would be parties Friday and Saturday night, too, but tonight was the biggest one, thrown by Glenn McCarthy himself at the Shamrock. He was trying to be spectacular after the embarrassment of *Giant*.

I slipped on a red Lucite bangle as a finishing touch; Ray wore a soft red tie. We were a handsome couple. Maria took our photograph before we left.

"Say cheese," she said, and we all smiled, even Tommy. Ray's hand was around my waist; his other hand was on Tommy's shoulder. He felt proud of us. *I* felt proud of us.

I still have that photograph — it's one of my favorites. The colors are garish. Tommy's grin is so wide his face is distorted. I look so happy I want to reach through the photograph and slap my tastefully rouged cheek.

Tommy had spoken again yesterday, called me Ma twice more, once in front of Ray. He'd said it first when I'd come to retrieve him from his nap. "Ma," and pointed to me. Then again that afternoon, after I'd called Ray to tell him and he'd canceled meetings and rearranged his mysterious schedule and come home early in the hopes that Tommy might speak again, in his presence. And he did: in his nursery, playing with his ever-present blocks, Tommy had looked at Ray, pointed at me with a block in each hand, and said, "Ma," as if telling Ray who I was. And just like that, what had seemed impossible for so long — what I had anticipated and hoped and wished for since it became clear that Tommy was behind — had become just another fact of life. Now that

Tommy had said one thing, there was nothing stopping him from saying another, and another, and another. Until the "Ma" became "Mama"; then he would say "Father," and "Maria," maybe. Until the words became longer expressions: of desire, of want.

"Thank you," I said to Maria as I took the camera from her. She nodded but would not look me in the eye.

"We're lucky with Maria," Ray said as he backed the car down the drive. Maria and Tommy stood at the door, waving. "Tommy loves her."

I nodded and patted his thigh. I felt like I was supposed to feel, is how I remember it. Pleased by my family. Pleased by the way my flower beds had been perfectly edged by the gardener yesterday. Pleased by the way my breasts felt beneath my dress: smooth and pert.

"This'll be fun," I said, and I believed it: the first party Ray and I had been to in a long time that would not involve Joan. "Joan won't be there," I said.

Ray nodded. "You've mentioned."

I couldn't read his tone, not quite. But then he reached down and squeezed my thigh, gently, and I knew we were fine.

Our perfectly ordered world passed by as

we drove. Our route would take us by Evergreen but not by Joan's house. In a few years we would move out of our house and into a bigger one. We might even buy a plot of land and build our own dream home. Ray was calling where we lived now our "starter home" more and more frequently; there was no reason to think he wouldn't continue rising through the ranks in his company, accruing greater degrees of influence and power and money. I would be right by Ray's side, of course. Did I care about a bigger house? A nicer car? More extravagant vacations? Of course I did.

We were getting closer and closer to Evergreen. I had called Joan on Monday, taken the phone into the pantry even though Tommy was upstairs, asleep, and Maria was folding laundry. I had been so good! It had been nearly two weeks since I'd been by her house and talked to her by the pool. But it couldn't hurt, I'd reasoned, to talk to her for just a minute.

"Joan?" I said when she answered, and if I sounded incredulous it's because I was. Sari usually answered, especially — I checked my watch, 10:03 a.m. — this early.

She laughed. "Did you expect President Eisenhower? It's me, doll. I've been up for hours."

"What have you been doing?"

I could picture her shrugging. "Wandering. Reading. Smoking." And, as if that had reminded her, she inhaled deeply, then exhaled. She didn't bother holding her mouth away from the receiver, but that was okay, I was glad to hear her breathe. She was still Joan, still smoking and reading and wandering and talking to me, her best friend, on the phone.

"Tommy spoke," I blurted.

"Did he?" she said, and she sounded distracted, and I felt as if she'd reached through the phone and slapped me across the face.

But then she seemed to gather herself. "That's wonderful, Cee. I'm so pleased."

"We were pleased, too," I said, and it was all I could do not to cry. I hadn't realized how pleased, how *relieved* we were until this very moment. That was what Joan did for me: she brought things out for me. Clarified my situation.

"Are you going to the Shamrock on Thursday?" I asked, though I knew the answer. Of course she was. She hadn't ever missed that party.

"Thursday? Oh, right. The Fourth. I don't think so, doll."

Sid. They would go somewhere else. To

Galveston, perhaps.

"But you always go," I said, and I tried to silence the note of franticness I could feel creeping in.

"Well, that's the funny thing about always. Always until it's not."

And then I heard her murmuring to someone. I pressed the phone to my ear but couldn't make out a word they were saying. I couldn't even tell if the voice was male or female.

Tommy cried out upstairs.

"Joan," I said, "Joan? Are you there?"

"Hold on, Cece," she said, annoyed, and then the muffled conversation again, and Tommy overhead, crying, and me in a pantry, talking in secret. I felt desperate, unmoored. Suddenly, I was a little girl, trying to get Joan's attention in the school lunchroom.

Then the pantry door swung open, and I was caught, the telephone cord wrapped around my wrist.

Maria stood there, Tommy on her hip. Her brow was furrowed. I took the phone away from my ear, unbraceleted the cord, stepped out of the pantry, and held out my arms for Tommy.

"I'll trade you," I said, and handed her the phone. Once I held Tommy and Maria held the phone she looked at it, curiously.

"Ma'am?" She tried to give it back to me.

"I don't want it!" I said, and Maria stepped back in surprise. "Hang it up, please. Just hang it up."

What else could she do but what I told her? I was jealous of her, in that instant. Of my Mexican housekeeper and babysitter. People told her to do things, and she did them. It was simple, easy.

Maria awkwardly replaced the phone in its cradle. Contacting Maria when she left here required phoning a cousin; Maria phoned back an hour later, either from her cousin's house — I could hear the same dim cacophony in the background, children and adults yelling at children — or from a pay phone near a busy road, car horns in the background.

"You don't have a telephone, do you?"

Maria's face crumpled like a piece of tissue paper. It was so easy to hurt people. I understood exactly why I had done it: Joan had hurt me, and so I turned right around and hurt Maria, who looked so small now. It wasn't what I had said, exactly. It was how I had said it. It was easy to be cruel. Far more difficult to be kind. How did Joan feel, after she was cruel to me? Powerful? Regretful? But then I understood, Tommy's warm cheek on my shoulder — he wanted his milk now, was waiting patiently for it — that Joan felt none of these things. She did not know she was being cruel, not like I knew it now; she would not feel the powerful surge of regret that I felt at this instant.

"I'm sorry," I said, and moved toward her.

But Maria stepped back. All those years of trust, built up so carefully — when Maria had come here, five years ago, she was so shy she would barely look me in the eye — destroyed in an instant.

"That is all?"

And I could do nothing but nod. "Yes," I said. "That's all."

And I had hung up on Joan! She had returned to the phone expecting me to be there, waiting. Always waiting, that was me, Cece, the most faithful of faithful friends. But instead of my voice she had met a dial tone.

She had not called back. She might not have cared that I had hung up, might have blamed it on a faulty line or a bad connection. But she had to know, deep down, that I had been bold.

Once, before we were married, Ray had told me there was no point trying to figure out what made another person tick. "Maybe," he'd conceded, "you can figure out what makes the person you're married to tick. But only if they want you to. Everyone else" — here he had held his hands up and shrugged — "it's impossible."

I disagreed. We hadn't been speaking directly of Joan, but our conversation had occurred during that time when Joan was going off the rails, when I was spending most of my time trying to figure out where she, or I, had gone wrong.

I'd understood her once, when we were young, when I'd stood on the Galveston beach and watched her plunge into the sea. But that had been a long time ago.

Now I wanted to hurt her. I wanted to show her I could.

Maria aside, I felt buoyant. Maria would not be at this party tonight; neither would Joan. Just me and Ray and the rest of our friends. Darlene would be there with her husband, and Kenna, too, and Ciela, along with everyone else in Houston. Ray was happy because I was happy, and because there would be dancing.

Evergreen was upon us, but I wasn't going to say anything. I was simply going to watch it pass from the window. Then Ray spoke.

"Furlow must have a thousand people

working on that yard alone," Ray said.

It was, I admit, a little bit of a fight, in my head, to decide whether or not to correct Ray or leave it alone. Surely he knew Furlow wasn't capable of making decisions these days, that the days in which he had been in charge of anything were but a distant memory? He didn't even dress himself anymore. He certainly wasn't corralling lawn men and conferring with the head gardener over what might look best in the winter beds.

But then Ray turned on the radio and started to whistle along to the opening of "Love Letters in the Sand," and it was clear that he didn't think very much about Evergreen, or Furlow's mind, or Mary's role in landscaping. He didn't think very much about the Fortiers at all, except that he wanted me to spend less time thinking about Joan.

There was pomade in his hair, and I spotted a little dried piece of it clinging to his temple. I brushed it away, and Ray grabbed my hand and kissed it, and then I expected him to let it go, but he held on to it, and I was moved. He held on to it all the way to the Shamrock, where he only let it go to pull into the valet line, which was backed up to the street.

"God almighty," Ray said, as he took his place in line and put the car in neutral. "Elvis himself must be here."

"No," I said. "Just Diamond Glenn."

We found, once inside — the line moved surprisingly quickly, the valets soaked with sweat and hustling — that Elvis was not there, but everyone else was. Diamond Glenn McCarthy was indeed in the corner, holding court at a cluster of tables. He was tossing his solid-gold lighter, dotted with a large diamond, from hand to hand. He never went anywhere without that lighter. The Shamrock, of course, didn't belong to McCarthy anymore — he'd lost it during one of his financial lows — but he still owned the Cork Club. McCarthy had aged since our early days — his cheeks were looser, his hair thinner. The years had not been kind to him.

"Poor waiter," Ray said, nodding his head toward the tall, tired-looking man taking orders at McCarthy's table. "I heard he doesn't tip."

"A man as rich as that?"

Ray shrugged. "What you have and what you give don't always match up, darling." He kissed my cheek. The sympathy I'd just felt for McCarthy vanished.

I saw Ciela and JJ right away, near the bar.

Ciela waved us over and I led Ray through the crowd of glistening bodies. We were all a little sweaty; "gleaming" was a better way to think of it. I passed a heavy lady who was drawing a handkerchief over her forehead; I could see the orange smear of her foundation on the delicate fabric. The room was air-conditioned and the fans were on, but they were no match for the scores of people stuffed into the Cork Club.

"Are you burning up?" I whispered to Ray. "I don't envy you your coat."

"Or my pants," Ray said, as we reached the bar. "For once, I'm jealous of the ladies." He grazed my collarbone with his finger, stopped at the dip in my dress. I thought, for the second time, that Ray was feeling forward tonight.

"A daiquiri and a G and T?" Louis asked. I was home.

Ciela slid into a tight spot next to me while Ray gathered our drinks.

"Ray's handsy tonight," she said, and I blushed.

"He's feeling his oats a little bit."

"And why shouldn't he? Tonight's the night, if ever there were one. I heard McCarthy spent ten grand on the fireworks display. There's enough liquor to fill the pool. JJ's already sloshed. And I'm on my way."

I wanted, suddenly, to tell Ciela about Tommy, could feel the words already forming at the back of my throat. *He's spoken!* I'd say. *Took him a little longer than everyone else, that's all. But you know Einstein didn't speak until he was five.*

Ray had told me about Einstein yesterday.

Ciela leaned forward attentively. She wore an off-the-shoulder dress with a diamond brooch in the shape of a starburst pinned over her right breast.

"Cat got your tongue?"

I shook my head, touched her brooch. I could never tell her about Tommy, but that was okay. It was a secret, mine and Ray's. Tommy would never even know how worried we had been.

"I like this," I said.

"It's supposed to be a firework."

"Ah," I said. "That's right."

"And Joan?" Ciela asked. "Where is the lady of the hour?"

"I have no earthly idea," I said, and swallowed my daiquiri so fast it made my throat burn.

We danced. We drank Blue Hawaiians in honor of the Fourth, even the men, and ate little canapés as they passed by us on endless silver trays guided into our midst by white-gloved hands: meatballs stabbed with red toothpicks; sausage puffs baked in the shape of rectangles, etched with miniature stars and stripes; tiny, rare roast beef sandwiches dotted with blood and blueberry compote. I must have swallowed a thousand hors d'oeuvres, washed down by a dozen cocktails, but my dress didn't feel any tighter, my makeup didn't run, and when I darted into the bathroom my hair was still pulled back into its French twist.

Ray held me as we swayed back and forth to the same song we'd heard on the way over — "Love Letters in the Sand" — a song I thought was corny. *How you laughed when I cried, each time I saw the tide, take our love letters from the sand.*

"What does it even mean?" I asked Ray, over the music.

"What does what mean?" We had to shout to be heard, but there was an intimacy to the shouting, because we could be as loud as we wanted and people stood right next to us and couldn't understand a word we said.

"This song!" I said. "It makes no sense."

"It's not supposed to make sense," Ray said. "Just let yourself be carried away." And he took my hand and placed it over his heart, and smiled dramatically, and I realized we were both drunker than we thought, but in a good way.

I only thought about Joan to confirm that I wasn't thinking about her. I only wanted to think about me, and Ray, and this night we were having, one for the books.

Then there was a crush of bodies, all moving toward the door. Ray grabbed my hand and we followed everyone outside. A man with a horrible comb-over stepped on my foot; a chinless woman with a glass of champagne in each hand mouthed "sorry" over his head. I shook my head and waved the apology away.

"What are we going to see?" I asked Ray.

"Better be something good," he said.

"Fireworks!" a young man in a white sports coat shouted. "We've been called outside for fireworks!"

It was cool outside, mercifully so.

"This," I said, "is divine."

Ray had shed his jacket long ago, and his tie was loose around his throat. We stood a safe distance from the pool and admired hundreds of floating candles in red, white, and blue, in the shape of our flag, bobbing in the water, the wind blowing them this way and that, so the flag looked blurry, more beautiful because of the blurriness.

The scent of gardenias, which lined the patio in giant concrete planters, filled the air. Someone was handing out lit sparklers; revelers were waving them above their heads.

"Listen," Ray said, and pointed to a waiter with a silver tray of champagne. "I'm going to snag us a couple of glasses. Look, here's Ciela and JJ. Wait here. I'll be back in a flash." And he disappeared into the crowd.

"Do I look half as drunk as I feel?" Ciela asked, and I shook my head, laughing. She did, in fact, but we all did. I smoothed a stray piece of hair from her forehead. Her skin was damp. I never touched other women, besides Joan. But tonight I felt expansive.

The crowd began to murmur; the murmur turned into a dull roar. People began to point, then shout.

And that's when I saw her. On a raised stage behind the pool, where the band played. The back of her head, but I would have recognized it anywhere. Sid was with her.

Ciela shouted something in my ear and I shook my head; I had no idea what she'd just asked. She leaned in again.

"Ugly-handsome fellow, isn't he? He's got it, though. Whatever it is. He has *it* in spades. Just like Joan." Her voice had turned serious without my noticing when. "I almost have it."

"Maybe he got it in Hollywood," I said.

"Hollywood? Sid Stark?" She laughed. Clearly Ciela had done her homework — a few weeks ago she'd never heard of the man. "I hear he's as Texan as they come. Born and raised in Friona."

"No." I shook my head.

"He made his money in cattle, then casinos," she said.

"No. You must be wrong," I repeated, though I was losing heart in my declaration. Joan had lied about so many things. Why not this?

"Maybe I am," Ciela said finally. "I've still never met the man. Just gossip."

Then the bandleader, Dick Krueger, dressed in a white suit, shouted into the microphone, his voice so loud I pressed my palms over my ears.

Joan smiled and laughed with Sid while Dick tried to quiet the crowd. We were drunk, rowdy. We did not want to be quieted. Joan wore a white collared dress, and it hurt me to admit how beautiful she looked. Or, more precisely, that she looked beautiful without my help. The dress showed most of her bare, tanned chest: the top of her breasts, the space in between them. She wore earrings shaped like feathers: wisps of sapphire growing from a diamond spine.

"Are you in a trance?" Ciela asked, mock-whispering in my ear.

"Her earrings," I said, and touched my own ears, the diamond earrings Ray had given me for our first anniversary suddenly inadequate. "They're new. They must be a present from Sid."

"You can see them from here?"

"I can see everything," I said, and it was true. I could see Sid's pinky ring, crammed onto his meaty finger. I could see the way his sideburns were cut more than a little unevenly, as if his barber had been hasty with his shave that morning. Or perhaps Joan had shaved him, in a romantic moment.

"I guess we're not that far away," Ciela said, and I wished she'd shut up and take JJ and leave me alone to observe Joan. I felt suddenly sober.

And then I knew what I had to do; it was suddenly clear as day.

"I have to go," I said to Ciela. "I have to find Ray and go."

I darted away before she had a chance to respond. My purse, where was my purse? I remembered that I'd given it to Ray, who had checked it with his coat. Then there he was, walking toward me, a flute of champagne in each hand.

"I thought we'd better slow down," he said, and held out the glass for me to take. "Champagne's only a little stronger than ice water."

Had we always talked to each other like this? I felt disgusted, suddenly, by how young we were pretending to be. We were old enough to know better. Ray read my disgust with confusion, first; then Dick Krueger shouted into the microphone over the crowd — "Well, you won't quiet down so I'll just yell. We have here Miss Joan Fortier along with her beau, Sidney Stark, here to light the evening on fire for y'all."

Joan had been showcased like this before, at big events: at the Houston Fat Stock Show and Rodeo, at grand openings, at ribbon cuttings. She must have been doing this as a favor to Glenn McCarthy.

Ray's confusion turned to comprehension, then disgust to mirror my own. I felt a surge of hopefulness. I could save this night.

"I want to leave," I said. "I want to go home to Tommy." Tommy, my son, who was spending the night with Maria. What if he woke, and silently beckoned someone to come to him, as was his habit? Maria would not know to go to him. She was not his mother, after all. I was.

301

I smiled at Ray. "Come on. Let's get your coat and my purse and skedaddle."

At first I read his smile as gratitude. That I was choosing home over Joan.

I was wrong. He tipped his champagne back and emptied the entire glass in a single swallow. Then he wiped his lips with the back of his hand; normally I would have told him not to, but now I just stood there, and waited.

"We're not going anywhere," Ray said, and nodded to the stage.

Once, when we were dating, we'd gone to a ball game in Alvin and some roughnecks had bothered me when I'd gone to the refreshment stand for Cokes. Ray had stalked down from the stands; the boys — they had been boys, really, not men — took one look at his face and scattered. Ray was big, but he wasn't a man who used his largeness to impress. Although I guessed all men used their largeness to impress, whether or not they knew it. Back then Ray's anger had made me feel safe; now it scared me.

The fireworks display was indeed spectacular. But the night had turned sour. Joan had left the stage and disappeared into the throng of bodies. I danced with Ray for a while by the pool, but we were both just going through the motions. I was grateful when JJ signaled to us from the edge of the floor.

"JJ wants something," I said to Ray, who was leading me determinedly. I had a feeling he would not let me out of his sight for the rest of the night.

"We're lighting up some Cubans," JJ said to Ray, and it seemed I had misread my husband entirely, because he followed JJ into the Shamrock with barely a glance behind him.

This might be a test — what would I do, now that Ray was gone? Would I find Joan or Ciela? How would I let the night unfurl?

He walked away, my tall, handsome husband whom I was lucky to have. I could have been stuck with a man who was light in his loafers, like Darlene, or even someone who knocked me around sometimes, like Jean Hill, who lived on the outskirts of River Oaks, showed up to Garden Club meetings with too much makeup and shadows under her eyes. Ray truly loved me, even though I wasn't always sure he knew me, through and through; he hadn't known me in my darkest days, the way the Fortiers had — but did he really need to see that side?

Joan was nowhere to be seen. I shoved myself in between drunk people, withstood the press of sweaty torsos and sloppy pats to the rear end — that was what happened, when you traipsed around without a man — and said "pardon me" more times than I could count. But still no Joan.

Finally I went to the lobby and collapsed on one of the green sectionals. This was where people came when they wanted to be heard. It was rowdy in here, with plenty of people, but there was room to sit.

Joan must have left. She had come last-minute, because Glenn had begged her, and then when she was finished with her appearance she and Sid had sneaked into their waiting car and gone back home, which was the only place, it seemed, she wanted to be these days.

This scenario meant that Joan had not lied to me, had not avoided me once she was here. I began to relax on the couch. My eyelids fluttered. Ray would come fetch me soon, and he would be so, so pleased: I would be waiting for him, like a good wife. We'd had our fun, and then I'd let him have some more fun without me. I was a good wife. I was a Texas wife.

And then I heard Joan's voice, and saw her slip into an elevator with three or four other people, and I rose.

■ ■ ■ ■

The elevator operator couldn't have been more than eighteen. I touched his green tasseled sleeve as I stepped inside.

"Floor eighteen," I said.

He paused. "That's the penthouse," he said, stammering a little bit on the *P.* "Are you — ?"

"I'm Miss Joan Fortier." I patted my French twist, sighed, checked my tiny watch.

It worked. The air in the elevator changed once I said Joan's name. He didn't know who Joan was, of course. He was too young. But her name had always had a magical effect: people listened.

I'd never been to the penthouse before. The elevator came to a halt and I waited as the gold gates slid open for me. Waited like I was Joan: as if I'd forgotten I was waiting. As if it were nothing: interrupting a private party on the eighteenth floor of the Shamrock. Walking into a room uninvited, where I knew not a single soul except someone who probably didn't want to see me: it wouldn't have fazed Joan one bit.

It was all so easy, if I pretended to be Joan.

"Thanks, hon," I said as I left the elevator, and I could feel his eyes on my back as I walked away. The room I was in was dominated by a dark, mahogany bar, and I was surprised to see Louis, whom I had only ever seen downstairs, tending it. You'd think I'd have been grateful, to see a familiar face, but I wasn't. I couldn't pretend to be Joan around someone who knew me as Cece.

"What'll it be?" Louis asked, and I was grateful he hadn't assumed I wanted my usual.

"Gin martini," I said. "Dirty. Up." I would only pretend to sip it. If I drank any more I might pass out before I found Joan.

So far, nobody seemed to have registered my presence. This was only the entry room; I had expected it to look like the Specimen Jar, which was completely open, where it would have been difficult for Joan to hide. But I'd already spotted several doors, most of them closed. I had no idea which one Joan had disappeared behind.

There was a cluster of mixed company, men and women, near a curved couch, some sitting, some standing. I half hoped that one of them would turn around and ask who I was, but nobody did. They were engrossed in their own conversation, and I was simply another body in a roomful of bodies.

"Gin martini," Louis said. "Straight up."

I wished I could give him a tip but I didn't have my purse. And maybe the penthouse wasn't a place where you tipped. I wouldn't know. I wondered how often Joan came up here, and with whom. I wondered if Sid was new, or if Joan really had known him for a long time.

I no longer felt betrayed, as I had when I'd first seen Joan. My hurt had been replaced by a feeling of intense curiosity. A desperate curiosity. The thought I'd had while cleaning that endless grout with Maria circled my brain: *Good practice for when Joan is gone.* I wanted to find out what was happening to her, what had happened to her, before it was over.

"Where is everyone?" I asked Louis, stirring my martini with the green, shamrock-topped swizzle stick, trying to sound casual, as if I didn't much care where everyone was. I wasn't Joan anymore. That had only lasted long enough to get me up here. Now I was Cece, and the sip I took of my martini was so terrible and astringent it was all I could do not to spit it out.

Louis said nothing, and I felt my cheeks redden.

"I don't know why people want to be up so high," I said, staring into my drink. "If

307

Russia drops the bomb we're toast, up here. Better to be down there" — here I raised my eyes to Louis. He was watching me, quietly. I pointed to the floor — "than up here, closer to the sky." I couldn't stop. I opened my mouth to go on, but Louis reached across the bar and put his hand, cool from handling ice and cold metal shakers all night, over mine. Louis was as old as my grandfather would have been. I decided his hand over mine was a kindness.

"Miss Fortier is behind that door," Louis said. He took his hand away and pointed to the door closest to us. "She's not alone."

I went to the door and, before I could convince myself not to, flung it open. At first I couldn't see a thing, and then, gradually, my eyes adjusted to the dark. I had screwed up my courage for nothing. I was in a long, empty corridor with another door at the end.

I clutched my martini to my chest, spilling some on my dress. The carpet was plush, tricky to navigate in heels. I couldn't help but think of the long hallway in Sugar Land, Texas, all those years ago. I had gone somewhere unknown for Joan then, too. And here I was, five years later, a wife and a mother, doing the same thing.

The scent of the Sugar Land house came

back to me: potpourri, the plastic that covered the furniture, the ghost of Joan's perfume.

When I reached the second door I pressed my ear against it, but heard nothing.

I twisted the knob, half expecting it to be locked — Sid and Joan might have been in there together, having sex, but I didn't care.

The door wasn't locked, and I saw right away Joan wasn't in the room, either. Only Sid, and three men who faced me as I entered. They were standing by a glass table, looking at something. Papers. I spotted a briefcase, a crystal decanter of brown liquor. A pen. The various accoutrements of men.

"Sid," I said, my voice shaky. I tried to steady it. "Cece. Cecilia Buchanan."

I held out my hand — for him to shake? To kiss? I didn't know. But Sid's face was impassive, his vitality, which had been on public display just an hour ago, a distant memory. This was Joan's Sid, but he seemed like a different person entirely.

His friends — his associates? — watched me with the same blank expressions, and I remembered the first time I'd seen him, how he'd scared me and I hadn't known why. I set my martini on the brass side table near the door and turned to go — "I'm in the wrong place," I murmured, or something to that effect. I was a woman among strange men. I had thought Joan might disappear, but now it occurred to me that I might disappear, too. We could all disappear, so easily.

I was so close to leaving — my hand was on the knob. But no, I had to find Joan.

I turned back around and met the eyes of one of the men, idly spinning a cigarette between his fingers. He stopped, gave his attention to Sid, and I understood that I had nothing to fear from Sid's company, only from Sid himself.

"Joan," I said, and I was proud of how clear my voice was, like a bell in this silent room.

"She's in there," Sid said after a moment, though I had no idea where "there" was. He needed to make me wait. I would wait. "In the bedroom," he said after another moment, and pointed to a pair of French doors at the far end of the room. And then he waved his hand, dismissing me.

This was a suite, I realized as I entered: Sid and his associates were in the living quarters, and Joan was in the bedroom. This was where Sid would retire when he was finished with whatever it was that occupied him out there; he would send the men away, and come into this room and wake Joan and they would have sex. Or perhaps he wouldn't wake her. Or perhaps he wouldn't send the men away. All those years ago Joan had let herself be used by men she barely knew. She'd done it once. Who was to say she wouldn't do it a second time? Hadn't already?

Joan was asleep on the bed in her beautiful white dress, her makeup perfect except for a speck of ash, from the fireworks, on her cheek. I gently wiped it away with my thumb. There. She looked perfect now.

I stood over her for a moment, two. Or maybe it was ten. I lost track of time. She was inert and vulnerable, and I felt a protectiveness I had not felt since Tommy's birth. I checked my watch; it was three thirty in the morning. Ray was surely downstairs, looking for me, but Ray might have been a million miles away.

Joan opened her eyes. She stared at me in silence for so long I thought she might be dreaming.

"Cee," she said. "You shouldn't be here."

She seemed lucid enough. That was the first thing I noticed. And then she sat up, and I saw a bruise on her shoulder, where her dress had shifted.

She followed my eyes, touched the bruise, then returned her hand to her lap.

"I found you," I said, as if we had been playing a game, and Joan was the prize. "Who are those men out there?" I asked.

Joan said nothing.

"Who is Sid, Joan? Tell me who he is."

Still she said nothing.

"Joan," I said, "you need to leave. Come with me."

"Where do you want to take me, Cee?"

I hadn't thought about where I'd take her.

"Home," I said, firmly. "I'll take you home."

"My home or yours?"

Taking her to my home was out of the question. And her own home — it was Sid's domain now.

"Evergreen," I said.

She grimaced. "Evergreen. I think you and Mama are the only people who call it that anymore. My father would, of course, if his mind hadn't turned to cotton."

I held out my hand. "Let's go there."

She stared at my hand, then looked up at me. "Cece, I need you to leave."

"Leave?"

She nodded. "Leave here. Leave me alone."

"I can't," I said, simply. "Don't you know that by now?"

She rose, walked steadily to the window

— she wasn't drunk — then drew back the deep-green curtain. She rested her cheek against the glass, and I could almost feel the delicious coolness against her hot skin.

"Evergreen's the last place I want to be, and you're the last person I want to see."

"Evergreen is your home," I said, ignoring the barb.

"I left my home a long time ago."

Beyond Joan the city was lit up with a million glimmering lights, evidence of its industry, its breadth. Joan had a home: Houston. The city she could not live without, the city that could not live without her.

"I'm afraid Sid is going to hurt you." I went to her. "I'm afraid for you," I said at last.

"The last time you were afraid you went and told Mama, and I was sent away, and I came back and I was good for a while, wasn't I? I was golden. But now I'm tired." She closed her eyes again.

She'd never before spoken of being sent away; we'd never mentioned that night in Sugar Land. We had so much history, Joan and I, that it had always seemed easy to pick and choose which parts of it we recognized.

Yet here Joan was acknowledging what had remained unspoken for so long. Perhaps the similarities between then and now were obvious to her, too.

"How are you tired, Joan? Tell me."

"I'm tired of all of it."

"I've seen you like this before," I said, and I knew I was coming close to dangerous territory. I'd never spoken so frankly of that time in her life before. Of that time in our lives. "Do you remember the night I found you? In that — that house." It felt thrilling, to finally talk about it. I couldn't stop. "You were dead to the world. With those men. They could have done anything to you." My voice broke; I brought my hand to my mouth. "Maybe they did."

She opened her eyes. I thought she might be crying, but she wasn't. Our faces were so close I could see the mole on her right temple beneath a thick layer of powder.

"I liked what they did to me. Is that so hard to imagine? I wasn't made to do anything I didn't want to do."

I shook my head. "I don't believe you."

"Believe what you want. But I'm not like you, Cece. I never was."

"What I believe," I said, "is that you convinced yourself you liked it. Because you were different that year. You came back from California and you were changed.

"Something happened the first time you went away. California was cruel to you, that was it, wasn't it? Something happened to you there."

She watched me.

"Hollywood didn't treat you like Houston," I said.

"Pardon?" But she'd heard me. She was daring me to go on.

"You weren't a star there. You were just like everyone else. You thought you were going to make it. And you didn't. And —"

"Oh God," Joan interrupted, her voice shrill. She turned and picked up a silver cigarette case from a small table — her back was shaking. I had made Joan cry. I tried to think — had I ever made her cry before? I felt ashamed; I'd gone too far. I moved to hug her, but she spun around to face me. She was laughing.

"Why is Dorie back?" I asked.

She jerked her head up.

"Dorie," I said. "I saw her in the kitchen. At Evergreen. What was she doing there, Joan?"

Joan shook her head. "I have absolutely no idea."

"But you do!" I cried. "Tell me, Joan. Please tell me."

Joan looked from me to her cigarette, which she stubbed out on a silver coaster. There was an ashtray by the bed. Even in my state I'd noticed it. Because that's what women like me did: noticed things. Kept the world in order. And women like Joan were always undoing our careful, hard work. Women like Joan were always creating messes for other people, unthinkingly, like children. But you couldn't be mad at a child for being a child. How could you be mad at a woman like Joan, who was all action, no thought? It was like being mad at a horse for running, at Ray for wishing I would leave Joan alone. At me for being unable to comply.

"Leave, Cece. Go back to Tommy. He needs you. I don't."

I stood there helplessly, my hands by my sides. Our moment was over.

"Go," she said, her voice firm. I nodded. There was no sense in staying.

"Cee," Joan called out when I was opening the door. "What did he say? Tell me."

" 'Ma,' " I answered. "He said 'Ma.' "

I let myself out of the suite. Sid watched me leave, winking as I passed by him, and I was so confused. Sid was a horrible threat, or Sid was just a man with whom Joan was entertaining herself while she waited for the next man, or Sid meant more than I understood, or Sid meant nothing at all.

Downstairs, I checked with the valet: Ray

had already gone, but left the car. Neither of us was in any state to drive. I was too tired to care that Ray had abandoned me. I took a taxi home, let myself in with the spare key hidden beneath the back mat, and went straight to Tommy's room. I put my hand on his warm back and he stirred; he would have no memory of this night, of his mother coming into his room so very late. But I would remember it always.

Chapter Twenty-Two

1957

Ray was gone when Tommy woke me the next day. I had passed out in his rocking chair. I decided to pretend it was a workday. That was probably where Ray had gone, anyway, even though his office was closed for the holiday. Where else would he go? I trusted him. That he did not trust me in the same way was a thought on which I tried not to linger.

I called Maria's cousin and waited for Maria to call me back, and then promised her double pay if she would come in. She hesitated, and I felt guilty — who knew what she had planned for today — but she wasn't in a situation where she could refuse extra money, so she said yes. Maria bought her own food, the fabric for the clothes she made. She paid her own bus fare. She needed money not for fine dresses, or to eat at private clubs: she needed it to survive.

When she arrived she smiled at me, and it seemed genuine enough. What choice did she have but to forgive me? My family was how she made a living.

I knew where Idie was working now, because I had provided a reference. It was the second family she'd been with since she'd left ten years ago. She was a live-in at a house in West University, over by Rice, near Ray's parents.

It was all easier than I thought it would be. A maid answered the phone. I knew from the way she said "Hayes residence" that she was not a Hayes herself — and a few moments later, I heard Idie's voice.

"I'll take the children to Hermann Park after lunch," she said, after a moment. "You can meet me there."

Her tone was clear, unaccommodating. If I wanted to see her I would have to come to her.

There hadn't been any reason for Idie to stay, after my mother died. I had left, for Evergreen. But Idie wouldn't have stayed with me even if I'd begged, even if my father had doubled her salary. She knew what Joan and I had done.

The houses here were nice, but they weren't River Oaks. They felt more a part of the outside world; River Oaks was its own world.

Idie was still pretty. I noticed that first as I drove up, parked my car by the edge of the park. In another world — a world in which Idie was white — she would have been the wife of an oil executive instead of nanny to an oil executive's wife. She was slender, with a high forehead and clear, alert eyes. I'd forgotten how young she and Dorie must have been when they'd been our nannies. Idie had never married. Dorie had — her husband had worked as a gardener in River Oaks. But Idie remained alone. Neither sister had children of her own. Nannies rarely did.

She sat on a park bench, her hands folded in her lap, watching her charges — three straw-colored blondes — play on a swing set. Seeing her turned me into a child again, six years old and standing by her bed because a bad dream had woken me. Eleven years old and playing down the street, turning my head at the sound of Idie's voice, calling me home. Fourteen years old and sitting at the kitchen table, avoiding Idie's glare, in trouble because I smelled of cigarette smoke. I had thought Idie would remain with me forever, that she would be a nanny to my own children when I was an adult. And it might have happened as I'd imagined it, had my mother lived.

Idie was like a mother, except that she had been paid to attend to me. Except that after I had disappointed her, she had removed her affection.

When I was seven she had spent days at the sewing machine creating a miniature wedding dress, for no other reason than I'd asked for it. There was no beginning, with Idie — in my earliest memories, Idie is present. But there had been an end.

Her attention was on her charges, completely. And then, when my car door slammed shut, she turned that focus to me. I remembered that focus. My mother always seemed half available, half here, half in another world. But Idie had always seemed completely present.

I had chosen my outfit carefully. I wanted to appear modest for Idie, evidence of my life as a mother. And yet I wanted my clothes to carry me, as they always did. People said I had a knack for dressing but really I had a knack for wearing clothes that made me two or three notches superior to plain old Cece. So I'd worn a pale yellow skirt that came past my knees, tailored to make my waist look small. Then a simple white blouse that was so light it felt like wearing air. The blouse was silk, the skirt custom-made, and both had cost a fortune. But Idie would never guess that. She would, I hoped, take me in and decide I was dressed appropriately. Like the young mother of a young child. Like a good person, a person deserving of her love.

I presented myself to Idie gracelessly, my hand in an awkward half wave; the sight of her turned me breathless with want. I waited for her to stand, to hug me, but she simply observed me, and I felt foolish.

I saw, now that I was close to her, what I could not see from a distance: tiny wrinkles around her eyes, a missing tooth when she smiled. I saw that she had aged, and I was, for an instant, unspeakably sad. I turned to watch the children so Idie wouldn't see the tears in my eyes.

"They're beautiful," I said, and then immediately wished I hadn't spoken. These weren't Idie's children, and perhaps hearing them complimented reminded Idie that she had no children of her own. In that other world, Idie would have been a mother as well as a wife. Motherhood suddenly seemed like an unfairly allotted privilege.

But I had been mistaken. "Thank you," she said, and there was pride in her voice. "I've been with them since the oldest —

Lucinda there — was a baby."

"A long time," I said, and Idie nodded.

"I haven't seen you in forever," I said, as I tucked my skirt beneath me and sat next to Idie on the bench.

Idie shook her head. "No."

"Ten years."

"Has it been that long? I suppose it has. Lucinda," she called out, across the playground, her voice a warning. "Don't."

I laughed. I couldn't help it.

"It's just, I remember that voice," I explained. "I remember it very well. It meant I should stop whatever I was doing immediately, or else."

"Or else," Idie repeated. "You didn't know what 'or else' was. But you were a good girl."

"Was I?"

"Oh, yes," she said, and the fervor in her voice surprised me. "Very good. You wanted to please, Cecilia. You always wanted to please, and that's all you can ask for in a child." She pointed. "Ricky and Danny want to please. Lucinda doesn't care. She's a fireball."

I was jealous of Lucinda the fireball. It was ridiculous, but *I* wanted to have been a fireball, not the child who wanted to please. I wondered who I was now, as an adult. Surely I had changed.

"Joan was a fireball," I said. Idie stiffened next to me. "She still is."

The wind picked up and I caught Idie's particular smell, a mix of the lotion she used to rub into my skin after bath time and something unidentifiable. The urge to lean into her was so strong it was nearly unbearable. I had felt a certain electricity between us since I'd sat down: we had once loved each other, after all. Idie had brought comfort to my life.

I would do no such thing, of course. Idie was gone from me, had been for a long time. If I leaned into her she would scoot away as if burned; the moment would not be tender. It would be strange, intolerable.

"Joan was a fireball because she had a mother who cared about her. You wanted to please because your mother didn't notice you." She turned to me. "Children are simple creatures, Cecilia. The simplest creatures in the world."

"My mother cared about me," I said, and I wondered why I felt the urge to defend her. "She was a difficult woman."

Idie nodded. A colored woman in a white uniform pushed a stroller and waved in our direction. Idie nodded back. This was Idie's domain; the woman was deferential, stayed at a respectful distance, did not stare at the nanny talking with a well-dressed white woman. This was Idie's life, as I had once been.

One of her charges — the younger boy — ran up and announced he was hungry.

"You're always hungry," she said, but her voice was kinder with him than with me. "We'll leave soon. Get a snack at home."

He pouted for a second, and then turned to me. "Who's that?" he asked, pointing.

"Don't point," Idie said. "This is Miss Cecilia."

"Where did she come from?"

Idie laughed. "Cecilia, where did you come from?"

"I came from nearby," I said, grateful for the boy's presence. He softened Idie. The boy eyed me warily; he hadn't liked being the object of Idie's laughter. "Idie used to watch me, when I was a little girl."

"It's true," Idie said. She leaned forward and dusted off the boy's shorts, straightened his shirt. He looked from me to Idie, not so much confused as uninterested. That Idie, whom he clearly loved, had had a life before him, would have a life after him, was beyond his comprehension.

And then he darted off, without warning, in the way of children.

"I have a child," I said. "Thomas. He's

three years old."

"I know."

"Dorie told you?"

She was silent. "Why are you here, Cecilia?"

I closed my eyes against the sun. We were sitting in the shade, but still, if I sat here too long I would burn.

"I came to see why Dorie is back." I had nothing to lose. I might as well be honest. Idie might appreciate my honesty.

"I figured as much," she said. "I haven't heard from you in ten years." Her voice tightened as she spoke. "I knew, the instant I heard your voice, you wanted to know something about Joan."

I thought about defending myself, but Idie wouldn't believe the truth, which had been apparent to me as soon as I'd seen her: I'd wanted to see Idie for a long time. But I had known she did not want to see me.

"You've always disapproved of Joan," I said instead. "Since we were girls."

"Is that what you think?" She stood, and the children, as if tethered to her invisibly, spun around to face her. "One minute," she called out, across the playground, and tapped her wrist, though she wasn't wearing a watch. "One minute and then we go home.

"I only cared about you, Cecilia. Joan

326

made no difference to me. She was Dorie's. You were mine."

"But why did Dorie leave? Where did she go?"

Idie shook her head. "If you don't know, I can't tell you. It's not my business."

"Please," I said. "I need to know."

Idie raised her hand. "It's not mine to tell." She touched her neck, and I noticed her tiny gold cross was gone, lost to the years. "It's not for men to interfere in matters of God."

A deep unease rose in my throat, and I felt like I might vomit into the grass.

"Matters of God? What are you talking about, Idie? Please." I clasped her hand. "Please tell me."

"The children will be here soon," she said, taking back her hand. They walked toward us, timidly, as if they did not want to interrupt us. I wondered, briefly, what they made of us.

"Please," I said again, though I knew it was useless.

"Ask Joan. It's her story. And your own story, Cecilia? I often wonder if you regret."

"No," I said. And it was true. I did not. "I don't regret it. Joan did what I could not. I'm forever in her debt." I paused. "It was what my mother wanted."

"She didn't know what she wanted."

The children reached us; they no longer looked curiously at me. For a moment I had been interesting, but I had stayed too long.

Idie straightened the children's clothes, neatened Lucinda's hair, then spoke again.

"Go play," she said to the children. "I'll call you in another minute." Then she sat back down beside me, and I was thrilled, though I knew I shouldn't be. "I heard what your mother told you."

"What my mother told me?" My mother had told me so many things; at first I didn't understand.

"When she was dying. I listened sometimes, outside her door, to make sure she wasn't being cruel."

"She wasn't."

"I know." She paused, brushed a speck of something from her lap. "She told you not to let Joan take you."

Ah. I remembered exactly. My mother had just swallowed her pill. I had blotted her chin with a napkin.

"She was sick," I said. "She was losing her mind."

"But she hadn't lost it completely, had she?" She met my eye, in a way that meant I had to answer.

"No," I said. "No, she hadn't." Because it

was the truth.

"She told you to be careful with Joan."

"She told me Joan would rip me in two." I remembered the heat of my mother's room, the cloying smells. She was always cold, as she was dying, and I was always warm, as I was nursing her.

"Yes. What would happen to you after she died was her great fear."

"No," I said, reflexively. "It couldn't have been."

"Why? Because she could be cruel? She wasn't meant to be a mother. I grant you that. But she had a mother's instincts, all the same."

"A mother's instincts," I repeated. I was close to tears. "What are those, I wonder? I couldn't move through the house without her telling me I clomped like a horse. I still think of that, sometimes. I remember how much she hated the way I walked."

"Your mother loved you."

"I can't remember her ever telling me so. *You* told me. You told me all the time. But never my mother."

"All the same." Idie pressed her finger to her lips, as if to stop herself from speaking. But she went on. "I used to think it might be God's providence, that she died just as you were becoming a woman. She couldn't

329

have mothered a young woman. She didn't have it in her."

"Do you still think it was God's providence?"

"You know what I think." She stood. "Children," she called. "It's time to go home."

Idie had been my home. I put my hand on my chest. I was a child again, waiting to be led somewhere safe.

I imagined my life had Idie remained in it. She would have been at my wedding. She would have helped me when Tommy was an infant and I could not, for the life of me, please him. She would have helped me in all manner of ways. She would have left less room for Joan.

"I was fifteen years old," I said. "A child."

She pointed to her charges, who were running toward us.

"*They* are children," she said. "You stopped being a child the moment your mother got sick."

The children reached us; Idie patted Ricky's shoulder, distractedly.

"And has she, Cecilia? Has Joan ripped you in two?" Her voice was calm, even. She did not want to alarm the children. I'd forgotten Idie's poise. I'd never once seen my mother rattle her. "I had hoped you wanted to see me for another reason. Any reason, besides her. But I knew in my heart it was Joan."

I was silent. I was still in my mother's room, watching her die. Or no, I was younger than that, a little girl Lucinda's age, unable to defend myself against the accusations of an adult.

"You're twenty-five years old, Cecilia. A grown woman, chasing after another grown woman's secrets."

I looked up at her. The children stood beside her in a neat row. They watched me, solemnly, and Idie leaned down. I put my hand up, unsure of what she wanted, but then her warm, dry lips met my cheek.

"I wanted to see you, Idie," I whispered, when her face was next to mine. "*You* were my mother."

"Oh, child," she said. I could tell I had pleased her. She shook her head. "How I wish I had been." She held out her hands and the younger brother claimed the right; the older, the left. "You taught me that."

"I taught you what?" I asked, my voice high. "Tell me." I would do anything to keep her there, in front of me, so close I could see the faint wrinkles in her crisply ironed skirt, the scuff on the toe of her white shoe.

"That you're never really mine." She lifted

her hands, and the boys' hands also rose. "How I wish you were," she said, and her voice was rich and honeyed, like I remembered it. The wall she had erected between us seemed to have collapsed, all at once. She'd wanted to keep her distance for her own sake, I realized. Not because she hated me.

I made to stand — to what? Take her hand from one of her charges? Idie watched me, sadly. It was all too late.

"Good-bye, Cecilia," she said, and walked away, the boys on either side of her, Lucinda behind them. Again, I wanted to be her. Then Lucinda ran ahead, eager, for what, I did not know. She didn't know, either. Eager to see what came next.

CHAPTER TWENTY-THREE

1957

I made it to the car before I began to cry.
Idie had kissed me, as she had when I was a
child: my forehead, the final step in tucking
me in at night; my hand, when it was hurt
and I held it out to her; my cheek, before
she left Sunday mornings for church. I
pressed my head against the steering wheel
and tried to compose myself.

There was nothing Tommy could do that
would cause me to remove myself from his
life. My love for him was absolute, final.
But now it occurred to me that it was not
Idie who had left. I had chosen Joan; choosing her had been my strongest instinct. I
did not regret my mother. Joan had helped
me, and I was grateful. Even if my mother
had died naturally, in the next week or two;
even if I had let nature take its course, as
Idie had desired — still I would have chosen
Joan, the Fortiers, Evergreen. My mother

had told me not to let Joan take me. And what had I done? I had gone with her, willingly.

Last night I should have searched the hotel for Ray. Instead I had lied my way up to the penthouse to see a woman who had told me to go away.

I heard the shout of a child, and looked up to see a flock of children running to the swings. They reminded me I had my own little boy to attend to. I couldn't sit in this car all day and weep.

I thought I might see Ray's car in the driveway as I turned down our street, but he was still gone, nursing his wounds, nursing a drink, attending to his work — doing whatever it was he did when he needed to distract himself from me. But maybe — and I clung to this possibility — I hadn't behaved as badly as I'd feared. Ray, after all, had no idea where I'd gone last night.

After I stepped inside the house I listened for sounds of Maria and Tommy but heard nothing at first, and a panic rose in my throat. But, gradually, Maria's voice emerged. They were in the kitchen, Tommy in his high chair, Maria watching him feed himself green beans. He smiled when he saw me.

"Are those good?" I asked, and felt light-headed. I leaned on the kitchen counter and closed my eyes.

"Are you all right?" Maria asked. I could feel them both watching me.

I opened my eyes and smiled to show I was fine.

"Tired," I said.

"Ah." She turned back to Tommy. "There's my boy," she said in her accented English as she watched Tommy pincer a bean, bring it to his mouth. "There he is."

Motherhood meant endlessly imagining the misfortune your child might encounter. And then endlessly thinking of ways to avoid such disaster on your child's behalf. Yes, my mother had loved me, in her own way.

I watched Tommy and felt like I could see the future: he would raise his hand in class and supply an answer. He would go out to get burgers with friends and ask the waitress for onion rings instead of fries. He would tell a girl he loved her. I was allowed to be happy at the thought of Tommy's future. I deserved that happiness.

Again I envisioned my life with Idie in it, instead of Joan. My mother would have suffered for another week. Still she would have died. I would have lived in the old colonial with Idie, who would not have told me I clomped like a horse, who would have been happy to see me in the mornings, who would have made sure I was home at a decent hour, not gallivanting around town on Joan's arm.

The intimacy of waking up every morning to Joan's light snoring; the heady feeling of anticipation right before we entered a party, a club; the knowledge that I was special because Joan loved me, because I had been granted the privilege of moving through the world in her spectacular company and she had chosen me, from all the people she could have chosen: all of it gone, vanished. Instead: Idie's even, loving presence. Instead: the sound of Idie downstairs making breakfast, long before I was fully awake. Instead: her cool lips on my forehead, kissing me good night.

I'd never doubted Idie's affection for me. I'd had to work for Joan's: I'd stepped into the shadows so she would not see me spying. I'd stood alone at parties after a boy had caught her eye from across the room. All my life, I'd been careful with her, a prudence that had only made me want her more fiercely. Because without Joan, I would have been just another girl, with none of Joan's radiance to claim as my own. Because I wasn't radiant. I wasn't anything, without Joan. I believed the world would have been indifferent to me without her.

But now I wondered what was wrong with me, that I had wanted, still wanted, a girl, now a woman, who'd always held me at a certain distance. What need in me was so great, so yawning, it could only be satisfied by Joan Fortier?

I thought of the wedding dress Idie had made me. I still had it, in a box in the attic somewhere. The details were exquisite: A line of tiny pearl buttons down the back. A lace collar, a floor-length veil. I had worn it nearly to death.

Would the world have been as indifferent to me as I had believed? Had I chosen Joan because I had been young and careless? Because Idie's steady patience was no match for Joan's wild charisma?

"There he is," Maria said again. Tommy blinked. "Mrs. Fortier called," she added. "She says to call her back immediately."

Mary showed me into Evergreen's formal sitting room, instead of the den, or the breakfast room. I didn't want to be there, but I needed — for my own sake — to finally close the business of Joan with Mary. I was twenty-five years old. I could no longer be Joan's keeper.

Mary seemed agitated. I perched on a silk-covered settee, Mary directly across from me on a high-backed chair. It was one hundred degrees in there, and Mary didn't believe in air-conditioning. An electric fan sat in the corner of the room, cooling nothing. She didn't offer me a drink, the first time I could ever remember her forgetting.

I crossed my ankles and smoothed my skirt over my thighs.

"It's so hot," I said, and then regretted saying anything. But Mary didn't seem to notice I'd spoken.

"I called you because I need help, Cece. I need help."

I waited. Mary seemed very old all of a sudden. She looked her age. Older than that, even. She was not the mistress of Evergreen, who had presided over River Oaks for decades. No, she was an old lady, too thin, wearing a shirt that showed her prominent collarbones, a skirt that needed to be taken in.

I did not like the transformation. Shame was not a feeling I'd ever associated with the Fortiers. It was a feeling I'd only associated with my own family: my mother, who could not be trusted in social situations; my father, who lived at the Warwick with his girlfriend.

"How do you need my help, Mary?"

She looked up, alarmed. I realized I'd never called her by her first name before.

"Joan's been distant," she said. "She hasn't come around for weeks. And then she stopped by, yesterday. She didn't look well." She fretted with a small, needle-pointed pillow beside her. "Sidney Stark," she said, her voice lilting up at the end, as if asking me a question. "She's been with him."

"Yes. With Sid." There was something not quite right about the man, but it was time I stopped caring about Joan's beaus.

"Sid? On such intimate terms already."

I shook my head, irritated. "Not at all. I've barely spoken to him."

"So you agree, that Joan has made herself scarce as of late?"

I felt myself losing whatever edge I thought I'd had.

"I don't know!" I cried, frustrated that she was pulling me back to this old, familiar dance. "I don't know. Sometimes Joan disappears, grows distant, whatever you'd like to call it. I don't know why." And what I thought, but didn't say: *I've got to stop caring why.*

Mary held up a hand, weakly. My outburst seemed to have drained her.

"You know I do not come from the kind

of family that Furlow comes from. That you, Cecilia, come from. I used to think I meant less in the world, because of my lack of — what should I call it? — lineage." She sounded more like her old self now. "But now I understand how very lucky I was. I don't owe any debts to anyone." Her voice rose, almost imperceptibly, but not quite. "Joan is a target, you understand, because of her family. She always was. Something she inherited from Furlow, not me."

"How is she a target?"

"A girl that beautiful, with that much money. She's always a target, whether she knows it or not." And then, suddenly, Mary was completely present again. "You see, dear, Joan has been too absent. We haven't seen her in weeks. Sid is keeping her from us."

I hated how she'd called me "dear," as if I were a child. "Maybe she's exactly where she wants to be."

"You're not afraid for her?"

"How are you afraid for her, Mary?"

Mary shook her head. "I don't know."

"Are you afraid he'll hurt her?" I thought of Joan's bruise.

"He'll hurt her reputation," she said, sharply. "He'll hurt her pride. He's using her, can't you see?"

There was a mahogany wardrobe in the corner of the room that held an assortment of amber-filled decanters. I wanted a drink desperately. I decided to get one. I stood, strode to the wardrobe, opened it, and poured myself a neat finger of scotch.

Mary looked astonished. Good. For the first time in my life, I wanted to astonish Mary Fortier. I was tired of her talk about Family and Money and Responsibility and Burden. Joan was acting badly. That was the long and the short of it.

I took a sip of my drink. It burned, pleasantly.

"What if Joan likes being used?" I asked.

Mary clasped her hand to her breast. "Cecilia!"

"You're worried people will start to talk. That's all we do, isn't it? Worry about Joan. But Joan doesn't want my help. I don't think she ever did." I thought of her last night, in bed, the bruise on her shoulder. I thought of her asking — no, *demanding* — that I leave.

"But you *love* Joan," Mary said. I'd never heard her voice so full of emotion. "You need to help her."

"What do you think I can do? Remove her, limb by limb, from Sid?" I let the question linger. "I do love her." Tears pricked my eyes. I thought of Joan as a golden-haired child, leaning against Dorie, laughing, watching the birds in the birdbath. So many years ago. Days are gods to years, my mother used to say. And it was true.

"People are already talking. Joan will do what Joan wants to do. Do you want to send her away again?" I could feel my cheeks flush. "She's twenty-five years old. If she were a child you could have Dorie clean up her mess, couldn't you, since she's back in your kitchen?"

I didn't expect an answer. Mary stared at me, stunned.

"I do love Joan," I repeated. I thought of Tommy, at home, taking his bath. I thought of Ray, who would surely leave work soon. "But I can't help you. I have my own family, my own life." I set my crystal glass on the low table between us. Mary picked it up and set it on a silver coaster, a gesture that seemed to bring her back to herself.

"Thank you, Cecilia. That will be all. I trust you can find your own way out. This house was yours once, as much as it was ours."

I stood.

"It was never mine," I said. "I think we both know that."

"Is that so?" Mary asked.

342

I looked her in the eye.

"I was a live-in who helped you manage your daughter."

I lit a cigarette before I started the car. My back was damp with sweat.

The world was very still, as it always is the day after a holiday. Halfway home I almost missed my turn onto Troon, forgetting the way to my own house. The silver car behind me honked.

"Sorry, sorry," I muttered, and waved my hand above my head. I steered the car to the side of the road, stubbed my cigarette in the ashtray that pulled out of the dashboard. It needed to be emptied. I hadn't ever cleaned it. Ray took care of our cars, had hired a man who came to our house every other Sunday to simonize them.

The sureness I had felt at Evergreen evaporated. Mary would never forgive me.

My head began to throb. The world turned blurry, for a second.

I doubled back on the next street and pulled into the Avalon drugstore, where I picked up a pint of chocolate ice cream.

"Was your Fourth worth celebrating?" the old man behind the counter asked, winking at me. He and his wife had owned this store since I was a little girl. Joan and I used to

343

come sit at the counter and drink Coke floats.

"It was," I said, as he scooped. He was practiced at it, the way you get good at something you've done your entire life. "Was yours?"

"Oh yes." He smoothed the top of the ice cream with the back of his metal scoop, as neatly as if he were putting the finishing touches on a wedding cake, then shut the glass case. The cold air felt heavenly. He handed me a brown paper bag. "And where are you off to now, dear?"

"Home," I said, without hesitating.

If Ray was surprised to see me he didn't show it. I held up the brown paper bag as proof. "Ice cream," I said, "to celebrate the day after the Fourth."

Maria left early and Tommy stayed up late and it seemed that last night at the club was going to remain unmentioned, for which I was grateful. We lit sparklers when it was dark enough and let Tommy hold them, which he did with a carefulness beyond his years.

I watched Ray help Tommy and I knew I was lucky. Joan didn't belong to me the same way they did. She never could. She belonged to her mother, her father. To the man who would eventually marry her. Because surely she would marry, someday. And if she didn't marry, well — eventually she would belong to no one. And that was her choice.

"I'm keeping my distance from Joan," I told Ray, as we lay in bed. "I've decided."

Ray patted my hand beneath the covers. I could tell by his touch that he wanted to believe me, but couldn't, not quite.

"We can't keep this up."

Keep what up? I could have asked. *What do you mean?* But I knew what he meant.

"I know."

"Do you remember when you married me?"

"Of course I remember, Ray." His tone made me wary.

"Do you remember our witness's name?"

"No." She was a nice, stooped old lady. with white hair, but I did not remember her name. Maybe I had never known it. "She was a stranger." Our wedding certificate was somewhere in my files. "I could look it up, though. I could —"

"Her name was Rhonda Fields. I still remember that. Strange, the things that stay with you."

I squeezed Ray's hand. He was making me nervous. Ray wasn't nostalgic. He didn't sit around and remember for memory's sake.

"Rhonda Fields," I repeated.

"We couldn't have any of my family there. Because Joan wasn't there. So we had Rhonda Fields."

"I'm sorry," I said.

"All the time I've known you I've played second fiddle to Joan Fortier. Haven't I?"

I wanted to turn the light on. Ray wouldn't say such things to my face. Or perhaps he would.

"Joan is more than a friend. Joan is —" I could not explain it. I would have traded a lifetime of friendship with Ciela for fifteen minutes with Joan, in a heartbeat. And I liked Ciela; I enjoyed her company. But no one made me feel like Joan.

"Joan is what?" His voice was eerily calm. "She's not everything, is she?"

"No!" I said. "No, of course she's not everything. You and Tommy are everything."

"Are we?"

"You are!" I cried. "You are. But Joan . . ." I tried to think of how to phrase it. "She's a mystery," I said, finally. "A mystery."

"No more a mystery than you or I. No more a mystery than anyone in the world."

Maybe that was true. I could not see myself as clearly as Ray could. I couldn't see Joan as clearly, either. I was too close to her. She was like something inside my skin and bones, something I could feel but not see.

She was my mother, my father, my sister, my friend. She was everything that came before. But even then, in that moment, I wanted to keep Joan private. I wanted to keep what she meant to me hidden. *She's a mystery I've been trying to solve since we were little girls,* I could have said. *She's the great mystery of my life.*

"I told you," I said. "We won't be as close. It's been happening for a while. Joan has her own life. I have mine."

"You've said things like that before."

"I mean it this time." And it was true, I did. "I can't help her anymore. I see that now. I can't help her anymore."

Ray let go of my hand beneath the sheet. At first I thought he was angry, but he began to lightly rub my forearm, up and down, following a rhythm known only to him. It felt like the most tender gesture that had ever passed between us.

"I'm not lying," I whispered.

"I know."

"I'm done."

"You have to be. Completely done, Cece. Not like the other times."

I lay awake a long time after Ray had fallen asleep. What did it mean to be done with a person? What exactly did my life mean, without her? I touched my stomach, where another child might rest soon.

I used to think that if I told Ray what Joan had done for me so long ago, with my mother, he would understand what I owed her. But he would not. He would say we were children, that we had not known what we were doing. That things happened when you were young, that life went on, that I couldn't live forever in debt to a fifteen-year-old version of myself and a friend.

I opened the *Chronicle* and flipped to the "Gadabout" section on Sunday morning and saw Joan, with Sid, smiling grandly from their perch above the Shamrock's pool. I stared at her long enough to burn a batch of pancakes.

Ray sniffed the air when he came down, still in his pajamas. I'd already tossed the pancakes into the trash, refolded the news-paper, and laid it by Ray's plate, already made a new batch of pancakes, heated the syrup in a saucepan on the stove.

"Everything's ready," I said. "If you eat now it won't get cold."

Ray kissed me on the cheek before he sat

down. I cut a pancake into eighths and put it on Tommy's high chair tray.

"Mmm," he said, and Ray and I looked at each other with the kind of pleasure unique to parents. *We* did this, the look said. There wasn't a Thomas Fitzgerald Buchanan before us, and now there was, and he did things that he hadn't done a week ago, like say "Mmm" when presented with a pancake.

Ray had surprised me when he'd told me to choose, between him, between our family, and Joan. I waited for him to surprise me again now. I sat down across from him and helped Tommy eat while Ray read the paper. He was a skimmer; he came to the women's section in no time. He turned the page as if a giant photograph of Joan had not confronted him. I felt strangely disappointed. But what had I wanted? For him to light a match and burn the paper? Ray wasn't going to make a spectacle. He was going to let Joan fade from our lives, so slowly you might not notice if you weren't paying attention.

He turned back to the front of the paper and went through it again more deliberately, as was his habit. What could he possibly be reading about that was more interesting than Joan? School desegregation, perhaps.

Nuclear bombs, the Russians.

The truth was, I didn't care about school desegregation. I didn't care about the Russians. Joan did, or at least she pretended to: this winter she'd given me an article about disarmament she'd clipped from the paper. But who really knew what Joan cared about?

"Thank you for the pancakes," Ray said, after he had finished the paper, and had turned his attention to his food, finished his short stack, like he did every Saturday and Sunday. He always waited to eat until he'd finished skimming the paper, which meant the pancakes weren't hot any longer, only warm. First he buttered them, every single one; then he poured syrup *around* the pancakes but not directly on them; then he sliced them into a dozen pieces; and then, finally, he ate. In fifty years he'd still be buttering and eating his pancakes in the same exact way. And I would be there to see it, every Saturday and Sunday for the rest of my life.

"I think I might meet JJ at the Houston Club today," he said, and this did not surprise me, either. The Houston Club was a regular haunt, where men went to broker deals.

"And I'll be here, with Tommy. We'll go to the park, won't we, Tommy? We'll swim, when the sun's gone in a little bit."

I would not surprise Ray. That was the new pact of our marriage. No surprises. The same version of yourself, day after day after day.

CHAPTER TWENTY-FOUR

1957

A week passed. I wondered if Joan would call. I hoped she'd call. I wondered if Mary would call. I wondered if I'd hear some news of Joan — from Ciela, from Darlene, from a neighbor. But I did not. Whenever I thought of Mary and all the things I'd said to her at Evergreen, I'd cringe, sing a little song to distract myself, convince myself that I had been correct, that Mary had needed to hear what I'd had to say.

What power did she have over me? I waited. Nothing happened. Gardenia Watson, who lived three streets over, did not call to tell me my Junior League membership had been rescinded for reasons she could not disclose. I did not receive a letter from the River Oaks homeowner's association informing me my hedges were not clipped to regulation height. I did not receive a letter from Mary, listing all the things she and Furlow had done for me, page after page after page. I did not open the door to find Mary herself, begging me for help; only the postman, with a package too big for the mailbox.

I began to feel free. Magically, I was able to see us all as characters in another person's life. Mary as the sad old mother, trying to help a daughter who refused it. Furlow, the fading patriarch. Joan, the aging socialite, so high and drunk most of the time she didn't know which end was up. Sid, the wily businessman who thought he might sleep with Joan and get something else from her, too.

I saw it all. And I saw myself. An observer. Separate from it all.

The next Sunday I invited JJ, Ciela, and Tina over for drinks and a cookout. "Just us?" Ciela asked. "We'd be delighted."

And it was true, I didn't often entertain single families. Joan used to come over nearly every weekend night, and she wasn't interested in making small talk with a man like JJ. When I wanted to throw a party it was usually huge, like the Valentine's party I'd had earlier that year, where I'd tinted the pool water pink and invited twenty families for red gin and tonics and heart-shaped filets. The nannies had wrangled the children upstairs while the adults had gotten drunk by the pool.

This, by contrast, would be intimate and casual. I'd made potato salad that morning, had Maria make a lemon cake the day before. A simple affair, but even simple affairs were twice as much work as you thought they would be.

When the doorbell rang that evening, I removed my apron, touched up my lipstick in the reflection of the stove, surveyed the kitchen.

"I'll get it," Ray shouted, and I saw him go by the kitchen door in a blur, Tommy on his hip.

You're going to have fun, I told myself. *You're going to enjoy yourself.*

And I was having fun, after a few daiquiris. JJ had appointed himself bartender, which annoyed me a little, since it was Ray's house, but Ray didn't seem to mind so I resolved not to, either.

Ciela and I stood by the pool, smoking, watching Tina and Tommy play on the swing set. She'd brought her nanny, and so I was unexpectedly absolved of the responsibility of Tommy for the night.

"What's her day off?" I asked, gesturing

toward the children.

"Tuesday. She'd prefer Sunday, church and all, but there's always something to do on Sunday, you know?"

I nodded.

"And," she continued, "I have a little surprise. We're expecting again! Hopefully a little JJ. The doctor just called yesterday, though I already knew, of course." She took a sip of her daiquiri, smoothed her palm over her stomach.

I'd known since she first walked in. She wore a figure-hugging white sundress, no visible tummy yet, but she kept brushing her stomach with her fingertips, as only pregnant women do. And Tina was two, which was the age, around here, that you tried for another one.

"That's wonderful news," I said. "Tina will be a wonderful big sister." I couldn't think of any word besides "wonderful."

Ciela laughed. "She'll be awful. She thinks the world revolves around her. And it does. That's the way of first children." She paused, fanned her face with a napkin. "You and I were only children, so the world always revolved around us. Probably would have done me good to have a little brother or sister."

"Probably," I echoed. I'd never felt the

355

world revolved around me. It revolved around my mother. And Joan.

I waited for Ciela to say that Joan was always like a sister to me. *Say it,* I thought, *say it.* But Ciela simply took a drag of her cigarette; when she spoke it had nothing to do with Joan.

"And a little sister for Tommy? When will she make an appearance?"

I patted my stomach, instinctively, and noticed that the thought of a second child didn't fill me with dread.

"Oh," I said vaguely. "We're letting nature take its course. But hopefully sometime soon."

I surprised myself with that admission; I could tell I'd surprised Ciela, too. I felt giddy with the possibility of it, suddenly. Another child! And maybe Ciela was right, maybe it would be a little girl.

Worrying about Joan had done my figure good: I wore high-waisted shorts, and a sleeveless top I'd knotted at my belly button. "Skinny Minnie," Ciela had said when she'd seen me, and Ray had looked at me appreciatively when I'd emerged from the bedroom.

Later, after we'd eaten our steaks — rare, all around — and the children had nibbled on hot dogs and large helpings of cake, and been taken upstairs by the nanny, we sat around the outside bar, lit only by the glow of tiki lanterns. I was drunk but not sloppy. I felt no pain. I was smoking my millionth cigarette, and in the soft light of the lanterns, everyone looked beautiful. Especially Ray, who kept touching my knee underneath the table. The heat, which had been a wet blanket all day, had turned cozy once the sun disappeared. There was even a faint breeze, though I might have been imagining it.

I could see glimpses of our neighbors' perfectly kept houses: A television set, a cat sitting in a window. A Spanish-tiled roof, an ivy-clad brick wall.

I felt good, is what I mean to say. Satisfied. I felt like Joan was very far away, doing what she would do with Sid Stark. *Her life is not my life,* I thought, and the phrase, pleasing in its simplicity, stayed with me as we sat there. I hadn't yet reached the point where I wanted Ciela and JJ to leave.

"Did you see the *Chronicle*?" Ciela asked.

I straightened, suddenly alert. I knew immediately. Not exactly what she would say, not precisely, but I knew from the tone of her voice it was going to be about Joan. I tried to send her a silent signal — *don't, don't, don't.*

Surely Ciela knew that Joan was a tense subject between me and Ray. I hadn't mentioned her the entire night. But perhaps she didn't know; perhaps she had no idea how deeply Joan had threaded herself, or been threaded, by me, through our marriage.

"Skimmed it front to back," Ray said, and JJ laughed. Ray was clueless. I thought Ciela was going to say that Joan's absence from the paper today was notable, because she hadn't been in the "Gadabout" column this morning — I had looked, first thing! My hackles rose. I tapped my cigarette on the ashtray. Ciela looked garish, too much eyeliner, and were those fake eyelashes?

Ray and JJ were talking about business, man stuff, and I wanted to hit them both. I needed to hear what Ciela had to say.

"I didn't," I said, interrupting JJ. "I didn't get a chance."

"It was a gigantic picture of Sid Stark! At the opening of a new place — the Hula Hoop." Ciela laughed. "I wonder if the waitresses will wear grass skirts."

"Stark?" Ray asked, stupidly, and I realized he had no idea who Sid was. I hadn't ever told him.

Ciela looked at me, then at Ray, and I could see it dawn on her: that I'd kept

358

something from Ray. I felt ashamed; the guts of my marriage had spilled in front of her.

"Not from around here — he's in the gambling world," JJ was saying. "Wouldn't trust him as far as I could throw him. I hear he's taken up with our Joan, lately," he said, raising his eyebrows. "Can't see that coming to any good."

Our Joan? Men were so stupid. He was simply parroting what Ciela had told him; he wasn't capable of an original thought concerning Joan, or men and women, or all the complexities that existed between them.

I kept silent. Ray looked at me. He didn't seem angry, and for that I was grateful. But overriding my gratefulness was confusion: I hadn't seen any picture of Sid in the *Chronicle* that morning. Ciela must have been mistaken.

As if she'd read my mind, Ciela continued. "Joan was there, too." I half wanted to slap her, for continuing the story and bringing Joan into it, front and center, and I half wanted to hug her. I ached for news. "Standing between the men, beaming. It must have been a hundred degrees but she isn't sweating at all."

I nodded, trying to absorb and assemble this information, recast the events of last week in my mind.

Joan wasn't holed up in her house, high and drunk. Oh, she might have been high and drunk, but she was presentable enough to attend ribbon-cutting ceremonies. She was being seen; she was out and about.

"I guess things are still hot and heavy with Mr. Stark," Ciela said.

"I wouldn't know," I said, killing the conversation. My voice was harsher than I'd intended, but I wasn't sorry. I stubbed out my cigarette and leaned back in my chair. Now I wanted Ciela and JJ to leave.

JJ stared into his martini, and Ciela smoked her cigarette, and Ray — well, I didn't want to look at Ray. I heard a child scream upstairs, and I cocked my head toward the sound.

"That might be Tommy," I said, rising, and Ciela stood in tandem.

"But it might be Tina." And we were off.

When we were in bed Ray turned to me, touched my breast, and I lay there and let him have sex with me. My mind was downstairs, in the trash can where Ray had already put the paper. My mind was with Joan, four streets over, or maybe she was out tonight, somewhere special with Sid. The Petroleum Club, cutting into a steak.

By the pool at the Shamrock, laughing merrily while sipping champagne.

After Tommy was born I had no interest in sex for months. Not even the slightest urge. My mind was always with Tommy, then. But I never refused Ray. Not then, not now. Ray wasn't the kind of man to push himself on his unwilling wife, but I wanted him to think of himself as a man who was always desired.

Ray flipped me over, entered me from behind. I didn't particularly like this position. He'd not mentioned Joan after Ciela and JJ had departed. He'd acted like his normal self, chatting about a fishing trip he and JJ might take in August with some other men from Shell.

Now I wondered if he might be punishing me, unconsciously. It hurt, him behind me; I tried to change my position, lift my stomach up from the mattress, but he was pressed so hard against me I couldn't move an inch.

His mouth was on my ear, his hot breath, his smell of toothpaste and whiskey. And then he was done, the pressure of him, on top of me and inside me, suddenly gone.

He kissed my cheek, more tenderly than usual, and I knew: he had been punishing me. But that was good. He had punished me and forgiven me. And now he could forget.

I was elbow-deep in garbage when I found the paper down at the bottom of the kitchen trash, beneath all the old food from the past week. I'd felt such a satisfying sense of accomplishment when I was through cleaning the fridge, its shelves gleaming and orderly and clean.

Now I was on the floor, sitting next to a pile of noodles and wilted iceberg lettuce, clad in yellow plastic kitchen gloves, a smear of ketchup on my forehead from where I'd unthinkingly scratched an itch. The garbage overturned and open before me like a tunnel: I reconsidered. *Go to bed.* It was just a picture in the paper.

I couldn't.

And then there it was, dotted with eggshell and bacon grease.

I flipped through each page, first to last. I saw the picture nearly immediately, in the "Our City" column. No wonder I'd missed it. I don't think Joan had ever been in any section but the women's section. I laughed. Joan Fortier was either becoming less or more important, depending on how you looked at it.

Houston native and socialite Joan Fortier

with friend Sidney Stark at the opening of a local Hawaiian-themed nightclub, the Hula Hoop, which promises "a genuine Hawaiian ambiance."

That was all. Joan had gone to club openings before, a thousand of them.

I almost missed it: Sid's pinky ring, big and gold, on his finger — he was shaking someone's hand. The ring drew my attention to his hand, then to his arm; his arm drew my attention to a long, ugly scar.

I felt hot, too hot. I stood, clumsily, disrupting the pile of garbage near my knee.

I would have recognized that scar anywhere.

Joan had lied to me. The scar was proof. Had she ever been honest with me?

Sid was from the past, but not from Hollywood. What Joan had told me was a half-truth, one of many Joan had fed me over the years. But why lie about him?

It occurred to me, standing there in the detritus of our household, that Joan only fed me her lies because I wanted them. Because I was hungry for them. I would clean this mess and pray it didn't leave a stain. I would rinse off in Tommy's bathroom and return to bed, slip in beside my husband and forget Joan.

All those years ago, my mother dying,

dead. But I had paid Joan what I owed her. I could give her no more. I would not let her rip me in two.

CHAPTER TWENTY-FIVE

1957

I woke to a splash in the pool. It was Tuesday, two nights after the cookout. I went to the window, peered through the blinds. Joan, in her bra and panties, floating on her back in the turquoise water.

"Ray," I whispered. Mercifully, he did not respond. If he slept through this, I would start praying.

"I promise," I whispered, and hurried downstairs.

"Joan," I said, my voice low, as I stood at the edge of the pool. Her skin glistened in the moonlight; her hair floated behind her and framed her face. Most of us never got our hair wet, in the pool. Too much trouble. But Joan always did.

Her eyes were still closed. "Joan!" I said again.

She opened them, smiled at me like nothing about any of this was unusual. As if she had just dropped by to say hi and have a drink and then would be on her merry way again.

"Have you lost your mind?" I asked, furious. "It's two o'clock in the morning." I pointed to my watch. "Where are your clothes?"

But as I spoke I could feel my fury subsiding. Joan disappeared underwater, and I watched her blurry form swimming toward me across the length of the pool. She came up beside me, gasping for air. Despite everything, I was happy to see her.

"In the water is the only place I want to be these days," she said, and she patted the concrete. "Sit."

I sat. It was dark, and her eyes were bloodshot; I couldn't tell if it was the chlorine or if she had taken something. I wiped a piece of hair off her forehead, cool in the night air.

"Are you on something, Joan? Let's not —" *Play games,* I was going to say, but she cut me off.

"Yesterday," she said, "yesterday, I think. But not today. And I haven't lost my mind. It's very much here, unfortunately." She smiled ruefully. It was so rare that I saw Joan rueful.

Now that Joan was here I didn't want her

to leave. She seemed easy around me, for the first time in a long time. My old friend. I never could stay mad at Joan.

She thrummed her fingers on the blue tile. There was a new ring on her right ring finger, an emerald-cut diamond between two diamond baguettes. I touched it.

"From Sid?"

"No." She examined it. "Something Daddy gave me years ago."

"Really?" I'd never seen it.

"Really. I should sell it."

I laughed. "For what?"

"The money, what else?"

"You don't need money," I said.

"You have no idea what I need. Anyway, it wouldn't be enough." She twisted the ring around her finger. "Why have you stayed away, Cece? You've never stayed away like this before."

"No," I said. "No, I guess I haven't."

"You're surprised I noticed? Of course I noticed. You're always there."

She pushed off from the edge of the pool, floated on her back again. It was easier to talk to her like this, when I couldn't see her eyes.

"You told me you didn't want me there."

Joan said nothing. Her silence made me bold. What did it matter, if I mortally offended her? She didn't want me anyway.

"I know who Sid is."

"Do you?" Her voice had laughter in it, as if she were speaking to a child who had made an obvious discovery.

"He's not who you said he was," I said. "*Nothing* is what you said it was."

"I've told so many lies," she said, after a minute had passed, after I was beginning to think she wouldn't answer me at all. She no longer spoke as if I were a child. "That I can't keep track. I knew you'd figure it out, eventually. That I was lying about Sid. That I was lying about everything. I wanted you to," she added.

"Really? You could have just told me the truth." I thought of the way she had dangled Sid in front of me, meeting him in the most public of places. She hadn't tried very hard to keep him a secret. But I had not solved the mystery.

"No," she said, and shook her head. "No. That would have been impossible. You know what I wish? I wish I weren't a Fortier."

"Who would you be if you weren't a Fortier?"

Again, it took Joan a long time to answer. "I suppose I might be happy," she said, finally.

I watched my friend float on her back. She

368

wasn't happy, it was true, hadn't been that way for a very long time.

"That house, Joan." I still didn't know how to phrase it. *That place. That horrible place.*

She continued to float, five, six feet away from me.

"Where I found you with those men. And then your parents sent you away."

"My *mother* sent me away," Joan said, and her voice was hard. "And my father let her."

"You were destroying yourself." She did not disagree. "I found you with Sid, half-dead. And another man. Sid's scar." I traced my forearm from wrist to elbow. "I saw it that time. And then I saw it again, in the paper on Sunday — he had his sleeves rolled up."

"What if I wanted to destroy myself? Wasn't that my right?" She swam to the stairs. She emerged, gleaming and wet, her back to me.

"What are you playing at, Joan?"

Joan shook her head. Still I could not see her face.

"Sid's not a beautiful man," Joan said, "but he's vain about that scar. It was so hot. That's why his sleeves were rolled up. The only reason." When she turned to face me there were tears in her eyes.

"Lucky you, Cece. Lucky you. You get to know everything, now."

CHAPTER TWENTY-SIX

1957

I'd like to say I thought twice about following Joan out the side gate, into the front yard, where Fred waited next to the curb. He tipped his hat to me as I opened the door, and I understood that Fred knew everything, always had, much more than I. I'd like to say I thought about telling Fred to wait. I needed to at least make up a story for Ray. To leave a note. I could hedge my bets, that way, hope that we would return in time for me to destroy it. I needed not to go at all, I needed to think about all I risked by going wherever Joan led me.

I handed her the towel I'd grabbed from the stack I kept in the outdoor bar. She didn't even seem to notice the fact of her own wetness; she would have slid into the car half-naked had I not handed her the towel, waited while she dried off; had I not taken her hair and twisted the water out before she slipped on her dress. She let me touch her. There was that. She said nothing, and I said nothing. I simply followed her.

"Glenwood," she said to Fred, and he nodded.

"For?" I asked, but Joan shook her head, and my question disappeared in my throat. *For my mother,* I was going to say, because Glenwood was where my mother had been buried, ten years earlier. I'd visited her grave a handful of times. Once with Ray. I paid for fresh flowers to be placed near her headstone once a month, but that was all the sentimentality I could muster.

I lay back against the cool leather seat. This car was always a relief, always signaled a return home, a respite against the heat, quiet and order after a noisy night in a club. This car was a comfort.

I closed my eyes, and waited to be delivered to our destination.

We stepped outside the car, Joan first, shivering in her dress, even in the humid nighttime air. I reached back in the car and retrieved the blanket Fred kept by our feet; Joan let me cover her shoulders with it. When we started walking she pulled it tighter.

Glenwood was enormous and stately,

where everyone in River Oaks was buried. Where I would be buried one day. Ray had already purchased two plots. Buffalo Bayou was nearby, and you could hear the water moving, always; I remembered it from my mother's funeral.

Fred called for Joan from the car. "Ma'am," he said, "Miss Fortier," and Joan turned, irritation on her face, but then he handed her a flashlight, and her look turned to gratitude. Fred did not meet my eye. *What are we doing here?* I wanted to ask him, because it was clear that he knew.

Joan walked through Glenwood's enormous iron gates, which had never in my memory been closed, and at first I didn't follow her, didn't want to follow her. I thought of Idie and I did not want to be there. I did not want to see my mother's grave, to recall her last night on earth. I looked back for Fred, but he was already in the car, and I couldn't make out his face in the darkness. Joan disappeared into the night, and I stood where I was. The cemetery was closed, of course — a small plaque next to the entrance said so: *Visitors welcome, from sunrise to sundown.* We weren't supposed to be in there. There were rules for every single thing in the world, some written, some simply understood, but it didn't matter: Joan broke all of them.

Then she came back for me.

"Come with me," she said, and that was all she had to say.

As we walked, our path lit by the shaky beam of the flashlight, I tried not to think about Ray, at home; I tried not to think about Tommy. Surely I would be back by sunrise. I would insist. Yet I knew that I would be home whenever Joan took me there. No sooner, no later.

Two nights earlier I had been entertaining Ciela and JJ on my patio, drinking daiquiris and feeling sure that I had given up the habit that was Joan. I was pleased with myself, pleased with pleasing Ray. And now I was traipsing through Houston's finest cemetery after midnight, walking on the carefully groomed pathways between grave sites.

We were walking toward my mother's grave, on the south side. I didn't know exactly where to find it, but I supposed Joan did. Had she been coming here for years? Was she guilty over what we had done? If anyone could make Joan feel guilty it would be Raynalda Beirne. She was a ghost who haunted, a ghost who demanded her pound of flesh.

I wasn't silly, I wasn't hysterical, but I was

scared. I caught up with Joan, who was walking very quickly.

"Joan," I said, "why are you taking me here?"

She shook her head. Her hand clutched the blanket beneath her chin; her diamond ring was the only adornment that hinted at her place in the world. Other than that she looked rough, a little insane: damp, sloppy, on a mission known only to her.

We walked. My mother was buried near a child, whose grave was adorned with a weeping angel. The angel was large, bigger, I imagined, than the child she protected. I noticed the angel now, off to our left.

"Joan," I said, and pointed, "this way?"

She didn't bother to answer, just led me deeper and deeper into the cemetery. The air smelled fishy, a little swampy, thanks to the slow-moving river. Mother Bayou, we called her, the water a chocolate brown. It went all the way to Galveston, emptied into the bay. Joan had told me this, long ago. She'd read it somewhere.

Finally Joan slowed, brought her free hand out to signal we were turning. We were in a tiny enclosure, surrounded by bushes and low-lying tree branches. One small plaque was embedded in the dirt; it gleamed in the black earth, only sparsely dotted with grass.

I wanted to be home, with Ray, Tommy down the hall. I wanted to be there very badly. I felt like a child who'd gotten what she'd desired — the thing she'd coveted all her life — and then, upon receiving it, wanted to return it. I could almost feel Ray's presence beside me, warm and substantial at night. I could reach out a hand and touch his back, his shoulder — and he would murmur, he would respond to my touch without ever waking up. I had made the wrong choice, coming here.

"Joan?" I asked, my voice loud and jarring in the quiet stillness. "Take me back."

She was looking down at the plaque, the plaque I did not want to see. She looked up at me, but she was elsewhere, in a daze, a trance, somewhere unknown.

"You can't ever go back."

She pointed, down. To the gleaming plaque embedded in the earth. "Look at it," she said. "You wanted to know. You wanted to see." Her voice had turned high, ugly. "Now you see. Now you know."

I looked up at the flat night sky, bloodless, not a star in sight. Then I looked down at the earth, and I knew I was losing something.

David Furlow Fortier
Born August 19, 1950
Died May 10, 1957

"A child," I said, staring at the dates. Then I turned cold, as the truth dawned on me. But that's not true. The truth had been dawning on me for years and years.

"My child," Joan said. "Mine."

CHAPTER TWENTY-SEVEN

1957

I knew Joan the best of anyone in the world
— I still believe that, all these years later —
but in the end Joan was a secret, a cipher, a
myth. She did not want to be known.

That one night she told me everything. I
don't know why. Perhaps the planets
aligned. She didn't need to tell me, certainly.
She had grown accustomed to lying. She
was our most famous socialite, our most
beautiful friend, our brightest star. She was
a Fortier. I think she loved me.

Joan wasn't sad. She wasn't tragic. She
was a woman with a dead child, a status
that lent no intrigue, no glamour. A status
that would have made her, in our circles,
untouchable.

That night six years earlier, when Joan
dove into the Shamrock's pool, stood on
her tiptoes at the edge of the board, sus-
pended in time and space, my black gown

clinging to her body like a coat of wet paint — you didn't know what would happen. But oh, you wanted to go there with her. You wanted to stand on the board, you wanted to feel the air at that height. You wanted to look down and see all the people, watching. You wanted not to be one of those people. You wanted to be Joan.

You didn't know if she would dive or die trying. It didn't matter. There was only that single moment: Joan, poised. That was Joan Fortier's greatest gift. She made a moment feel endless. She made you feel endless, too. You would never age, as long as Joan was nearby. Never grow old or experience sadness or wake up to the knowledge that someone you loved was no longer on this earth.

A tragedy would have ruined Joan. And so a secret was kept, for seven years.

Yet Joan told me. She let me be her friend, that one night. I was something else, too. I was her witness.

"I left because I was pregnant," she began.

She told no one, at first.

"Not even the baby's father?"

"Especially him," she said. She shrugged. "He was just some boy. He could have been anyone."

She stared at her child's grave. I waited.

This was what Joan required of me: my patience. I've never believed in ghosts but I could feel my mother, lingering somewhere nearby, and in those strange hours, I was pleased by her nearness. The idea of her brought me comfort.

Joan was silent for a long time.

"I let my mother have her way, like I always let her have her way," she said. "I used to think that I would get used to it. Used to having a child but pretending I didn't. To keeping a secret. But I didn't. The secret became a part of me, until I didn't know what was a lie, what wasn't a lie. Which lies were important, which didn't matter."

"They all mattered," I murmured.

"I know that," she said, sharply, and then she began to cry. To weep. I went to her. It was my instinct: to relieve Joan of her pain.

She was stiff in my arms, at first, but then she relented, and I understood, as I held her, that Joan Fortier was a stranger whom I loved.

"Look at me, Joan," I said. She would not. "Please."

Slowly she lifted her head. "I'm ashamed," she whispered, her voice thick with grief. Even though I was right next to her, I could hardly understand her.

"Tell me why," I said. "Tell me your story."

It was all I'd ever really wanted, to hear Joan's story. For Joan to tell me the truth.

And so she did.

When Joan discovered she was pregnant, her life was sliced in two: there was her old life, which still required her participation. It was March, and we would be graduating in a few short months. Lamar was wrapped in a celebratory spirit: boys were deciding where they would go to college. Girls were busy planning the senior prom. Mothers were reserving back rooms in restaurants for graduation lunches. It was an ending, but we were young enough that endings felt like beginnings.

I felt something else. I knew that once we graduated, Evergreen would not be available to me in the same way. The safety of high school, the routine: the same halls, the same teachers, the same boys. That would be gone, too. Fred depositing us in the morning, picking us up in the afternoon. All of this would disappear. It would be a new world. But Joan would be there with me. I would see her each morning when I woke, each night before I fell asleep.

Joan participated in her old life. But her real life, she felt, was very far away from the halls of Lamar High School. Her clothes still fit. She had thought they would stop fitting immediately, and so she was relieved each time she zipped her cheerleading outfit, each time she buttoned a blouse over her breasts. She had never known a pregnant woman. She knew, vaguely, that Mary's pregnancy with her had been difficult, but she did not know how. She did not know what to expect from her own changing body.

The sudden intensity of the sickness was a surprise. She stayed home from school one day, sent me off with Fred, told me she had a bug. Mary was supposed to be at a Junior League meeting. She came home early. It would have happened sooner or later; Mary was always going to learn that Joan was pregnant. It was just a matter of when.

"My mother," Joan said, "knew everything."

Joan was surprised by her mother's kindness. She had expected fury. Instead Mary had quickly concocted a plan, and Joan was grateful. She had no feeling about the baby. It was, at this point, an absence: of her regular cycle, of feeling well. The baby was not yet a baby to Joan. That would come later.

Joan wanted one thing from Mary: a

promise that Furlow would never know. It was 1950. Furlow had been born in 1875. She had let a man have sex with her, and this man had not married her after she learned of the child. It would ruin Furlow. His Joan had always existed well above the rest of the world.

He'll be none the wiser, Mary told her, and Joan believed her. To have a baby out of wedlock, back then — there would have been nothing left of Joan. There wasn't any question of Joan marrying the father. The father was one of two boys, but there was no way to tell which one, and anyway, the thought of marrying either one of them, tying herself to him for life, going to him, begging him — it filled her with disgust. Mary seemed to understand that marriage wasn't an option; Mary seemed to understand everything.

"We decided I would leave when everyone would be busy. And you would be gone." We were sitting now, on the hard ground. "That was another reason. You would be in Oklahoma." Easter came and Joan disappeared.

I remembered returning from Oklahoma, Mary picking me up, Fred driving. It was all a farce.

"Did Dorie know?" I asked.

"If you didn't know," she said, "then no one knew."

And I was proud, sitting there in the dark cemetery. That I was the person, out of everyone, Mary and Joan had most wanted to fool.

Joan moved to Plano, outside of Dallas, and lived at a home for unwed mothers. The house was Victorian, winding. The old pine floors were uneven, the windows narrow and tall. Joan's room overlooked the front yard, which was shaded by oak trees. The view reminded her of Evergreen. She thought of Furlow when she thought of Evergreen.

"I missed Evergreen," she said. "I hadn't thought I would. I was glad to leave it. I had begun to hate it. But then I went away and I realized it was home. The place I went, in Plano — it wasn't so bad. There were other girls there, like me. We played cards. We ate meals together. We all got fatter and fatter. We wore loose, shapeless clothes. Rags. You would have hated it."

She smiled, shyly, in a way completely uncharacteristic of Joan.

"I was grateful for their company. If the other girls hadn't been there, I might have lost my mind."

But mainly, Joan read. There was a stack

of old magazines: *Harper's Bazaar, Life, Modern Screen, National Geographic.* Joan read each one, cover to cover. She read about the place she was supposed to be. She read about other places, too. When she'd finished with these she asked Mary, who called once a week, for more. Mary sent the most recent issues and Joan disappeared into her bedroom.

"I'd never pretended I was anyone else," she said. She rested her chin on her bent knees, a child's pose. "And now I pretended all the time."

"Who did you pretend to be?" I asked.

"*Who* didn't matter," she said. "*Where* mattered. I went to Hollywood, yes, but other places, too: London, Cairo. The places I saw in the pictures." She laughed. "Can you imagine?"

I could imagine, that was the thing. I saw it so clearly now: without a baby, Joan would have gone, eventually, to one of these places — not Cairo, but New York, LA, even Boston or Miami. She would have married a wealthy man — Joan wasn't meant for a life without money — a businessman, or maybe a successful writer. Someone who wouldn't have bored her, someone who could have given her a piece of the world: Taken her to Thailand to tour his textile factories. Taken her to Paris, to an artists' colony. Taken her away from me, and the life I had built so carefully. I loved the details of my life, most. That Maria arrived each morning precisely at eight. That Tommy would go to River Oaks Elementary, just as Joan and I had. That we all served the same pimiento sandwiches, from the same recipe, at luncheons. That our husbands disappeared onto patios to smoke cigars while we ladies cleared the table. In the end, the details weren't about beauty or status. They never had been, for me. They were about feeling at home in the world. And Joan hated these details. She thought my existence relentlessly tedious. What she couldn't see was that the details *were* life. That was how you loved someone: every day, without fail, over and over.

Joan waited for me to answer, but I couldn't speak. It felt like I was seeing her, and myself, clearly for the first time since we were children.

"Maybe you can't imagine. But I had a plan, Cece," Joan continued. "For the first time in my life, I had a plan. Mama thought I was coming back to Houston. But I was never coming back. There was nothing left for me, here. I was going to go someplace where no one knew me. Where no one knew

386

the Fortiers."

I had thought Joan needed Houston, *needed* to be worshipped, known, adored. Imagining her in Hollywood, seeking the adoration of strangers, had barely required any imagination at all. But Joan did not need to be adored. It was we who needed to adore her.

"You wanted to go where the ideas were," I said, remembering what she had told me so long ago, as we stood on the steps outside Lamar.

"Yes," Joan said. "Yes! That was exactly where I wanted to go. But I never quite made it, did I?" It wasn't a question I was meant to answer. "Instead I had a baby. Such a cliché: the unmarried girl who gets pregnant and ruins her life. But I wasn't going to let this baby ruin my life. There was one baby before mine. The girl — her name was Katherine, from St. Louis — labored for a very long time before she went to the hospital. And then we never saw her again. That was the promise of the place: you had a baby and then you left. It felt like a promise, anyway."

The next time Houston saw Joan, this period in her life — this sleepy, unchanging routine she found herself in — would be a memory. It would be less than that, because her new life would be so different she would be unable to recall her old life. She would not be able to remember staring at a photograph of Ava Gardner for so long, with such intensity, she saw her face in her dreams. She would not remember asking her mother for a French dictionary over the phone, and her mother's response — a quick burst of laughter — which had been worse than no. She would not remember the way the girl from St. Louis had grabbed Joan's hand one morning and put it on her stomach; the undeniable movement she felt beneath her hand, nor the guilty grin on the girl's face. She would not remember how her own baby felt within her.

"I would wake up in the middle of the night and he would be moving, constantly, as if he were trying to somersault out of the womb. He made me feel less alone." She shook her head. "Isn't that foolish? He wasn't even a baby at that point. He was half a baby. And he comforted me. I tried not to feel comfort. I knew I would give birth with a cloth over my eyes. I wouldn't even know if he was a boy or a girl. He would be taken, given to his new parents, right away."

She spent four months at the home for unwed mothers. She went into labor a month early, in August. When she woke, she was in a hospital in Dallas. Before she opened her eyes she heard a woman's voice say it was a shame, one of God's dirty tricks.

"The nurse said he wasn't right. That's how I knew he was a boy. And then they took me to him. I demanded it." She looked at me. "I'd never wanted anything, until that point, in my entire life. All I wanted was my baby."

The nurse took her to the nursery. Joan's baby was the only one there, and Joan understood, without anyone telling her, that it was where sick children went. His eyes were closed. He felt stiff against her hands. His hair was dark. Joan was surprised by its thickness. His cheeks were dotted with red spots.

The baby opened his eyes, and they were a color Joan had never seen: blue, nearly black. Joan reached inside his glass bassinet, touched his dark eyebrow, a smudge on his face. She felt she loved him more, because he wasn't right. She needed to protect him.

"There was a problem with his breathing, during the birth. Oxygen. He didn't have enough." Her sentences were short, clipped. "He had a feeding tube." She touched her nose, where, I understood, the tube had entered her child's body. "He had seizures.

He shook, terribly. He was never going to be what we imagined him to be. And what did we imagine him to be?" She shrugged. "We imagined he would be perfect. That's what I imagined, anyway, all those hours in the home. I imagined I would have a perfect child and he would go to perfect parents and I would be able to leave, then, go to one coast or the other, or Europe maybe, and not ever have to think about him, because I knew his life would be perfect." She made a strangled sound, somewhere between a laugh and a sob.

If you ignored the fact of the feeding tube, the baby looked like any other baby. Nobody used Joan's name in the hospital; it became clear, after a while, that the doctors and the nurses didn't know it. There seemed to be an arrangement. Joan wasn't really there. She wasn't an unwed mother. She certainly wasn't the mother of a damaged child. She was no one.

Joan thought of California, of how the baby would feel the warmth of the pretty sun on his small cheek. Before she knew it, her plans included this tiny infant.

Mary came after Joan had been in the hospital for nearly two weeks. Joan woke and found her standing over the bassinet. The baby had been brought in from the nursery, for Mary. Joan felt a surge of terror so intense she thought she might vomit.

"She told me he was beautiful. At first it seemed like she might let me keep him. But I was wrong. She told me he would go to a home. 'The best money could buy.' I told her no." She laughed. "She wasn't used to me telling her no. To anyone telling her no. She went back to Evergreen. I knew I hadn't won the war. Only the battle."

Mary installed Joan in a furnished apartment in an old neighborhood in Dallas, near the hospital. The neighborhood was pretty, gracious. The houses, including Joan's small apartment, red brick, with neat lawns.

When the doorbell rang her first morning, Joan opened the door to Dorie, a suitcase in her hand. Mary had sent her.

David required round-the-clock care. He was constantly uncomfortable. When he was held, he arched his back, wailed. But when he was set down he seemed bereft. He cried then, too. No surface — not the soft mattress of his crib, not his mother's arms — could make David comfortable. His left side was so stiff it seemed made of wood.

"One night I took him in the bath with me, because I didn't know what else to do. He stopped crying, immediately. I felt happier than I'd ever felt. I spent hours with him, in the bath. He loved the water."

"Like his mother," I said.

Joan and Dorie took turns with David. Joan could see that Dorie loved David. He was impossible not to love, this helpless, rigid child with her father's features. She'd written *Furlow* as his middle name on his birth certificate. She'd known Mary would not approve and she had done it anyway.

Joan had spent her pregnancy imagining herself into another life. Now it seemed impossible. She was never going to go to Hollywood, to Paris, to Istanbul. But perhaps the life she had imagined had always been unlikely, just out of reach, and David had only helped her realize it.

"They were the happiest and saddest months of my life. I lived and breathed according to his needs. My own needs? They disappeared. When it was just me and David, at night, it seemed manageable. When he was calm, when he wasn't in pain, it seemed manageable. After Dorie held him he smelled like her lotion, the same lotion she used when we were children." Joan smiled. "Right before I left, he could reach up and touch my cheek when I held him. Other times he cried and it seemed like he would never stop. He was in pain and I could not make him feel better. We couldn't spend every waking moment in the bath. I could only wait for him to cry himself to sleep. Sometimes he did, and sometimes he cried for hours, and then my plan seemed inconceivable."

"What was your plan?" I asked. There was a rustle in the bushes, and Joan startled. "Just a squirrel," I said. "There's no one here."

She was exhausted, spent. Telling her story cost her something, just as it cost me something to hear it.

"My plan was to take David and Dorie, if she would come, and go somewhere else. Raise David on my own. Are you wondering how I could imagine I was capable of being David's mother?" She practically spat the words.

"No," I said. "You were his mother."

She shook her head. "He deserved better. I tricked myself into believing that I could raise him. Mama left us alone those three months. She had to pretend I was in Hollywood. She could tell Daddy nothing. It was a mercy. It meant she couldn't get away to see us. She called, but it was a party line, so she had to be careful about what she said. She wrote letters, but I refused to read them. And then, one day she came again, when David was thirteen weeks old. I told her I didn't need her. I told her I would take David and live on my own, far away from her. From Houston. I told her to leave, to never come back."

I thought of that long year. Mary had lied to me, to her husband, to everyone about where Joan was. In retrospect, it did not seem possible, that we had believed her. It did not seem possible, that no one had found her out, had glimpsed Joan in Plano or Dallas, had put two and two together. And yet.

"That's when Mama told me that I had no money. At first I didn't believe it. Daddy would never leave me without money. But Mama told him that was the only way I would come back from Hollywood. She's a smart one, Mama. I could have all the money in the world as long as I did what she wanted."

Joan was astounded. *I* was astounded, listening to her. Furlow Fortier was one of the richest men in Texas. They had so much money Joan never had to think about it, which she would later understand was the truest sign of wealth.

That day, Mary was dressed in her usual uniform: a slim-fitting skirt, a crisply ironed shirt. The drive from Houston had not rumpled her clothes. Nothing rumpled her mother, Joan realized. Nothing interfered with her plans.

"Sometimes I couldn't make myself believe something was wrong with him. It seems so silly. But so much about caring for him was normal. You would know, with Tommy."

She gave me a desperate look. I tried not to cry.

"David dirtied his diapers. He was calmed by my touch. I wanted to tell my mother this, but she didn't give me a chance. She repeated what the doctors said. That David would never talk, would never walk or crawl. Would never achieve intelligence. Would likely die before his first birthday. I felt like my skin was being peeled from my body as I listened. I thought of all the things I bought, each week. Dorie, for one. She would need to be paid. Groceries. The doctors. All of this required money. I saw that there were two worlds: One for those with money. One for those without." She laughed. "I had always taken it for granted that I belonged to the former. But I didn't, not truly. Not like you."

"I would have traded the money in an instant for a mother who loved me. For parents who stayed put."

Joan nodded. "I know you would have.

395

And that's the difference between us, Cee." She plucked a piece of grass from the ground, twirled it between her fingers. "My mother was going to come back the next day, to take David away. Before she left she hugged me. She told me to trust her. I was going to go back to Houston with her. Have a grand homecoming." She smiled. "For a minute I thought about fighting her. I could take him, money or no money. I could make a life for us. If I'd been a different kind of person, a better person, I might have.

"I left that night. I took three hundred dollars from Mama's purse, and a suitcase of clothes. Dorie was with David. I could hear her, singing to him, as I passed by his door." She paused. "Leaving was easy. The easiest thing I've ever done."

"I don't believe you," I said, quietly.

"It's true. Afterward it was awful. But when I left that tiny apartment I felt — how can I explain it?" She gave me a pleading look. "It felt like I was shedding a second skin. It had become so hard, Cece. And it was only going to get harder. David was only going to get bigger. I knew every crack in the ceiling of that apartment, every loose floorboard, every scuff on the wall. I had never lived in a place so small. Mama made everything clear: I wasn't meant to raise a child like David. I wasn't meant to raise any child. And she was right. So I left. I should have left with David. I should have fought. I didn't. It was a relief, to leave."

"Maybe you left so you wouldn't have to say good-bye to him."

"No." Her voice was firm. "That's not why. I know you can't fathom it: Leaving your child. Being glad to leave him. It's another way we're different. Some women are meant to be mothers. I was glad to leave him, Cece."

"But you wanted to raise him?" I asked, confused.

"I did!" she cried. "I did. I wanted both things. I wanted to raise him and leave him. I left. Like I said, I wasn't meant to be a mother."

I thought of my own mother. "What *are* you meant to be?"

Joan shook her head. "I don't know."

At the bus depot Joan bought a ticket to Amarillo. It seemed as good a place as any.

David seemed very far away. Her breasts ached, the way they did when David cried, though Joan had never fed the child from her breast. But then the ache disappeared, and Joan slept. And slept, and slept.

When she woke she was in Amarillo. She got off the bus, decided that this city was too big. Mary might look for her there. So she bought another ticket, to a smaller city nearby: Hereford. No one would look for her there, she was sure.

"Everyone thought I was in Hollywood. Instead, I was in the least glamorous place in the world. Everything was painted green. I didn't understand why, at first. But then I figured it out. It was the color of money."

Hereford was surrounded by feedlots. She could smell it before she saw it. *Beef Capital of the World,* read a cow-shaped sign. There were thousands of cows, as far as the eye could see. No, Mary would not think to look for her there.

Joan was grateful for Texas's expansiveness. The sheer size of it. She pressed her forehead to the window and tried to see beyond the cows, beyond the feedlots. Tried to see her way into another life.

"I stood in the bus depot. And that was when I decided."

"What did you decide?"

"That I would trust no one. I went from the bus station to a diner. I drank coffee. As I was leaving, I saw a *Help Wanted* sign, and I asked the waitress if I could see the boss. She laughed in my face. She touched the sleeve of my coat and told me I might get it dirty. Do you remember that white coat? I wore it that year, before I left."

"Cashmere, with pearl buttons."

"And a fur collar. It probably cost more than that waitress made in a year. Five years."

She had never felt contempt like that. Joan was no one, nobody, never had been, never would be. In Houston her father's money had made her someone. And now that was gone, and Joan felt her place in the world shift, fundamentally.

Mary would know she was gone by now. David would be on his way to a home. Joan was worth nothing. Less than nothing.

"It was easy to rent a room. I got into the bed and I slept, and slept, and slept. I didn't even take my clothes off. I only woke up to get water from the bathroom. And then I woke up to a knock at the door. I opened it. I thought it might be Mama; I thought she might have found me. But it was a tall man."

There were four rooms in the boarding-house, and Sid lived in one. The other two were occupied by farmers, men who worked long hours and kept their heads down at mealtimes.

Sid was clearly not a farmer. Joan wasn't quite sure what he was. He told Joan he was in town to see about some cattle. He wasn't wealthy — that much was clear, or he wouldn't have been living in the same boardinghouse as Joan — but he seemed like the kind of man who was destined for money. Joan had known men like that all her life, driven men, men who were powerful even before the world had given them power. It was easy to recognize Sid as one of them.

That first week, they established a routine: Joan slept until lunchtime. They ate their sandwiches together. Mrs. Bader, the boardinghouse mistress, left out cold cuts, bread, pickles. A plate of oatmeal cookies for dessert. Sometimes they took their sandwiches outside, and sat on the front lawn. Mrs. Bader's house was another rambling Victorian, like the home for unwed mothers had been, and for the rest of her life Joan hated the sight of an old Victorian. She did not find them gracious, nor elegant.

"I had paid for two weeks. And when I went to pay for the next two, Mrs. Bader had left me a note, telling me Sid had taken care of it."

She didn't want it to be so simple: Life was easier, with money. Life was easier, with someone to take care of you. And yet she understood that it was that simple. If she wanted to leave Houston forever, she could have a life like the waitress, work her fingers to the bone, never get ahead, never achieve any measure of comfort. Or she could let men like Sidney Stark take care of her.

Joan wished for nothing now. She had stopped wishing once David was born and she understood that he was damaged. Another girl in her situation might have prayed, might have wished away his impairments. But Joan did not have that kind of hope in her any longer. She never would again.

So she let Sid Stark take care of her. She never got a job, never experienced the working woman's travails. She never knew the pleasures of earning a paycheck. Of being independent. None of us did, of course. Joan was no different in that way. But she came so close. And she wanted it so fiercely. Listening to her, I wondered whether, if Sid had not appeared, she might have led a different sort of life altogether. She might have fought harder. She might have found a way.

But Joan didn't think so. Joan knew that if Sid had not come to her room that night, she would have simply disappeared. Not eaten, not left her room, not made any contact with the world outside the boarding-house. It would have been easy, to disappear. She wanted to, in a way.

That night, after Mrs. Bader had returned

the money, Joan went to Sid's bedroom, which she had never done before. He had always come to her.

"I had sex with him. It was the first time." I did not understand. "The first time?"

"Since David's birth. I thought it would hurt. I'd expected pain. I'd *wanted* pain." I thought of how I had dug my fingernails into my cheeks the night Joan had left, seven years ago; how the pain had seemed right. "But it didn't hurt. It felt like he was erasing David. I lay there beneath him and thought of how my baby was disappearing."

"And this is the man you invited back into your life?"

"It wasn't Sid's fault. It was my fault. I was no better than a whore. But I had never been better than that, Cece. I had never been anything more than a girl whose entire life had been paid for by men."

"That's ridiculous," I said. My cheeks felt hot. "You were eighteen years old. You didn't have a choice."

"Maybe I did. Maybe I didn't. Either way, I took Sid's money."

She tried never to think of David, but she thought of little else. The way he tried, and failed, to lift his head when he lay on her shoulder. The sucking motion he made with his mouth, though he was fed through a tube. The way she, and only she, could calm him when he was beside himself. He did not want Dorie. He wanted her.

Despair. She said it was her purest feeling, in those days, when she thought of David at the home, crying, nobody there to tend to him. Nobody there who understood him.

"I had wanted to leave. And I had done it. But in Hereford, all I wanted was David. If I'd had a normal child, I would have given him up and when I thought of him I would have pictured a happy child, living a happy life."

"You would have missed that child, too," I said. "You were someone's mother."

"No," Joan said. "No. I don't think so. You're a mother, Cece. You were meant to be someone's mother. I wasn't. But I couldn't quite get rid of the guilt. I hadn't fought for my son. I imagined the woman who would take care of him at the home. She was strong, sturdy. Capable. Everything I was not. But in my mind she wasn't kind to David, because he wasn't hers. She didn't let him float in the tub for hours, to distract him from his pain. She didn't hold him while he sobbed, his hot head burning her forearm. *I* would have done that. I did do that. Because I was his mother."

403

"It was your instinct," I said. "To make him safe. To soothe him."

"Yes. It was. But it was also my instinct to abandon. To leave." She gave me a sideways glance. "I'm good at leaving. You know that best of all. At first, David made me more than I was before. And then I left. And it made me less."

I thought of what Idie had told me, that I'd stopped being a child when my mother fell ill. Joan had stopped being a child when David was born.

"You regretted it," I said. "You made a mistake."

She ignored me. "I can't fathom how he felt. All that was familiar to him: gone. I know nothing about where I sent my child." She brushed her hair from her forehead. "I couldn't live with him. And I couldn't live without him. When I allowed myself to think about what I had done, I wanted to die. And when I felt that way," she said, "I took a pill. Or a drink. The drink worked faster, but the pill lasted longer. It was simple. Days passed. Months. I moved into Sid's room. I turned nineteen. I waited for Sid all day. I didn't read anymore, but it didn't matter. I could wait forever. There was no future there, no past. And then my mother found me. I don't know how. But she came to see me and I gave everything up."

Mary told Joan her plan. David would live with Dorie in Galveston. First the beach house, while a more suitable house, without stairs, was built nearby. Dorie's husband, a large man, would live with them. He could lift David as he grew, carry him from room to room. Joan could see David whenever she wanted. On two conditions. She would return to Houston, to live her life as if nothing had happened. And she could never tell another living soul about him.

"And then she told me something that made me say yes. Dorie had told her David loved the water. And in Galveston, of course, he would always have the beach."

"Houston," Joan said. "She got me back where she wanted me. I would have done anything for David, at that point. Gone anywhere."

She had been paralyzed in Hereford. Sometimes she woke in the middle of the night and wondered if she was dead; she knew she would die soon. And then Mary came and offered her another chance. Joan realized, as her mother spoke, that she would do whatever her mother asked of her. If it meant seeing her child again. If it meant that David would not live in a home. If he could have the beach. Dorie had loved Joan.

Dorie would love David, too. She already did.

Maybe, if Joan had had her wits about her, she would have refused. Would have demanded money, and then she could have taken David somewhere else. But where would she have gone, with a boy like David? What corner of the earth? Perhaps she would have told Mary that David was not to be hidden away, that she was not ashamed. But Joan could not conceive of what concealing her child would mean, how it would change her. She could not foresee the shame.

Joan would never know, what she could have gotten if she had pressed Mary. She would always wonder. She would always understand that she'd had one chance, in that tiny room in Hereford, Texas.

"And I lost it. But I didn't even know what I wanted. And I had already failed David once. I thought if I argued, if I tried to negotiate, Mama might just disappear."

"That's when you came back."

"Yes."

"But you kept in touch with Sid."

"Yes," she said. She lifted her hair from the back of her neck, sighed as the air hit her sweaty, salty skin. I felt it, too. "He took care of me, when I couldn't. We kept in touch. He's the only person besides Mama who knows everything."

I was always here, I wanted to say. *I was always waiting, wanting to know you.*

"And then David died, this May. In his sleep. Dorie found him late at night, when she went to check on him. I was out, with you and the girls and your husbands. I didn't know he was dead until hours later."

The gravestone read *May 10.* I tried to place it but could not. We had been out, probably at the Cork Club. Ray had been with me. Ray, whose presence meant that I would never have to endure what Joan had endured. He would endure with me. For me. Joan had been alone.

"The doctors were wrong. They said he wouldn't live to see his first birthday." She smiled, proudly, and I thought of Tommy, and I felt a pure, deep sadness. "He didn't walk, or talk. But he knew who I was. I like to think he loved me."

"Of course he loved you."

"When he died I called Sid. Because he knows me."

This hurt, but my feelings were the least of Joan's problems.

"Joan," I said. "What did he look like?"

"Oh," she said, and put her hand on her

throat. "Just like me. He was a beautiful boy."

We sat awhile longer on the hard-packed ground. I felt some inexplicable combination of dread and giddiness. Joan had told me, had finally trusted me. But her story — for a brief moment, I wished she hadn't told me anything at all.

"Do you blame me?"

"For what?" I asked, though I knew perfectly well what she meant.

"For leaving David."

"No," I said, and it was true, I did not. I took her hand. Joan stared at it, then up at me. It felt like the first time she had looked at me in years. "I feel sorry for you."

Joan smiled, a sad smile. "Don't," she said.

But that was impossible. I always would.

"Your mother let you bury him . . ." I gestured at the grave. "Here?"

"My one victory. I told her if she denied me this I would leave and never come back. She allowed it. She probably thought no one would notice. What's one more grave, in a cemetery full of them. I'll be buried here, one day." She touched the earth. "Here. With him."

The sky was changing from black to gray. We would need to leave soon, before Ray noticed my absence.

I wanted to ask Joan how she had borne it, when I'd had my own child. Also a boy, a boy who must have, despite his lack of speech, seemed perfect to Joan. She had come to the hospital, and held him. What that must have cost her. I wanted to ask how she'd done it, all these years, how she'd kept such a secret, how she'd denied herself her child's love, day after day after day.

"I don't think I ever really knew you," I said suddenly.

"You knew me," she said, and I waited, and I could see she was deciding how to finish her sentence. "The best of anyone," she said finally.

It might have been true, that I knew her the best of anyone. I was certainly persistent. I was certainly dogged. I knew Joan as well as she wanted to be known.

Joan stood. Her palms were covered with dirt. I wanted very badly to take her hands in mine, clean them. But I did not.

"I'm going to leave," she said. "I have to."

"Where are you going to go?" The news did not surprise me. Joan would move away. Go somewhere she was not known. Somewhere cold. Busy.

"I'll tell you tomorrow night," she said. "Let's go to the Cork Club. For old times' sake."

■ ■ ■ ■

Fred pulled over three houses before mine, in front of the Dempseys'.

"Ray," I said, as an explanation to Joan, whose eyebrows were raised. I was embarrassed to tell her that Ray wouldn't approve.

But Joan didn't care about Ray. I saw, in that moment, what David had robbed her of: caring about anybody else in the world. She hadn't, since his birth. But now that he was gone, the life she had imagined, living in the home for unwed mothers: was it hers?

Her hair was completely dry by this point, and it fell in waves around her face. The plaid blanket was still wrapped around her shoulders, and she sat slumped in her seat, exhausted and swollen eyed.

"I'll see you tomorrow," I said, and it seemed like such a strange thing to say: as if we were leaving a party, a club.

"Midnight," Joan said. "I'll be there."

I slipped back into our house just as I had hoped. It was five o'clock in the morning. Tommy wouldn't be up for another two hours. Ray wouldn't be up for one. Both of them sleeping: Ray on his back, just as I had left him, and Tommy with his head pushed into the corner of his crib, the corner of his blanket in his mouth.

I stood in his room for a long time without touching him. I didn't smooth his hair away from his brow, which was, I knew, hot and moist, the way it always was at night. He slept fervently, had since he was a tiny infant. I tried to imagine my life had Tommy been absent from it — had he been raised by someone else, nearby but not with me — and could not. It seemed like a punishment handed down from God: having your child both near and unreachable. A child who was a terrible secret. I tried to imagine Joan's life, all these years without her child, and could not.

When Tommy was born, I had refused Ray's offer of a baby nurse. His mother had stayed away, perhaps sensing that I didn't want her help. I wanted no one's help. This infant was *mine.* In those first days, he was a collection of sounds and odors: His cry, which sounded more like a sad song than a wail. The vaguely eggy scent of his dirty diapers. The soft murmurs he made as he slept. The sweet smell that emerged from the red well of his mouth. But what I remember most is the hot weight of him, as he lay on top of me for hours, gently rising and falling according to my breath. Tommy made me feel needed, for the first time in my life. He could not survive without me. Then Ray would come home from work, and kiss Tommy's hand — he said he didn't want to kiss him on the forehead and chance making him sick — and I could tell he was proud of me, for loving his son. Loving Tommy was the most natural thing in the world.

Loving David had been an instinct for Joan, as well. But Tommy was an anchor. David had been a snare.

I'd spent so much time, years and years, trying to imagine my way into Joan's brain. Trying to see the world as she saw it. Trying to understand it as she understood it.

The next day I took Tommy to the park, went to Jamail's to pick up a few extra things instead of sending Maria. The day did not pass quickly, but it passed.

Ray and I were usually in bed by ten, ten thirty at the latest. Tonight was no different. We had eaten dinner outside — burgers on the grill, corn on the cob — put Tommy to bed, and had a glass of wine in the living room in companionable silence. I had lain beside Ray and listened to him fall asleep, one breath at a time.

At eleven o'clock I rose, went downstairs to the laundry room, where I had stashed an outfit.

For the rest of my life I would wonder about Joan's true motives. Did she want to meet at the Cork Club for sentimentality's sake? We had been happy there. She had been happy there, the queen of Houston. Or maybe she hadn't been happy there. Maybe this had all simply served as a distraction.

I was going to meet Joan tonight because I wanted a conclusion. I zipped my dress, applied lipstick by feel.

I envisioned our future in clear terms: She would move away, and I would see her a few times a year, when she came back to Houston to visit. We could write letters. We could talk on the telephone. Ray would be happy.

I patted my hair, straightened my dress, which was brand-new, silvery blue and off the shoulder, a dress I would not normally have wasted on a Wednesday night. I smoothed the fabric over my hips and flipped off the light switch before I opened the laundry room door.

Ray. Standing there in his striped pajamas, his hands balled into fists by his sides.

"Oh," I said, and felt for the doorknob behind me, as if I could simply disappear back into the laundry room.

413

"Oh," Ray said. "Oh." He was mocking me, I realized. Ray rarely mocked me. It wasn't his style.

"I'm just going out to meet . . ." I trailed off.

"To meet Joan," he finished for me.

I nodded.

"And you were with her last night, too?" He waited for me to answer. When I said nothing, he continued. "You weren't in bed. I'd hoped you were in my office, sipping scotch, being sad. I didn't get up to check because I didn't want to know. But I knew." He looked away.

"She's told me a lot of things, Ray. She's explained herself. She's —"

"What did she tell you?" he interrupted. "What exactly did she say?"

I looked down at my hands, at my week-old manicure, my purse. I couldn't tell Ray what she had told me.

"Cece?"

I looked up at him. "She's leaving," I said. "She's moving away."

"I don't care." And then: "You promised me."

"I promise I'll be back," I said. "I promise things will be different." As I said it, I wondered how many wives had said this to how many husbands; how many husbands had said it to how many wives. I could see that Ray wanted to believe me.

He said nothing, simply watched me as I made my way to the front door. I was halfway out when he spoke again.

"What's going to happen, Cece?"

I stopped. "What do you mean?"

"When does this end?" He raised his hands, let them drop. "Is there an end, to Joan?"

He understood. There was not an end to Joan. She went on forever and ever.

But that was not what he meant.

"Yes," I said. "I've ended it. I just need to see her one last time."

He shook his head in disgust.

"I'm trying to be honest," I said.

Ray snorted. "Do you want a prize? No. You only want Joan." I could tell he wanted to ask something else of me. I was going to be late, but answering Ray's question seemed the least I could do.

"Do you love Joan," he asked, quietly, "like you love me?"

I stopped. "How could you think that?"

"It's a fair question," he said.

Was it? I tried to think. I tried to clear my head.

"I've never loved anyone that way but you."

Ray nodded. "If you leave, I can't promise I'll take you back."

I didn't look at his face, didn't pause or ask him to repeat himself so I could make sure I understood him. I understood him. If I looked at my husband's face, the face I knew best of anyone's, besides my own, and my child's, I would not leave my house, I would stay and never know what Joan wanted.

If I'd had to choose between Ray and Joan, a lifetime of one or the other, I'd have chosen Ray. Of course. But I wasn't really choosing, not truly. Ray would take me back, he would let me in again. I would explain; I would make him see.

And perhaps that was why it didn't feel like a choice, that night. Ray was too steady, too good and earnest. He always wanted me. He was always there.

I left because I didn't think he meant it.

The Cork Club was quiet that night. There were businessmen scattered throughout the place, sipping scotch, making what I supposed were important decisions. One of them, a bald-pated man with the red cheeks of an alcoholic, stared at me frankly, but mainly I was ignored. I wore a wedding ring, for one; and two — well, at twenty-five, I was getting too old.

I sat down at a little table, meant for two; Louis came a second later with two champagne flutes dangling upside down from his hand, a bottle of champagne.

"Oh," I said, not wanting to hurt his feelings. "I didn't order this."

"Miss Fortier called ahead," he said, not meeting my eye, focusing instead on the ceremony of the champagne, cradling it in a white cloth, as if it were, I couldn't help but think, a baby. "It's been in the Fortier locker for years," he murmured, running his hand across the label, upon which was scrawled a lot of French words that meant nothing to me. "Bollinger R.D., 1952," he said. "Champagne."

"We should wait to open it," I said. "Until Joan comes."

"Of course," Louis demurred.

And just then Joan did come, as if I had summoned her. A deep, calm pleasure settled over me, and I realized it had been so, so long since Joan had made me happy in this way. But here she was, coming to meet me, on time, even — she burst into the room in a strapless red silk dress, a matching capelet tied around her shoulders. I wondered, of course, where she had gotten it — New York? Paris? I wondered when

417

Joan had had time to think about fashion, in the past few months. And then I knew that Sid had bought it for her.

"Sid," I said, as she sat down. I reached across the table and felt the stiff, fine material of her capelet between my fingers.

Joan nodded. "He loves me in red." What else did he love her in? Joan chatted with Louis while he opened the champagne and I took her in, my friend who seemed so different from the friend I had encountered last night — so much less vulnerable than the Joan in Glenwood.

I startled at the pop of the cork, muffled under Louis's white napkin.

Joan beamed. "It's a celebration," she said.

"Of what?" What exactly were we celebrating? Her sad story? The secret she had kept since we were teenagers? That she was leaving me, for good?

"You, Cece! We don't celebrate you enough, do we?" There was something false in her voice.

We touched glasses: a light clink. I thought of Ray, who surely wouldn't be sleeping — he would be pacing, or paging through a book, trying to distract himself — and I had the sudden impulse to smash my glass into Joan's, but the urge passed almost as soon as it had appeared.

I sipped my champagne. Joan sipped hers. We were quiet, a rarity for us. We both felt the same lack of verve, the same undercurrent of melancholy.

"I need," Joan said, and her voice caught. She was nervous, which touched me. "I need to tell you some other things," she said, "and I need you to listen." She drained her glass, and Louis was beside us again in a flash, refilling it.

She lit a cigarette, inhaled deeply. The cigarette, the smoke, seemed the only thing that stood between Joan and her hysteria. The cigarette was a comfort, a way for her to remain calm.

"Here's what I have to tell you," she said. She cleared her throat. I flicked my champagne glass with my finger.

"I need money," she said. She paused, took a deep breath, followed by a long drag from her cigarette.

I had guessed, before she told me. Perhaps I had known all along.

"You can have mine," I said, though I knew as I offered that she would never accept.

"No, Cece. I can't."

"Oh, Joan," I said. "What are you planning?"

She stubbed her cigarette out in the green

glass ashtray, took another sip of champagne.

"Joan," I said, and my voice was desperate.

She looked me straight in the eye.

"I need to disappear."

I listened, quietly.

"Sid saw how unhappy I was, when he came here. He agreed to help me. It's good for him, too. He needs money, too."

I laughed. "He has money, Joan." I thought of his big Cadillac, his flashy suits, his gold money clip. "I thought that was the main attraction." It was mean to say, but Joan didn't notice.

"He made money in Hereford," she said, "and then he lost it. He has the trappings of money. But not much more."

"Like you."

She nodded. "Exactly like me."

"How is he going to help you?"

She glanced behind her, making sure nobody was within earshot. The way she had walked in this evening, the clothes she was wearing, the champagne she had called out of the locker — it was all bravado.

"You can tell me," I said, though I was afraid to hear what she had to say.

She laughed, agitatedly. "I'm going to disappear, with Sid. And Sid is going to ask

Mama for money."

"You're going to blackmail your own mother?" I asked. "What makes you think she'll pay?"

"She'll pay."

"But why would she pay?"

"Because," she said, and she would not meet my eye, "Sid is going to tell her he'll hurt me if she doesn't. He's already hinted."

I was confused, then stunned as I slowly assembled Joan's plot. The bruise, Mary's admission that she was afraid for Joan. Afraid of Sid. This was why?

"Oh," I said.

"Oh, what? I'm not above anything."

"No," I said. "It seems you're not."

She shrugged. "Sid and I have a mutual purpose. He's going to help me disappear. We'll go somewhere else, start over."

"Disappear," I repeated. The idea was unfathomable. "You're going to disappear." I laughed. I couldn't help it. "You've never not been Joan Fortier, do you know that? Since we were little girls, everyone knew who you were before you walked into a room. You think you can give that all up, so easily?" I snapped my fingers. "Like that? I think you're mistaken." I grew angrier and angrier as I spoke. "You tried once," I said. "That didn't work out so well." I knew as soon as the words left my mouth that I was being cruel. But I didn't care. Joan had been cruel to me, hadn't she? Letting me think I knew her, that I understood her, for so many years.

"I *hate* being Joan Fortier," she said. "I hate her. I hate what she did."

My anger disappeared. "You were so young," I said.

She shrugged. "I need to leave, Cece."

I thought of Mary. "This will kill your mother."

"Yes," she said, without hesitating. "Yes, it will. But you'll learn to live without me."

You'll. "We'll see each other a few times a year," I said. "We'll talk in between." I could already picture it: telling Ray that I was going to see my father, then stealing off to a bright new city. Joan picking me up at the airport, ferrying me to her penthouse.

"No," Joan said.

"No?"

"I can't."

"You can't," I repeated, slowly putting the pieces together. "Or you won't?"

Joan looked pained. "You know me too well," she said, finally, "and I need to be unknown."

"You don't get to start over!" I cried. "We're not children. This isn't a game. You can't decide to start again, just because you want to. Just because you've decided that you don't like your old life anymore."

"There's nothing for me here," Joan said. "There was David, but he's gone."

"So you met me here tonight to tell me good-bye. In a public place, so I wouldn't make a scene."

She reached across the table and grabbed my hand, her grip desperate.

"I have to," she said. "I think you *do* get to start over, when your child dies."

Joan watched me like I was the only person in the world. It had been so long since she'd looked at me like that. She would never look that way at me again.

I heard her call my name as I half walked, half ran through the club, my heels sinking into the carpet. I felt as if I were running through sand. This time I was running away from Joan, when it had always been the other way around.

"Excuse me, miss," a man said as I slipped past him, through the doors. I was making a spectacle of myself.

I wanted to be somewhere else. I didn't know where — not at home, with Ray, who hated me. I would get my car and then decide. A hotel, maybe. Somewhere I knew no one. If Joan could disappear, then so could I. Why not? Who was stopping me?

Then I was outside. The heat greeted me, an old, familiar friend. The air so thick it felt like you could cut it. I slowed to a walk. A valet tipped his cap.

I didn't know where to go. My plans vanished. I was lost.

Then Joan's hand was on my shoulder. My own hand went to hers, instinctively.

"I don't want you to leave," I said. It was one thing to imagine her in a different city, with an address, a phone number. A way I could reach her. It was quite another to imagine her gone forever.

"I know." She guided me onto a little bench next to the valet stand, the coolness of the iron beneath my thighs, through the silk of my dress, a relief. This was where ladies in heels sat and waited for their cars to be brought up by the valets. You could see Houston from here. Its industry, its breadth. I would never live anywhere else. I belonged to this place, as Joan did. As we all did. But unlike Joan, I could never leave. I didn't want to. My child lived here, and so did my husband.

For the first time in my life, I had something over Joan. I could destroy her plan in a second.

"Why tell me?"

She began to speak, then stopped short.

"Why tell me?" I asked again. "I could go to your mother. I could go to the police."

Joan shook her head. "I trust you."

"How can you say you trust me? When you've told me nothing for years and years."

"I'm sorry," she said, and her voice was mournful. "I'm telling you because I want one person in the world to know. To know me — I want you to know me, Cece."

I was moved. I couldn't help it.

"Can you trust Sid?"

She nodded. "Don't worry about Sid. I've known him for a long time. Don't worry about me."

"Oh, Joan," I said. "You think this'll work? You think you can just disappear? You think your mother will ever stop looking for you?"

"The world is large. I'll find a little pocket, slip into it. It'll be as if I never existed. I almost did it, once before. I could have done it, if I'd had money. It's a plan I've been thinking of for years."

"Years," I echoed. "I thought you were happy."

Joan squeezed my hand. "Did you really?"

"I really did."

It was Joan's gift, or curse — I didn't know which — to be so unfathomable.

I had failed her. We had all failed her.

I heard a rumbling off in the distance; a black Cadillac rounded the corner. Joan stiffened, alert. It was Sid's car.

"Promise," Joan said, "promise you'll help me."

Joan had helped me, when we were young. If I could go back in time, what would I tell the younger versions of ourselves? I would tell Joan to be careful. I would tell her not to be so careless with her love. I would tell myself the same thing. I knew I needed Joan gone as much as she needed to be gone. My life was not my own, when she was in it.

"All right," I said.

"Say it."

"I promise."

Years later, I still don't understand what happened next. Sid drove up, in his Cadillac the size of a boat. He stormed out of the car, said a couple of hurried words to the valet who approached him for his keys; Sid did not relinquish them. I felt sorry for the valet, the same valet who had tipped his cap at me. He looked devastated — he wasn't a familiar face — and then I saw why: Sid's car was blocking the route for other cars. So there was that pressure, immediately: Sid needed to leave. His car needed to be moved. He could cost the valet his job.

I watched it all as if from a distance.

I put my hand on Joan's knee. "You don't have to do this," I said, but I knew she would.

"Don't be scared for me," Joan whispered. "I'll be fine. It's all for show."

Did Sid scare me, that night? Other people there said I seemed frightened. A young woman who had come to the Cork Club for a nightcap with her fiancé — she told a reporter from the *Chronicle* that both Joan and I seemed terrified. "And that man — Sid Stark. He grabbed Joan Fortier's arm like she was a doll. Like she was nothing."

But there was nothing doll-like about Joan that night. She was solid. She was strong. My hand was still on her knee.

"Sid," I said, "Sid." It was the first time he had looked me in the eye since that sunny morning so many years ago, when I had convinced myself I'd rescued Joan from the bed in Sugar Land. Maybe I had rescued her, maybe I hadn't. I'll never know.

"She's a good girl," he had said then, and I would never forget those words.

"What do you want me to do?" I asked, and Sid answered for Joan, seething — "I want you to sit there and watch." Heat radiated from his body. I could feel his fury. I could smell his distinct odor: sweat and cigar smoke and rage. But was any of it real? Was Sid as good an actor as my beloved Joan?

"I wasn't talking to you," I said. I could feel Sid move toward me, feel his presence surround me, but I didn't care.

"Joan," I said. "Joan. What do you want me to do?"

Tell me, Joan. All these years later and I still don't know.

"Joan," I said again, "please answer me."

But Joan seemed riveted by Sid, by what he might do, where he might take her.

"Joan?" I said again, this time more tentatively. "Please?"

She didn't answer. She never answered. I sat and watched as Sid half dragged, half escorted Joan to his car. Truly, it was hard to tell. Did Joan want to go? Was she a participant? A victim? Was she something in between?

I watched.

Once Joan was in the car Sid dropped his keys. He fell to his belly and slithered around on the ground, his hand underneath the car, blindly searching. His carelessness bought Joan time. She rolled down her window, brought her hand to her mouth, then pointed her outstretched palm at me.

Only at me. It was as if the whole world except the two of us had disappeared, which was the way I had always wanted it. There was a crowd of people now, watching the spectacle, but I only had eyes for Joan. She only had eyes for me.

It was only after she drove off — was driven off — that I realized Joan had been blowing me a kiss.

Joan was done with me. And I with her. I tried to memorize her face, the last time I would ever see it. Her hair, her arms, the way she had walked into the Cork Club tonight.

But all I could see was Joan's back. We were six years old and she was running into Furlow's arms. We were thirteen years old and she was disappearing into the ocean. We were fourteen years old and she was climbing out a window. We were fifteen years old and she was closing the door to my mother's room a final time. We were seventeen years old and she was walking off the dance floor on a boy's arm. We were eighteen years old and she was slipping into a bedroom at a party. We were twenty-two years old and she was exiting a club, this time on a man's arm. We were twenty-four years old and she was leaving my house with a promise to be back soon.

We were twenty-five years old now, and Joan was looking for something else. This time I hoped she would find it.

CHAPTER TWENTY-EIGHT

1957

Our front door was unlocked, as I had left it; perhaps Ray was inviting me back inside. *This is my home,* I thought as I stepped through the foyer, and rested my keys beside the green vase I had purchased before Tommy was born and still took pleasure in every day. I picked it up now, admired it: it was small but heavy, unadorned, with none of the fussiness of an object from my mother's home. It was meant to hold nothing. Meant only to exist on my entryway table as a thing to admire.

I went to Tommy's room first. I could feel Ray's presence; he was in the house with me, but I didn't know where.

Tommy was fast asleep, as he always was at this hour. He could be counted on for so many things: to sleep and wake at certain times, to eat what I fed him. To convey himself as a sweet weight against my chest, his damp cheek against mine, his breath in my ear. To bring pleasure to Ray and me without trying, simply by existing. That was what being a mother was, or should be, I thought, as I combed Tommy's hair behind his ear: existing as a resting spot for your child. Acting as a tether between him and the world. Joan had not wanted to be tethered to anyone or anything. She would stay with Sid as long as he helped her. And then she would leave him, too, as she left everyone.

I had been a burden to my mother, as David had been a burden to Joan. And I had made myself a burden to Joan, too. But I was twenty-five years old, a wife, a mother. I was no one's burden any longer.

I felt Ray enter the room behind me. I wanted to stand here like this forever: Ray behind me, Tommy in front of me.

"Cece," Ray said, and his voice was soft, because Tommy was sleeping, but it wasn't kind. "Look at me."

All my certainty vanished. I had nothing without Ray.

"I can't," I whispered. I thought, If I don't look at him, he can't tell me what he wants to tell me. If I don't look at him, he'll leave, and I can steal into bed beside him, later, and when we wake in the morning he'll have

432

forgiven me. He'll have forgotten.

It was two o'clock; I felt as if I were moving through a dream.

"Leave," he said loudly, and Tommy stirred in his sleep. Ray sounded close to hysteria. I'd never heard his voice like this before.

Ray was angry, but angry because he was hurt. This insight made me brave, and I turned and went to him. I stood very close but stopped short of touching him; it was clear he didn't want me to touch him.

The first night I'd slept over at Ray's bachelor pad I'd woken in the early morning and Ray had been standing at the foot of the bed. It seemed like he had been there awhile. I'd said nothing, simply closed my eyes again. No one had ever watched me sleep before.

We were young. We were newly in love. Ray was trying to know me, observing me in my most unguarded state. When Joan and I were teenagers we thought relationships were a vehicle for passion and romance. We knew nothing of marriage and domesticity. Men were still that, for Joan: Passion, sex. A thirst for something she could not name.

But I knew what I wanted. I wanted *this.* I wanted to be with the man who had wanted to know me so badly he had watched me sleep. I wanted what I already had.

"Ray," I said, and I stared at the soft, navy blue rug I'd splurged on after Tommy was born. I'd waited until he was born — until I'd known if I had a son or a daughter — to buy it. "I want to have another child."

He wasn't rough exactly, but he wasn't gentle, either, as he grabbed me by the shoulders.

"Say it again."

"I want a child." I couldn't look him in the eye.

"Say it and look me in the eye."

There wasn't any liquor on his breath. He wasn't the kind of man who tried to soften things by drinking. He wasn't the kind of man who made idle threats, either. He wasn't the kind of man who should have ended up with me as his wife. I had lied to him, more times than I cared to remember. I had given him no reason to trust me.

"I want a child," I repeated.

"It seems convenient," Ray said.

It did seem convenient, and perhaps it was. But it was true. The want was deep in my bones.

By this time my eyes had adjusted completely to the darkness. I could see hollows beneath Ray's eyes, evidence he hadn't slept. Something shifted between us; Ray believed me.

"Is it different this time?" Ray asked. His voice was plaintive instead of hard. He still wanted me. Still needed me.

"I'm all yours now," I said. "I promise."

A promise from a woman like me meant nothing. I needed to prove it, somehow. I went to Tommy's crib, put my arm through the slats, and touched his head. It was still, after all these years, always a relief to find he was breathing. When he was a newborn I would come into his room in the middle of the night, certain that I would touch his cheek and find coldness instead of warmth. I'd thought I was the only mother who did this, because I couldn't imagine my own mother wondering whether or not I was still among the living. I had slept in Idie's room as an infant. One day I'd mentioned checking on Tommy to Ciela and she'd laughed, told me she had done the same exact thing a dozen times a night when Tina was a newborn. I used to think Joan was exempt from all the worries of motherhood. I had felt sorry for her, and sometimes, when I'd had a particularly bad day with Tommy, I was jealous of her. But of course Joan had checked on David, too.

I could feel Ray watching me. I took his hand and led him from our son's room and into ours.

"Come here," I said, and patted the space next to me. "Come sit."

He came.

The mattress shifted under his weight. The bed was unmade — it seemed impossible that I'd slept in it hours ago. I ran my hand over the smooth sheet between us, our sheets that had been changed every week, like clockwork, since we'd married.

"Ray," I said, "I want to tell you every-thing." My voice caught. Outside the win-dow, the sky was still dark, but it would become lighter, soon. Tommy would wake. I only had so much time. Who's to say what we deserve, what we do not, in this life? I did not deserve Ray. He deserved more than me, a wife so willing to go where he could not follow.

"Joan," I began. "I thought I knew her completely. I thought I understood her."

Ray asked no questions. He simply lis-tened.

I told him about Evergreen, the strange tension that I always sensed between Mary and Joan; about how fervently Furlow had doted on his only child. I told him how generous the Fortiers had been with me, but how I had always suspected that, in certain ways, I was Joan's handmaiden: half as beautiful, half as lucky. He knew some of this, of course, the facts, but I'd never been this honest with Ray, with anyone, about Joan.

He winced when I called myself half as beautiful as Joan. He made as if to correct me but I shushed him. It was a fact, that I was not as beautiful as Joan. And what had her beauty earned her, in the end? Her mother's pride. The attention of every man, including the wrong kind. The spite of every woman.

If he was surprised when I told him that Joan had taken me to Glenwood on Tuesday night, he did not show it. Nor did he express shock, or wonder, at the fact of David: his life or his death.

Finally, I told him of Joan's plan: to take Mary's money, and run. Or, more precisely, to run, and then take Mary's money. By the time Mary sent the money, Joan would be long gone.

I almost stopped there.

"Cee?"

I went on. "You know my mother died," I said, "but you don't know how."

When I was done he took my hand. His palm was as cool as mine was hot.

"I loved her," I said. "But I never knew her."

"Loving and knowing aren't the same thing," he said, with a rueful smile. "You can't know someone who doesn't want to be known."

He was talking about me, not Joan.

"She left him," he said.

I tried to see the world as simply as my husband did. I had exhausted both of us. I pressed my hand to his chin, rough with stubble. Ray was what I wanted. And I had almost given him up.

"It wasn't that simple," I said.

"No," he said. "It never is. But I don't care, Cece. She helped you, but it was a long time ago. I want you back."

"You can have me," I said. "If you want me."

"I want you. I've always wanted you." He stroked my hair. "You know what you have to do," he said, and it was not a question.

"Yes," I said.

"And what is that?"

"I have to do nothing at all. I have to let her go."

Ray nodded. I smiled; I couldn't help it. "You and Joan want the same thing."

Ray kissed my forehead, and I bit back tears.

Ray let me sleep that morning. He waited

with Tommy, fed him breakfast and played with him while I dozed in our bed. I left the door open so I could hear them. My sweet son and his doting father. Ray's voice, Tommy's noises — once he even laughed — almost lulled me to sleep.

What was Joan doing in that exact moment? I'd done this all my life. I am here, I would think, eating pancakes with Idie, and Joan is at home, washing her face with a washcloth, Mary nearby, making sure she does a thorough job. I am here, in bed at Evergreen, while Joan is breaking curfew with John. I am here, eating tuna fish sandwiches with Ray, while Joan is lounging by the pool, a drink in her hand. I could taste the vodka as it slid down her throat. I could feel the heat of the sun as it hit her oiled shins.

But now I found I could not imagine what Joan was doing. I saw her with Sid, in a car somewhere, driving toward — well, I did not know. The pain I felt, as I lay in bed, was physical: in my stomach, in my shoulders. I felt it everywhere.

I would never see my friend again. I told myself this, silently repeating the words until they felt like a prayer. But I couldn't quite believe them. Surely I had not seen the last of Joan Fortier.

CHAPTER TWENTY-NINE

1957

This time, Joan's disappearance was a scandal of the highest order. Three days after I'd last seen her, I rose early and walked outside in my bare feet. The driveway was already hot, though it was barely five o'clock and the sun had not yet risen. I opened the *Chronicle* to a picture of Joan's face and a headline: JOAN FORTIER VANISHES. It was an old photograph, one of my favorites: we were at the Cork Club, and Joan was looking over her shoulder. Had she been looking at me? I could not remember.

I'd been waiting for this. I read the article while I stood outside, the concrete warming my feet; I hadn't even put on a robe. The article was brief. Joan's maid had contacted the police after Joan had not come home on Wednesday night. I thought of Sari, making Joan's bed, smoothing the sheets with her practiced hand. I wondered how much she had guessed.

Joan's clothes were still in her closet. I lingered on this detail. It made sense, of course — if you were going to stage a kidnapping, you wouldn't pack a suitcase — but the detail made me unspeakably sad. I had assembled Joan's wardrobe. Most of it, anyway. When she wore a skirt I'd chosen, a dress I'd had made for her, I liked to think she thought of me.

I wondered if Mary was looking at the paper at this very moment. She was an early riser, especially as she'd aged. I wondered if Mary slept at all now, or if sleep, when it came, was fretful and brief, like my own.

Sid would have told Mary not to contact the police. Maybe she had told Sari to do it. Maybe she had already sent the money, was hoping Joan would reappear any day now, as perfect and unblemished as the day she disappeared. Maybe Mary suspected that Joan was deceiving her. Mary was nothing if not shrewd. But if anyone could trick Mary, if anyone could make her act ardently instead of judiciously, it was Joan.

I brought the paper inside, left it on the kitchen table while I went upstairs and locked myself in the bathroom.

I stood in the shower until the hot water

ran out. I leaned my head against the tile while the freezing water hit my face. I wept. It felt like another death: first my mother, then Joan. For this death, I did not have Joan here to comfort me.

The day the story broke the police came. They were kind. They were treating Joan's disappearance as a kidnapping, with Sid, of course, as the prime suspect. It was all unfolding just as Joan had wished.

I told them that Sid seemed a little rough, that Joan seemed not entirely herself. But that was all I knew, I said. I didn't know Sid Stark very well at all.

"But you knew Joan," a policeman — the older one — said. "Was she aware that she was in danger?"

"She brought out the best bottle of champagne from her father's locker. That was unusual." They watched me, eagerly. "But I can't say why she did it."

They would return periodically in the weeks and months that followed, and then they would stop.

The first time Joan had disappeared, we weren't worried. I'd wanted her back, but I knew she was safe. She'd sent a postcard. We thought she'd gone to Hollywood. A rumor that Mary had planted herself, but still, we believed it. Joan was somewhere glamorous, being glamorous. It all made sense, and, of course, Mary was in on it.

This time, her disappearance was ominous. She wasn't eighteen years old anymore, ripe, ready to be plucked: by a studio head, a rich businessman. Joan's world was no longer limitless. And there was Sid, an outsider, with an unpleasant reputation. No one trusted an outsider.

In some moments I hoped the police would show up on my doorstep and catch my lie. But regardless, Joan would never come back. Money or no money, she had found a pocket of the world and slipped into it.

A week and a half after Joan disappeared, Ciela came by. She'd called several times, but I hadn't answered the telephone since Joan's disappearance. I skipped the Garden Club meeting, sent Maria to Jamail's in my stead. The *Chronicle* had called for a quote from me, Joan's best friend. I didn't return the call. Darlene had left a coffee cake on my doorstep, surprising me with her sensitivity. I'd expected her to knock, to barge in and demand gossip. I didn't want to talk to her, or Ciela — I didn't want to talk to anyone except Ray — but mostly I didn't want to talk to Mary. I wasn't sure I could lie to her. I wasn't sure my heart would allow it, tied as it was to Evergreen. Twice, a woman had called and declined to leave a message — her words. Ray had answered both times. He said the voice could have belonged to anyone, seemed irritated by my certainty, my insistence that he repeat the exact words the caller had used. But who else would have declined to leave a message but Mary Fortier?

I was swimming laps in the pool when I opened my eyes and saw a woman looming over me. For an instant I thought she was Joan. But my eyes adjusted and the thrill — of dread? joy? — disappeared. It was only Ciela, peering down at me.

I didn't glide through the water, like Joan had. My stroke was sloppy, unpracticed. I'd never swum laps before. The pool was for lounging, for dipping your toes in. For sitting beside with a drink. But I had to distract myself. The sitting still, the waiting for news, the daily ritual of unfolding the *Chronicle* in the driveway — I couldn't bear it.

And yet I knew it would be worse when Houston began to forget, when the news of Joan migrated from the front page to the last; when some other, newer scandal took up our attention.

"What are you doing here?" I hadn't meant to sound hostile, but the sight of Ciela, here when I had clearly wanted to be left alone, disarmed me. "I mean," I said, "I didn't know you'd be stopping by." I tried to make my voice nicer, smoother.

"I haven't been able to get ahold of you," she said, lightly. "I thought I'd swing by. Maria said you were outside."

I climbed out of the pool. I took my time drying off, twisting the water out of my hair, smoothing oil on my legs. The coconut scent reminded me of Joan.

"Do you mind sitting out here?" I asked. "I want to get a little sun."

I wanted no such thing. I hated tanning. The oil was for when Joan came over. I wasn't sure why I was using it, except that I didn't want to go into the house with Ciela.

Ciela waited until we had perched ourselves, awkwardly, on the red plastic lounge chairs. Though Ciela didn't look awkward, even dressed as she was, in a slim-fitting yellow dress. She wasn't showing yet.

"You must be falling to pieces," she began. I hadn't expected sympathy.

I began to cry, and she sat down next to me.

"You'll ruin your dress," I said, and pointed to the oily spot blooming on the fabric above her hip.

Ciela shook her head. "It's a silly old dress. What about you, Cece? Are you bearing it?"

"I miss her," I said.

"Of course you do. And not knowing . . . where she is." She chose her words carefully. "And poor, poor Mary Fortier. Joan was her life."

"Yes," I said weakly.

Ciela continued. "She was your life, too, wasn't she? I used to envy you and Joan your closeness," she said.

"And now?"

"And now I feel sorry for you." She let go of my hand, smoothed her hair behind her ears. She wore ruby and turquoise starburst earrings. She could wear jewelry that would have looked gauche on anyone else.

I didn't mind Ciela's pity; I welcomed it. I wanted her to touch me again. I reached for her, but Ciela turned and I let my hand fall into my lap.

"Cece, I have to ask you something. I know you saw Joan before she disappeared."

Everyone knew that. It had been in the paper, and even if it hadn't Ciela would have known. Word traveled fast in our circle, and Ciela knew everything anyway.

"Did she tell you anything before she disappeared?"

Later, I appreciated Ciela's cleverness. If she had asked if I knew where Joan had gone, I could have told her no, honestly.

But she'd asked the right question, which meant she suspected. I felt grateful that she assumed Joan had confided in me.

I almost told her.

But no. I looked Ciela straight in the eye, and lied.

"She did not," I said.

Ciela nodded. "Poor Joan," she said.

"Why?" I asked.

"She was never really happy. We were never really enough for her, were we?"

My legs, gleaming in the sun, were already turning darker.

Ciela waited for me to answer.

"Do you think she's dead?" I whispered.

"That's what everyone thinks," Ciela said. "I'm sorry. It's just that the longer she's gone, with no word — it's not promising, is it?"

I didn't answer. Promising. What an odd way to put it.

"What do you think?" Ciela asked softly.

"I don't know," I said truthfully. "I thought I knew her," I said slowly. I wanted to tell her something, something true. "But in the end, I did not."

The glass door slid open. Ray was home.

"Hi there, Ciela," he called from behind us, in his easy, considerate way. "Did Cece offer you a cocktail?"

That afternoon I lay in bed, the curtains drawn. I hadn't turned on the fan. Tommy was napping, I'd let Maria go home early. Ray was in his study.

Then the room was flooded with light.

"Someone here who wants to see you," Ray said. The mattress shifted under his weight as he sat down. A hand on my back. I didn't want to be touched. I wanted to be alone with my grief.

But this hand was small, the touch light.

I turned over. "Hi," Tommy said, which he had been saying a lot lately. He was already in his footed pajamas, his hair damp and combed sweetly away from his face. He smelled of baby powder. I held out my arms and he came to me without hesitation.

"Hi," I said back. "Hi."

The next day the news was about Sid's previous arrest, years before, for tax fraud. There was nothing violent in his past, not officially, but who knew? Houston loved to speculate.

I had just come in with the paper when the phone rang. I don't know what compelled me to answer it.

"Cecilia," Mary said, after I had said hello.

"Yes," I said, "this is she."

I pressed the receiver to my ear, half expecting to hear the sounds of Evergreen — a servant, taking away a cup of coffee; Joan, scampering in the background. I heard nothing, of course. Those were the old sounds of Evergreen.

"Mary?" My voice was tentative. She turned me into a child so easily.

"I trust you have seen today's issue of the *Chronicle.*"

"Yes." It was in my hand, the musty scent of newsprint in my nose.

"You have a child of your own."

"Yes," I said softly.

"Then you can imagine —" She stopped short. "I called to say that I know you don't know anything, Cecilia."

I said nothing.

"About where Joan might be. Because if you did, you would have told me. Told someone. You love Joan too much not to."

I clutched the phone.

"Cecilia? I am correct in these assumptions?" Still, I couldn't speak. "Cecilia? Are you there? Please." Hearing Mary Fortier's voice break — she sounded, finally, like what she was: a distraught, sixty-seven-year-old woman — allowed me to respond. She had brought it on herself. She had helped ruin Joan.

"Yes," I whispered. And again, louder: "Yes. I would tell. Of course I would tell."

"I thought so," Mary said wearily. She sounded so old. "I thought so, Cecilia. I thought so. Joan is lucky to have a friend like you."

I think I would have pleased Mary Fortier had I been her daughter. I wanted the same things she wanted: to stay put, namely. Was it Mary who had ruined Joan? Perhaps it was Furlow, who had made Joan believe in the fiction of her own power. In this way, he had treated her more like a son than a daughter, letting her believe that she could have anything. Everything. She had only to want it, and it was hers. For a while, it had been true: a pony, a diamond, Furlow's endless adoration. But then Joan was no longer a child, and her needs became more complex: she began to want a world that Furlow could not have predicted. And he had not given her the means to move within this world, because he hadn't truly wanted her to. Furlow had given Joan plenty, but he had not given her a bank account in her own name.

Or was it David who had ruined Joan? A child who could not help the fact of his own life. A child born of his mother's reckless desire. It might have been a fantasy, but I wanted to believe that David had given Joan something. That Joan might have regretted her life, but not her child: that she could separate one from the other, the pain from the gift. David had given his mother his trust, even when Joan had not deserved it.

But who knows?

None of us wanted Joan to leave. She was a daughter. We — her parents and I — believed she belonged to us. Daughters sat tight. Daughters abided. They never left.

But in the end, Joan was no one's daughter.

Ray found me at the kitchen table, staring out the window.

"It'll be all right," he said.

It might be, I thought, or it might not. Only time would tell. But there was this: Tommy's warm hand in mine, every day. Ray's solid presence next to me, every night. Joan's life was unknown to me now. But Tommy and Ray were alive, safe. Mine.

CHAPTER THIRTY

1958

I lived a year without knowing what had happened to Joan. Alive or dead, I had no way of knowing. Houston moved on, as it always did; I'd overestimated the city's interest in Joan Fortier. I should have known better — I'd lived here my entire life, after all. Sometimes I thought it was better that Joan left when she did. There were younger, fresher girls rising up to take her place. At first, when the girls and I resumed going to the Petroleum Club for our monthly dinners, we were a spectacle. Joan's friends. Then, gradually, people stopped looking. They would have stopped looking at Joan, too, though now I knew she wouldn't have cared.

I never spoke to Mary Fortier again. I tried, once. I went back to Evergreen, when I was four months pregnant and just starting to show. I'd gotten pregnant in the month after Joan left, and at first I'd feared for the child growing inside me, that I might ruin this new life with my sadness. I was sick, as I was with Tommy, but this sickness was different. It felt cleansing. I spent entire days sprawled on the cool tile floor, only rising to my hands and knees to vomit. My misery served a purpose, in stark contrast to the futile longing I felt for Joan. My longing would not bring her back.

I never knew what Mary understood of Joan's disappearance. And in the end, I couldn't decide which was worse: never to know your daughter's fate, or to know that your daughter had swindled you. That your daughter had staged her own disappearance, at least in part, because she never wanted to see you again.

I'd read Furlow's obituary in the *Chronicle.* There was to be no funeral, no service. The picture that accompanied the obituary was the same one I had seen so many times: a young Furlow standing in the oil field, his life ahead of him, Joan not yet a thought in his head. It was a mercy, that Furlow's mind was lost before Joan was lost. He would not have survived her absence. I hoped he'd died living in a world in which his daughter was present and beautiful and loved him.

I began to forget. It is either the mind's

greatest mercy or its worst trick: that we forget those we love. If I thought about her a thousand times a day in the months after she disappeared, then I thought about her nine hundred ninety-nine times in the year after she disappeared, and so on, until I had to look at a picture of her to remember her face. But her voice — deep, a little gravelly — I could always call up her voice.

I went to Evergreen to pay my respects. Ray waited in the car, with Tommy. I touched my stomach constantly now, evidence of what I had gained in sacrificing Joan. And Tommy — Tommy blossomed after Joan left. I wished she could see him, wished so badly she could take pleasure in the little boy he was becoming. He spoke beautifully now, had preferences I could not have imagined: he delighted in the birds that fed at the bird-feeder outside our window, hummingbirds especially. He loved music, the sound glasses made when they clinked together, which Ray and I had discovered one night as we toasted our anniversary with flutes of champagne. He toasted our water with his milk every night before we ate. I no longer hid him away; I felt guilty for ever doing so.

Dorie answered the door.

Mary was in Galveston.

"That's where she lives now," Dorie said.

"Alone?"

Dorie nodded. "All alone."

I stepped away — Dorie had not invited me inside — but then I changed my mind.

"I want to see a picture of him. A photograph."

"Of who?"

"You know who," I said, in a low voice.

Dorie did not move. She'd never really liked me, even when I was a child.

"I know one must exist," I said.

She nodded, almost imperceptibly. When she returned, a minute later, she carried a small silver frame, polished to gleaming.

She opened the screen door and dropped it into my hand.

"David," I said. Joan's eyes, the curve of her mouth. "He was beautiful." And he was.

"You don't know the half of it," Dorie said, but her voice was soft.

"He looks like Joan. A miniature Joan." He was smiling, looking to the side. He looked around four years old — no longer a baby, but not quite a child. I wanted to think he was staring at his mother, at the woman who had only really loved one person, her entire life: him.

He looked like any child. He could not have conceived of the depth of his mother's love. I handed the frame back to Dorie.

"Where is this kept?" I asked.

"On my bedside table," she said. "Mrs. Fortier had one on hers, too. She took it with her."

I nodded, and took a step backward. Being here, at Evergreen, undid me. I half expected Joan to walk around the back of the house in her red bathing suit, smile, wave me to the pool.

"He was loved," Dorie said, with fervor in her voice, before I turned to go. "He was adored."

My daughter was born in April, as the azaleas were blooming. We named her Evelyn, after Ray's grandmother. Ray asked me if I wanted her middle name to be Joan, but I did not. I wanted that name to die with Joan, with me.

When Evelyn was six months old, and Houston was no longer so hot you felt half in hell, I opened an envelope with no return address. I almost didn't see it: Joan's necklace, the one Furlow had given her so many years ago. I hadn't seen it since that night in high school.

"Look," I said, and dangled the delicate chain from my finger. The star was tinier than I remembered, the diamond smaller.

Evelyn reached for it.

AUTHOR'S NOTE

I spent a great deal of time researching the colorful, storied past of Houston's Shamrock Hotel, and though I've tried to be, in most instances, faithful to the historical record, fact always serves at the pleasure of fiction in this book. One instance of note: In March of 1957, the Cork Club was moved out of its location in the Shamrock Hotel to a spot in downtown Houston. In the book, of course, it remains a part of the Shamrock. I didn't have the heart to move it.

ACKNOWLEDGMENTS

Thank you to my agent, Dorian Karchmar, whose dedication to writing in general — and, to my great fortune, my writing in particular — is so passionate I am still occasionally astonished by her commitment.

Thank you to my editor, Sarah McGrath, whom I feel lucky to work with. She made this book so much better. There is no eye more discerning. Without her patient, calm presence, along with her incisive, brilliant editorial suggestions, this book would not have gotten written. I am forever grateful to her.

At Riverhead, thank you to the entire spectacular team, but especially to Geoffrey Kloske, Jynne Martin, Danya Kukafka, and Lydia Hirt.

Thank you to my publicist, Liz Hohenadel, whose love for books is infectious, and who is so good at getting them noticed. I don't pretend to understand all the hard

459

work that goes into publishing a book, but I am incredibly thankful for all the effort Riverhead and Liz have put into mine.

At William Morris Endeavor, thank you to Tracy Fisher, Anna DeRoy, Simone Blaser, and Jamie Carr.

Thank you to the English department at Auburn University, where I am surrounded every day by fine students and colleagues.

Thank you to Tim Mullaney for reading a draft.

Thank you to Roy Nichol, for his generous help in explaining the world of River Oaks.

Thank you to my mother and father and sister, as always, for their love and support.

Thank you to my husband, Mat Smith, for everything.

This book is for the two Peters in my life: one past, one present and future.

ABOUT THE AUTHOR

Anton DiSclafani is the author of the *New York Times* and nationally bestselling novel, *The Yonahlossee Riding Camp for Girls*. She was raised in northern Florida and now lives in Alabama with her husband and son, where she teaches at Auburn University.